ALAMO

NORTH DAKOTA

A DAN NEUMANN MYSTERY

Dear + Trudy,
Enjoy the read.

Phil
Rustad

Fast Dog Press • Minneapolis

Published by Fast Dog Press
www.fastdogpress.com

Editing by Patricia Morris
Book design by Dorie McClelland, www.springbookdesign.com

ISBN: 978-09840413-0-5

First edition
05 04 03 02 01 11 12 13 14 15

Publisher's Cataloging-in-Publication available upon request.

To Cindy, who puts up with me.
I still do.

Prologue

December 13
Alamo, North Dakota

Pete and I lay in the snow under the pounding blizzard. The snow was racing in horizontally, whipped by forty-plus-mile-per-hour winds screaming out of Canada. There was literally nothing to stop them as they poured southward from the Arctic Circle; an Alberta Clipper was what the TV weatherman called it. Somewhere across the parking lot FBI Special Agent Will Sanford was behind cover, nursing a wound from a high-powered rifle. My mind was going a thousand miles per hour as Pete and I tried to figure out what to do next. As I drew a breath of the icy air, I mused that murder wasn't the only crime without a statute of limitations.

Part One

Minnesota

Chapter One

Thursday, October 30
Robbinsdale, Minnesota

Fall in Minnesota is a great time of year. Today's weather forecast was OK, around seventy with some gusty winds, perfect for finishing those late summer chores that had been put off, followed by a late afternoon grilling of hot dogs or steaks. It's a super time for outdoor activities and I try to get all I can in before winter. If I had my way, we'd have one month of winter, say March, for the snow and cold, even though that hurts a lot of Minnesota-based industries like snowmobile manufacturing. Yeah, I'm a fan of global warming.

Of course, there was the Halloween of '91 when it started snowing and didn't stop for over two days. When that storm got to the East Coast, it combined with a late season hurricane that had come up from Bermuda and turned into what author Sebastian Junger dubbed "The Perfect Storm." By the time that storm left Minnesota the temps had gone from the mid-fifties to close to zero and there was nearly three feet of the white stuff on the ground. I thought today looked nicer than that.

My name is Dan Neumann. I'm a semi-retired Minneapolis cop and author of a few books on forensic ballistics investigation. I live in Robbinsdale, Minnesota, a first-ring suburb of Minneapolis, as the real estate people say. On this particular Thursday morning I was enjoying a few days of that "semi" part of retirement by raking my yard.

My house is a newer one for the area, having been built in 1996, compared to the 1920's to mid-1940's houses in the rest of the neighborhood. It sits on a lot that was previously occupied by one of those 1920's houses that had gone to seed and wound up being torn down.

As a result, I've got a new house on a big old lot and that means big old trees—really big trees with lots of branches that produce lots of leaves. It all makes for a good fall workout.

You have to get the leaves up in the fall. If you don't they just lay there rotting under the snow all winter; come spring, you've got a mess. So there I was, raking away, wishing there'd never been a ban on burning in the city. I'm just old enough to remember the smell of burning leaves in the fall and I miss it.

I didn't buy the house for the trees. It came with a two-car attached garage, but the old-style neighborhood meant there was an alley down the back and room for another garage. I put up an oversized three-car one with a built-in workshop. This gave me room for "toy" storage and the shop became the center of my efforts to become a carpenter/cabinet-maker/furniture maker. I'm a Norm Abram wannabe.

After thirty years with the Minneapolis police department, now I only work cases that involve unusual firearms or ballistics investigations, or that just interest me. The department thinks it's OK—they don't have to pay me except when I'm on a case. With my books selling to forensic libraries across the country, I've gained a little fame within the law enforcement world. The result is I get calls to help out with cases all over the place and I still get to carry a shield and firearm nationwide.

I've also started consulting in Hollywood on TV and movie projects. Those people want to know about the latest and greatest in the firearms world, things like "If we shoot this guy with a shotgun, how big a hole will it make?" or "Can a bullet fired from a pistol really make a car's fuel tank explode?" I always give them the truth—shotguns don't really make very big holes at close range and it's just about impossible to get a car's fuel tank to explode even using incendiary ammunition, which is not available to the general public. They pretty much go with whatever looks the best on the screen anyway. I guess I don't care. Like everything else about Southern California—it's all make-believe.

It was just about time for a mid-morning coffee break when my cell phone went off.

"Neumann," I answered.

"Dan, it's Pete. I need to talk to you," the urgent voice said.

Pete Anderson is one of my oldest buddies. We went to high school and the University of Minnesota together, although in different directions. He wound up rich and I wound up a cop. Something was wrong—I could hear it in his tone.

"Yeah, Pete. What's up?"

"I need your help, buddy. Grams is dead."

"Grams? You mean Grandma Anderson? Your grandmother—*our* Grams?"

Grams was Pete's grandmother and everyone else's best friend. She had played an important part in raising Pete and just about everyone he knew. More than once Grams gave me reason to question my own judgment.

"Yeah, Grams." Pete's voice was quivering. "Someone broke into her house and killed her."

A switch snapped in my head, sending me straight into cop mode.

"Are you there now?"

"Yeah."

"Have you called the Edina PD?"

"They called me. The housekeeper found her."

"Hang tight—I'm on my way."

I went around the house, locking the back door on the way by, walked into the second garage and tossed the rake on a wall hook. No need to grab a gun, I was already armed. After nearly thirty years of carrying a gun it's a hard habit to break. I hopped on my city bike, a Harley Davidson Night Rod Special. It's big, black, loud, fast and equipped with lights and siren. I figured I could make it to Grams' house in about ten minutes.

I buzzed over to Highway 100 and headed south to the home of Emma Bjornstrom Anderson. As I rode, I thought about Grams.

I'd heard pretty much every story Pete had to tell about his grandmother. She was born in some way-out-there town in the northwest corner of North Dakota called, believe it or not, Alamo.

Emma had grown up in the northwest corner of the Peace Garden state. It was a time of great change for the entire country and Alamo was no exception. Just one of many children of a local farming family, she had married Pete's granddad, Elmer Anderson, in 1938.

Elmer always did his best to stay on top of world events by reading everything he could get his hands on. Seeing what was coming better than most Americans, he enlisted in the Marine Corps shortly after Germany invaded Poland in September 1939, just six months after Grams gave birth to a son, Karl. Grams bundled up Karl and moved to Fargo to work as a bookkeeper in a Wells Fargo bank during the war years.

After VJ Day, Elmer made the long trip home to his bride and now six-year-old son, Karl, but not many jobs. Taking advantage of the just-passed G.I. Bill, the family moved to Fargo, where Emma had spent much of the war, so Elmer could attend North Dakota State. A degree in agricultural science led to a job with General Mills in Minneapolis.

Elmer was a product manager in the cereals division and helped the country develop a habit of a quick "boxed breakfast." The family wound up in the house I was riding to in the Country Club area of Edina, a very upscale old-money suburb of Minneapolis.

Karl stayed in Edina when he married, eventually building on acreage in west Edina, where Pete and I hung out. In 1972, when Pete was fifteen, his grandfather died in a boating accident and Karl moved his family into his parents' house so he could keep an eye on his mom, Pete's Grams. As it turned out, it was a fortuitous move. Four years later, a drunk driver killed both of Pete's parents. Pete was attending the University of Minnesota at the time but his younger sister, Ruth, was still in high school.

Grams finished raising Ruth and when Ruth went off to college, Grams continued to live in the big house by herself. Eventually, she hired a housekeeper named Agnes, who came in every day to help with household chores and to drive Grams around to the many meetings and activities she still enjoyed.

Pete continued the family tradition and bought his first house in Edina, near Pamela Park, a bit south from Grams. Three years ago, with his son at college and his wife on the road much of the time selling her cookbooks, he made the move he'd talked about for years and bought a place right on Lake Minnetonka, as high-end as property gets around the Twin Cities.

I rolled into the driveway with my shield in my hand. An Edina cop was standing in a position to block anyone trying to enter. Two TV trucks, half the local stations, were already setting up. I guess the word was out. This was a big story—not many murders in Edina. The driveway was full of cop cars and vans so I parked the Harley on the sidewalk.

Grams' house was a 1930's Tudor-style two-story that backed up to the Edina Country Club, giving it the feel of having a huge backyard. Years ago, Pete and I had the exact limits of the real yard pointed out to us by irritated golfers a couple of times.

Another Edina cop was keeping a log of everyone who came into the house. I checked in then made my way through the foyer full of Hennepin County crime scene people and found Pete in the living room. He was standing off to the side in kind of a daze. His sister Ruth was sitting on the couch, sobbing softly. I sat down next to her and wrapped my arms around her.

"Oh Dan, how could something like this happen?" she cried.

It was a question I'd heard at hundreds of crime scenes. I just never thought the family would be my own, after a fashion.

I have a married sister who has produced two fine young boys I enjoy playing uncle to but they live in Wisconsin, so I don't see them too often. With my parents gone and Sis on the wrong side of the St. Croix River, I'm pretty much alone, except for Pete's family. Growing up under the influence of Grams made me an auxiliary branch on their family tree. These two people, now trapped in the depths of the sudden loss of the family's anchor, were as much family as I had.

As I gave Ruthie a squeeze I felt my jaw clench. I was already feeling the heat of a case that was more than personal. "Honey, I don't know yet what happened, but I guarantee you, and you too Pete, I will find out."

I stood up and guided Pete away from his sister. "Where's Carol?" I asked.

Carol is Pete's wife, the cookbook author. With all the experimenting in the kitchen she does, I had no idea how Pete stayed in such good shape. Of course being retired at fifty helped—he had plenty of time to workout.

"She's in L.A. at a book-signing thing. I called her and left a message to call me back"

"What have they told you?"

"So far, not much."

"Was it a robbery? Did they clean the place out?"

"No, and that's what's got the cops puzzled. Nothing's missing that we can see. It looks like whoever did this left everything they should have taken. I don't get it." He was getting agitated. "Grams gets killed and they don't even take anything? It doesn't make any sense."

"No, it doesn't," I agreed. "Listen, I see the Edina chief over there. I've known him for a while. Let me go over and see what he'll tell me."

Dave Houkkinen, the Edina Chief of Police, was standing in the hallway talking to an investigator from the state Bureau of Criminal Investigation. I made my way over and waited for a break in the conversation.

"Hey, Dave," I announced myself.

"Dan. What brings you out here?"

"Friend of the family. I went to high school with Pete. They're practically my own family."

"Bad business, this. First homicide since I've been chief."

I'd known Dave about ten years—since he'd become the top cop in Edina. I knew his wife too. She was also a LEO, or Law Enforcement Officer. In fact, we were sitting at the wedding reception of another cop we both knew when she turned me on to cleaning my guns by tearing them down and throwing them in—no shit—the dishwasher. You still have to brush the barrel and do a good job of oiling everything afterward, but it works.

Dave started quizzing me. "So you knew the deceased?"

"Like she was my own grandmother."

"Anything you can tell me that might help? You know what I'm looking for, anything that could point at motive, anyone for suspects, anything at all."

"I got to tell you, Dave, there's nothing. I know Grams has some nice stuff, stuff that would attract a burglar, but only a pro would try to hit a house like this. I've got to figure that this was random. Just some guy who thought he'd hit a fancy Edina house and Grams was unlucky."

"According to your buddy Pete," he said, nodding in Pete's direction, "most of the 'good stuff' is still here. A pro would have surely taken the jewelry and maybe some of the art. But, then again, a pro wouldn't have killed the old girl. He would have made sure no one was home. Right now it looks like an amateur broke in, maybe thinking no one was home, and Pete's grandma surprised him. Can you check with the family and find out if she was scheduled to be out of the house."

I knew what Dave was getting at. If she was supposed to be gone it would indicate some kind of inside information. We'd have to check with her lawn service, paperboy, the post office and such. All kinds of people are informed when someone is going to be gone and often a burglary can be traced to these people.

But I doubted that could be it. I knew Pete well enough to know that the only service providers he'd allow would be fully bonded, insured, their personnel vetted and reliable. That meant either a random burglary or someone who targeted Grams. With only Pete and Ruthie left, there was no one in the family who could possibly want to do Grams harm. And money wasn't the motive. Pete's got more than he'll ever spend and Ruthie's husband Steve is a very successful real estate broker. And Ruthie is an artist—she makes stained glass windows and sells them for what I think are unbelievable numbers. I know she's booked up for the next two years. Neither of them looked good for this.

Normally, the housekeeper would be high on the suspect list. But Agnes was a seventy-something gal who had been around for close to twenty years. I also knew that Grams paid her more than she could have made anywhere else in this town, including health and dental insurance, vacation and even some kind of retirement plan. Plus Agnes was as nice as they came, had no family of her own, and was, at this moment, sitting in the dining room crying her eyes out. Nope, it wasn't Agnes. Still, I knew Dave would have her on the suspect list along with Pete, Ruth and Steve.

That's part of the job. When a family member is killed, the family is first on the list of suspects, no matter what, especially spouses. But you already knew that. Every time a woman is killed, her husband, and/or boyfriend, is number one on the list of who to check out. But that's true for dead men too. The wife/girlfriend (in some cases—both) is number one. Same with children, parents, grandparents, aunts and uncles—everyone is a suspect. I knew it wouldn't go anywhere here, but that doesn't mean you vary from standard procedure. In fact, I was wondering where Steve was. Ruthie's husband should be here.

Of course, that's when he walked in, accompanied by an Edina patrol officer. Dave waved the cop over as Steve went straight to comfort Ruth, wrapping her in his arms.

I'd known him almost as long as he'd known Ruthie. "I was at the office when Ruth called. What happened?" he asked, turning to me.

Pete joined us. "That's what we're trying to figure out, Steve," he said.

Dave spoke with the patrol officer. Dave looked at me and I nodded so he knew that I was giving the OK on Steve. He walked over to us.

"Mr. Hammer, I'm Dave Houkkinen, Edina Police Chief." He shook Steve's hand. "I can't tell you how sorry I am at your loss."

Steve wasn't really paying attention. His eyes flitted around the room as if he was looking for something.

"I just don't understand why anyone would want to hurt Grams," he said. "It just seems . . . surreal."

"Why don't you three sit down and catch your breath for a moment while I talk to the Chief?" I said.

Dave and I walked back through the house to the kitchen, where Grams' body still lay. She was covered with a sheet, but a small trickle of blood could be seen edging out. Dave allowed me to take a look.

I've seen a lot of bodies in my career. People leading their lives, living their hopes and dreams one minute and then, without warning or reason, they're suddenly brutally rendered into visions from a horror movie. But this was different. This was Grams. My body stiffened as Dave pulled back the sheet.

Grams was lying on the floor as if she'd decided to take a nap. Her arms were up surrounding her head, which was turned to the left. She had a startled expression on her face, but her open eyes were the dull lusterless grey of the dead. Through a blood-encrusted mat in her hair, I saw a wound typical of blunt trauma. In spite of over thirty years of seeing murder victims, I felt bile rising in my throat.

Looking away for a moment and taking a breath, I brought myself back to the case. I could tell the blow had been from a lateral swinging motion, like a baseball bat, as opposed to an overhand blow, like chopping wood. The impact was at the base of the skull. By hitting her there the attacker caused immediate damage to her lower brain where all the autonomic functions are, causing a very quick death. Shooters call this the "apricot" because that is what the organ resembles. If you shoot someone in the apricot, they check out immediately with no chance to fire back or hurt a hostage. It's just like turning off a light switch.

I know this because I am a shooter and considered an expert. My latest book covered wounds and blood spatter caused by gunfire. In the research for that book I discovered that you can tell a lot about how someone was killed by the amount of blood that comes out of the body after they've been shot. It's a direct indication of how long it took the victim to die. Abdominal wounds are the worst for bleeding and dying can take hours. Heart wounds take less time but still bleed quite a bit because the heart tries desperately to do its job. A shot to the head can sometimes be survived, depending on the caliber of the bullet and the location of the impact. But a shot to the apricot and the person is dead before they hit the floor. That's the target snipers are looking for, especially in a hostage situation. Like I said, it's just like turning off a light switch—click—you're gone.

"At least it looks like she went out quick," I said.

"I concur. With a blow like that she would have been at least unconscious before she went down. Also, the lack of blood indicates a quick death," Dave added.

Adrienne Hunter was a Hennepin County crime scene investigator whom I knew from previous cases. She had been standing aside while we looked over things.

"It always does my heart good to know that the experts agree with my analysis," she said, giving me a little wink.

Dave and I let her get back to work and continued through the house toward the main floor office.

"The rest of the house is almost untouched but someone spent some time in here," Dave said as we entered the office. "We found a lot of the disturbed material in here."

I looked around. It was immediately obvious to a trained cop's eye that someone had been going through the office. Although the office was still neat—no one had pulled out the drawers and dumped the contents onto the floor the way a quick in-and-out burglar would have—things were out of place. I knew Grams well enough to know that she would never have tolerated her office looking like this.

First off, the chair was pulled away from the desk instead of being tucked under it. Papers were spread on the desk, not stacked neatly. Several books in the bookcase were tipped over. One of the file cabinet drawers was ajar. These were all things that were out of place for Grams. She had a thing for order.

"Has Pete had a chance to come in here yet?" I asked.

"No. We've been preserving the scene until County gets done with it. They haven't dusted for prints or collected fibers yet," Dave answered.

That meant that I couldn't dig around in here either. Until the crime lab people finished, there would be no touching anything. I understood and knew that they had to do their work, but I also thought, based upon the rest of the house, that there was little chance of finding anything. A person as careful as this one had been would not leave a bunch of fingerprints in here after leaving nothing in the rest of the house. But that wasn't what was bugging me.

"Dave, you were saying that it looks like a lot of probable loot was left behind?"

"Correct. There is no visible evidence that the bad guy was even in

Mrs. Anderson's bedroom, which is where she kept her jewelry. If he had gone in there he would have found quite a collection of very valuable stuff that is, basically, just lying there in unlocked boxes. No safe, no lock box, just sitting there in regular jewelry boxes. There is also a nice collection of art that would be worth taking. And I saw a coin collection in one of the hutches in the living room. I'm no expert on that, but they looked well stored and that, at least, is an indicator that someone thought they were worth something.

"There is also a safe," he said, gesturing toward a steel brick the size of a two-drawer file cabinet. "It appears that an attempt was made to open that. Since it's part of the investigation, we haven't opened it yet. When the CSIs are done, we'll have your friend open that if he can. The contents will be cataloged and, if they are interesting enough, taken into evidence. It's going to be a long morning."

That was an understatement. This was going to take at least until early afternoon. I asked Dave if he was going to stay for the whole thing.

"Probably not. It's usually best to let the experts work by getting out of their way. My office is only a few minutes away if they need me. And there is going to be the media to deal with," he said with a sigh.

I knew Dave well enough to know that, like most cops, he loathed the press. The problem isn't the people; it's their job. Their job is to get a nine-second sound bite. Print press people are better at what they do; they have the luxury of being able to take more time. But print media is going the way of the horse and buggy—it takes too long. Now we have the Internet and a 24/7 news cycle on television. TV is the here and now. TV wants a flashy visual and a statement that incorporates the facts and some emotion—immediately. Actually, as long as it's got emotion, the facts don't really matter.

That's why you see so many interviews with people who have no facts to contribute. They aren't even asked for the facts; they're just asked for their emotions. After a park shooting in which some no-skill gangbanger fires a dozen rounds at an enemy gang member from a distance of, oh, ten feet, and misses the intended target but hits an eight-year-old a block away, you'll see an interview with the eight-year-old's mother/

aunt/sister/cousin, none of whom saw the crime or could offer any explanation of what happened. All they do is cry and scream and moan for some kind of justice. Grandmothers are the best. They never know what happened but always can be counted on for a description of the victim's prospects for a successful future. Hey, maybe the kid would have been president, but we'll never know now—she's dead.

The point is, modern news has nothing to do with the facts—the who, what, where, when and how that used to be taught in J-schools. It's all about emotion. That's what people want to see. And cops hate it.

Here's an example: everyone remembers the airliner that had to land in the Hudson River after both engines were taken out by a flock of geese. Sully, the captain, used all his experience and training to get those people down safe—an incredible feat.

Months later, The History Channel had a special on the event. I recorded it in anticipation of a show along the lines of what I've come to expect from them—a review of what happened, why, and how the crew performed a miracle.

That's not what I got. The entire show was interviews with the survivors. While they had the unique perspective of having been on the airplane, they were not pilots, aerodynamicists, engine specialists or even ornithologists. They were regular people whose whole experience was limited to the seat they were sitting in. They related their feelings—they were scared, they were angry, they were preparing to die—all reasonable feelings for someone in that situation, but there were no facts about what actually happened. Facts are cold and flat, not emotional. This is why most cops look bad on TV.

Dave was facing one of those TV moments. The electronic media was assembling outside and they wanted their nine seconds. It was Dave's job to deliver a brief but engaging statement that included what had happened to whom (the where was obvious, other than where in the house), when it happened, and how it happened. Anything beyond that was not news and would not be coming from him. As a result, anything he was about to say was going to come across as cold and flat. That was OK. Cops prefer cold and flat. There are a few exceptions to that—big-city police chiefs or big-county sheriffs, who are really politicians and relish the spotlight—but not the grandson of Finnish immigrants standing before me here. One thing about the Finns, they know cold and flat.

"I don't envy you that assignment. You OK with me hanging around?"

"Yeah, you know what you're doing, and," he gave me a stern look, "you will stay out of the way." A command, not a question.

I nodded. "I just want to stay with the family and be here when Pete opens that safe. If I have any ideas, I'll run them through your investigator or the County people."

"Sounds good. Stop by later and let me know what you think. This one's a mess."

I nodded again and we shook hands. He sighed and headed out toward the microphones.

Chapter Two

I went back to sit with the family while the mechanics of the murder investigation took place in the next room. It's pretty hard on a family to see this exercise, which is why most crime scenes are immediately off limits to everyone not employed by the investigating agency. The technicians remain calm and professional but it's hard for them not to talk about last night's ball game or who's dating whom just as anyone does at work. This kind of small talk can be very offensive to the family when the victim is still laid out stiff on the kitchen floor.

Pete and Ruth were sitting on the couch in the living room, while Steve was pacing around. Steve's always been a pacer, so I didn't connect anything to that. He's a very active guy—up early every day whether he's working or not, always takes the o'dark-thirty tee time and always has some project he's working on. I think the pacing helps him think, sort of like my going to the shooting range helps me think. Some people think in the shower, some think over coffee. Everyone has his own way of coalescing thought.

"Pete, we've got a little time until the County people are done. Can you think of anyone who would have had a reason for doing this?"

"That's all I've been thinking about since I got here. Who would do this? But there's no one. Gramps has been gone for so many years that I can't believe this would be related to anything about him and Grams is, well—Grams."

I knew what he meant. Everyone loved Grams. She was active in her church, in women's clubs, at the local community center, still on the board of the country club that adjoined the backyard—all the usual upper crust sort of activities. In addition, she was very busy with humanitarian causes. She helped out at the local food bank, worked to raise money and materials for Habitat for Humanity and volunteered at Meals on Wheels. She was busy all the time. The idea that she could have made an enemy who would be willing to kill her over any of these matters was absurd. No, I kept coming back to a random break-in burglar who thought no one was home.

"Does the house have an alarm system?" I wondered aloud.

Pete answered, "Of course it does, but Grams didn't use it."

Steve jumped into the conversation. "Like most people, she didn't want to bother with it. It's a passive-active system so it provides fire coverage whether it's active or not. Grams knew this and she told me that as long as the fire alarm worked, that was enough."

"She told you this?" I asked.

"Yeah. I was trying to teach her how to operate it and she just wasn't interested. She kept saying that no one in the neighborhood had ever been robbed and she knew that her neighbors would keep an eye on the house when she was gone."

"What about when she was home?"

"She said no one would break in when she was home because that never happened. She said that she watched the crime shows on TV and that all you needed to keep burglars away was a sign that said you had an alarm and the bad guys would go to the next house. She said she kept up the service in case there was a fire, so it would call the fire department."

"Well, that's sort of correct," I said. Crime experts say that one of the big values of an alarm is the sign in the yard. They also say that you have to have an alarm to have the sign, that the alarm should be on all the time and that you should also have a dog. A firearm close at hand is a good idea, too, if you are trained and have the personality to use it if you have to. Actually, I thought Grams would have had the personality to pull the trigger. She'd been a tough North Dakota bird before moving to the comforts of the suburban Twin Cities.

I had another thought. "Pete, let's take a walk. There's something I want to check out."

Pete got up and we headed out the back of the house. "What's on your mind, Dan?"

"The alarm. Grams was right. She had a sign in the yard but that didn't stop the guy. And he couldn't have known that she didn't use it. Where does the phone service come into the house?"

Pete led me around to the west side of the house. The power poles had disappeared from this neighborhood years ago when everything had gone underground. Two light green boxes were nestled between some bushes that had been planted to hide them on the property line between Grams' house and the neighbor to the west. One was power, the other phone and cable. We walked over to the boxes.

The phone box showed scratches on the screws that held on the cover. I pulled out the Leatherman tool I always carry (a very handy device—everyone should have one) and pulled out the screwdriver. After removing the screws, we looked inside.

A small electronic device had been attached to the phone wires for Grams' house. I whistled the nearest Edina cop over and asked him to send the lead investigator out to us. He leaned his head into the radio mike on his shoulder and a few moments later a nice looking thirty-something woman came out of the house. She walked over.

"You must be Neumann?" she asked as she shook my hand. "I'm Liz Reddy."

"I'm Neumann," I admitted. She shook Pete's hand, too, but I got the feeling they'd already met. "Take a look at this," I said, pointing into the box.

"Well, that explains the alarm. We checked the system and called the monitoring company. The alarm was not activated last night. In fact, they said it hadn't been on in years. Either the intruder knew the alarm would be off or there should have been some effort to disable it. There's a big sign in the garden by the front walk that anyone would have seen. In fact, anyone planning to hit any house around here would assume it had an alarm. We checked the line where it enters the house to see if it was cut or tampered with and there's nothing. So this is it."

Indeed it was. I recognized the gizmo and so did Liz. It was a commercially available device that would keep an alarm monitoring company from being able to do its job.

The way most alarms work is that, when the alarm is activated, it sends a signal to the monitoring company through the phone line. Cutting it would prevent the alarm company from discovering that a break-in or fire or anything else was going on at the house. So the alarm company sends a random signal back through the line every five or ten minutes to make sure the line is still active and hasn't been cut. If it's been cut, it triggers a call to the cops. Cutting the line wouldn't keep an alarm from sounding a siren or horn. But many systems are silent, or became that way after the homeowner had enough false alarms and got so tired of the damn horn going off that they neutered the thing with a wire cutter.

Someone had tried to bypass the alarm. This meant they knew there was an alarm, wanted to get in anyway, and went to the trouble of finding this gizmo and attaching it to the wire. If he did it right before the break-in last night it would have been dark and the bushes could have hidden his activities. I thanked Liz and left her to photograph and remove the gizmo. Pete and I walked back to the house.

I sighed. "She was targeted—someone wanted into this house. We have to figure out who would target Grams. What did she have that they wanted? It apparently wasn't her jewelry, the art, or Gramps' coin collection. Those are all still here. What was here that someone wanted? And why did they figure they could get in and get it last night? Was there anything on Grams' schedule that would have had her out of the house last night?"

"I've been thinking about that. It's a little strange, but she did usually leave the house toward the end of the month."

"Left? Where?"

"She's in this group of older gals that has kind of a travel club. They go around to bed and breakfasts and explore antique shops. They're usually gone for three or four days."

We were back to the porch and walked into the house via the living room. Pete went over to Ruthie.

"Ruth, do you know anything about Grams' B & B club?"

"Yes. What's that got to do with this?"

I asked, "When did she go on her trips?"

"The last weekend of the month, every other month. They leave on Thursday or Friday morning and come back Saturday night so they can make it to church on Sunday. She went nearly every time they had a trip planned.

"So she was planning on going on this trip?"

Pete answered, "I'm sure she was."

Steve whipped out his phone and in about a minute he was showing it to everyone.

"Here it is."

We crowded around Steve, Pete looming behind him, taking full advantage of his six-foot-four-inch height. The phone showed a picture of Grams' church with the usual web page accessories. Steve entered a series of clicks and wound up on the B and B club's page. The phone showed the web page for the "Golden Girls Antiquing Club." The first and biggest picture on the page showed some of the club members. Grams was right in the middle of the picture.

A calendar showed the weekends the group went out. There was a banner headline atop the calendar that said "Remember—Due to September's cancellation, we have an even grander tour planned for October. We'll be leaving from the church at noon on Wednesday, October 29th."

"But she was home. Why didn't she go?"

"She decided to stay home for Halloween night, tomorrow. You know how much she loves to see the kids in their costumes and give out candy."

"She won't be handing out any candy this year," I thought. The coal burning in my soul glowed a bit hotter.

"I guess we know how someone could have believed Grams was going to be out last night," Pete said.

Inspector Reddy came into the living room. "We're done with the office. If you can open the safe, we'd appreciate it."

Pete nodded and we all trundled into the office. The safe was visible to anyone who came into the room. While it was not bolted to the floor, it was too large and heavy for an individual to move alone. Pete knelt before it and dialed in the combination. The dial spun without a sound, a testament to the quality of old technology. He looked at Reddy. "Should I open it or do you want to?"

"Go ahead and crack it, then let me take a look."

Pete grabbed the big handle and turned it ninety degrees. The safe made a clunk sound and the door swung free. Pete stepped back.

Liz Reddy bent down and took a quick look. She snapped a few photographs, then started removing the contents. Another investigator had followed us into the office and was cataloging the contents as Liz removed them. A third investigator snapped a picture of each item as it came out of the safe.

"Two passports, a small jewelry box . . ." she droned on as she methodically emptied the safe.

"What's this?" she said as she removed a heavy rag-wrapped lump. She unwrapped a Colt 1911 .45-caliber semi-automatic pistol in the remains of a holster. The pistol was well worn and the holster was literally falling apart. She removed the pistol from the holster and, in a reflex action typical of someone familiar with firearms, removed the magazine and cleared the action. A large shiny .45-caliber round flipped out of the ejection port when she racked the slide. With the fluid movements of an expert, she caught it in mid-air.

"Oh my goodness," Liz said. "Someone believed in being prepared."

I put my hand out and she handed me the pistol. It had "U.S. Marine Corps" engraved into the frame below the slide. "I'll bet this was Gramps' pistol from World War II."

I handed the pistol to Pete who hefted it. "I've seen this thing maybe twice. Gramps wasn't much for stories but I knew he was in the Marines and saw a lot of action."

Liz had pulled a wide flat box from the safe. She opened it to reveal

Gramps' awards. "Wow, will you look at this!" There was a very impressive collection of ribbons and medals, including three Bronze Stars, a Silver Star, and a Navy Cross along with the usual "I was there" awards. It was a part of Gramps none of us ever knew.

Pete, who had spent most of his business career working with military contractors and, therefore, the military, looked at the collection of what the military boys call "fruit salad" and started to tear up. He knew more than the rest of us what Gramps had been through to earn this box of trinkets.

Pete collected himself and said, "I've known a lot of warriors in my life and most don't talk about it, especially not to people who weren't there. We weren't there, so he didn't talk to us about it. I wish he would have."

The other investigator had finished with the inventory and looked at Liz for direction. Liz nodded and he left. "There doesn't seem to be anything here of interest to us. I'll leave this stuff with you. If you could go through it and see if anything is missing, I'd appreciate it."

Pete shook his head. "I won't know if anything's missing or not. I didn't know the gun or the medals were in there. I don't know what's supposed to be in there."

Pete was getting a bit upset by all this so I took over. "Liz, I'll stay on this and let you and Dave know if we come up with anything."

I walked the family back to the living room. "There's really nothing left for you to do here today."

Pete asked, "What's the process from here? We need to plan the funeral."

In every homicide case, there is a mandatory autopsy. There was no way I could delicately tell them that the state was taking over possession of their grandmother's mortal remains, which they were then going to slice and dice until they had pulled every detail about her death they could from her cold body. Of course, I couldn't tell them that. But . . . well, that's the process. I was reaching a level of pissed off I had never experienced before in my life. Whoever had done this was going to pay.

"Well, when they've completed the job here of trying to find everything they can about what happened, they'll transport Grams to the

Hennepin County Medical Center where they'll conduct the autopsy. That's required by law in any homicide. It will be a few days before you'll be able to take Grams to the funeral home."

"She wanted to be cremated," Ruthie said.

I thought that would at least make things a bit easier, considering that an autopsy sometimes leaves the remains less than viewable, especially when a head wound is the cause of death.

"Then you can make the arrangements now and the Cremation Society can pick up Grams when she's available."

I had always been bothered when people referred to the deceased as if they were still alive. They seemed to be hanging on to some sliver of hope that their loved one would somehow "get better," as if they were just sick or something. I'd heard a thousand of them and never knew why people talked that way. Now I knew. The coal burned on.

"You should all go home and just take the rest of the day to wrap your heads around this. You need to contact people. And Pete, you need to talk to Carol. And call the Academy. They'll let Jim come home for this.

"As soon as the police let you, you need to go through all of Grams' things very carefully. Let me know if you find anything that might be of interest, anything that seems even the least bit out of place or unusual. Something in this house attracted her killer and we need to find it."

"I'll go through everything. It's going to take a few days, but I'll do it," Pete answered.

"Good. And don't forget her safe-deposit box. Whatever it is might be in there," I said.

I gave hugs all around, something I'm getting better at in my dotage, and made my way out of the house. I fired up the black bike and took Wooddale up to 50th. The ride took me through one of the most elegant of the Twin Cities' suburbs. Along Wooddale are beautiful homes dating back to the turn of the last century; the Edina Country Club is on the west side of the street. The turn at 50th is like something out of a Norman Rockwell painting, with a big church on the southeast corner and the country club on the southwest. I took a left and zipped up the hill to the Edina city offices, heading for the cop shop.

I grew up in Edina, so that makes me a local. Growing up in the '60s was to grow up during the time of change. I was too young for Viet Nam, much to my parents' relief, but not too young to be at the University of Minnesota during the war protests. The news coverage was thick with stories about the war and the protests. This environment produced people with polarized points of view. You were either pro or con, Republican or Democrat, square or hip. There was no in-between.

My parents' plans for me involved going to the U and then going on to some graduate program, whatever I had to do to stay undraftable. Then I'd get married, have a career, make babies, get a dog and live in Edina with everyone else. It did go that way for a while.

I got married before my senior year, just a bit ahead of the schedule. My bride, also a senior, was in pre-law. I majored in sociology with a minor in abnormal psych. We both graduated in the standard four years and she was accepted to John Marshall in St. Paul for her legal training. I didn't apply to any grad schools; instead, I applied to the Minneapolis Police Department. This act of defiance completely baffled my parents, my in-laws, and my wife, even though we'd talked about it while we were dating. I guess she thought she'd talk me out of it or I'd grow out of it. After graduating from police training, I spent three years riding the graveyard shift in the toughest neighborhoods of the city. She'd had enough and used her new legal degree to file for divorce.

So, I've been on my own for most of my adult life, not an uncommon situation for a cop. It's a tough life for relationships. Cops have one of the highest divorce rates in the country. Understandable, but not acceptable. Something needs to be done to help these men and women lead more normal lives. I'm not sure what it is, but it's something to work on.

I parked the Harley, walked in and asked for Dave. He was in a meeting so I left a note saying we hadn't found anything interesting and that I'd stay in touch.

Chapter Three

Tuesday, November 11th

Two weeks went by quickly. The county released Grams' body back to the family after five days. An enormous crowd honored Grams at the memorial service. It often seems that the older a person is, the fewer people come to their funerals, but Grams had nearly 1,000 people come to either the wake or the service itself.

In the ten days since the funeral I'd been all over the country. While Pete tried to figure out if anything was missing from Grams' house, my other job as an expert witness had kept me busy. I'd just finished a two-day deposition in a Florida murder case that I was going to appear in as an expert witness. A man was on trial for killing his former girlfriend. The victim had died of a gunshot wound to the head that, at first glance, looked to be a suicide. But, after looking at the crime scene evidence and writing the postmortem protocol, the medical examiner listed "Homicide" as cause of death and the wheels of justice started rolling. In the report she submitted, the ME found one key piece of evidence that told her the young woman had been murdered.

The killer had done a good job of setting up the scene. The victim had been taking anti-depressants and blood work showed she was on them and drunk at the time of her death. She had purchased the gun for personal protection about a month before her death and had taken the time at the local gun range to learn how to use it. The wound indicated that the muzzle of the pistol was in near contact with her head, the angle of the shot looked right, and the gun was still in her hand.

The suspect had a pretty good alibi. He said that he was about forty miles away at a strip club. That's where the story began to fall apart.

The girls at the strip club remembered him because he was a regular and a big tipper, but none could be sure he was there the whole time. It seemed there was almost two hours missing. He had used his credit card, a sure way to establish alibi, but there were no charges from 9:30 p.m. until 11:45 p.m. The transaction at 11:45 was a closeout charge the waitress had rung but had not turned in until she was leaving. There was no way of knowing when he signed it. No one could be sure that he hadn't left then returned to the club.

And, a friend of the dead girl testified that the victim had bought the gun at the insistence of the suspect, that he had, in fact, paid for it, and that he had been with her at the range teaching her how to use it. The witness said the victim was more afraid of the suspect than she was of anyone else.

That raised some doubts for me when I was consulted. Another big concern was the choice of weapon. Most women will purchase a small-caliber gun for self-defense, a .25 or maybe a .380 automatic. They are easily concealed and don't have a lot of kick. And both are good for self-defense, if escaping an attacker is your primary concern. But the victim hadn't bought that kind of gun. She'd purchased a .357-caliber revolver with a two-inch barrel, the short length making it easy to conceal. It was a special model, light and easy to carry, made out of titanium. It's about one-third the weight of a standard model of the same caliber. Still, it's heavier when loaded that the aforementioned guns, more expensive to purchase, and much more expensive to practice with. In fact, its only positive attribute over the smaller caliber is that it is much more likely to inflict a fatal wound. The final problem is that its light weight lets the gun kick like a mule.

That kick was the final kicker for me.

I'd run tests, complete with video, and shown that the gun should have been thrown out of her hand, perhaps as far as ten feet away. I'd even suggested to the prosecution that we should all go to a range and let the jurors shoot the gun, an idea they were sure the judge would not allow. Anyway, in my expert opinion, there was no way she could have held onto it after shooting herself in the head. She had all four fingers neatly wrapped around the grip—nothing on the trigger.

Anyway, it was a good trip. I got to go to Miami in November and even worked in a three-day weekend in Phoenix on the way home. I have a friend there I'd met on a case last summer, a detective with the Maricopa County Sheriff's office who was a big help in solving a mystery. We didn't get the doers convicted, and never would, but we figured out what happened. That happens sometimes. Did I mention that the detective is a woman?

I had just put the breakfast dishes in the dishwasher when the phone rang.

"Neumann," I answered.

"Dan, it's Pete."

"Hey Pete, how you doing? Things getting back to normal yet?"

"I guess so. At least things are back to normal at home. Carol's heading out to finish the book tour. I've got pretty much all of Grams' stuff sorted out. I'm talking to a Realtor about selling the house. Ruthie's not sure she wants to let it go yet and the Realtor says we'll have to disclose that Grams was murdered there. That ought to help the price, right? Maybe we'll wind up waiting for a while, try to find somebody to rent it. I still need to look at the safe-deposit box. I was wondering if you'd be available to go downtown with me to check that out."

"Sure. When do you have in mind?"

"Can you go this morning?"

"Pick me up in an hour?"

"I'll be there."

Another thing I'd done since that sad morning was stop by the Edina PD to talk to Dave Houkkinen again. They weren't getting anywhere with the case.

The previous morning

I walked into the Edina PD reception area and told the young lady behind the bullet-resistant glass that I was there to see the chief. She called, then told me he'd be right down. A minute or two later Dave greeted me with a wave, then came over and opened the security door.

"Good to see you again, Dan, although I wish it was under better circumstances."

I shook his hand. "I agree. How are you doing otherwise?"

"You know, the usual. This job is more paperwork than police work."

We went back up the stairs to his office. It's a nice office for a cop's; enough room for three or four people if they're friends, a functional desk, and a table area. The only really unique thing about it was the view of the north end of the Edina Country Club's golf course. Not many cop's offices have that. If we'd had a really good scope we could've seen all the way south to Grams' backyard.

We sat down across the table from each other and Dave gave me a rundown.

"County went through that place with a fine-toothed comb and came up empty. The only real clue is that gadget you found on the phone line. It turns out that it does just what you said—it interrupts the phone line but keeps a signal going back, which makes the alarm company think there's nothing wrong even if the phone line is cut. Your friend Pete couldn't identify any missing items but he was still working on the office. Cause of death is just what it looked like, blunt force trauma to the back of the head resulting in immediate loss of consciousness and death. No one saw any unusual vehicles, nothing's come up for anyone having any kind of motive. You know, I've got five investigators in this department, two of them trained homicide investigators, but neither of them has ever worked a homicide. Not that I'm complaining, you understand, we just don't have the horsepower or experience to get anywhere on this. Everything dead-ends. Do you have any ideas?"

"Dave, I've given this a lot of thought," I said. In fact it had been in the forefront of my mind every day since Grams died. "Since the only room disturbed was the office, it has to be the burglar's target. I'm pretty sure he expected Grams to be gone, so he probably figured he could jump the alarm, and get in and out without any interference. Whatever it was he was looking for, he thought it was in the office. Maybe it was, maybe it wasn't. Maybe he got it. We may never know. But for now, I think we concentrate on the office."

"Do you have time to work on this?" Dave asked.

"Dave, I'd work on this even if I didn't have time. If you can put me on officially as a consultant, I'll do it for a dollar."

That's where we left it.

I finished the breakfast chores, then hit the treadmill for a quick twenty-minute trot. I don't run on it; my knees have seen too many moguls for that. Maybe I should try biking; that's pretty popular now. Anyway, twenty minutes of light jogging followed by sit-ups and pushups keep the old bones in shape. I showered and dressed in what I consider business casual for November, gray wool slacks, a light blue long-sleeved dress shirt, no tie and a navy blue cashmere jacket. I was ready when Pete rolled into the driveway.

I locked up and hopped into Pete's eight-year-old Cadillac.

"Aren't you ever going to get a new car?" I asked.

"Why? This one is working great. Actually, it's prima facie evidence of what's wrong with car companies today."

Pete had been in manufacturing all his adult life. He loved to talk about it.

"And what's that?"

"In the late '70s the Japanese started to take market share from Detroit. It started with gas mileage, but what worked best for them was quality. You remember the American cars in those days—they sucked. So all through the '80s, Detroit worked hard to catch up. By the '90s they were almost there, but the Japanese had established a solid market share and were introducing new high-end brands like Lexus to compete with Caddies and Lincolns. This pushed quality even higher. When this car was built in 2002, it was built to last at least 250,000 miles with little maintenance and no major repairs. Those 1970's cars we drove could barely limp to 100,000.

"So what happens? If you make a product that lasts two or three times longer, is it logical to expect to sell as many as you used to? Now you do have to factor in some overall market growth, but you still have to expect that sales will go down by a bunch. It's counterintuitive—here you are making a better product and selling fewer. How does *that* work?"

"And that's why the car companies went to DC begging for help?" I asked.

"Well, they're not asking for money to make the cars better; they're making a case for just staying in business."

We were driving south on Broadway, heading to downtown Minneapolis. Pete was keeping his mind off the business at hand by talking about something in the abstract. I'd seen him do it before and I did it myself on occasion.

"You see the problem, don't you?" he went on. "No one likes to think that the product they are making is not going to be needed. In this case, it's not that cars are obsolete, it's that they are better and last longer. But the result is the same—they can't sell as many as they could before. It kind of makes a case for planned obsolescence. If they don't wear out, how are you going to sell more of them?"

I helped him along. "Do these kinds of changes happen often?"

"Sure. My favorite example is this. Can you name the product that was made by 238 companies in 1900 but only four companies were making it in 1920?"

I thought about it. What did you need in 1900 that wasn't needed1920? Hmmm. I could think of a lot of things that were being made in 1920 that weren't being made in 1900, but not the other way around. I said "No."

"Buggy whips. The entire industry collapsed when people started buying cars. Should the government have bailed out the buggy whip industry? No. The product was no longer necessary. Buggy whip companies either adapted to make something else or they went out of business."

"So what should the car companies do?"

"Bite the bullet, slim down, and keep making great cars. Otherwise, foreign companies will take over the market.

We pulled into the bank's parking area and locked up. I followed Pete into the bank to the information desk. Pete explained the situation and pulled open his briefcase. He had the paperwork the bank required to allow him to get into Grams' safe deposit box. Pete asked for a vice president.

Another young lady approached and asked, "Mr. Anderson?"

"I'm Pete Anderson," Pete answered and shook her outstretched hand. "This is Dan Neumann of the Minneapolis Police Department. He's a friend of the family, not here on business."

"I'm Judy Timmers. I can help you with your grandmother's accounts. We were all sorry to hear about her death. She was well known here at the bank and we all liked her."

That seemed to sum up Grams' life—well known and liked.

We followed Ms. Timmers into the deposit box area. Pete gave her the paperwork and she retrieved the box. It was large, about twelve inches wide and six inches deep by at least thirty inches long. We took it into a private booth and closed the privacy curtain.

Pete inserted the key into the box and gave it a turn.

Chapter Four

The key clicked smoothly and Pete opened the box. Nothing sprang out like it would in a horror movie, so we both took a breath and looked inside. It was the stuff you'd find in any safe-deposit box—papers, a few small jewelry boxes, a stack of old photos, a tea towel-wrapped something, a bundle of old letters, some legal-looking papers and more papers. No wrapped packages of powder-covered $100 dollar bills, no kilo of cocaine, no guns—none of the stuff I usually found when I opened a safe-deposit box with a warrant.

There was a mortgage stamped "Paid July 14, 1974," and a deed stamped "Recorded," both for the Edina house. Receipts for work done on the house in the '60s and '80s, an employment contract between Gramps and General Mills dated 1958, a deed conferring mineral rights from something called "F.Y.S. Land and Cattle" to Emma Bjornstrom Anderson, a copy of the front page of the Minneapolis Tribune from VJ day in 1945, and their wedding license. We opened a jewelry box next.

"It's empty," I said.

"I'm not surprised. Grams wore most of her jewelry frequently. She used to say, 'I didn't buy it to keep it in a box.' So it was at the house. She probably came in here, put it on and wore it out."

"Yeah, that makes sense." I couldn't think of a time Grams wasn't wearing jewelry. I could even remember seeing her gardening with big rings on her fingers. She was a Depression survivor and liked to keep her valuables close.

Next was the something rolled up in an old tea towel. Pete

unwrapped it and found a framed photo of a young couple standing under a tree. The photo was very old and faded. I didn't recognize the young man, who looked to be about eighteen, but the young woman looked familiar.

"Any idea who that is?" I asked Pete.

"Sure. The girl is Grams. Look at her, that's got to be Grams. But I haven't a clue who the guy is. I don't think it's Gramps."

"How about the location?"

"Beats me. Why's it matter?"

"It matters enough that Grams kept it in her safe-deposit box. That makes it matter to me."

"Good point." Pete looked at the photo a little longer. Nothing seemed to be registering. "I don't know. I'm pretty sure that's Grams. The guy—I don't know. I can't say it's not Gramps."

Pete set the photo aside and we turned to the last thing in the box, a bundle of letters. They were tied with a silk ribbon. Pete untied the bow and unfolded the top paper. He said, "It's a letter dated September 26th, 1945. Well, well. Looks like Gramps had a romantic side." He read from the letter.

> *My Dearest Emma,*
>
> *I have returned to the United States and hope to be with you soon. The war's interruption of our lives has ended and now, with the grace of God, we will be able to resume our lives as we planned. My family has told me that you had to leave Alamo to work in the war effort and that you had not been able to reply to my earlier letters. It is with all my heart and soul that I am confident that we will find each other again. A love like ours cannot be denied.*
>
> *Forever Yours*

"I never figured Gramps for something like that," I said.

"Me neither. There's a whole stack of these. She must have kept everything he ever sent her."

Pete started flipping through the letters looking at the dates. "These are from the '50s, the '60s and the '70s."

We looked at each other in wonder. It was a Gramps we didn't know.

"A lot of these are from after they were married," Pete said.

"Could be. I've seen that in couples. They keep up the habit to keep the romance. It's not that unusual for folks who're already writing each other."

I fanned through the stack. "These might make a nice little book—you know, a 'Letters from the past' kind of thing. But I doubt it has anything to do with Grams' death," I said.

"Maybe I could take them and use them on Carol for birthday cards and anniversary gifts—things like that."

I chuckled. "You could at that. You'd be the best-laid husband on the block if you could write like this."

"I never knew Gramps had it in him. It looks like Gramps was a secret romantic. You know they got married in the fall of 1938. He was eighteen and she was only seventeen, but that wasn't out of line for then. The war got in the way of their lives for a few years but afterward, they just picked up where they'd left off."

"Is he the guy in the picture?"

Pete picked up the photo again. "Could be. The ages would be about right. You know, it's sad to say, but I'm just not sure what he looked like then. I only remember him as Gramps.

"Grams was born in 1921. That would have made her twenty years old when Pearl Harbor got hit. She looks about eighteen in the picture, so he could be Gramps."

I reached over and picked up a couple of the letters. As I read them something started buzzing in the back of my head. It's a feeling I get when I come across some important piece of evidence but can't compartmentalize it yet. There was something here. If only I could figure out what.

Chapter Five

The buzzing thing has been going on throughout my entire law enforcement career. Some might call it a cop's instinct or a sixth sense; I don't know what it is, but it has served me well over the years so I pay attention to it. The problem is it's a "Wake up and pay attention, buddy" signal, not a "This is it!" signal. So sometimes I miss the important part. This time I was sure that it was signaling that something in the safe-deposit box should be lighting up my inner alarm.

I looked at the photo again. Who was this mystery man? I shook my head and set the picture aside and said, "We need to get back on point here. Is there anything here that could help us find Grams' killer?"

Pete said, "Not that I can see. There's a bunch of old documents and heirlooms, but nothing worth killing for."

"Even so, we should take all this stuff and catalog it for Dave. Just in case something comes up later."

I started a list. We identified, photographed and listed each item. The bundle of letters was listed as a single item—"Bundle of old letters." We labeled the photograph as "Photo believed to be of deceased unknown man, possibly Elmer Anderson, the deceased's husband (also deceased). Age at time of photo unknown, estimated to be circa 1939."

We put everything except the framed photograph, the loose photos, and the letters back into the box, locked the cover, and took it out to Ms. Timmers.

"All done?" she asked.

"Yes. Could you put this back for us?"

"Of course. And again, let me say how very sorry everyone here at the bank is about your grandmother's death. We will all miss her very much."

"Thank you," Pete said, handing her the box. We said our goodbyes.

As we pulled out of the parking lot, I told Pete, "I have to get this list to the Edina PD. You want to come along?"

"Sure. Nothing better to do. I just wish we would have found something."

"Maybe we did."

We headed out of downtown on I-394, took Highway 100 south to the 50th–Vernon Avenue exit in Edina, crossed the highway and turned into the parking lot. I led Pete into the building.

"Dan Neumann to see Chief Houkkinen, please" I told the receptionist.

She said, "I'm pretty sure he's in a meeting."

"Could you check? I have evidence to turn over to the Anderson murder team."

She called upstairs and, after a brief conversation, said, "He'll be right down."

A moment later I saw Dave coming down the stairs behind the lobby area. We met him at the security door.

"Good timing," he said after the customary hellos. "The team is meeting right now."

We followed Dave back up the stairs and down the hall. Just past his office we entered a central meeting area surrounded by other offices. It too had a window overlooking the Edina Country Club. "That would be a distraction for me if I worked here," I thought.

The investigative team was gathered at a large dog-bone shaped modular table facing a large white-board upon which was written a timeline and pertinent facts about the case. There weren't many. It looked like a scene from the "Without a Trace" TV show, only without the fancy computers, nice dark décor, pretty faces and plenty of cleavage. There was one other difference. This team was without a clue as to who had killed Grams.

Chapter Six

Detective Team Room
Edina Police Department

The three men and one woman all had the look of career law enforcement types—good physical condition, intelligent eyes and somber expressions. They looked up as Dave made the introductions.

"Guys, some of you may know Dan Neumann of the Minneapolis PD. He's an old friend of mine and of Mrs. Anderson's family. And this is Pete Anderson, Mrs. Anderson's grandson. They're here at my request to see if they can provide any insight into a possible motive. Pete and Dan, This is Arthur Henderson, Jack Sprague and Randy O'Falvey. I think you met Liz out at the scene."

All the detectives said hi or nodded in our direction. Liz got up and came over to Pete.

"Mr. Anderson, I just want to tell you how sorry I am that we haven't been able to get anywhere on this."

Pete shook her hand. "Thank you. Dan's told me how hard this is and I've known him long enough to know that he doesn't always solve his cases."

I spoke up. "We've just checked Emma's safe-deposit box. I've got to say that there wasn't anything that really jumped out at me. We made a list."

Liz spoke for the team. "Let's have the list and we'll see if anything ties together."

I handed over the list and she quickly made enough copies for everyone. As the team looked it over, the youngest-looking one—O'Falvey—said something to Sprague.

"You have something, Randy?" Liz asked.

"This stuff is pretty old." He held up a picture of a man standing next to a bi-plane on skis at an obviously snow covered airport. "I think you should send this stuff to the North Dakota Historical Society. There's nothing here for us but they might want it for a museum."

"Where did Mrs. Anderson grow up?" Sprague asked.

"Alamo, North Dakota" Pete answered.

"Alamo? Alamo, North Dakota? That's for real?"

Pete explained. "Alamo is a real place. It's about thirty miles from Montana and thirty miles from Canada."

"That's about thirty miles from the middle of nowhere," O'Falvey replied.

"It was actually a hopping burg in the early part of the twentieth century. Had stores, two banks, everything."

Henderson had been typing on his laptop. "Well, it's not so hopping now. Says here the population is fifty-one."

Pete surprised me by saying, "It *was* a hopping burg. The area is agricultural—hay and cattle. Back in those days there was a lot of farming up there but the farms were a lot smaller than they are now. Nowadays, the farms are huge and are run with a lot of automation so the local population is way down from what it was."

"Do they do anything else up there?" Liz asked.

"Not that I know of," Pete said. "There might be some mining or something. There was an old mineral rights deed in the safe-deposit box, probably something to do with some old gold mining or something like they do in the Black Hills. I don't think there's any real mining going on up there now."

"You know a lot about the area. Ever been there?" O'Falvey asked.

"My grandfather told me all about it, wanted me to know where our people came from, but I've never been there. I looked it up on Google Earth once. It doesn't look like much is left of the town."

Dave cut in. "What do we have?"

Liz took the lead. "We have the murder weapon. It was a candlestick the killer found on the premises. It was recovered from the floor of the kitchen where it had rolled under the table. There was a faint blood trail from the point where the bad guy had dropped it. Its matching partner was on the scene on a side table. Pete's sister Ruth identified it as belonging to the deceased. And we have the gizmo that was attached to the phone box. That turned out to be a commercially available device that is pretty much untraceable. It was probably purchased at a Radio Shack or other electronics supply place. The serial plate had been removed, so we can't trace its origin.

"No other trace was found on the scene. No prints, fibers or usable DNA trace of any kind.

"We have no motive other than burglary. But there is no evidence that anything is missing so there's nothing to look for at the usual stolen goods outlets—pawnshops, thrift stores.

"Unfortunately, Pete and his sister have been unable to determine if anything is missing from the files in the office. So we believe we are looking at a botched burglary. The bad guy had just gotten started when the victim interrupted him. He grabbed a weapon of convenience and struck the victim, killing her, then took off. That about wraps it up."

Liz was clearly troubled by the lack of success. This murder might be the only one they ever worked on and no one wants to go down in history with a batting average of .000.

"There may be something else we should keep an eye on here," I said. "Since we can't figure out what the bad guy was after, we don't know whether or not he found it. He may have found what he came for before Emma came downstairs. If that's right, he's done. If not, he may still be a threat. We should keep an eye on the house for a while." The buzz was louder. I didn't want to scare anybody but the cop in me was twitching. I looked at Pete and said, "And you and Ruthie should keep your guard up, too. If the bad guy didn't get what he wanted from Grams, he may come after you."

Pete startled. That was an angle he hadn't considered.

Chapter Seven

Shorewood, Minnesota

At nearly the exact moment Dan was telling Pete to stay vigilant about home security, Pete's home security was about to be tested. But not by a professional burglar.

The thin sandy-haired young man with thick glasses who was about to break into Pete's house was an engineer. He had a B.S. in Geological Engineering from South Dakota State and an MBA from the Carlson School of Management at the University of Minnesota. Burglary had not been included in either curricula.

It had been two weeks since the break-in at Grams' home. The engineer in him had required a detailed plan before that attempt and Grams had not been part of the plan. The old woman had always gone on the church-lady tours of B & B's and antique stores the last week of every other month. He even knew that the September tour had been postponed to October. She always went. Pictures on the church's website of each tour showed her in every picture. He had every evidence that she would not be home. All he had to do was bypass the alarm and he would have all night to find what he was looking for.

But it hadn't gone that way. He easily got around the alarm system and made the entry just fine. He'd just gotten started on his methodical search of the office when he heard the old woman. Either she had awakened or had heard him—whichever didn't matter. She had come down the stairs and into the kitchen. He grabbed the closest weapon handy—a candlestick of all things—and hit her from behind, thinking it would knock her out. Instead, it was like something from Clue, that old kid's board game—Mrs. Anderson in the kitchen with the candlestick. Except Mrs. Anderson wasn't one of the characters in the game. Mrs. Anderson had died and that complicated things. The result was an abbreviated search, which came up dry. Not good. Not good at all. Not good for business.

Business was what this was all about. In addition to being an engineer, he was a businessman. He certainly wasn't a burglar. He'd had to research the whole concept of burglary on the Internet. He'd found everything he needed to know about bypassing the security system and opening locked doors. Of course, Mrs. Anderson's door was unlocked anyway. But he had defeated the security system and took some pride in that.

The entire episode was filled with what ifs. If he could have found what he was looking for and destroyed it, there would be no further problems. If the old woman had not been home, he could have finished his search. If the family had been reasonable in the first place, none of this would have been necessary.

He'd spent the last two weeks reviewing what had happened during the first break-in and began working on Plan B. He had reached these conclusions: his search—brief as it was—should have yielded the item if it was there, but it had not. Therefore, Pete Anderson, the old woman's only grandson, must have it. There was also the granddaughter, but he thought that was a long shot. That the grandson would have it was logical, and the businessman-burglar was nothing if not logical.

So the research started anew. If he was going to attempt to recover the item from Peter Anderson's home, he had to know what the house looked like. This he got from overhead imagery available on the Internet. Nice place on the lake, he'd thought, viewing the photo from Google Earth.

Next was the floor plan. As with many municipalities, a copy of the floor plan was on file at the city hall. All he had to do was go in and tell the people in Inspections and Permits that he was a contractor who was going to be doing some work on the house.

The home had an alarm and he researched that as well. He was confident he could overcome it if it was, in fact, armed. The only remaining question was how long it would take him to find what he was after.

Unfortunately for him, there was one additional security feature in Pete's home that he didn't know about.

For the third time in six days the businessman-burglar turned the plain white contractor-type van off County Road 15 toward Pete Anderson's house. Before his first trip down this road he'd studied the maps and overhead photos and concluded that the road was a very long dead end. Once he made the turn from Wilshire onto Tuxedo he was on the cul-de-sac. The road connected a chain of islands that terminated on Shady Island, one hop past Enchanted Island, where the Anderson house was situated. He drove carefully, not wanting to attract the attention of either law enforcement or watchful citizens. He reached down between the seats and switched on a specialized radio set. Once on the island he turned onto Enchanted Point—the last street he'd need.

His reconnoitering had not only prepared him for the lay of the land and water; it had also revealed some other interesting information.

As he drove he reviewed the plan is his mind. He'd already gone over it three times while waiting in a nearby Caribou Coffee parking lot. Three times was required for him to feel comfortable. When under stress he would count things in groups of threes until he felt comfort from the routine. Each time he reviewed, he counted the steps. There were twenty-four. He had recited each one, counting them as he went. Now he reviewed them again in his head: 1. Park in the drive like any other repairman. 2. Remove the toolbox from the rear of the van. 3. Walk to the front door and knock to see if anyone might be home . . . He would continue this until the plan was completed.

His research had revealed a neighbor's Wi-Fi system, which included a security camera that was directed on the home's driveway. Fortunately, from the businessman-burglar's point of view it also showed Pete's driveway. He'd been able to hack into the local server through the camera feed and had downloaded a week's worth of that view. The recording revealed that Pete Anderson left nearly every day by 9 a.m. and went who-knows-where until at least lunchtime. Two days he'd come home at noon; on four he had not. Either way was fine with him; he had allocated one-and-a-half hours for the search. He'd be long gone by the time Pete returned home.

After verifying that the house was vacant he would walk around to the left side of the house where he assumed the phone line came in. He would neuter the security system as he had in Edina. Continuing to the lake side of the house, which appeared secluded in the overhead imagery, he would make his entry, search the home, find the item, and leave. This time he'd be sure to take the device off the phone line when he left.

He pulled boldly into the drive and parked the van. Counting to himself, he said "One." Getting out of the truck, he went around to the back and pulled out the toolbox. "Two," he said, trying to look to the world and any interested neighbors like a repairman. The front walk, a wide sweeping curve of paving stones, was lined with a variety of northern perennials. He counted to himself, "Three," as he rang the bell, then knocked loudly on the door. He waited.

Pete's study, a dark heavily paneled office with two walls of book-shelves held a large desk with attached computer stand. The desk faced a forty-inch plasma screen. The final wall faced the lake. The lake view was made possible through a set of antique poured-glass windows recovered from an early 20th century Minneapolis home that had been demolished. They stretched from two feet above the floor to the ten-foot ceiling. Variances in the poured glass gave the lake a wavy appearance whether the wind was blowing or not. Behind Pete's desk a dark shadow moved at the sound of the knocking.

The would-be burglar satisfied himself that no one was home. He would have been surprised if someone had been—he'd seen Pete drive away that morning. But he was prepared, just in case. He had donned a false beard and wig obtained from a local theatrical costume supplier. He wore typical serviceman's clothing of khaki cotton, even had a name tag—"Bob"—on his chest. He also had a phony work order for a house with the same address number but located on Enchanted Drive, not Point. He was pleased—the event was going as planned.

He continued his count as he walked around to the phone box and quietly bypassed the security line. Then he walked around to the lower level French doors on the lake side. He scanned the lake for any late-season boaters. Seeing none, he tried the door. As with the Edina house, it was unlocked. He entered.

The dark shadow in Pete's office had followed the burglar's progress. The shadow had exceptional hearing and knew exactly where the man was as he circled the house. The shadow moved with him until it was at the top of the stairs when the door opened. The shadow slipped behind a couch as the man crossed the lower level family room and climbed the stairs. When the man reached the top, he stopped and looked around. The shadow pounced.

Sinbad, a seventy-two-pound jet-black Flat-Coated Retriever was a dog show champion in his youth. Now nine years old, he was in great shape despite his age and spending most of his time indoors. Pete walked him four or five miles almost every day. They always left through the side door—a door unobserved by the neighbor's security camera. While he was normally a friendly, happy, and very social dog—typical of the breed—this was an unusual situation. Like many dogs of any breed, he was territorial and had a very different personality when someone entered his personal space when his master was not at home. He was defensive.

Sinbad leapt from the shadow of the couch with a roaring bark and caught the burglar full in the chest. The burglar's instincts had kicked in as he detected the motion. He brought his left arm up just in time to protect his face. The pair, plus the toolbox, tumbled down the stairs and crashed into the wall at the turn of the bottom step. Sinbad rolled off to the side and the burglar jumped to his feet and dashed for the door, never looking back. He slammed the door behind him and ran for the drive. As he rounded the side of the house he remembered the phone gizmo and stopped long enough to pop the box open and rip it off the wires. He slammed the box shut and ran for the van.

Still terrified and reeling from the burn of an adrenal gland dump into his bloodstream, he threw the van into reverse and hit the gas. He spun the wheel to turn around in the broad driveway, but didn't brake quickly enough to keep from running over the shrubs at the end of the turnaround. Shifting gears, the van leapt forward, making a screeching turn onto the street.

The burglar drove, willing himself to breath. He suddenly remembered that he couldn't afford to draw attention to himself, so he slowed. He replayed the last minutes in his head. Where had that dog come from? There had been no sign of a dog—no fence, no tie-out cable, no droppings in the yard.

He'd left the toolbox. Fortunately, it was just a prop. He'd paid cash for the whole prepackaged kit at a local big box home improvement store. There was no tracing that back to him.

He began to feel a dull ache in his side and noticed a gash on his arm. There was a tear in his shirtsleeve at his left forearm. Driving with his knees he pulled the fabric around to see how bad it was. Puncture wounds and a three-inch tear in the skin. With any wound inflicted by the dirty mouth of an animal, his preference would be to get professional assistance. Obviously, he couldn't get do that. "What if the dog hadn't had his shots?" he thought. No. He knew the owner by reputation well enough to know that the dog's shots would be up-to-date.

He would have to fix himself up. A quick stop back at the hotel room he'd rented under a false ID to clean up and change clothes, then a visit to a drug store and he'd be fine. But then what?

Chapter Eight

Wayzata, Minnesota
Heading for Pete's house

Pete and I decided to grab some lunch at a spot on the lake out near his place. is a newer style upscale restaurant with a nice view of Wayzata Bay. I ordered the daily special, tuna melt on marble rye with the house kettle chips. Pete had a Cobb salad with roast chicken. I can still delude myself with the idea that anything called "fish" is healthy—mayonnaise and deep-fried potatoes notwithstanding. Pete actually had a healthy lunch. I guess that pretty much defines our differences in cuisine; I think healthy, he eats it. I did wash it down with an iced tea—no sugar.

We sat next to one of the windows that overlooked the lake. A rail line runs between the restaurant and the lake and you can plan on a long freight slowly rumbling by in the middle of your meal, blocking the otherwise magnificent view for a few minutes. It's the oxymoronic nature of a new/old town. I love it.

After lunch we drove over to his place to mull over the mystery of the contents of the safe-deposit box.

We rode through the eclectic collection of homes that surround Lake Minnetonka—some old, some new, some run down, some worth millions—all depending upon whether or not they were on the lake. Lakeshore is the key. I heard from a real estate buddy of mine that one place on the lake went for 2.3 million and the first thing the buyer did was tear down the old house. I guess it's true what they say about location.

As we turned into Pete's driveway I saw a crushed shrub. "Hey Parnelli, what happened to the bush?"

"What are you talking about?"

"Take a look, bro. You hit it good."

Pete looked over at the bush and pinched his eyes. "It wasn't like that when I left this morning."

Then I saw something else that probably hadn't been there that morning—tire marks on the driveway, marks made when someone left in a big hurry. I said, "Stay in the car and call the local police. Tell them you may have had a break-in and that I'm with you and I'm checking the house."

I got out, patting the pistol on my hip. I didn't draw—too much paperwork. But I put my hand on it.

When you've been on the job as long as I have, you think you'd get used to situations like this. The unknown. The only data is that there's been a disturbance in the drive and someone apparently left in a hurry. You don't know if anyone is in the house. They've probably left, but assumptions like that get you killed. The door is locked and you are doing your best to peek in the window without making yourself too much of a target. Your focus is so intent that you can lose situation awareness, or SA, as the tactical boys say.

Situational awareness is the ability to know what's going on all around you. Fighter pilots, combat soldiers, policeman, race car drivers, quarterbacks—anyone who needs to "picture" what's going on all around them—are trained to develop this sixth sense. Lack of it gets you killed by someone you never knew was there. Great quarterbacks always seem to know when to duck to elude that blitzing linebacker coming from their blind side. Great fighter pilots have it in three dimensions plus overtime so they can see not only what's going on right now, but where half a dozen jets flying at over 500 miles per hour will be five and ten seconds from now. I've always had great SA and it's saved my butt on several occasions. Not today, though.

I peered into the entryway. Nothing. I tried the door—locked. I took another look into the house and felt something that made me jump.

Pete was about to open the door. He'd come up behind me after I'd gone into tunnel vision, leaving me open to the heart-stopping surprise.

"Jesus Christ, Pete!" I wailed. "I told you to stay in the car."

"Like hell. This is my house. I'm going in."

Pete opened the door. The old house was solidly built and once we were inside all the sounds of nature and civilization were turned off as if someone had thrown a switch. It was quiet except for the beep of the security system. Suddenly we both heard the patter of feet on the floor. Sinbad.

"Hey, buddy," Pete said. "How's my boy?" He bent and gave his black furry house partner a firm thump on the side. Sinbad responded with a low but friendly growl, like the purring of a big cat. Pete went to turn off the security system while I gave the dog a rub on the head—we'd been friends for years.

I heard a car in the drive. A South Lake Minnetonka police cruiser had arrived. I went outside with my shield and ID in one hand and my other hand up in plain sight.

"Dan Neumann, Minneapolis police" I said, standing still on the walk.

The suburban police officer was very young. "Does this kid's dad know he has borrowed his uniform?" I wondered. He opened his door and stayed behind it for cover—a smart move that many older officers forget about. He spoke into his radio, then came from behind the door. I kept my hands in sight as he walked up to me to check my credentials. He relaxed a bit as he saw my ID was the real McCoy and motioned me that it was OK to put my hands down. "So, what's up?" he asked.

"Not sure yet. The bushes at the end of the drive are crushed and there are fresh tire marks in the drive. We thought there might have been a break-in. Looks clear now."

Pete came to the door and called, "Hey Dan—get in here."

The South Lake cop and I trotted up the walk while I told him the owner was in the house.

"What's going on, Pete?" I asked, as we entered the foyer.

"I went to shut off the alarm and the panel says there was an entry."

"Where?"

"Downstairs door. But I didn't get a call, so I don't know what the deal is."

I looked at the keypad readout and it said "Lower Level Patio Door: 9:58 a.m."

We looked at each other and then, as one, moved to the stairs. I beat the cop there and pulled my gun as I went downstairs. At the bottom of the stairs I scanned the room and saw a toolbox and tools strewn on the floor near the bottom of the stairs. A floor lamp was knocked over in the same area. The cop, his Glock out, moved to my left, covering that part of the room, Then Pete appeared with a Kimber 1911A1 .45-caliber pistol in his hand, which he'd retrieved from his bedroom.

"Sir, I'm going to have to tell you to put that away," the cop said.

"Like hell," he said, repeating his earlier claim. "This is my house and I am going to defend it."

"Pete, I know you can handle that pistol, but for my sake, please put it down and let us do this, OK?" I said.

Reluctantly, Pete complied. He lowered his hand and tucked the big pistol into the small of his back. That apparently satisfied the cop, who went back to searching his side of the room.

I checked out the furnace room, then checked the bathroom and the lower level bedroom. "All clear on my side," I declared.

The cop came out of the media room and nodded agreement that his side was clear too. We regrouped at the bottom of the stairs where the toolbox and tools were scattered.

"I think Sinbad spooked him," Pete said.

I looked at the cop and said, "Call this in. The house was burglarized and we need the Hennepin CSI out here soonest."

"We usually investigate our own small-scale stuff out here. We don't call County unless it's something big like a homicide." He seemed pretty nervous about all the help he was getting.

"I understand your S.O.P.s, son, but this is probably connected to a homicide. Mr. Anderson's grandmother was murdered about two weeks ago during a burglary in Edina and I think this is connected."

"That was your grandma?" the cop asked.

"Yes," Pete said to the cop. "Are you sure this is the same guy?" Pete asked me.

"I've got that feeling. Not a pro—no pro would have a toolbox like this."

I bent over and looked at the tools. "They're brand new. Look at them —there's not a mark on them."

Pete and the cop stooped and, without touching anything, inspected the tools and the box. A half-peeled-off price tag on the box told us it had been purchased at Home Depot.

That was enough for the cop. He went outside and I could see him talking into his microphone.

Pete looked at me and asked, "What the hell is this guy looking for?"

"That's the million dollar question all right." A light flickered in my mind. "The alarm control panel said there was an entry and you said you never got called. Call the alarm company and ask them why."

Pete went upstairs as the cop was coming back in. "I talked to the chief about it and he said he'd get the County people out here. I think he's coming over himself."

"Good. If this is what I think it is, we'll need a very thorough sweep of the house by the CSI folks and some heavy-duty police work on the part of your department."

The young officer struggled to stay nonchalant. "We can handle it," he said with a smile.

Chapter Nine

Enchanted Island,
Shorewood, Minnesota

I went upstairs and found Pete on the phone. All I got from his end was "Yes. No. Yes, the system was on when I got home." He stood watching the alarm's control panel. After a few seconds he said, "Yeah, the thing says 'Status OK.'"

He hung up and looked at me.

"They said they never got a call. They downloaded the onsite memory and it says there was entry and that it tried to call the base, but they never got a call."

"You have a siren?" I asked, wondering if there was an onsite screamer.

"No, I hate those things. They shriek and bother the whole neighborhood." He looked a bit sheepish and said, "I guess that would have been a good idea, huh?"

"Yeah, pal. It would have been a good idea. Hey—if they didn't get a call maybe the guy used that phone bypass thing again."

We ran outside to the phone box. It showed tool marks indicating it had recently been pried open. I flipped out my pocketknife and popped it open. No joy. No gizmo on the wires. I uttered "Damn" under my breath.

Pete said, "Wait a second. Take a look at the wires."

Pete's had a lot more experience looking at wires than I have. He worked in the local manufacturing industry for years, and the companies he worked for all made stuff that had wires. I didn't see what he was looking at and admitted it.

"See here?" he said, pointing. "See where there is a little nick in two of the four wires? Something was attached to them."

Sure enough, when he pointed them out I could see the nicks. Great eyes, my buddy has. "We'll have to make sure the CSI folks get this. You may not have phone service for a day or two."

We went in the house to have a beer while we awaited the arrival of scientific technology.

Chapter Ten

The burglar drove back to his hotel wondering if he was out of his mind. Maybe he should just go ahead without it and take his chances. After all, these people didn't know him—hadn't ever contacted him. For all he knew they had no reason to expect anything from the project he envisioned. But the stakes were so high. If things worked out as he thought they would, it could mean billions of dollars to him. The numbers were staggering.

The low estimates were 1.5 trillion dollars. Obviously, he wouldn't get all of it—only the royalties on the part recovered from his property. But that fraction would still be huge. He had dreamed for months about what he could do with that kind of money. He could build a decent airport so he could keep a private jet locally, he could have a yacht on Lake Superior and a home on the North Shore, he could drive anything he wanted—maybe an Aston Martin or a Ferrari. No, screw all that. He could finally leave the godforsaken place of his birth and see the world, live somewhere warm year round—maybe Hawaii. That would be a good place for a jet and a yacht.

No, he liked North Dakota. It was in his blood. He'd be able to stay there and travel anywhere he wanted to when he felt a little cold. That would be all right.

At the hotel he draped his jacket around his arm to hide the blood. He went to his room where he removed his shirt and washed the wound. There was a tear on the outside of his left forearm and a series of puncture holes lined up in a row. The dog had gotten a pretty good grip on him before they both went ass over teakettle down the stairs. Fortunately, he hadn't bled much, just a little rivulet that ran down his arm into a frozen stream. He checked the rest of his body and found a number of bruises starting to swell and color. Grabbing a bottle of ibuprofen he gulped four of the 200-mg pills and washed them down with a bottle of water. He'd have to get to a drugstore and buy some Bacitracin and a decent bandage. Until he could do that, wrapping it with a hotel washcloth and taping it with some duct tape he had in his trunk would have to do.

He slumped down into the overstuffed chair to contemplate his options. He had twice attempted to recover the document or documents—he didn't know how many there were—and had failed both times. And, now he'd left things behind . . . again.

He did a quick mental inventory. He knew about the toolbox of course, but what about what the TV people called "trace." Trace was what they solved crimes with. From TV he knew they could find anyone with something as small as a drop of sweat or blood. And he had certainly left blood in the house.

Or had he? He didn't know for sure. When the dog bounced off him at the bottom of the stairs he'd gotten out of the house very quickly. Maybe there was nothing left behind. Could he be that lucky? He was due some luck after the way everything had been going. He had always believed that luck ran in streaks. Was this the turning point or was he still on a run of bad luck? He didn't know.

He needed to leave town. He packed his things neatly and checked the room carefully three times, each time counting the places he'd checked—bathroom, under the bed, each of the bureau drawers. Carefully. Even though he'd used a phony name to check in and paid in cash, he didn't want to leave anything behind. He loaded his car and checked the GPS for the nearest drugstore. It would be a long drive home and he needed to take care of the dog bite before it became infected. And he'd need more painkillers.

Lake Minnetonka

The Hennepin County crime scene team arrived about 2:00 p.m. and took over. The South Lake cop and I had done the tape thing to secure the scene and Pete had taken Sinbad for a walk. When they returned we put Sinbad in Pete's Cadillac.

I spoke with the crime scene team leader and gave her a rundown on what I thought had happened—break-in at the rear door (unlocked, much to Pete's chagrin), entry and climb to the top of the stairs, possible Sinbad attack and fall down the stairs, scattered toolbox at the bottom of the stairs, retreat, and retrieve the gizmo on the phone line. We were standing in the lower-level family room.

"Where's the dog?" she asked.

"The homeowner put him in his car. Do you want to see him?"

"Perhaps. If the dog bit the intruder there may be a chance we could recover DNA from his mouth, but it's been a pretty long time since the incident so that's a real long shot. We'll look for blood in here first."

I left her to do her job and looked for Pete. I found him sitting out on the veranda. Being mid-November it was a bit chilly but the house faces southwest and he had the sun on his face as he looked at the lake.

"Man, I am really screwed up. What the heck is going on here?" he asked.

I plopped down in the chair next to him and said, "I don't know, man. This is about a 9.2 on my weird-shit-o-meter. I'm still wondering what Grams or you have that would attract a burglar. I mean, beyond the obvious stuff. Once again—someone breaks in and takes nothing. This time Sinbad might have run him off before he could take anything, but he had plenty of time at Grams.'"

Pete looked out across the bay, squinting into the low sun. A flock of coots moved low over the water. They were funny little birds to watch as they flocked in large groups and scooted across the wave tops. Dark steel grey with bright yellow and white bills, they are difficult to see against the slate cold water. Only their bills give them away. Now in mid-November they were gathering for their trip south. Winter was knocking on the door and they were smart enough to leave before the door opened to a true Minnesota winter.

Minnesota in November is simultaneously one of the most interesting and depressing places in the country. Sunrises come after 7:00 and sunsets before 5:00. The days are cold and short but often, as is the case this year, there is no snow yet. Snow can come anytime between early September and the end of never.

Then there are the aforementioned blizzards. They can be killers, literally. And unpredictable. The day of the Armistice Blizzard of 1940, the temperature dropped fifty degrees in a few hours with the wind gusting to seventy miles per hour. Two and a half feet of snow fell. With the high wind, the snow didn't really fall, it blew into enormous drifts, covering anything sticking up from the ground—buildings, trees, hills, cars, and people.

The 1991 Halloween Blizzard had more snow and less of a temp drop but the biggest difference was public notice. In 1940, guys had gone out bird hunting that morning wearing what you'd wear for hunting in forty-five to fifty-five degree weather, not knowing that the temp would drop to zero, with wind chill down to minus thirty. One hundred fifty four people died that day—more than half were duck hunters. In 1991 we had radio and TV forecasts. Yep, autumn in the Midwest can be interesting.

The other part of a Minnesota autumn—depression—sets in for many people. The trees are barren; if there's no snow, the grass is brown, if there is snow the color is even more monochromatic. The sky often has a charcoal patina and the lack of sunlight gives the entire panorama a sort of black and white quality. I'm one of those people who get hit by something called "seasonal affective disorder" or SAD. What that really means is that people like me slow down and hibernate when the days get short. We crave more daylight, get moody and, in some cases, depressed during the short days. A local radio show host has the same thing but he has developed a way to deal with it. He started something called "The Order of the 21sters." It's for people like him who count down the days to the various astronomically important days of the calendar like the equinoxes and solstices. For those people, December 21—the shortest day of the year—is actually the last day of winter. Once the days start getting longer, they feel better. It can be twenty below in January or February but the sun appears earlier, the days slowly get longer, the sky is blue and the colors of nature seem somehow more intense in the crystal clear air. Getting to that date is the point. Focusing on the fact that the days are getting longer helps you get through it. The radio guy even has a sign-up place on his website. I'm a charter member.

Sitting here with Pete, looking out over a soon-to-be-frozen lake, I continued to work the mystery. But, I'm stumped. Maybe a Scotch would help.

"I read a few more of those love letters from Gramps to Grams. They're really touching. It was a side of Gramps I certainly never knew," Pete mused as we sat in the warmth of the low sun. Between the heat-absorbing slate of the terrace and the lack of wind, it was nearly toasty. "It's kind of strange, you know, reading those things that he wrote when he was probably younger than we are now. He was a romantic at heart."

"That may be, bro, but I just don't think that has anything to do with what's going on here," I said.

The crime scene gal came out of the house. "We found a little blood at the bottom of the stairs. There's also a smudge mark on the staircase wall. Looks like someone took a fall."

"I'll bet Sinbad either spooked him or jumped him," Pete said.

"You're probably right. If Sinbad was on him he'd have run for his life," I said. I looked at the CSI and asked, "You want to take a look at the dog's mouth?"

"Sure. I won't know what we get until I do the lab work. It's a long shot."

"That's what I figured. But—you never know."

Sinbad was sitting in the front seat behind the wheel of Pete's car and looked like he was ready to drive off. He's a pretty smart dog. He was a dog-show champion and had some obedience titles. He just might be able to drive. Too bad he couldn't talk.

Pete helped Sinbad down from the high front seat saying, "At his age I don't like him landing on his front end so hard. I read something in a dog magazine about 'jump down syndrome.' Someone did a study and found that dogs jumping out of trucks and cars had more shoulder problems in later life. Makes sense to me."

Sinbad looked at the CSI tech with a big smile as she took a swab from her tackle box. Pete commanded Sinbad to sit, which he promptly did. Pete took hold of Sinbad's lower jaw and held the dog's mouth open so the tech could get a good look inside. She swabbed both sides of his mouth and said "Let's look him over for anything else. He may have picked up a skin sample or fibers if he came in contact with the burglar."

Pete told the dog to stand, which Sinbad immediately did. I'm amazed by this. The only dogs in my life were a few that were owned by female friends over the years. None of them showed the least inclination toward this kind of ability. Sinbad just stood there looking like the stud muffin he is. He could have been a statue.

The tech examined Sinbad very closely, starting at his nose and working methodically rearward. She stopped at his right shoulder and asked, "Did he have this before?"

Pete took a look. There was a spot on Sinbad's shoulder blade where the fur and skin had been rubbed off—like a road-rash burn on a motorcyclist's shin after a fall. Pete said, "No, that's new. He must have hit something with his shoulder."

"That could explain the blood in the stairwell," the tech said as she swabbed the area. "I'll check it against this sample to be sure."

The tech completed her check of Sinbad without finding any other wounds and closed her tackle box. We all walked back into the house and Pete put Sinbad in his kennel crate in a small room off the entry. The crate is big enough I could use it for camping.

"Anything else you need to work on?" I asked the tech.

"I think we are pretty much finished. I'll need to get prints and blood from all the occupants of the house for elimination."

"Elimination?" Pete asked.

"We have to eliminate you as the possible source for the blood or fingerprints—you and anyone else who is frequently in the house—wife, children, housekeeper, weekly poker buddies—anyone you can think of who might be the source of the evidence."

"My wife is out of town until this weekend. Our son is at school. Except for coming home for a couple of days for Grams' funeral, he's been there since mid-summer."

"We can wait on your wife. I'd like to get your son's, though. Sons have a tendency to bleed a lot. Where is he?"

"Annapolis—the Naval Academy."

"That works. They'll have a medical facility and some kind of military police office. They can get what we need and send it to us secure enough to support chain of evidence."

The South Lake cop came into the foyer. He looked around and must have figured I was still the highest-ranking guy in sight. His boss wasn't on site yet. "Detective Neumann, there's a guy out front I think you should talk to."

I hopped up from the side table I was half sitting on. "Yeah? What's his story?"

"He says he's the next-door neighbor. He just got home and I guess he saw the squads, so he came over asking what was up. I told him there was a break-in and asked if he'd seen anything unusual this morning. He said he'd been gone since about 7:00, but he has a security camera that covers his front and driveway area. He said that camera covers Mr. Anderson's driveway too."

"Well, isn't that special?" I said, looking at Pete. "You want to tag along?" I asked the CSI.

"Sure. This could be interesting."

Chapter Twelve

We all traipsed back to the front door where an average looking guy in his sixties was standing patiently. He appeared to be examining Pete's entry-hall art—an original Terry Redlin oil painting. It was worth, maybe, $50,000. If I had one of these it would be in a place of honor in my family room, not the front hall. Of course, if you have a half dozen pieces like this, one of them has to go by the front door.

"Hi, Jim," Pete said.

"Hiya, Pete. You know, I've always liked this one the best," Jim replied, referring to the painting.

Pete made the introductions. "Dan, this is Jim Arthur, my next door neighbor."

"I just got home and saw the cop cars. This fellow over here," Jim nodded to the cop, "said you'd had a break in." He looked at Pete. "Well, I've got that security system I put in two years ago and the camera that covers my drive also gets a pretty good look at yours. I thought maybe you'd like to take a look at the recording."

Why can't my neighbors be like this guy? I could go on vacation for a month with no worries.

"Sure would, Jim," I said. "You have time right now?"

Actually, he'd have to make time whether he knew it or not. Information like this could be critical and I wasn't going to let this guy out of my sight until his recordings were locked into a chain of evidence.

He said he did and we walked next door. Jim's place was completely different from Pete's. It had been done in classic Prairie Style—Frank Lloyd Wright at his peak—a broad ranch-style home with extended overhanging eaves, natural stone and terra cotta colors on the trim, and long horizontal windows. It was set into the back side of the hill so it faced the lake and received a full ration of natural light. About the only thing visible from the street side was the drive and garage doors. There was an entry door next to the garage.

"Two years ago we had some break-ins that turned out to be high school kids looking for prescription painkillers. That's when I decided to put in the system. It's first class—video on all exterior areas, contact sensors on all points of entry, including windows, glass break and infrared-motion sensors inside, plus onsite recording. But, as you can see, I can't really monitor the garage and drive area from any windows, so I made sure to have a camera monitoring this area."

I thought about the fact that most video recordings were junk because the cameras moved, the lenses were dirty, or the tapes were shot and asked, "Do you take a look at what you're recording once in a while?"

"Oh yes. I check it almost daily."

"And your recording media—you replace the tapes once in a while?"

"Actually, the recording media is digital. The recordings are pristine."

Glory be—that's a switch. I can't count how many crime scenes I'd been to over the years where a camera in the perfect location to record the entire event was either malfunctioning or pointing the wrong way. Maybe this was our lucky day.

Jim opened the door and immediately hit the alarm panel to deactivate the system.

"You armed it even though you were coming right back?" I asked.

"Of course. It makes no sense to have a system and not use it." I looked at Pete who looked chagrined again.

Jim led us into the house and down a hall to a storage room that held the security system equipment.

Jim said, "Give me a moment to call up the computer program." He went ahead of us. Pete, the CSI tech and I stopped in the hallway—I had the feeling that Jim prized his home security and wanted to keep his log-on procedure to himself. Sure enough, after a few seconds we heard, "OK, you can come in now."

On the right side of the room was a fairly standard looking computer station like you'd see in any high school kid's bedroom. On the desk was a monitor and keyboard, and to the left was a computer tower. I could see cables running behind the desk to a box mounted on the wall. More cables ran out the top of the box and disappeared into the wall through a neatly cut hole. I've seen banks that didn't have this level of security. Jim was at the desk.

"The camera you'll want to see is number eight. You can see here that it covers my driveway and, at the edge of the picture, you can see Pete's drive. I just have to enter the time coordinates you're interested in." He looked up, expectantly.

"Pete, when did you leave this morning?" I asked.

"About 9:00."

I looked at Jim and said, "Start at nine."

Jim hit a few keys and the monitor came to life. We could see Pete's drive about halfway up from the street and just a bit of his walkway. The counter read 9:03 when we saw Pete's truck back out of the garage, change direction in the turnaround and drive off. Jim hit a few more keys and you could tell that the replay had gone into fast forward—the trees started moving in a time-compressed jiggle and shadows were moving across the drive. The timer in the bottom corner of the picture was a blur.

"It will stop automatically when it senses something different in the picture."

I mean, this was one of the top home systems I'd ever come across. Automatic scanning—it's a wonderful thing.

At 9:50 the timer abruptly returned to normal. A moment later, the entire screen turned to hash. It was as if we were watching TV when the channel suddenly went off the air.

"That's odd," Jim said. "The signal seems to be gone."

"You mean the system went on the fritz just when we need it?" I asked. "That would be about par for recording systems in my world," I thought. Maybe it *wasn't* my lucky day.

"No, you can still see the timer reference in the bottom right-hand corner. That means the main processor is still functioning. It's just not getting any feed from the camera."

"How can that happen?" I wondered aloud.

"Well, I don't really know. The company that installed this system said it was foolproof and infallible."

I thought about that for a second and asked, "How many cameras do you have on this system?"

Jim said, "There are two on the lake side of the house, one on each end of the house, a front-door camera and the one on the driveway."

"So six exterior cameras?"

"Correct."

"You said this was camera eight," I continued.

"Correct. There is room for ten feeds in this system. My original plan needed only five but I numbered them based on which feed port they go into. This one feeds into slot number eight."

A little too complicated for me. "And each one has a line running in here?"

"Actually, they are wireless. They transmit into this receiver box," he said, pointing to a black plastic box atop the stack of boxes, "and the signal is decoded and sent into the CPU."

"Hmmm. The whole thing looked like a late 1980's stereo setup to me. And the music goes round and round, wah-o-wah-o . . ." I thought. Something was coalescing in my head.

"Can you check the feed from the other cameras?"

"Sure." Jim hit a few keys and the screen changed to show six individual windows. Each had a different, but clear, view of the exterior of the house—except the one. It was hash.

"That's interesting," Jim said. "The other cameras recorded just fine."

That got me wondering. "You said they're wireless?"

"Yes, it made the installation easier."

"Do you know if there's any way to intercept the signal or jam it?" I asked.

"Beats me. I was told that this is the best way to do this. I'm going to have to call the company and ask them about this missing time."

I shook my head in frustration and thought, "I bet you are."

We watched for eight minutes as Jim tinkered with the keyboard. Suddenly, at 10:02, the picture returned.

"Great job, Jim. Maybe we'll see this guy after all," I said.

"I don't think so. The picture came back by itself. I didn't do anything to bring it back."

"What do you mean? You've been hammering away the whole time. You must have fixed it."

"Unfortunately, I don't think there was anything to fix. I think the system was recording the signal it was receiving. As you can see now, the recording is clear. I think the signal was being jammed."

I looked at the picture and could see the crushed shrub and tire marks.

"We're too late. He's gone," I said.

Pete spoke up. "You mean that the signal for just the garage camera was being intentionally interfered with for just those few minutes? And then it came back when the jamming stopped?"

"That's what it looks like. I think your burglar somehow knew I had this system and blocked it while he was here," Jim said.

I asked, "How would he do that?"

"I don't really know. What I know about this system is that it is supposed to be state of the art. Apparently, I was misinformed."

Pete looked at me and said, "This guy is pretty good, isn't he?"

"Yeah, I'll go with that. The question is, how did he find out about Jim's system and what did he do to block it? Jim, you have any ideas at all?"

"No, but I'm going to call the alarm company and try to find out. I was sold this system based upon its infallibility. I may want a refund."

So that was that. No help from technology. But as with any development in a crime investigation, a fact had been learned—our guy knew how to disable a sophisticated security camera. I started thinking about who I knew who would have those skills. I came up with only one possibility—old friend, after a fashion, a guy I was sure could do it, just as sure as I knew there was an empty airplane lying at the bottom of Lake Superior. Ben Harris could do this. "In my sleep," I could hear him saying. I knew I'd better give Ben a call.

Chapter Thirteen

We thanked Jim as the crime scene tech got a disk copy of the recording for the investigation team. It might be helpful somewhere down the line, but I doubted it. We were going to have to do a lot more work on this. Catching a lucky break didn't seem likely.

Walking back to Pete's, I asked, "Have you had any ideas at all—even crazy ones—about what this guy's after? I mean, he's got to be looking for something specific. First he looks at Grams' house and now here. What is it?"

Pete's head was down as we walked back to his house. I could tell he was thinking. Just before we went in he looked at me and asked, "What would I have that could have been at Grams'? I just don't know."

"We've got to go over everything in detail—everything that connects you and Grams. And the stuff in the safe-deposit box."

I remembered that my inner alarm had gone off when we were going through the safe-deposit box earlier that morning so I said, "Let's start with the stuff in the box."

Pete's car had been left in the drive since we'd pulled in hours ago. The list of the safe-deposit contents was on the seat with my camera and the bundle of letters. We collected everything and went into the house.

I tossed the letters onto the side table in Pete's office and started hooking up my camera to his computer. He made a copy of the evidence list as I was downloading the photos of everything onto his hard drive. He looked over my shoulder as the pictures came up.

"I don't think it's the jewelry or the old photos or letters. All that leaves is the legal documents. Why don't you take a look at them and let me know if anything jumps out at you," I said as I got up.

Pete asked, "You taking off?"

"Yeah. OK if I take your Caddy? I gotta see a guy about some radios."

Chapter Fourteen

West of St. Cloud, Minnesota, on I-94

About a hundred miles to the northwest, Paul Swanberg was driving home. It had been a long day and he knew he had a long way to go before he could rest. I-94 stretched out before him like an undulating carnival ride—rising and falling over the remains of the last glacial ice age. As he drove, he worried.

Overhead, he saw the contrails of passing aircraft making their daily runs from New York to Los Angeles, Boston to San Francisco. Most "Coasters," as he called those who did not live here in "flyover land," did not appreciate the variety of sights and sounds available on the northern plains, sights and sounds that told natives everything they needed to know about the season, the weather, and the kind of day they'd be having. The Coasters simply looked down from their little windows up there at 36,000 feet and saw colored shapes—mostly squares and circles with a few rectangular wavy squiggles thrown in for variety. The colors and shapes depended upon the season. A blank canvas of white winter snow led to the light green and dark brown of wet earth in the spring and early summer that changed to a dark green interspersed with patches of the bright yellow of sweet clover and Wedgwood blue of the blooming alfalfa, before the tans and browns of fall took over as the crops matured and were harvested. Then the snow returned, erasing the memory of the year's palette. All of it started again every year like some crazed global decorator who couldn't make up her mind. The colors of the seasons had great meaning to the people who cared for the land and raised the country's crops but they meant nothing to the airplane riders.

Normally, Paul would enjoy this drive. It took him back to his roots, his life. But today, he was worried. Worried to the point of distraction. Paul didn't care about the flyers. He knew that theirs were different lives than his. He'd been born in North Dakota in 1973 and raised on the Plains. His family was old-style "big fish in a small pond." His great-grandparents became one of the largest ,landowners in the area. Of course, all things are relative, and being one of the largest landowners in Williams County, North Dakota, was not on a par with, say, one of the largest landowners in Nassau County on Long Island, or owning waterfront in Malibu. They were hard-working people in a land of such people and they built an empire of sorts in what some called the "flat northern wasteland." Swanberg knew the land.

Paul, the only child born to Oscar and Betty Swanberg, was the heir apparent to what had become a ranching and farming conglomerate. He had gone to local schools through high school, then went to North Dakota State University in Fargo for his degree in agricultural systems management, then to the Twin Cities to the Carlson School of Management at the University of Minnesota for an MBA. The plan was that he'd wind up running a corporation that raised cattle and crop hay, controlling 640,000 acres in Williams and Divide counties.

Paul's parents always had confidence in Paul. Even with his "affliction," as they called it, they knew he could handle the family business when the time came. They were worried about something else, though. They worried about whether or not he'd ever marry and have children. He wasn't gay; he seemed to have a strong interest in the opposite sex. The question was whether anyone of the opposite sex would ever have an interest in him.

Paul's affliction was real. He had a mild case of obsessive-compulsive disorder, or OCD. As a child it hadn't caused any real problems. In fact, his parents had studied what little literature there was on the subject when he was young and learned that many famous people had had OCD as children. People like Edison, Howard Hughes and, maybe, Einstein, great thinkers and inventors and engineers, people who came up with the things that moved our civilization forward.

So they didn't worry about him too much. Like most who have it, it became more prominent when he was under pressure or stress, such as that rare date with a girl.

But there was a price to be paid for a mind that worked outside the box. People with OCD develop little rituals and habits that they use to keep their mental balance, so to speak. They became counters or checkers or obsessed with cleanliness. Many people knew the story of Howard Hughes, especially after his life story was made into a popular movie. Unfortunately, the movie depicted OCD as a debilitating psychological disease that ultimately ruined Hughes' life. It can be that severe, but most cases are just annoyances—the urge to check to see if the garage door is down, to turn the car around and make sure they haven't run over the neighbor's cat, the compulsion to count events to a specific number—all are the everyday kinds of OCD, occurrences that most people never notice. Paul had this type of the disease. It was just enough for the girls in his life to classify him as quirky, nerdy, or a little odd. His parents knew he'd have to find someone who understood his condition and accepted it, and there weren't too many prospects in Williston, North Dakota.

Even so, Paul knew the riches the land held in agriculture and, more recently, mining resources. Now, in his early thirties, he wasn't counting on a wife and family to make him whole. He was counting on something called the Bakken Shale Oil Reserve for his future.

Chapter Fifteen

Plymouth, Minnesota

The cell phone on his belt rang and Ben Harris answered it.

"Harris."

"Ben, Dan Neumann, Minneapolis Police Department. I was wondering if I could pick your brain a little over a radio problem." I was standing in Pete's driveway. I didn't really want Pete to hear who I was going to see.

"Detective Neumann, how nice to hear from you. It's been, what, three-and-a-half months?"

"But, who's counting, right? Listen; if you've got some time, I'll buy you dinner if you can fill me in on some radio tech stuff. What do you say?"

I figured Ben was weighing the possibilities. On the one hand, we had sort-of become friends last summer when I was investigating a series of murders that were related to a bank robbery during which Ben's wife was murdered. No, "friends" isn't the right word. But we weren't enemies either, and we were certainly more than acquaintances. It was a tenuous relationship at best.

"All right. But it's a bit early for dinner. Why don't you just come out to the house and we'll talk. If it goes late enough, we'll go get something."

"Deal. I'll see you in about twenty minutes."

Pete's Caddy is about thirty feet long. Fortunately, my own Yukon XL Denali is almost as long, so I'm comfortable in the big rig. Not wishing to try the turnaround, I backed it straight down to the street. There's almost no traffic on this dead end off another dead end so that wasn't an issue. I got the bus onto the street in one piece.

Winding my way down the narrow roads between the channels and bays of the lake I finally came to Highway 12, which turns into I-394. At the I-394–I-494 intersection I took the loop to north I-494 and zipped up to Plymouth. At the County Road 9 exit I got off, turned left to cross the highway and headed for Ben Harris's house.

Like I said earlier, Ben and I met last summer when I was investigating a bank robbery during which his wife had been killed. What should have been a slam-dunk case resulted in an acquittal, which was followed by the deaths of the suspects and several other interesting folks. Since Ben's wife had been killed in the original case, he was a prime suspect for the subsequent murders. Turned out to be a guy who died in a plane crash, but that's another story.

The case wasn't a total loss from my point of view. During the course of the investigation I'd met Maria Fernandez, my friend in Phoenix, and it looks like the relationship actually has a chance. So far it's still growing—albeit at long distance. We're working on a vacation in Alaska next May. We'll see how that goes.

Along the way to Ben's I called Sharon Rademacher at my office. Sharon is a specialist in the research end of law enforcement, an unrecognized and unappreciated field. She spends long days sitting behind a desk or digging through records trying to piece together threads of information, like a part of a name here, a job history there, and maybe throw in membership in some social organization like the Elks or the Crips. Tie in a few associates and proximity to various pieces of physical evidence and you might come up with likely suspects. The information is handed to the detective in charge of the investigation and he or she gets to go out and grab the bad guy. The technician might get a few days in court, but she's pretty much out of it after giving the results of long hours of mind-numbing work to the hot shot. He gets the glory; she gets another case to work on.

Apparently, Sharon's phone had caller ID. That, or she just liked turning everyone on.

"Hiya, honey, how they hanging?" Sharon answered in a sexy voice that could earn her a couple of hundred an hour doing live phone sex.

"Sharon, you are going to be in so much trouble if you ever guess wrong about who is on the phone" I answered.

"But I'm never wrong."

"What's that over-sexed weightlifter doing tonight?" I asked, referring to Sharon's husband, who worked with the Hennepin County Sheriff's Department.

"He's working. Want to come over?"

I knew she was kidding; Sharon was pre-PC and would never be indoctrinated. And her husband was about six foot five, two-sixty, worked out often, and was armed.

I envied their relationship. Sharon's husband was one of the few men in the state who could understand her job. I guess that was one of the main reasons Maria entranced me. She was a fellow LEO.

LEOs are not people born under a certain star. They are Law Enforcement Officers. These men and women work nasty hours dealing with people whose attitudes vary between "Why can't you solve my problem?" to "Leave me alone or I'll kill you," and do so without expectation of fame or glory or making much money. They do it in spite of being the first budget cut when money gets tight at city hall. It is a culture of people who wish only to serve their fellow man. But dealing with people who are lying to you every day has a devastating effect on cops.

It happened to me. After disappointing my family and my wife's family, I was left young, single, and available. I tried the office romance thing years ago. It just doesn't work, at least not for most cops. The work itself is too intense—*real* life and death. You have some days that put you on top of the world, emotionally speaking, but you have more days that leave you dragging your dobber in the dirt. On those days you need someone who's had a good day and will fix you a drink and a steak and not ask about why you are acting the way you are. That kind of spouse is awfully hard for most cops to find—thus the extraordinarily high divorce rate among peace officers.

Last summer's case involving the guy I was on my way to see resulted in the long distance romance with the aforementioned Phoenix beauty, Maria. This had been working pretty well and I'd stay on the case until it was resolved. "Resolved" was starting to look like maybe someone would be moving. Might as well be me. Maria is younger than I am and still has a ways to go until retirement. And I could get used to living in Arizona.

Regarding the guy I was heading to talk to, it had been about two years since the bank robbery and his wife's murder. As I drove I wondered if he'd given any thought to getting out and trying the dating waters. Certainly a guy like Ben would be considered quite a catch in today's singles market—good looking, intelligent, fit, early fifties, no kids or other attachments, save a cute dog, and retired early from a great job that left him with money No apparent bad habits like drugs, smoking, too much drinking or gambling—I'd checked all these things out when I was investigating the murder. But I digress.

I said to Sharon, "Actually, I was thinking about having you over. My buddy Pete's coming. We're working on his grandmother's murder case. He's got some documents we don't understand well enough to know whether or not they are important. I'm going to call Olson, too. Maybe among the four of us we can make something out of this stuff."

"Sounds OK. Does this include dinner?"

"Sure. What would you like?"

"You just have your money ready. I'll bring dinner. I'll even talk to Olson for you; he's here right now."

"OK. See you about 6:30."

I turned into Ben's long driveway and rolled to a stop behind his big Winnebago RV. I wondered if he'd be going south like so many other Minnesotans do in winter. I've lived here all my life but my recent trips to Phoenix have made me appreciate the southern climes. Maybe I could write my next forensics book in Phoenix? It was a thought.

Ben's dog Mikey greeted me with a bark. A Shetland Sheepdog, he's sort of a miniature Lassie, although I'd learned along the way that Sheltie people react violently to any suggestion that a Sheltie is a miniature Collie. Mikey is a very friendly dog who demanded attention. I gave him a quick rub between the ears and looked around for Ben.

He appeared at the back door and gave me a wave. He looked just the same as last summer. Six foot, average-but-fit build, a little snow on the roof but still a full head of hair—all in all, an average Minnesotan.

"You look like you've had a nice fall, Ben."

"I really thought I might see you up at the lake," he countered as we shook hands.

In the course of the case, Ben had invited me up to his cabin on Bay Lake for some fishing. I never took him up on it but I might next year.

"Well, I was writing a book about blood spatter and my publisher started pushing the deadline button. We'll see how things go next season."

"You're welcome anytime," Ben said. "So what can I do for the Minneapolis Police?"

"Actually, it's the Edina Department and the South Lake Minnetonka Police. There was a break-in and burglary that turned into a homicide about two weeks ago in Edina. A woman was killed. The victim was the grandmother of a very good friend of mine, a guy named Pete Anderson." Ben nodded his understanding. "Today, my friend Pete's home was burglarized. His neighbor has a security system that includes a camera that covers Pete's driveway. We checked it out. When we rolled back the recording to the point when the burglar apparently came onto the property, the playback turned to hash. It's supposed to be a top-of-the-line wireless system, so I've got a few questions about wireless security systems and such that I hope you can help me with."

"As you know, I do have some expertise in that area. Come on in. Can I get you something to drink? I seem to recall you're a Scotch drinker."

That's a pretty good memory considering the only time I had a Scotch with him was sitting on the porch in front of his cabin on Bay Lake last July as we wrapped up the case. Did I mention this guy is exceptionally bright?

We walked into his house. It looked the same as it did the one time I'd been in it last summer—very neat with eclectic decorating combining comfortable middle class furniture and Scandinavian teak, Midwest wildlife art and some nice modern pieces.

I passed on the Scotch but accepted a Diet Pepsi. While Ben got the drinks I made myself comfortable on the couch. Ben came back into the room, handed me my glass and sat down.

"Did you get a good look at the system?" he asked.

"I did, but I'm not sure what I was looking at. I can take you out there if that would help. The homeowner said it was state of the art."

This drew a harrumph from Harris. I guess he had a different concept of state of the art.

"There is one thing I can show you," I said as I took out the photos of the gizmo we recovered from the phone junction box at Grandma Anderson's house. I handed them to Ben, explaining where we found it.

"This is as you found the device?" he asked.

"Correct. It was on the wires as you see it there. The later close-ups were taken after it was removed. We think it was there to trick the phone line into thinking it was still hooked to the alarm system."

"I believe you are correct. This is a simple jumper that would feed the signal back into the sending line, showing a complete circuit. If the alarm company's base system had sent a test signal to the house system to check that it was operational, this device would trick it into thinking everything was fine, even if the phone wires had been cut at the house. If the local alarm had been triggered, the device would prevent the system from making contact with the base, preventing the monitoring company from knowing anything happened. As a result, no check call to the house would have been made and no call to the police."

"That's what we figured, but we didn't have the expertise to state it as fact."

"Well, now you do."

Now I did. I knew this would be a good place to get information.

"Ben, that was two weeks ago. Today, Pete's house was broken into. Pete's alarm says there was a door opened, but the alarm company didn't get a call. And his neighbor's system has a camera that should have recorded anyone who came up the drive to the front door."

"Yes, the neighbor's system. First, let me ask you a few questions. You said the system is wireless. That would be the camera feed?"

"Correct."

"How many cameras are there?"

"The neighbor said six. And that's one of the strange things. When Jim, that's the neighbor, played back the recording, the other five cameras had clearly recorded everything that had happened in those areas during that time. Only the one that covered my buddy Pete's driveway was snowed out."

"All right. Are there other security devices—things like door-open switches, motion detectors, glass breaks—that sort of thing?"

"I suppose so. Pete's system readout said that the lower level patio door had been opened."

"That would be a door switch on Pete's system. What I'm interested in is the neighbor's. Since the homeowner, Jim you said his name is, said that the system is 'state of the art,' it probably doesn't matter. What you are concerned with is the camera feed. While Wi-Fi is a wonderful modern invention that allows many people access to the Internet in a broad variety of venues—airports, restaurants, coffee shops and such—it is fraught with security problems. It can be easily hacked and allows the hacker into the user's computer in a way that most users will never detect. The key is a strong password and an encryption system. The same threats exist for security systems."

"Do you have any ideas on what might have happened with Pete's neighbor's system?"

"I can't give you anything concrete without examining the system, but here's a probable scenario: your burglar—I believe the term is 'cased the joint'—before attempting entry. If he was thorough, he may have scanned the neighborhood for Wi-Fi transmissions."

Now, I'm not the most "techie" guy around but, I have a clue on most of this stuff—not how it works but what it's called and what you're supposed to do with it. I even have a phone that gets my email. But I didn't understand what Ben was trying to explain.

"Why would he do that?" I asked.

"He was probably looking to see if the target house had Wi-Fi, but found the neighbor's instead."

"And how does one look for a system like this?"

"There are many commercially available receivers, including some cell phones, that can find Wi-Fi systems. Most are just to locate them so someone can use them, but they are pretty easy to modify to allow a person to hack into the systems they find. It's a growth industry."

I'd had some training on this and had learned that it is, indeed, a growth industry. Police departments are now training their officers to look for something that goes like this: A cop is driving a squad around the neighborhood on a regular patrol watch, just like they do every day, looking for traffic and parking violations, answering calls for cats in trees and little old ladies who need help crossing the street—normal everyday cop work. They are also looking for anything suspicious, which can range from a bunch a kids walking down the street late at night carrying rolls of toilet paper to a crazed-looking character running through backyards with a machete.

Now it also includes an otherwise regular-looking guy wearing a tie or a repairman's uniform sitting in a vehicle with a laptop open on the seat beside him. He may be just what he looks like or he may be breaking into people's Wi-Fi systems looking for identity items. Cops are now stopping and asking these people for identification and asking what they are doing. Naturally, the legitimate business people are annoyed by this and, in the typical American reaction, consider their privacy is being invaded, their day being interrupted and their integrity being questioned. I mean—think about it. You are a guy canvassing a neighborhood to drum up business for your boss, a fellow who owns a legitimate roofing and siding company. There's been a big storm in the area and you know that many of the residents will need new roofs. So, you sit in your truck recording what you've done, who you've talked to, and which people want repair quotes. Along comes some cop who wants to know what you're doing, pulls you out of your truck to check your ID and asks you a few questions. How do you suppose this looks to the potential customers he just signed up?

But the alternative is to let the bad guy sit there. The class I attended taught that in as little as fifteen minutes a trained and talented hacker can get into your computer, locate and download your driver's license numbers, credit card numbers, Social Security numbers, passwords, etc., for you and anyone else who has used the computer for online work or purchases. And he can do it all while sitting in a vehicle parked down the street from your house—no breaking and entering necessary. In some neighborhoods, one day of work can produce a windfall of saleable information.

The instructor told the class about one case where the victim taken for the most didn't even have a Wi-Fi system. He was using his neighbor's without the neighbor's knowledge. But he and his wife did a lot of online shopping using credit cards, had renewed their driver's licenses online and had paid their taxes online. The bad guy got all their numbers and they didn't know. When the cops found out about it and went back to the neighborhood to talk to people, the first thing they asked at the door was, "Do you have a Wi-Fi system?" People who said no got a "Sorry to bother you" and off the cops went. So the guy who lost everything didn't even get notified because he was a hacker too. Now the cops are asking if people have a system and if they say no, they ask if they might be using someone else's.

I said to Ben, "I've had some training on what to look for if someone is loitering in a neighborhood but I don't know how this works. What would I have to do if I was the burglar? How would I go about scanning a neighborhood?"

"You have an iPhone, right?" he said pointing at my belt.

"Yeah, but I really can't take advantage of everything it can do."

Ben laughed and said, "You need a fifteen year old to get a full understanding of all the phone's features. He was right. I knew in an intellectual way that it could get the Internet on Mars, but damned if I knew how to do that. I could make phone calls and check email, and my nephew showed me how to listen to music, which he downloaded for me. Slick for plane rides, something I hated, but was getting used to the more I took them.

Ben continued, "But I believe there is a commercially available app that will allow you to use your phone as a scanner to find a Wi-Fi system."

"An app?" I asked.

"That's an applications program you can download off the Internet. Most cost a few bucks but some are free or are just upgrades the manufacturer makes available."

Ben went on. "So your bad guy does something like this. He cases the neighborhood, that's the word, 'cases,' right?"

"Correct" I replied.

"So he cases the neighborhood to see the lay of the land, how secluded the house is, if there are any alarm company signs, if the neighbor lady is out in her garden all day, stuff like that. But this guy also has his phone on, looking for a Wi-Fi system. When he finds it, he gets into it and figures out that it's the next-door guy's alarm/surveillance system. A quick look in there and he finds the camera feeds, isolates the camera on the driveway, downloads some history so he can get a feel for your friend's comings and goings, and so on. He also figures out what frequencies are involved so he can jam it when he comes back. That's what happened based on what you told me."

"You think he'd look for the Wi-Fi net?"

"That's what I'd do, hypothetically speaking."

Of course, when this guy was speaking hypothetical, I took him at his word. I speak hypothetical too.

I looked at my watch. It was closing in on 6:00. "You mind if we talk to a few other people about this?"

He glanced at me with a look that could have been caution or could have just been surprise. I'm pretty sure he wasn't expecting it.

I explained. "Tell you what, I promised dinner. I'm having a few people over to talk about this case and I'd appreciate it if you could just listen and throw in your two cents when you feel like it."

Ben got up, then said, "OK, Dan. I'll come over for dinner. But I'll drive myself," he said. "It'll save you having to bring me home."

"Works for me. I have to run back down to Minnetonka to pick up Pete anyway, I've got his car. You can follow me if you want, but my house is pretty easy to find—right down Rockford Road to Robbinsdale. Why don't you just meet me there in about an hour?"

"I remember, even the address."

That's when I recalled that while I had been checking him out, Ben had researched me last summer. He had said at the time that he wanted to know who was investigating the murder of his wife's murderer. He had learned about my department forensic investigation books, he knew I was single, and he knew I had the highest case-closure rate in the department. He was a cool customer then and would be now. I was hoping I could get him to use that fabulous mind of his to help us figure out what was going on with Pete's family.

Chapter Sixteen

Williston, North Dakota

Matthew Turner was everyone's friend. He was the guy you went to when you were in a jam because he'd know someone who could help you out; he'd find a way to fix things. He'd been that guy all his life.

Born in 1968 during America's summer of violence, he was a living antithesis to that season of unrest. Always calm. Always mellow. Always right. His parents raised him to be trusting of strangers, accepting of differences and tolerant of those with whom he disagreed. An all-American kid, Eagle Scout, leader in his high school band, student council president, debate team captain, he lettered in three sports. His whole life seemed pointed at some higher calling.

Matt, however, didn't go into the clergy or the military. His father had started a business in the early '70s when he foresaw the emergence of an oil industry in North Dakota. The formation of OPEC and the resulting gasoline rationing in the mid-'70s made it clear to those willing to see that the American oil industry had to expand and find new sources within the U.S. A broad expansion of oil exploration in the Gulf of Mexico, off the California coast, and in Alaska followed. Then someone discovered a little-known record that there was oil in the middle of the North American continent—oil that had been known about for a long time but had been ignored due to the rock formations that sealed it deep in the earth.

About two miles beneath the North Dakota prairies, not all that deep as oil fields go, lies the Bakken oil field. This formation, discovered in 1953 and named for Henry Bakken, a Montana famer on whose land the discovery was made, was ignored for years because of the type of rock it is.

Drilling for oil in the North Atlantic or the north slope of Alaska is fraught with many more difficulties than drilling in the Bakken. The problem with the Bakken is the rock. It captures the oil in a way that makes it nearly impossible to just dig a well and expect a Texas-style gusher. The Bakken oil is in the shale.

On the other hand, the oil in the Bakken is highly desirable to refiners. According to the experts, it is "high-gravity crude" and "some of the cleanest crude oil to be found anywhere." "The Bakken is a world-class source rock," those same experts say. If only they could get it out of the ground.

Matt's father had correctly figured that, sooner or later, someone would solve the engineering problems and the oil would flow. When that happened, money would be made. So he looked around for a way to get in on this future bonanza.

He didn't own vast tracts of land from which the oil could be removed, nor did he know anything about the roughneck/roustabout end of the oil drilling business. The people who perform that tough field work would come from other places—Texas, Louisiana, or Alaska, to name a few. Likewise, the transportation of the crude was something that would go to trucking companies and there was no magic there. That would be a hard competitive business that Matt's dad wanted no part of.

Refining oil is enormously capital intensive and the big oil companies would do that themselves. He needed something local, not geo-engineering related. He had a bachelor's degree in agriculture and an MBA stressing ag-business management. He needed something more business related. And he found it.

There was a business slot for someone who knew people, could negotiate contracts and would get a little "taste" on both ends. It was called mineral lease management.

Property rights in the United States stem from old English law. They state that the owner of land owns not only the surface itself, but the air above it and the depths below. If a property is adjacent to water, the landowner will also have water, or riparian, rights. These rights are as old as the concept of property ownership itself.

The idea of owning the rights to the space above your land is fairly simple. Draw a line around your land and project that line straight up into space. Theoretically, you control that space all the way to the moon. Of course, if planes fly over your land at 38,000 feet, you're not going to get anything from the airline company for rental of the space above your land. But if the neighbor's tree grows over your land and the branches are interfering with your garage or simply block the sunshine from your tomato plants, you have the right to cut off the offending branch where it crosses your property line. It's usually a good idea to check with the neighbor first, but, "technically," you don't have to.

Likewise, riparian, or water rights, have a long history. If you have a river running past or through your property, you have the right to expect that it will continue to run. This means that someone upstream can't just block it off or use up all the water, thus depriving you of its use. In the dry high plains of the Old West there were many legal cases and gunfights over this issue.

Mineral rights, too, are recognized as belonging to the landowner, which means that anything of value that can be dug out of the ground belongs first to the landowner. If the landowner doesn't want to do this, he can lease the right to do so to someone with that expertise. The ability to negotiate these leases has become, over time, a specialized field requiring special individuals—individuals who charge a fee for their services.

A typical mineral lease is five to ten years for the right to prospect for a specific type of mineral on the land described in the lease. Say a farmer has two hundred acres and leases it to a drilling company for five years for $400 per acre. That's $80,000 to the farmer, whether the drilling results in anything or not. In fact, it's $80,000 whether or not a hole is even drilled. But if a well is drilled, oil is found, pumped out and removed from the property, the farmer typically got no more than the original $80,000. In some cases, though, if the likelihood was high enough, the farmer might be able to negotiate a lease that included a percentage of production. And even if there were no royalties, the farmer could readdress that issue when the original lease expired at the end of its five-year term.

It was the ability to predict which pieces of land would produce and which would not that would make or break a mineral-lease broker. If the broker represented the farmer and had a pretty good feeling that the land was barren and he could get a lease anyway, he made money for his landowner client and himself. If he represented the driller and could negotiate a straight fee lease on land that was sure to produce, he'd make money for his driller client and himself. He had to walk a tightrope between being too successful in one camp or the other. If the landowners thought he was taking advantage of them, they'd stop doing business with him, but if his leases never produced oil, the drillers would stop looking to him for leases. He had to be completely above reproach and had to maintain the trust of both the landowners and the drillers.

Matt's father saw this and became one of the most trusted men in northwestern North Dakota and northeastern Montana. He was able to make money for everyone, which kept everyone happy. To keep the family business going he guided his elder son into that arcane specialty. Matt earned a degree in Petroleum Engineering from the Colorado School of Mines, then went to the University of Minnesota's Carlson School of Management for an MBA with a specialty in contract law. He returned to Williston tempered by engineering internships in the heat of the Arabian Desert and the Australian outback. Under his father's tutelage he quickly developed the skills to negotiate mineral leases for clients, purchase leases for the company, and sell them to the highest bidders when they were in demand.

Matt also got on with the other part of his life, marrying April, his high school sweetheart in 1992. The two had maintained their relationship by long distance phone calls and writing letters, a long-lost art in the late 1980s in America. April was teaching at a local elementary school when Matt popped the question. She continued teaching and gave birth to twin boys while also completing her master's.

Everything changed when Matt's father was killed in a skiing accident in 2002. Matt was only thirty-four years old, but he was ready. His father had prepared him well by immersing him in the business as soon as he returned from Minneapolis. Matt continued to grow the business as the

Bakken Oil Field began to emerge as the super resource it had been projected to be. By 2007 the company was making an annual income in the mid-seven figures and had fifteen employees, one of whom was Matt's younger brother, Simon.

Like many siblings, Simon was the opposite of his brother. Where Matt was well liked by all, Simon had few close friends. Where Matt was the school's top team sport athlete, Simon disdained team sports and competed only in cross-country and chess. Outside school he participated in skeet and trap shooting—distinctly individual sports. He did spend some time in theater where he did well portraying other people. He became an accomplished manipulator and provocateur as was witnessed by his success with the girls who flocked to his unsettling good looks. He was, in fact, attractive to almost everyone who met him, male or female. Tall, fit, blonde, his broad smile and flashing eyes could immediately make anyone his friend—at least until he found out whether or not they could do him any good. If they couldn't he would cast them away with the ease of a fisherman tossing back an unwanted fish—the rejected never even knew they'd been tested and found wanting.

Simon also went away to school, but he went to the University of Colorado at Boulder, a party school of the first water. He completed a BS in sociology and went on for the requisite master's from the Wharton School. His entry into the family business was primarily on the oil industry side, where he proved to be the entertainer, schmoozer and as good a negotiator as his brother. His failing was working with the landowner side of the business. He identified far too strongly with the oil companies and felt the landowners should give up their rights for whatever the oil drillers were willing to offer. For that reason, Matt kept him hidden in the office or in the field with oilmen.

Matt knew his brother would never be able to run the company but that was all right. He'd be running it until after Simon decided he had enough money and retired. By then, one of his sons (maybe both, he hoped), would be ready and he could pass the reigns to the next generation with confidence. When that time came, Matt would retire someplace south and enjoy golf and swimming and his life with April.

Chapter Seventeen

Williston, North Dakota
The previous spring

The winter had been a fair one for North Dakota with plenty of cold and wind and an unusually deep blanket of snow to cover the winter wheat fields as they slept. Now the spring was peeking out from between the clouds and the temperatures were warming. A beautiful day was dawning as Matt left his office to run across the street for a cup of coffee.

He was going to meet with an owner of a large tract of land northwest of a little town about twenty-five miles north of Williston. This man was an acquaintance of Matt's, though Simon knew him better—they had been in the same class in high school. But, as was Matt's practice, he'd keep Simon out of this one. Simon didn't care if the land had been in the family for generations and there were personal histories associated with the rolling hills covered with bright yellow sweet clover or blue-flowered alfalfa. The open prairie land the cattlemen loved was to be cherished and cared for, but if you took Simon's attitude, that it was just a matter of documents and oil derricks, they wouldn't want you anywhere near their beloved land.

Matt knew this meeting would have to be handled delicately. The landowner was the grandson of one of the area's largest original rancher/farmers—a man who had accumulated vast tracts of possible oil land—he had hundreds of thousands of acres to lease. The only question was why he hadn't done so yet. In any case, the leases would total millions of dollars in fees for Turner Mineral Leases, LLC, and Matt had every intention of making this man his biggest landowner client.

Matt looked across the street to the coffee shop. He wanted to be on time. As he passed under the permanent awning of the barber shop next to his office, he failed to notice that yesterday's warm weather had melted the snow from atop the awning and that it had dripped onto the concrete sidewalk where it had refrozen, absolutely smooth. It was a textbook example of glare ice.

His intention was to pivot to cut across the street. There was little traffic and there hadn't been a jaywalking ticket in Williston in anyone's memory. As he pivoted with his right foot on the ice patch, physics took over and his foot went right out from under him. His entire 248 pounds first went horizontal, then dropped, rotating around his center of gravity. This motion combined all the force from his forward momentum, the rotational acceleration of his mass and the downward acceleration of gravity to the first point of impact with the concrete sidewalk. Unfortunately for Matt, that point was the back of his head. He was immediately knocked unconscious and the expanding sub-cranial hematoma caused by a half-dollar-sized piece of broken skull protruding into his brain, quickly ended his life. Control of Turner Mineral Leases, LLC, was now in the hands of his brother Simon.

Chapter Eighteen

Robbinsdale, Minnesota
Tuesday, November 11

My house is a late twentieth-century style called a modified two story. I guess it's modified in the sense that it only has about half the second story. That's the area above the kitchen and main-level bedroom and bath. There's room enough for three bedrooms and two baths upstairs so I don't miss the rest of the second floor. The area above the living room and the family room have only roof above, which allows those rooms to have ten-foot vaulted ceilings. That's not why I bought it, of course. I bought it for the garage space.

I had made the run out to Pete's to pick him up in good time and came down the street to find that Ben, as he had predicted, had no problem finding my home. He was waiting in the driveway. We walked into my house from the front door after parking Pete's car next to Ben's. There's plenty of on-street parking for my other guests and I'm known to the local police department, so I didn't think we'd have any issues in that arena. Ben followed me through the short hallway to the kitchen and commented on my decorating.

"Well, this is a guy's house if I ever saw one."

My decorating is not nearly as sophisticated as his. While I have some wildlife art, typical of the Midwest, mine is all in high-run-quantity prints, not originals like my buddy Pete's or Ben's. My furniture could best be described as in need of replacement. Not that it's worn out; it's just not very attractive. One of the things Maria has said is that if we should get together it would be OK with her if I sold my house furnished. At least I've forgone what I refer to as a "dead animal room."

That's a room, usually the man cave (I do have one of those down-stairs—wet bar, big screen, etc.), which is adorned with heads that attest to the owner's various hunting/gathering skills—deer, fish, that sort of thing. I don't hunt and the only things I've had to kill on the job I wouldn't want to have to look at every day.

The best thing I can say about my kitchen is that it's functional. From years of cooking for myself, I'm actually quite competent in the kitchen. This has recently been enhanced by some very good cable TV shows.

As I hung my jacket on a hook in the entry hall, the phone rang. Caller ID said it was the little butcher shop on Robbinsdale's main drag where I get all my meat products. I really like those guys and have been shopping there since I bought this house. I picked up the receiver.

"And how can I help the best butcher in Robbinsdale?" I asked.

"Hey, Dan. How you doing?"

"Doing fine, Jerry. You have some kind of special on Black Angus you're so overstocked on you have to call customers to get rid of it?"

"Not quite, although I do have some very good pork chops that would look good with your name on 'em. Listen, I've got a woman here picking up some steaks and she says to charge them to you. Said her name was Sharon something."

"That figures. Yeah, she works with me. I'm having her and some other people over tonight and she said she'd take care of the shopping. She's a specialist in data analysis so I guess I should have figured that she'd know where I get my protein. Go ahead and give her whatever she wants and put it on my bill."

"OK, Dan. Just wanted to check. Stop over and see me about those chops."

"See ya later, Jerry." I hung up.

Ben had wandered out into the screened porch that is connected to the back of the house. He was looking at the deck and backyard. I heard someone coming through the front door.

Robert "Don't call me Bob" Olson had been my last partner at the MPD. We'd worked together for over eight years and, like a lot of good cop teams, we complemented each other's talents. His seemed to be that he was a reservoir of trivial and useless knowledge. But you never knew when that knowledge would come in handy. Not a big guy at five nine, he is more of a typical Minnesota Scandinavian who stays in pretty good shape, still has most of his hair and still has little fashion sense. Since my career shift has produced some income, I've started wearing a little nicer level of wardrobe. Not $2,000 suits, mind you, just replacing things when they wore out and staying a little closer to the fashion curve. Olson looked like he was still wearing stuff he'd bought when he was in college.

Tonight was no different. He was wearing worn jeans and a battered tweed jacket over a button-down blue shirt with no tie. He had scuffed used-to-be brown Hush Puppies on his feet. As he came in with a bagged bottle in his hand, he said, "I didn't know what the occasion was so I got you a bottle of the Captain. So what's up?" He set the bag on the counter of the center island and proceeded to slip off his jacket, revealing his shoulder rig and Glock 17 with two spare magazines. That's when Ben came back into the house from the porch.

"Hello, Detective Olson," Ben said cordially.

"Mr. Harris. I must say you are the last person I expected to be dining with tonight." Olson cast an inquisitive look my way.

Olson was the first one to like Ben Harris for the murders of the two guys who clearly, at least in our eyes, had pulled a bank robbery and killed Ben's wife. But, as the case went on and more people died . . . well, it got a little foggy at that point.

"Ben is here to help me on the Anderson murder case. My buddy Pete is here too."

"All right, so this is a working dinner," Olson said.

"Correct. I've got Sharon coming because Pete has some documents from his grandmother's safe-deposit box that we can't make heads nor tails out of. Pete's house was broken into today, I think by the same guy who broke into Grandma Anderson's. Ben is here because I think the bad guy used some kind of radio technology when he set up the burglary at Pete's."

Just then, Sharon Rademacher came through the front door with her arms full of bags. "Hello, Hello" she announced, striding straight to the kitchen where she deposited the bags on the counter. She immediately began unpacking her treasures.

"Hello," she repeated again. "Here is your menu for tonight. We are having New York strips, which I will season for proper grilling, a great potato salad from my favorite deli, and fresh steamed broccoli with carrots and slivered almonds. We'll start off with a nice green salad and finish with a little cheesecake. While we're waiting for the steaks to assume room temperature, I've got an appetizer from my deli. This will be better for you, Danny," she said, looking my way, "than the half cup of cashews and two fingers of Scotch you usually have."

I couldn't argue with that. I'm going to have to watch those cashews as I get older, they're pretty high in fat. Of course, there's nothing wrong with a little scotch.

Sharon hadn't noticed Ben so I made the introduction.

"Sharon, this is Ben Harris."

"Of course it is. I recognized him the moment I walked in. Thanks for remembering to introduce us."

She walked over to him, offering her hand, and said, "I'm so sorry for your loss. It was a tragedy."

Ben took her hand in his and said, "Thank you. It was."

Sharon stepped back to the counter and resumed her preparations. She mentioned to no one in particular, "It was regrettable what happened to all those people, a shame the way things sometimes happen," referring to Ben's wife's murder and the subsequent murders. "Now, what are we going to talk about tonight?"

Chapter Nineteen

Williston, North Dakota
Tuesday, November 11

Simon Turner was not a happy man. He sat in his office and wondered how a guy could be such a fuck-up. It should have been a quick in-and-out breaking and entering. All he had to do was find the document and the two of them would be in tall clover. Why fate had saddled him with Paul Swanberg was unfathomable.

He'd known Paul all his life. The two very nearly shared a birthday, which would have put them both in the maternity nursery at Williston's Mercy Hospital at the same time. They lived only six blocks from each other, went to the same schools, studied in the same classes, and attended the same church all their lives.

When it became apparent that Paul was going to control the vast Swanberg land holdings, Simon was excited. Finally, he'd get a chance to show his high and mighty brother that he could handle the landowner side of the business. But Matt wouldn't let him. He had told Simon that he would handle Swanberg himself. Simon would stay on the producer side of the business, working with the drilling companies and haulers.

Looking back, that would have been fine. Although Paul was Simon's contemporary, they could not have been more dissimilar. Where Simon was outgoing and gregarious, Paul was a bookish introvert. Where Simon was an attractive ladies' man, Paul, though not unattractive, was a wallflower who simply had no social skills. This may have been due to the fact that Paul was "different."

Simon had known, as had all the children who had gone to school with Paul, that Paul was different from the rest of them. Not because

Paul's family had more money than any other family in Williston; children rarely think about money. Paul himself was different. He was odd. He had little habits that annoyed some of his playmates and drove others to distraction. He could be talking with a person one moment and completely out of it the next. Little things distracted him. He had difficulty concentrating in school, consequently drawing the attention of his teachers, who would write in his report cards that though Paul was an intelligent, likeable lad who did his work well and in a timely manner, he lacked attention in class and would interrupt other students with seemingly unassociated matters, disrupting activities with his attempts to straighten things or reorder items. And there was his counting. He liked to count everything.

Simon had known all this before he started down the current road. He knew that Paul could be odd but he thought he could handle him and get them both to the end game. That end game would result in vast wealth for Simon with Paul basically coming along for the ride. All Paul had to do was sign the documents and the royalties would start rolling in. Simon had the producers all lined up. All he needed were the signed leases.

Chapter Twenty

Robbinsdale, Minnesota

Over dinner I reviewed the case, starting with the break-in and murder of Emma Anderson and ending with this morning's attempted break-in at Pete's. I went over the lack of real evidence and our theories regarding the wireless security system. Ben then gave a dissertation on the structure of wireless communication systems and its application in today's computer world. He also covered its use in security systems. He was quite clear in their inherent fallibility when it came to hacking. He also went over his hypothesis of what could have taken place at Pete's. It was an eye-opening lecture for the group.

"You mean that all you have to do is drive around a neighborhood and you can find these systems, break into them and hack into people's computers?" Pete asked.

"Unfortunately, it is that easy and it's becoming a growth industry. Personal identity security is the next great criminal opportunity. It used to be harder to get the most important information—Social Security numbers, driver's license numbers, credit card numbers—but those things are on almost every home computer in the country. If you use Wi-Fi you put all that data at risk."

"And there's no way to protect it?" Olson inquired.

"Good encryption and passwords. Those are your only hope. And by good passwords, I don't mean your birthday or your kid's names. I mean a combination of alpha and numeric characters. Something like this— what's your wedding anniversary, Olson?"

"August 25th, 1984."

"And do you have any pets?"

"Yeah, we've got a dog named George."

"And what is George's birthday?"

Olson had to think a moment on that one. But, being Olson, the human hard drive, he was able to call it up.

"April 29, 2003."

"For you a good password would be something like 04Geo29rge825. That would be a combination of George's name, his birthday, and your wedding anniversary. Thirteen characters, alpha and numeric, mixed up yet something you could recall without too much trouble. It would be nearly impossible for the typical hacker to break."

Personally, I was impressed that Ben had come up with that without writing anything down. I'd forgotten the anniversary by the time he got to the dog's name.

We had moved to the family room, enjoying a little after-dinner snort—coffee for Sharon and Ben, a beer for Olson and Pete, a little Scotch rocks for yours truly. The coffee table held the treasures we had taken from Grams' safe-deposit box, and photos of the stuff we'd left behind. Pete had also brought along a photo of his grandfather taken when Gramps was in his forties to compare to the photo from the safe-deposit box.

Olson asked, "I still don't get this security system thing. If a guy like Pete's neighbor is going to all the trouble of having a system like that, why didn't he make it more secure?"

Ben answered, "Like almost all engineering failures, I suspect it was a failure of imagination."

"Imagination?" I asked. "Imagining what?"

"Pete's neighbor, or the people who installed the system, failed to imagine what could happen. After all, it's just a camera system and it's outside the house. No snooping or peeping Tom worries. Why bother with encryption, right?"

We all nodded.

"This is how engineering failures occur. The designers or engineers involved have worked very hard to imagine every possible scenario and decided that encryption was simply an overelaborate add-on. They decided, based on good reasons, that it wasn't necessary."

Ben looked at the group's blank faces and concluded an example was required.

"OK. Some of you are old enough to remember Apollo 13, right? The moon mission that had the little problem? Or at least you saw the Tom Hanks movie?"

We all nodded.

"That was a classic failure of imagination followed by a cascade failure. That's the other part of nearly every huge and famous engineering disaster. The tank exploded because of a chain of failures, then the explosion caused another series of failures—failures that no one had imagined could happen. It was a combination of great engineering and luck that got those three guys back.

"So this neighbor puts in what he thinks is the tip-top state-of-the-art home security system and it's defeated by a guy with a jimmied up cell phone and a transmitter that can jam the signals. I'll bet the company that made the system never imagined that someone would build cell phones with Wi-Fi location receivers."

This brought a chorus of harrumphs from the gathered experts. Our attention turned back to the collection of items from Grams' safe-deposit box.

Ben had turned his attention to the photos of the legal documents. He was perusing them one by one.

"Any ideas would be welcome, Ben" I said.

"I'm curious about one of them."

Chapter Twenty-one

Ben picked up the photo of the mineral rights deed. He carefully looked it over, straining a bit as the photo was 8½ by 11 and the actual document, still in the safe-deposit box, was 8½ by 14—legal size. This made the print a bit small for his fifty-something eyes. I watched as he read down the page. He scanned the edges as if looking for something.

"Something there, Ben?" I asked.

"I'm not sure. This is clearly an authentic deed, at least it looks good to me, but I'm not sure what it represents. We need someone with real estate knowledge to look at it."

I looked at Pete. "How about Steve?" To the others I said, "Pete's brother-in-law, Steve, is a real estate guru. Maybe he could shed some light on this."

"I'll call him. They live about a half hour away, but Steve may still be at his downtown office. He works late."

Pete went into the kitchen to call. The conversation was just far enough away that I couldn't make it out. I only got the feeling from Pete's body language that he'd reached his sister's husband and that they were discussing the paper at hand. Pete was getting more excited as the conversation went on. Suddenly, Pete was waving at me.

"Bring that photo over here," he said.

I did as commanded, getting up and taking the picture of the deed over to Pete. Standing next to him I got a better handle on the balance of the conversation.

"Yeah, it says 'the entire holdings of F. Y. S. Land and Cattle, including all of the Townships.'" He read off a bunch of things he called township and range numbers. "Does that mean anything to you?"

I watched as Pete nodded in agreement to whatever Steve was saying. "OK. See you then."

He hung up.

"Steve will be here in fifteen minutes. He says this could be something and asked about the location. That's what I was reading to him. He said he has to find a general survey map of North Dakota in his resource library and then he'll come out here."

While we waited, Sharon asked Pete about his grandparents. She had been perusing the stack of letters Gramps wrote to Grams and had already become a fan of Gramps, at least of his writing style.

"My grandparents were the classic 'American Dream' story. Both had been born to hard-working farm families in northwest North Dakota around 1920. Gramps' family had some land, not much, but enough to raise everyone. Grams' family was dirt poor. And families had a lot of kids back in those days, eight in her case, so there were a lot of mouths to feed. Grams and Gramps started courting in their teens. Then, in 1938, around Christmas, they got married. Just in time, too, because my father was born in May of 1939. But, as scandalous as that might seem, it wasn't all that uncommon in those days. Grams used to say, 'The first one can come anytime; after that they take nine months.'"

This drew a round a chuckles from the group. I was having a hard time drawing a mental picture of Grams as a pregnant bride. I'd known her nearly all my conscious life. She represented dignity, wisdom, tradition and morality—especially morality. The idea that she was once a sweet young thing and fooling around—it's just one of those things I can't wrap my mind around.

Pete went on. "Gramps went into the service in the fall of '39 after the Germans invaded Poland. He told me once that he could see that, sooner or later, the entire world would be at war again and he wanted to have a leg up on those who were 'coming to the party late,' as he'd say. He figured it would give him a better chance of surviving. So he went down to Williston and enlisted in the Marine Corps. I asked him about that, too, and he said that he figured that Europe would be the Army's problem and he could ride the war out someplace calm like, say, the Philippines. Well, he got the hemisphere right, but like almost everyone else, he forgot that the Japanese had been fighting in China since 1936. When the Japanese hit Pearl Harbor on December 7th, he was stationed at Camp LeJeune in North Carolina. He'd made corporal in two years, which was something of a miracle in those days. As soon as the war broke out, the Marine Corps decided they were going to need a lot more officers and they didn't want them all to be coming from the outside, so they launched an experimental program to run outstanding enlisted men through Officers Candidate School. Gramps was selected and the rest, as they say, is history. He was in on every landing from Guadalcanal through Iwo Jima. Got a chest full of decorations and was never hit, not even once."

The doorbell rang and I knew it was Steve. He was always formal about the bell, even though I'd told him, as I tell everyone I'm expecting, to just come on in. In this day of home invasions, that may seem a little casual, but pretty much everyone who's ever at my house is armed.

"Hi Dan," Steve said as he made his way into the family room. "I got here as quickly as I could."

"Steve, these are some people from my office. Olson, I think you've met. He was my partner the last nine years I was on the force." Steve went around the room, shaking hands and saying "Good to see you again" and "Glad to meet you;" as is his habit. I guess that's the standard procedure in the real estate business. "Sharon Rademacher works in research and this is Ben Harris."

I watched as Steve looked at Ben. I knew he'd recognize the name from last summer's events. He did and the recognition stopped him right in his tracks. He just stood there holding Ben's hand.

I went on. "Ben is here helping us with this, too. I had some questions about wireless systems and I thought Ben might have the answers. He did."

Steve rejoined us in the land of real time and let go of Ben's hand but apparently couldn't decide whether or not he was glad to meet him so he said nothing.

Steve had a hard-case tube under his arm, the kind an architect carries drawings in. I took it from him, nudging him back to reality, and started unscrewing the end cap. Steve came around, recovered the tube from me and began his presentation. At least, it seemed like a presentation to me.

"I grabbed this on the way out the door. You said you had a deed?"

I nodded.

"I'd like to see it."

I handed Steve the deed photo. He looked at it closely and began slowly rocking back and forth while mumbling under his breath. I heard a few "Hmmms" and "Ah ha's" and "That's interesting." After about two minutes he came back from communing with his spirit world and said, "This is very interesting. It could be very valuable or just a pretty piece of paper from days gone by."

"How can we tell?" Sharon asked. She was always ready to learn more about documents and records. It was her specialty.

"I'll give you the once-over, then tell you what it means. This is a mineral rights deed. A mineral rights deed conveys the right to ownership of and/or the right to remove minerals from beneath a specific piece of surface land. In order to be valid it has to contain the legal description of the property, describe the minerals to be covered by the deed, name the current, soon to be former, owner of the right, the name to whom the right is deeded—that's the new owner of the rights, in this case Emma—describe the time period for which the right is granted, and what happens when that time period expires. It may also contain information on what happens in the case of the demise of the grantor or grantee. Finally, to be enforceable, it must be recorded with the county records department in the county where the property is located. This document does almost all those things."

"OK. I'll bite," I said. "What's missing?"

"There's no recording stamp. We must assume it has never been recorded. It's still a valid deed, but if it were lost or destroyed, there would be no way to establish the rights of the person to whom the deed was issued."

"So, this piece of paper transfers the mineral rights of some chunk of land to Emma?" I asked.

"Correct,"

"How much land? I mean, is it worth anything?" The cop in me was wondering if it was worth killing for.

"As I said before, this deed refers to land by range and township, so it was divided up after that method became popular. And, I can tell you, it refers to a lot of land, at least 947 sections."

"How much is 'a lot'" Olson wanted to know.

"Well, a section is 640 acres or a square mile, depending upon how you want to look at it. So it's at least 600,000 acres or 947 square miles. That's a lot in my book."

"Nine hundred forty-seven square miles!" I said. I was astounded. "One person owns that much land?"

"It's not really that much once you do the math. It's about a thirty-mile square. That's a lot for around here, but there are ranches in Texas that are over a thousand square miles and there are ranches in Australia that are over five thousand square miles."

I nodded and said, "So the next question is, 'Where is it?'"

Steve got a map out of his case and rolled it flat on the coffee table. It was an outline of the state of North Dakota but looked like a big checkerboard with all the squares the same color. He was mumbling again and then started moving his fingers across the map. I watched as he noted numbers and names and kept moving his fingers north and west until he stopped, checked one last thing, then announced, "Here it is."

His finger had stopped on a little dot in the northwest corner of the state. The name by the dot said "Alamo."

Chapter Twenty-two

I looked around the room. Pete was looking at Steve with an expression that said he was sorry he'd waited to bring this to his attention. Steve was looking at Pete like he'd been left out of the winning lottery pool.

Sharon had evidently lost interest in geography and was picking through the love letters from the safe deposit box. The whole North Dakota thing fascinated Olson.

"This is where the mineral deed is from?"

"No real way to know where it's from, but this is the property it refers to. It looks to me like something called F. Y. S. Land and Cattle granted Emma Bjornstrom Anderson the mineral rights to a big chunk of this corner of the state" Steve said. "Pete, why didn't you mention this to me before?"

"We didn't think it was important. Is it?"

"No way of telling," Steve said. "The rest of the deed says the mineral rights are conveyed to Emma and all her progeny forever. If she has no progeny, the mineral rights revert back to the estate of whomever this guy is that wrote the deed."

"I'll give you $25,000 for those rights right now," Olson said.

It was a conversation stopper. The others didn't know Olson like I did. He wouldn't give you $10 for a guaranteed winning $25 scratch-off ticket. The guy had his picture in the dictionary next to the definition of the word "cheap."

"OK, Olson, I'll bite," I said. "Why is this worth at least $100,000, because it's got to be worth that much for you to be offering anything on it."

"I don't know that it's worth anything or not, but I'm willing to take a chance on this. It's in the Bakken Oil Field."

Now we were all stumped. "The what?" I asked.

"The Bakken Oil Field—the biggest thing to happen in domestic oil since Alaska. Don't you guys pay attention to anything?"

Olson had the reputation of being a walking encyclopedia, back when people used those things. I guess now he's a walking web connection. When it comes to trivial info, he's my go-to guy, to say nothing of sports statistics.

"The U.S. Geological Survey reported this past year that the Bakken Oil field, which is roughly a circle centered on Weyburne, Saskatchewan," he placed a finger on the map about forty miles north of the international border, just a little east of the line dividing Montana and North Dakota, "with a radius going south all the way to Dickinson, North Dakota." He placed another finger on Dickinson. "So, a circle drawn like this—" he drew a circle that covered most of northwest North Dakota, a big chunk of northeast Montana and an even bigger chunk in Saskatchewan, "that's the Bakken. Anyway, the USGS estimates that there is at least 3.65 billion with a "B," barrels of oil, 1.85 *trillion* cubic feet of natural gas and 145 million barrels of liquid natural gas in the U.S. part of the field. And Alamo is smack in the middle of it."

Pete wondered aloud, "Why hasn't anyone gone in there for it before?"

Of course Olson knew. "Because, although it's considered to be some of the very best oil available from the refining point of view, what they call 'high-gravity crude' from some of the best source rock on the planet, that rock has been the problem. It's not the easiest stuff in the world to get oil out of."

"This may all be true," I said, "but this deed was made out in 1948. It doesn't mean anything to us regarding why Grams was killed or if this deed means anything to the case."

Steve disagreed. "It could be everything to the case, if this is what the burglar wanted. We didn't know it was even there. If the F. Y. S. Land and Cattle Company wanted it back it could be worth billions, with a B," he said looking at Olson.

"So what, they get it back. Just having the deed can't transfer the rights back to them. One of Grams' progeny would have to do that."

"I don't think so," Steve said. "That's the other unusual thing about it. To be binding, a deed has to be executed, that means signed, then it has to be recorded. In effect, it's valid, but this piece of paper is the only proof of the grant. That's the whole reason county recorder offices were established—to keep track of who owns what, just in case the original paperwork was lost or destroyed. This one has the required notarized signature from the transferor; no signature by the receiver is necessary. But it's not stamped with a date stamp that would indicate it was received by the Williams County recorder's office. It's never been recorded."

"So all the other party would have to do to get rid of it is get rid of it?" I asked.

"Correct. If it has never been recorded and somehow was destroyed, it would be as if it never existed. Then, F. Y. S. Land and whatever would get their mineral rights back."

Steve said, "I wonder who F. Y. S. Land and Cattle is?"

The room fell silent, each of us thinking about what this could mean.

Sharon stirred in her seat on the couch. "I have another riddle, Pete. Didn't you say that your grandfather died in 1972?"

"Yes."

"Well, he was awfully devoted to your grandmother. I've got letters here dated through 1978."

Chapter Twenty-three

Williston, North Dakota
Tuesday, November 11

Simon Turner sat in his office, deep in thought. The office had been his brother's. He had taken it over upon his ascendency to the controls of Turner Mineral Leases, LLC. He liked the office and had kept it pretty much the same as his brother had had it—same desk and chair, same décor; only the nameplate on the desk had been removed.

He had also kept Angie Nash, his brother's secretary. She was extraordinarily competent and had been quite a help to him. At first he thought that her helpful attitude was an attempt to get close to him personally. She was mid-thirties, divorced and very attractive. But when he had suggested that he would enjoy an evening tryst with her, she had shut him down cold. Since then, he had started thinking that as long as he was the top dog here, he should get special treatment from his personal staff. He'd have to replace her, but that was life. Those who have, have.

Simon again pondered the latest news. Paul had screwed it up again. His phone call had been brief and concise—he couldn't get the document because there was a dog in the house. What kind of an excuse was that?

Simon knew it was now up to him. Paul couldn't do it. Paul's stress-induced pedantic methodology would always hold him back. He was simply incapable of thinking on the fly. Simon knew all of this because when he first realized how much money was at stake and that he would be forced to partner with Paul, Simon studied Paul's condition to better know how to handle him. As long as things were copacetic, Paul would be fine. But put him under stress and he had no ability to adapt.

Paul had excelled at schoolwork, which was highly organized to begin with. Teachers would give an assignment and Paul would do it perfectly, as long as he had the time to go through the steps one by one. Simon knew that one by one was how Paul would do it, counting all the way— one by one, two by two, three by three, and so on. Paul was a wizard at intellectual problems that had a logical set pattern moving toward a solution. He could even excel in a dynamic situation, one that required the individual to adapt, innovate and overcome, as long as the problem was theoretical. But if the situation was real, or involved personal stress, he could dissolve. As soon as he had to deviate from the plan, he was done.

Simon had no such issue. He was built to multitask. His mind was agile and free moving. He could immediately move from a phone call regarding an oil lease, to a trucking problem, to setting up a golf date. People would call him while he was on the golf course or in the middle of sex with his chick *du jour* and he'd have the answers to their questions without missing a stroke. He would have been able to recover the deed.

"Well," Simon thought, "there are two ways to skin this cat." Some of his acquaintances in the drilling business had connections that could be useful at a time like this. Not normally given to extremes, this was a unique situation. With so much money on the line, Simon was willing to do anything. Anything, that is, as long as he didn't have to get his own hands dirty. He'd always paid for "special services," things he didn't want to handle himself, but nothing this extreme. "So what?" he thought. This would put him in the big leagues in the eyes of certain associates and even bigger leagues in terms of money.

He picked up the phone and dialed a number from memory.

Just outside the office, Angie Nash noticed the light go on, indicating that her boss was making a call. She went on with her work as always, typing a contract for the lease of 160 acres south of Williston to a drilling company for exploration. She paused only long enough to jot down a number and the time, a small housekeeping chore she had always done when Matt Turner was president.

Chapter Twenty-four

Robbinsdale, Minnesota

The room was silent. We were all thinking exactly the same thing, almost as if a spontaneous séance had started. Who had written these letters?

I looked from face to face and saw the same expression. The map and deed were forgotten. All thoughts had turned to the pile of letters in front of Sharon. Who was the author?

Pete broke the silence. "Sharon, are you sure?"

"I've reviewed a lot of documents in my day and these are all written by the same hand. They start just after the end of World War II and the last one is dated July 3, 1978. In it, the writer discloses to the recipient that he has been diagnosed with something that is terminal and that this will be his last letter. He says:

> *My Beloved,*
>
> *This is my farewell to you. I have been informed that my new and constant companion will be the death of me. The doctors say there is no magic they can perform that will change the inevitability of this course.*
>
> *So, I have returned to that place which has always been my home. While I know that our lives have been full and fruitful, I cannot help but wonder what else they could have been, if only events had not played out as they did. What more fulfilling and more interesting lives we could have had.*

Here, now, at the end, I have come to a realization. I have always belonged here, I exist here, and I shall exist hereafter. And that you are here, too, a woman at seventeen. Though truly, you have had your own existence, in your own way, there so far away.

Think of me sometimes. Remember that I have always loved you, even when the distances have divided us,

I have always been,

Forever Yours,
Alamo, North Dakota
July 3, 1978

Silence again filled the room. Sharon dabbed tears from her eyes. "Boys, I don't know who this guy was, but he sure had a way with words," she said between dabs.

"Indeed, who was he?" I asked the group. "I think we should find out." I looked at Pete and Steve. "Any ideas?"

Pete looked puzzled. "OK, so Grams had a long-lost admirer. What does that have to do with her murder?"

"Could be everything," Olson chimed in. "Past love affairs have a way of reappearing when someone is killed. Could be the killer had something to do with this guy, whoever he is."

"But this guy died in '78. He's gone. He didn't do it," Pete said.

I held my hand up. "Olson's right. Past lovers are a common source for the suspect pool. And Pete's right, saying whoever wrote these letters is dead and, therefore, not a suspect. But there could be someone else associated with the dead poet. I'm a little reluctant to spend a lot of time on this, though, because everything about the crime scene says that the murder was not planned, that Grams just surprised the burglar, and taking a swing at her was reactive to his being surprised, not part of the plan."

Olson disagreed. "How about this—the burglary was not the real reason he went there. The burglary was misdirection to cover up the murder. The burglar didn't intend to take anything, just rifled a few drawers to make it look good. He could have done that specifically to lure Mrs. Anderson downstairs. She could have been the target all along."

This is why I keep Olson around—the ability to bring a fresh look at something. Many times, investigators get too close to a case and get stuck on their own first impressions. While first impressions are usually correct, in the case of an elaborate misdirection, you can stand there for months and not see something that's right in front of your nose, as we had in this case.

Years ago I had a case where a fellow had been murdered. Turns out he was a closet homosexual. He was a cop and there were people on the force, past partners and other guys, who knew, but for the most part it was still a secret in a time when that sort of thing had to be kept secret. The way this guy's body was left showed that it was a hate crime. He was left in public, after a fashion, and posed to highlight his sexual orientation. He was found in a public park, naked, with his genitals cut off and stuffed in his mouth and a mop handle had been inserted into his rectum. To a forensic psychologist this is the sure sign of a homophobic killer showcasing the victim's sexual orientation. I was sure of it as soon as I saw the body and so was the department's specialist in sex crimes.

Turned out we were wrong. The killer, who we got after two months of tough police work, turned out to be his lover. He was a cop, too, and knew that posing the victim the way he did would throw us off the trail. It did, at least for a while.

"So, how does this tie to the break-in at Pete's," I asked the group.

Olson, always there to contribute, said, "Maybe they're not related. Maybe Pete's house was just a coincidence."

"What about the jumper on the phone line?" Pete asked.

"Could be coincidence. After all, it's been two weeks. Today's burglar showed quite of bit of forethought with the way he or she disabled the neighbor's Wi-Fi system. The killer in Edina didn't show any more tech savvy than buying a commercially available phone jumper. And the guy today had burglary tools with him. There was no sign of tools being used in Edina. In fact, the Edina murder may have brought your house to the burglar's attention, Pete. They watch the obituaries for wealthy people, then hit the relatives, knowing that there's a payday in it. Was your name and city of residence listed in the obit?"

"Yes, it was. You mean that burglars read the obituaries looking for victims?"

"They sure do. They look for funerals and wedding announcements. They know the family will be out of the house during both. In your case, he or she waited a couple of weeks for the will to be settled and for you to get back to some kind of routine, to be sure you'd be out. But the same methodology applies."

"OK," I said. "Let's go with the idea that the two incidents could be unrelated. Let's go back to the letters. How can we find out who wrote them?"

Ben, who had been quietly listening to all this, spoke up. "Perhaps I can make a contribution here. My wife's mother had a stack of letters like this that we found when she passed away. No one knew about them, and, like yours, Pete," he said with a nod to my pal, "we found them in the safe-deposit box at the bank. They were obviously important to Ann's mother and secret enough that she didn't want them found at the house. Ann was just plain curious about who the writer was, so she searched him out. She contacted old friends and a couple of old relatives who were still around, and after talking with a friend of her aunt's, we discovered that they were actually written by Ann's father. He had a set, too. It turned out that her mother and father had written each other these letters over the years as a way of refreshing their relationship. There never was a 'secret admirer;' they were writing to each other."

Sharon said, "But we know that Pete's grandfather couldn't have written these. They're dated after his death."

"True, but the way to find out is the same one that Ann used. Go to her friends at church and any remaining relatives or childhood friends and ask them about Mrs. Anderson's early years. I'll bet you find that the writer is the same person as the man in the photo."

Ben gestured to the photo that had been sitting on the coffee table all evening. He and Sharon had been the only two to disagree that the two in the photo were Grams and Gramps, based on the picture of Gramps Pete had brought. Both thought it was Grams, but not Gramps. A mystery man.

Chapter Twenty-five

Monday, November 17
At a home on Bald Eagle Lake, Minnesota

Minnesota proclaims itself to be the "Land of 10,000 Lakes" on its license plates, but there are really far more lakes. It all depends on how you define "lake."

According to the state's department of natural resources, there are 14,906 lakes, nearly all over the unofficial minimum of one hundred acres.

Minnetonka, the lake Pete Anderson lives on, is set in the west edge of the Twin Cities metropolitan area. Long before it became a Minneapolis suburb, it was a summer destination for the Minneapolis well to do. In fact, the Minneapolis trolley line used to run all the way out to the city of Excelsior on the eastern end of the lake. From there, riders could switch to a boat that looked much like another trolley car and ride right up to their own docks. This arrangement made for gentler summers for those who could afford two homes back in the first quarter of the twentieth century.

St. Paul has its share of lakes, too, the biggest of which is White Bear Lake. This 2,427-acre lake is located north and a little east of downtown St. Paul. It has a long history of attracting characters—good and bad. Several renowned mobsters of the 1930s reportedly spent their summer vacations on the quiet shores of White Bear Lake.

Off the northwestern shore of White Bear is its lesser-known neighbor, Bald Eagle Lake. On Bald Eagle's eastern shore lived a modern day mobster. This all-concrete ranch-style house was purchased for cash two years earlier from a widow who had decided that seventy-two Minnesota winters were enough.

Sitting on the front porch, facing the lake and enjoying the late fall warm spell with a cigar and a Bushmill's Irish Whiskey was George Kline. He was looking at the low sun as it reflected off the surface of the water and his dock, which had been pulled up onto the shoreline in anticipation of the winter's ice.

Bald Eagle Lake was the end of a long road in George's short life. Only forty-two years old, George had enough experiences stocked up to fill several lifetimes for "normal" people. He had been born in Boston in 1966 during a time that saw America tearing itself apart internally. The Viet Nam War and the civil rights movement had the country's older generations questioning their core values, while the younger ones were rebelling by experimenting with new types of relationships and pharmaceuticals. George was the product of this experimentation, having been born to a single mother, something that was rather novel at the time. She was working part time while attending college to earn a degree in sociology. She wasn't sure who the father was, just approximately when she became pregnant, and there was no way of telling paternity from that. But being the new liberated modern woman she knew she didn't need a man in her life. After all, all they were here for was to donate sperm.

So she raised George the best she could, taking him with her to classes when he was a baby and then, when he became a toddler, leaving him in one of the new daycare facilities. This worked fine until George was in school. About the time most boys are delivering newspapers and dreaming of playing for the Red Sox, George started running with a gang.

Granted, at age ten, it was a low-intensity gang as gangs go. But it was Boston in the late '70s and there was still plenty of racial tension. George never really cared about the black/white component; he just wanted to make money. If that meant pushing around the blacks or the Korean and Vietnamese immigrants flooding into the country, so be it.

There was also, during this time in U.S. history, a fondness for supporting causes that would allow the supporter to feel like he or she was doing some good in the world. Many groups had been started to raise money for various causes like hunger and childcare in faraway places. Most were legitimate, but some were fronts for violent revolutionaries. In Boston, the most fashionable common cause was to support the down and out in Northern Ireland. With its heavily Catholic population, there were more than enough folks who wanted to feel good about giving some money to the poor children in Northern Ireland. That most of their contributions went to train, arm, and otherwise fund terrorist attacks on the British Army and non-Catholic civilians wasn't lost on the good people of Boston; they simply chose to ignore the obvious and take the "feel good" path. They met with the various groups and organizations at fundraisers in local pubs, where they drank and sang of the old sod and wrote checks. George's mother attended these ad hoc meetings and imbibed in the general merriment and festivities. She was in it for the parties, not the politics.

And so it happened that, in the fall of 1984, the year of Orwell's prophecy, after one too many scrapes with the law and only one step away from jail, George fled the country to the land across the sea. His mother sent him to Northern Ireland to spend the summer with relatives.

Chapter Twenty-six

**Somewhere in the countryside of Northern Ireland
July 13th, 1985**

George was fascinated. The detail and intricacy of the work was
entrancing. The person doing the work, teaching George how to do it
as well, was a patient, careful and skilled man. He had three young men
with him in this ad hoc class and George was proving to be the best
student among them. Too bad he was supposed to go back to the States,
as he called them, at the end of the summer. He could use a man with
George's quickly developing skills in The Cause.

The Cause, as he called it, was the Irish Republican Army. The
instructor was one of four at this camp that was disguised as an operating farm in the Northern Ireland countryside. It was remote enough and
had sympathetic enough neighbors that they could run firearms training without worry of an unannounced visit by the British Army. They
had classroom training on a variety of other topics such as intelligence
gathering, electronics and demolition. Today's class was demolition.

George returned to Boston in September he a changed man. Still only
nineteen, he had been to war. It was not the war his mother's generation had seen. This was a new low-intensity type of combat where the
enemies lived side by side and the combat took place between individuals at a very personal level. He'd learned firearms proficiency, bomb
making and intelligence gathering, and had experienced enough conflict
firsthand to be comfortable with it, after a fashion.

There wasn't much the American system could teach him, now that
he had "skills." But there weren't too many employers who needed
someone with his "skills." There was the American military, which was

completely out of fashion in the 1980s and was off limits if he had any appreciation of his mother's feelings. And there was organized crime.

George had already been through a unique curriculum during his summer in Northern Ireland, training that wasn't available at Harvard or the Wharton School, but it was valuable training nonetheless. After a few years running with a local organization, his group subcontracted George's talents to another New York group. He was good at what he did, so one job led to another. By the time he was thirty, George had become an independent contractor.

About a decade later, he bought the house on Bald Eagle Lake. He'd come to appreciate the Twin Cities while passing through on business and thought it would be a good place to live. It was quiet, he loved fishing, had loved it all his life, and it was far from most of his jobs, which tended to be located on the coasts. He'd told neighbors that he wrote for fishing magazines, which explained why he was often home for weeks at a time, then would disappear for a week or two. He came and went quietly, never bothering anyone, not exactly a recluse, but no one could really say they knew him. He was always invited to neighborhood parties and had attended two over the years. No wife, no kids, no obvious girlfriends or boyfriends. Occasionally, a neighbor would see a woman visiting, but more often men would stop by, usually in groups of two or more. They'd grill or go out on George's pontoon boat, and then they'd disappear. Never any trouble.

So here he was, far from the Boston neighborhood he'd grown up in, far from the business he conducted, at peace with himself and with the world. Just your average next-door contract killer.

He looked out over the chilling lake as he sipped his whiskey. He'd received a communication just two hours earlier and was going through the usual process of cost–benefit analysis.

Although the offer was tempting, there were many negatives to this offer. First, the logistics. The job required the deaths of two families. One was a childless couple; the other was a couple with a college-age son. All five were part of the contract.

Further, there was a time limit. The contractor wanted the job completed by December 1, only nineteen days away. Not much time for a background study and intelligence gathering. The cause of death had to look accidental, meaning he couldn't just go in and shoot them all, which is a lot easier than most people think. Bombing was out, too, unless he could make it look like an accident. He'd have to think about that. Could he get them all into one place then blow up the place? That was worth pursuing. Or maybe get them all into the same car and have an "accident." Another possibility.

Normally, he wouldn't even consider the job. It was much too close to home and the timeline much too short. But the remuneration was 2.5 million dollars, a million up front, the balance upon completion, if he made all the criteria—method and deadline. That was five times his usual fee. Of course, there were five people, so that made sense. He'd told the contact that he'd give the job some thought, do some research and let the contractor know his answer in the morning.

Chapter Twenty-seven

Sunday, November 19
Edina, Minnesota

Over a week-and-a-half had passed since the attempted burglary at Pete's and the impromptu dinner party brainstorming session at my place. It had been a busy two weeks, but not much had been done on Pete's case and what work had been done hadn't produced much. The CSIs had gone over his house but came up with no more than we had right after we got there. They took blood samples from Pete and his wife Carol and had the Naval Academy draw a sample from their son Jim to cross-reference with the trace they had found in the stairwell. It would take at least eighteen days, probably more, until those results came back. The toolbox had come from the local Home Depot, as we thought, and the nicks on the phone wires matched those left by the bypass gizmo on the phone wires at Grams' house. Pete and Steve were researching the mineral rights deed, looking for any clues there.

On the other hand, there had been no further break-in attempts at Pete's or his sister Ruth's, so maybe whatever was going on was over. I was beginning to believe it was at least a possibility.

I had been off to my much more fun and much less stressful job of Hollywood consultant for four days. One of the independent studios was making a movie with a big shoot-out scene for the climax. The director was a young guy who was determined it would be as close to reality as possible without regard for what looks better special-effects wise (also called FX). He wanted me there to keep the FX people under control.

The final major scene had a SWAT team storming a building where a bunch of bad guys were holding two hostages. The hostages, two cops—a man and a woman—had been beaten by the bad guys to get information out of them about the layout and security of the police station because the bad guys wanted to steal back all the weapons and drugs the cops confiscated from them in a previous scene in the movie. The bad guys were about to rape the woman when the cavalry arrived.

We had to figure out how to get the good guys into the building close enough to engage the bad guys without alerting them. All the bad guys' stooges had to be knocked off, then the top two bad guys. The hostages had to be freed so they could participate in the final climactic scene, where they get the top bad guy. It took four days to film what turned out to be six minutes, twenty-three seconds of the movie.

The director, who also wrote the screenplay, which helped a lot, had the logistics of the scene pretty well thought out and scripted. He also had a retired marine gunnery sergeant on hand as firearms instructor. This position is usually overlooked. Most directors think their actors can pick up a pistol or a rifle and handle it like a pro; after all, they're actors. But things like proper muzzle discipline, reloading techniques and just pointing and shooting the weapon are learned behaviors. Without proper training, the actors will appear amateurish to any viewer who's had any training at all.

My personal hot button is trigger-finger control. It's one of the four prime directives in gun safety. The finger is off the trigger until you need to pull it—it's as simple as that. Anyone who's been in the military will recognize poor technique.

So, I flew out to fantasyland to help them with the actual filming of this big scene. The actors playing the cops were well trained and had very good technique. The bad guys had also been trained, but they were trained to be bad guys, which means they had generally poor firearms skills. They would do things like hold their pistols with the grips sideways like all the hoods do in the movies. As a cop in real life, you can't always count on this. Sooner or later you are going to run into that one bad guy who has had training and still practices. That's a tough day.

Proper technique had been well taught by the gunny. All I had to do was help with the choreography. This involved figuring out who could stand where and not be in the line of fire, planning movements and determining how many rounds should be fired from here and there and where reloads would take place. It was a lot of fun.

Final result is that this will be a very realistic movie. I hope it can convey the intensity of actual one-on-one combat. Police work, thankfully, doesn't involve much of that. But I've been there a couple of times and it's as intense as anything you'll ever experience. As Winston Churchill said, "There is nothing in life as exhilarating as to have been shot at without effect."

At home, Pete and I did get a chance to have a sit down with some of Grams' church lady friends on Sunday after services. They were a lively bunch of old girls, the youngest seventy-two. We met at the church and had coffee in one of the Sunday school rooms.

I started the conversation by saying, "I want to thank all of you for taking this time to talk to Pete and me about Emma. As you know, we are still investigating her death and have kind of come to a dead end on leads. We're hoping you might have some information, things that you probably don't even think are relevant, that might help us."

Sitting around the table that day were Ellen Hagen, Maggie Grothe, Cora Stordahl, Edna Enger and Norma Eckmann. They were a typical collection of women, the kind who could be found in the basement of any Lutheran church in the state. Their hair was several shades of silver to blue, except for one obviously dyed, but attractive, strawberry blond. They ranged in size from withering to pleasantly plump. They wore comfortable shoes, sweaters and dresses—no slacks in this group. All of them were Emma's friends but I wanted to know if they'd been friends since the early '70s, the timeframe of the last love letters. I doubted Grams would have talked much about them after they stopped arriving, if she talked about them at all.

Cora spoke up. "I'm really sure that I don't know what could have happened. I've thought about nothing else since that day and I only wish there was some way to help."

"We aren't looking for help on what happened that day," I said. "We have a pretty good idea about the events that took place. We are looking for what we call background, things that might have taken place in other locations or years ago."

The mention of times drew a few knowing nods. This group knew that what happens in your life doesn't always take place in any logical order, that experiences from long ago can come back to help you, or haunt you.

"Tell me about Emma, things you remember about her from years ago. Any stories or events that stick in your mind." This got the group talking about Emma, remembering past experiences and episodes from her life that could offer insight into her personality.

I asked leading questions to keep the discussion going. This is an interrogation technique I call "Let 'em roll." The idea is to get the group to feed off each other, each trying to come up with another Emma story to top the last one. From the look on Pete's face he was hearing a lot of this stuff for the first time. After the usual stories about Emma's cooking for thousands and her church work, they got into her few car accidents, her cheating at golf (seems Emma had a foot wedge), and her love of music even though she couldn't carry a tune in a five-gallon bucket.

I got to the meat. "Do any of you know if Emma had any little romances?" I asked with a wink, a smile and as much charm as I could muster.

The girls looked at each other and giggled.

"Oh, I'm sure she didn't," said Maggie. "She was as faithful as they came."

I asked, "Even after Elmer passed?"

"Even then," said Edna. "And she was a prize catch."

Ellen spoke up. "Oh yes. She was still a handsome woman and had her own money. She would have had her pick."

"Yes, but we all know that there's not much to pick from," Cora added.

"That's because we live longer that you do," Maggie explained to Pete and me. "Women, I mean. Women live longer than men so, at the end, there are more of us than of you."

"How about when she was younger? Elmer was gone quite a bit with business wasn't he? Couldn't she have had a little fling then?"

"I've known her since she moved here and that's, what, at least fifty years ago," Cora said. "We've been in the same church choir all that time and you're right," she said, looking at Edna, who had previously criticized Emma's singing ability; she couldn't carry a tune by herself but she was a good choir singer."

The discussion returned to Emma's musical abilities, or lack thereof. While this was going on it occurred to me that one member of the group, Norma, hadn't said a thing since I brought up the possibility of infidelity.

We finished the discussion of Emma's life, including her devotion to Elmer. I felt a little empty. I'd had high hopes for this event and believed that the thread we needed to pull might be here. As the ladies left, I asked Norma about her hat, trying to stall her until the others had cleared the room. When Pete ushered the rest out, I blocked her way to the door.

"There is something, isn't there, Norma?" I asked.

Norma Eckmann, in her late eighties, was the vision of Minnesota stoic. Not many people outside the state know this, as we are usually thought of as being all Scandinavian, but there were actually more German immigrants to this area than Swedes and Norwegians. Being one of the Germans, I can spot another—they look like my relatives. I had watched Norma throughout the discussion and suspected she was holding something back.

She was pensive, obviously thinking it over, balancing the questions. Was it worth risking Emma's reputation to maybe help me find her killer? I hoped she thought so.

This is one of those moments they teach you about in negotiating school. Once you've laid your case on the line, you wait. The next one to talk loses.

I waited.

"I just don't know if it's important or not," she finally said.

"Why don't you tell me and let me decide. After all, Emma's gone and I can keep this a secret."

"I just don't know."

"Norma, I promise, I won't even tell Pete unless you think it's OK.

If you know something, anything, please tell me. We have to find the person who murdered Emma. We owe it to her."

Norma thought some more. True to her nature, she was torn between dedication to helping people and her devotion to her deceased friend. And, being of German descent, she respected authority. I waited.

"All right, I'll tell you. And I think it's all right if you tell Pete, too. I don't think it's speaking ill of the dead to help find her killer. Emma used to get letters from an old flame. She showed them to me."

"We found the letters. Emma kept them in her safe-deposit box."

"Then you know about him?"

"Only the letters. We don't know who he is."

"Well, I don't know, either, just that he was an old flame from her childhood, before she married Elmer. She wrote him back, too."

This was something. She wrote him back.

"Do you have any idea where he lived or who he was? When she knew him?"

"No idea who he was. Like I said, she knew him before Elmer, so I guess he would have been from where she grew up. Someplace way out west in North Dakota."

"Yes, she grew up in a place called Alamo. It's about as far out west as you can go and still be in North Dakota. Did they do more than correspond? You know, did they ever get together?"

"Not that she ever said. Theirs was a long distance relationship. As far as I know she never met him anywhere for, well, you know."

Norma was thinking hard and I knew it was tough on her to talk about this. She came from an age that just kept certain things private.

"No," she went on, "I'm sure they never met with each other. She was devoted to Elmer. I think it was just a young girl's infatuation that became a fast friendship. I think they were just friends."

"Norma, I've read the letters he sent her. They didn't sound like 'just friends' to me. They sounded like they were in love."

"Maybe he was, but she was in love with Elmer. I don't know. I'm sure she loved Elmer with all her heart. I suppose she could have loved someone else long ago and maybe he never let go of it. You know how men are; they fall in love forever. Women are stronger. They can love and move on. Men never seem to be able to do that."

I knew that was the truth. How many homicides had I investigated where an old boyfriend couldn't get over her and killed the woman? Women move on; men just never let go.

"Thank you, Norma. I know this has been hard for you but I want you to know that this could be important. Pete knows about the letters too; he's read them. So this isn't breaking any confidence, is it?"

"I guess not. I just want you to get the man who did this. He took away a very good friend and a very good person."

I nodded and we turned toward the door. Just before we left the sanctity of that private moment, she stopped and said, "You know, Emma had another friend, someone she grew up with. I don't recall her name, maybe June something, Engberg or Ingberg, something like that, another Norski. I think she still lives up north somewhere."

"Got it, June up north. Any idea where 'up north?'"

"I'm not sure. Somewhere between here and Alamo."

"OK. And why do I want to talk to June?"

"Because she might know who he is."

"The letter writer?"

"Yes, the man is who wrote the letters. I remember that Emma said that June was her best friend growing up and that she had lived there too. She might know who wrote those letters."

With these cryptic revelations, we parted company. My mind was going five different directions at once. On the way out to tell Pete, my phone rang. I answered it. Another trial testimony offer. This one was in Memphis, Tennessee. The prosecutor's office had a case in which the bad guy had shot someone using a left-handed AR-15-type rifle. Very unusual—left-handed rifles are very rare and cost more than the normal.

The prosecution had a lot of other evidence on this particular perp and just wanted me to come in and testify on the statistical rarity of left-handed rifles. They'd handle everything else, such as ballistics and wound analysis. I told them to send me an email and I'd check my schedule to make sure I was available. My rates are $300 per hour for research, $3,000 per day plus expenses for travel and testimony, less than most decent criminal trial attorneys. It could be somewhere around a $10,000 payday for less than a week's work.

Between the job offer and the having learned earlier that morning that Maria was thinking about coming up from Arizona for Thanksgiving, I was more than distracted. Somewhere along the walk to the parking lot, I forgot about June up north.

Chapter Twenty-eight

Robbinsdale, Minnesota
Thanksgiving Day, Thursday, November 27th

I was up bright and snarly on Thanksgiving morn. It looked to be
a wonderfully typical late November day in Minnesota, sunny and
twenty-one with clear skies, a bit of a breeze with a high temp expected
in the low forties. We were in that period where the temps danced up
and down over the freeze point and the lakes couldn't make up their
minds whether or not to turn to ice.

Great weather aside, my real reason for feeling so fine that morning
was that Maria was spending the long weekend with me. We had talked
about this possibility, but with her work schedule heavily dependent
upon her caseload, we didn't know until two days before that she'd be
able to break away. She did and I was a happy camper.

I got up later than my usual 6:30. I have an absolutely steadfast
rule—never leave a bed that contains a naked woman. So this morning
I stayed in bed until about 8:00 but Maria was operating on mountain
time, so she was still sleepy. I got up to prepare breakfast.

While I consider myself one of the premier grillers in the country,
I can do breakfast, too. This may consist of pancakes or waffles from
scratch, omelets, outstanding oatmeal, and all the usual sides such as
toast, rolls, muffins, biscuits, etc. I'll even cut up fresh fruit.

This day it was oatmeal. I do use the one-minute stuff, but here's my
secret. Start by sorting through your raisins. You have to make sure they
all look good and there are no stems. No one likes to bite into a raisin
stem in their nice creamy oatmeal. I dump about half a cup of raisins
into the bottom of a two-quart saucepan.

Next, I add one cup of water, one cup of milk (half and half is better if you can stand the fat), a heaping cup of instant oats, two healthy tablespoons of brown sugar and a good shake of cinnamon. You can add the sugar and cinnamon to taste. Then I turn on the heat and bring it just to a boil, stirring often. When it starts to bubble pretty good, I shut off the heat (gas ranges are better than electric—when you shut them off, they're off), cover the pan and let it sit at least five minutes. That gave me time to finish the toast and eggs.

Today will be a big day for Maria and me, so I'm being extra careful with everything. We are heading over to Ruth's, Pete's sister's, for dessert and a football game after Thanksgiving dinner. This will be the first sort of "family" thing we've done together. It's the next step in our relationship. We've been very private and kept our relationship between us, although we both have people who know about us, but this will be taking it public. I suppose if all goes well we'll be dining with her parents the next time I'm in Phoenix. We'll see.

After covering the oatmeal I went back into the bedroom to see if Sleeping Beauty had awakened. She had. As I came in she was stretching luxuriously, her dark hair tossed up on her pillow like a black halo. She yawned as she stretched. I could see her legs moving under the sheets. All in all, it was one of the most erotic sights I had ever seen in my life. Be still my beating heart.

"Well, look who's awake. Sleep well?"

"After I finally got you taken care of. Who'd have thought a man could do what you did last night? At your age? You're an animal and I love you."

Actually, those were my thoughts. What she really said in reply to my question was "Great. What's for breakfast?"

"I've got oatmeal ready with all the trimmings. I figured we'd better stoke up a little since the big meal won't be until about 1:00."

"Sounds wonderful. Now scoot out of here so I can get up and get dressed."

We'd been seeing each other for about four months, albeit long distance, and this wasn't the first time we'd shared a bed, but she was still shy about some things. I loved it. I left the room but hesitated just long enough at the door to peek back and see her as she exited the warm sheets. She's beautiful.

I trotted back down the stairs and checked the oatmeal, breaking one of the cardinal rules in the kitchen, which is to leave the cover on the pan. Sometimes I just can't help myself.

The brewing coffee was filling the air with a wonderful aroma. Combined with the toast, it just smelled like morning should. The only thing missing was bacon. Whoops.

I hurriedly grabbed the bacon from the refrigerator and put it in the frying pan. I like my bacon a certain way—just on the verge of crispy, not really crisp but not chewy. The only way to get that is to cook it in a pan over low heat. It takes about ten minutes, so I hoped Maria would take her time. She did.

Eight minutes later, as the bacon was getting close, she came down the stairs. She was wearing snug khaki slacks that painted the outline of her figure from the waist down. A deep burgundy blouse that must have been satin the way it reflected the light coming in the windows finished the image. A perfect work of art.

"Hmmm, smells great. Bacon, too?"

"Of course. It's all part of the standard morning fare I prepare for all my guests."

"Not too often, I hope."

"Not often enough."

I looked at her with affection as I pulled a chair out for her. She sat and I returned to the stove.

"What's your family doing today?" I asked.

"Wondering where I am."

"Are you in trouble for coming here?"

"Not with my mother. She knows all about you and even bought one of your books. I can't say she got anything out of it, but that may be just as well. If she wants to think that you are some big academic lecturer instead of a lecher, that's all right by me."

She giggled at her joke.

I served the oatmeal while the bacon drained. Oatmeal stays nice and hot so it can stand some dwell time in the bowl. Orange juice was already poured and the coffee could wait. Toast, butter and strawberry preserves were already on the table. She started buttering her toast.

I delivered the bacon, sat down and started in as well. We ate, taking turns looking at each other, both wondering where this was going. Neither of us knew, which was part of the adventure. Finally, I spoke.

"Maria, I have a trip to L.A. coming up in about two weeks. Do you think I could stop by for a day or two?"

"If you go to L.A. and don't come see me, you'd better plan on never stopping by again."

I'd just been learning about her Latina temper. She could play rough when she wanted too.

"Just checking. You know, I don't want to interrupt any other plans you might have."

"You come and this time we'll go see the family."

I had asked about meeting her family every time I'd been to Phoenix. This was the first time she'd brought it up. Oh my.

Chapter Twenty-nine

Ruth and Steve Hammer's house
Apple Valley, Minnesota
Thanksgiving Day

From George Kline's point of view, the house was sited as perfectly as any house in the suburbs could be. It was a good thing, too, because the other house, the one by the lake, simply would not do—too many problems. There were not enough access points. Any house on a lake automatically lost one side from which to approach. And the house in question sat on an island. Only one road in and out, no nearby cover point from which to sit and observe, unnoticed and, of course, the dog. All these details made the kind of event he had in mind impossible at the lake house. But the house in Apple Valley—that was another story altogether.

George had decided to take the assignment. The risks were still there but there is no big reward without risk. All through human history, those who took the risks reaped the rewards. He was ready to take the risk in return for the two-and-a-half-million-dollar opportunity.

As with any assignment, the first thing was research. George had researched the targets, looking for one thing—a chance to get them all together. Fortunately for him, the opportunity was right in front of him, timing wise. Thanksgiving is that truly American holiday when families can be counted upon to get together. All he had to figure out was when and where.

The when was obvious: Thanksgiving Day.

Determining where was a little trickier. While most families go to someone's home for this holiday, some families choose to leave the dirty dishes to the restaurants. A little hacking answered his question.

He contacted a hacker he'd used in the past who had no moral reservations about his work. He was in it for the paycheck. George told him to start tracking all the members of this family—Ruth and Steve, and Pete and Carol and their son, Jim. He gave the hacker all the information he had on the five—names, birthdates, addresses, etc., and told him he wanted a purchasing and travel information summary on the clan. After that, he also wanted daily reports.

The data started to pour in. Immediately, he had Jim's flight number home for Wednesday, plus a list of the most frequented gas stations, grocery stores and restaurants the family used. Then the daily reports started to show traffic patterns. Finally, George got the hit he was looking for: Ruth Hammer bought a turkey big enough to feed the family.

To a casual observer, this might not seem like an important piece of this particular puzzle, but to George it was the jackpot. He knew, with a high statistical probability, that the dinner would be held at the home of the person who bought and cooked the turkey. This year, it would be at the Hammer residence in Apple Valley, Minnesota.

George started making his plans based upon that assumption. First, he personally reconnoitered the site. The house was located in a typical moderately upscale neighborhood. A wooded creek wound its way through the neighborhood and ran right behind the Hammer's house. The creek could be accessed further into the neighborhood near a play area. The play area had a parking lot, where he could leave his car, then follow the creek to the rear of the house.

He had several ideas about what to do when he got there.

The most straightforward option was to sneak in at night and cut their throats. While effective for the residents of the house, it wouldn't guarantee getting the other family. He could rig a gas line into the house, wait until all had arrived, then introduce natural gas or LP gas, which would eventually find an ignition source and blow the house into next week. Effective, but someone might notice the gas smell and they'd leave. He could gas the house with carbon monoxide. But there is always the chance that someone will notice that they were getting light-headed or nauseous before they inhaled enough gas to pass out. Add to that the recent addition of CO detectors to many homes and he dismissed all of these scenarios.

The one he chose required both the approach to the home and an actual entry. It had an element of risk, but that went with the territory.

About 3:00 a.m. he'd left his car in the parking lot of the play area and walked down the creek toward the Hammer's home. It seemed that his good Irish luck was holding as the house right next to the parking area had cars overflowing its driveway. Two cars were parked illegally, for Apple Valley, on the street overnight and one other car was already in the parking lot. Must be a bunch of out-of-town guests in for tomorrow's feast, he thought.

The creek was nearly dry this time of year and there was a soft bank to walk on. There was enough moonlight to guide his steps and his eyes were as sharp as his genes and a good diet could make them. He made sure to walk on the downed leaves so he wouldn't leave any footprints in the mud next to the creek. This allowed him to miss any twigs that might snap at his passing. Just because the target house had no dog didn't mean the other neighbors didn't. A barking dog was that last thing he wanted to hear.

He carried a duffel bag and a backpack that contained everything he needed—tools, hose, food, water, and a few other props plus a camouflage thermal blanket. It would be cold, around twenty degrees, but the blanket was all he required for warmth and cover. Even if a group of kids playing in the creek came by, he didn't think they'd see him in the depths of the gully behind the house.

When he reached the hiding point behind the house he set up shop. Checking around to make sure that no one in another house could see him, he pulled the camo blanket out of the bag and spread it over himself. Then, using a small green penlight, he assembled a brace and bit, a very old-school tool, to be sure, but effective and, more importantly to George, silent. He crept silently up the backyard to the rear of the house, pulling with him a green rubber hose. The approach to the house was fairly steep but he had no trouble pulling the hose up to the house, crawling under the rear deck, then moving along the back of the house.

This would leave the hose completely out of sight unless someone actually walked around to the back of the house. He knew from his research that the floor plan of the house had the bedrooms upstairs on the east end. He pulled the hose to the lower level on the west, where the mechanical room housing the furnace was located. He drilled a ¾-inch hole through the siding, the house wrap, sheeting, insulation, vapor barrier and inside drywall, then inserted the end of the hose and secured it with some putty. The job was done in less than ten minutes. All he had to do now was crawl back down to the creek and wait.

Waiting was always the hard part. He'd been doing this for nearly twenty years and waiting was never easy. Fortunately, he knew he'd be able to sleep. Wrapped up under the blanket he'd conk right out until the sun came up. He knew there wouldn't be any activity until then, so he might as well do what soldiers had done for years whenever they got the chance. Sleep.

Chapter Thirty

Robbinsdale, Minnesota

Maria and I spent the rest of Thanksgiving morning lollygagging away the time. We watched the Macy's parade on TV and the start of one of the football games. It was a rare day off for both of us.

We were heading out to a nice hotel with a restaurant well known for their big and well-advertised Thanksgiving Dinner Buffet, then we were going south where we would be spending the rest of our holiday with Pete's family, watching football and eating leftovers at his sister Ruth's.

"Time to head out," I said as I got up while flipping off the TV with the remote.

"Give me a minute." Maria got up from her seat next to me on the couch and ran upstairs. We had been picking on and wrestling with each other like a couple of third graders during the football game. She was a Cardinals fan and I was an occasional Vikings fan, depending on their coaching, but neither team was playing. So we each randomly picked one of the teams playing to cheer for and used that as an excuse to play with each other. Young love, it's a wonderful thing.

Maria came down the stairs, her Barbie Doll figure now covered with a black dress jacket. I knew it was for more than what she considered the unspeakably cold weather. She now had a way to hide her firearm.

Like any serving law enforcement officer, or LEO, Maria had the right to carry her firearm nationwide. Most departments required off-duty carry and some encouraged it even when out of town. Most LEOs didn't bother when on vacation, but Maria was cut from the same cloth as I was. After so many years of carrying, you kind of feel naked without it.

Maria Fernandez had been a cop for almost twenty years. She had started as a sheriff's deputy with the Maricopa County Arizona Sheriff's Office right out of college. She had worked patrol, as had all her counterparts. When opportunities for advancement presented themselves she did the work necessary to move up the ladder. At forty-two, she was a full investigator. Along the way she had served on the County's SWAT team and had been the designated sniper and rifle-training officer. She also competed in United States Practical Shooting Association pistol matches and shot Master in three divisions. She knew how to shoot. And she observed an old cop adage—you never need a pistol until you really need pistol. So, she always carried a pistol.

Carrying a firearm all the time is, in fact, a real pain in the ass. When you are not in uniform you have to conceal it. Although concealing it is not required by law, even for those civilians with carry permits, it is truly the only way to go. Most people still get nervous when they see a gun, even when the person wearing it looks like any other normal person in the grocery store or at the mall. So every wardrobe selection has to take that into consideration. Winter is no problem, at least in the colder climes. Bulky cold-weather clothes can hide an anti-tank missile. Summer is a completely different matter. Of course, Maria was still gorgeous in her now complete outfit.

With the beautiful weather, I decided to drive my '69 Mustang 429. In Minnesota you drive your "summer car" whenever you can with the following provisos. It can't be raining. There can't be any snow on the streets. If it's spring and the streets are dry, you must wait until a good rain has washed all the salt and sand away. Today's conditions met all the criteria.

Our reservations were for 1:00 and we were a bit early, but they seated us right away. The meal was as advertised—outstanding. The menu included the standard turkey, mashed potatoes, gravy, dressing, cranberry sauce and pumpkin pie plus ham, roast beef and about any kind of vegetable you'd want. Wild rice soup and several salads were there for starters, plus an assortment of breads, fresh fruit and, to finish it off, a dessert tray that could pretty much guarantee a heart attack before you reached your car. We skipped dessert.

We got through the mountain of food around 2:00 but I wasn't planning on getting to Ruth's until after 3:00 because I knew their dinner was planned for 2:00 and I didn't want to interrupt the family time. So we climbed back into the Mustang and I pointed it east on I-694 to catch the I-94 cutoff to show Maria downtown Minneapolis. It was my chance to give her a little tour of my frame of reference. I looked at it as cop-bonding time, an important part of our relationship.

Chapter Thirty-one

**Ruth and Steve Hammer's
Apple Valley, Minnesota**

George Kline had awakened at dawn. There were still quite a few birds in residence, even this late in the season. They awoke before the sun came up and started their daily reaffirmation of territory by trilling their songs. George listened to the singing with typical human pleasure but he also knew what it represented. "All that lovely music is really a challenge to keep outsiders away," he thought. "Not all that different from us."

As he stretched and thoroughly woke up, he ran through a quick mental list of what he'd be doing in the next few hours, then an inventory of what he would need in what order. Everything was still where he'd left it. He took care of morning bodily issues by voiding into an empty water bottle he'd kept for that purpose and eating three energy bars. He'd been taught that he could get all the necessary nutrients for a couple of days of hard work from energy bars, along with some dried fruit and nuts. The upside was that the meal was considered to be "low residual," meaning he wouldn't have to use a toilet for the term of the job. The downside was that he'd had to start this diet thirty-six hours ago and would be quite constipated when he got home. Part of the price to be paid. He made sure to hang on to all the wrappers and the now-refilled water bottle. He would pack those out with him. No sense leaving any litter behind.

Back to waiting. He had made sure his hiding place had a good view of the street on both sides of the house so he could see when someone arrived. He couldn't see the actual driveway, but he could assume that someone had arrived by watching the street on both sides of the house.

When the neighborhood was platted, the third-acre lots were offset so no two houses faced directly at its neighbor across the street. The driveways were likewise offset. So any car that passed in front of the house and didn't come out the other side had to have pulled into the driveway. He also knew what kind of cars the Anderson family owned and could watch for one of those. He would also watch the back windows of the house.

The house had a large two-story great room on the east end. Kline believed that is where the entertaining would be done. He also had a good view of the kitchen. Since it was the north facing back side of the house and faced only the creek bed and trees, the homeowners felt no need for drapes or blinds.

The day wound on slowly. Kline, like any warrior waiting in ambush, had time to think. That's a problem for warriors, good intentioned or bad. Thinking brings doubts. Doubt brings indecision. Indecision brings failure. Kline thought about failure.

Chapter Thirty-two

Somewhere in the countryside of Northern Ireland
July 13th, 1985

George and his three fellow "students" followed along as the instructor completed the assembly of their first live bomb. It was a simple device, one that in later years would be referred to by the warriors it targeted as an "improvised explosive device" or IED, but the concept and function was the same. Build a bomb out of whatever materials were available, disguise it as something harmless, and put it where your enemy will either pass near it or come to investigate. In this case, they had built the bomb into the back of a small car, a 1983 Austin Metro. It was a rather new car for this mission, but they had to look like they fit in and an older beat-up junker just would not suffice. Plus the Metro, with its large rear hatchback area, could hold a lot of luggage. At least that's what it would look like.

When they finished assembling it, they drew straws to see who would get the honor of driving the car to its final resting place. A lad from Belfast was thrilled when he drew the long straw. His entire life had been lived under what he believed was occupation by a foreign force. At least that's what he had been taught since he could speak. It's a kind of hate that is hard to let go of, even when it seems things are changing. In his mind, he would now be the one changing things.

The chosen driver received last-second instructions on the route to take and how to arm the bomb when he got to the appointed place, a theater that Protestants often went to. The team leader was very specific about where he was to park, how to arm the bomb, and that he should just get out of the car and walk away. A film was playing that would attract off-duty British soldiers. That there would be plenty of civilians, some of them Catholic, was just the price that had to be paid. Collateral damage was a fact of any war.

The lucky driver got in the car and started out the doors of the barn. The rest of the team followed in two other cars. The little caravan made its way into town and started down the highway toward the targeted theater in Belfast. In the trailing car, George looked out at the beautiful day. This day they would make a statement. His car mates passed around a bottle and commented about how this was going to change things in their war. Up ahead they could see the sun reflecting off the bomb-laden Metro, moving toward its destiny. They were all looking right at it as it hit a small piece of debris, a chunk of rubber from a shredded tire. It wasn't much of a bump in the road and the rest of the team would never know why it happened, but something triggered the bomb. The car vanished in a tremendous fireball. The driver was vaporized.

Failure.

Chapter Thirty-three

Ruth and Steve Hammer's
Apple Valley, Minnesota

At about one o'clock Kline saw Pete's Cadillac approach. It slowed as it neared the Hammer residence and did not pass by. Kline knew the group was assembled.

His plan was simple. Let everyone gather for the fall feast, wait until they had eaten their fill and settled down for the usual *après-meal* coffee and dessert in the family room. His part of the festivities would be to open the valve on the gas canister connected to the hose. As he reviewed the plan in his mind, he observed through his binoculars that three people had, in fact, arrived, a couple in their fifties and a young man around twenty-one who had a very short haircut and appeared to be extraordinarily fit. This must be the Naval Academy son. Time to go to work.

He watched through the big windows as the family assembled and went through the usual greeting ritual—hugs and kisses all around. Steve Hammer vigorously greeted the young man.

The men went into the great room and flopped on the couch and chairs to watch football until the meal began. The women moved about the kitchen with last-minute preparation duties coming to a head.

It would be a wonderful last meal, Kline thought. The image made him hungry so he broke out another energy bar.

Outside the house

The family finished their Thanksgiving dinner and headed back to the great room where a buffet of dessert and drinks had been set up. As they all settled into the comfortable furniture, Kline released the gas.

Kline had maintained his contacts with IRA and was able to procure the canister of gas used today through those old ties. He had never used the gas before. In his line of work new technology was welcome. The material had been researched for its use as a calmative or incapacitating agent for years. It had been developed for use by the U.S. military and was supposedly not available outside the military. Kline was anxious to see if it worked as well as advertised.

The primary qualities Kline was looking for was quick and total incapacitation and a residual effect of twenty-six minutes. From what he'd been told, the gas would knock out the entire family within one and a half minutes. They would be out for about a half hour. Kline figured he needed about fifteen minutes after nighty-night time for the rest of his plan.

The entry point for the gas was the mechanical room, near the furnace. In his reconnaissance, Kline saw that the house had a high-efficiency furnace. That meant that the combustion air for the furnace came from outside the house and the exhaust was vented back outside by a similar system. These systems are identified by their signature use of white PVC tubing for the venting, which Kline had seen. On the side of the house two tubes protruded from the siding, one pointing up and the other pointing down.

Inside the house

The gas was immediately drawn to the cold air return near the furnace and pulled inside. The furnace burners were not lit, because the temperature in the well-insulated house was above the thermostat setting due to the oven being on all morning. But the Hammers had set their furnace fan to run constantly to keep the air in the house at a more even temperature and to continuously circulate the air through the furnace's filters—a good commonsense thing to do unless you are expecting a gas attack.

The gas traveled through the house's supply vents and was uniformly distributed throughout the house. It reached all five occupants of the great room about three minutes after the valve was opened.

Pete and Steve had taken seats on the couch that faced a 52-inch flat screen TV. Another NFL game was in the second quarter. Jim was just about to sit down when he noticed an odd look on his father's face. He smelled a slightly sweet odor and, acting on thousands of years of evolution, he did what most people do when they notice an odd smell—he drew a lung full into his body through his nose. As he did he saw his mother and aunt both nod off where they sat. The last thing he saw was his father, trying to stand, falling forward over the coffee table.

Outside the house

Kline observed the mass somnolence, then shut the gas valve and waited five minutes for the gas to begin to disperse before making his approach. He walked to the east side of the house. When he got to the PVC pipes he removed a large wasp nest from his kit and stuffed it gingerly into the downward pointing intake pipe. He placed it in the pipe carefully so he would not damage the fragile paper nest. He looked up the pipe to assure that it appeared as though the wasps had built it there. Satisfied, he moved to the rear of the house, which was guarded by tall pine trees that served to block the neighbors' view. He donned a gas mask, gained entry through the patio door, always one of the easiest to broach, and headed inside to complete the job. Leaving the door wide open to allow more ventilation, he quickly moved to the great room. After checking to be sure everyone was down for the count, he went around the house opening windows, then opened the front door. He needed the gas completely out of the house before he closed it back up. Satisfied that the late fall breeze would do the job, he picked up his tool bag and went downstairs.

Chapter Thirty-four

Downtown Minneapolis

I parked the beast in one of the police slots at Minneapolis City Hall, a city-block sized building that sits anachronistically between two very modern buildings built in the late twentieth century. The City Hall building was constructed near the turn of the last century out of rough-hewn Minnesota granite quarried on the Dakota border and hauled in by horse-drawn wagon. Windows were set deep in carved squares that gave evidence to the thickness of the walls. Its color reminds some of liver on its way to going bad but I thought it was an attractive color.

We locked the car and walked up 5th heading for the Nicollet Mall to walk off our meal. Window-shopping along the way, we made the turn south at 10th and a block later went back down Marquette Avenue. We stopped for a pick-me-up at one of the chain coffee shops. Maria had a turtle latte and I had a double mocha.

A half hour later we headed for Ruth and Steve's.

Apple Valley is only about ten miles, as the crow flies, straight south of downtown Minneapolis. But you can't drive the way that pesky crow gets to fly because he doesn't have to worry about how to get across the Minnesota River.

I didn't think the drive would be a problem today as we took the ramp to the eastbound Crosstown then drove just over a mile or so to the southbound ramp for Cedar Avenue. This path takes you right along the western edge of the airport, crosses I-494 then passes the Mall Of America. A beautiful sky, cool temps and holiday traffic made this a pleasant ride through the burbs. We had Bob Seeger's "Hollywood

Nights" cranked up loud. We zipped south on Cedar. We were only ten minutes out now. The only thing wrong was the Mustang's bucket seats, which precluded any cuddling.

We had a large bowl of cut fruit in the back—our contribution to dessert. I wondered how dinner had gone at the Hammer's. By now they'd eaten and were probably fighting off the usual post-turkey drowsiness.

In front of the Hammer house

We pulled into Ruth and Steve's driveway about 3:30, stylishly late for our 3:00 expected time.

"Nice place," Maria said as we strolled up the brick paver walk. "Is everyone here loaded?"

"No, just my friends. See? It's a great place to live, with rich friends and great weather, at least a few months of the year."

"I think the weather today is wonderful. How bad can the winters be?"

"I'm sure they're more than you've ever seen. Do you ever get snow in Phoenix?"

Maria's attention was diverted. "Looks like they're expecting us," she said.

The front door was open. In fact, both the storm door and the entry door were wide open.

"Must have burned something and they're trying to air out the place," I said as we walked up the steps. We stepped inside and I announced our arrival. No response. We looked at each other and instinctively drew our pistols.

I rounded the corner and looked into the great room where I saw five people down. It was now officially nasty.

The Basement

Kline heard footsteps above his head. "Damn," he thought, "Someone else must have been invited for dinner. He'd have to neutralize them, then leave them for stage two of the attack. He didn't fret about confronting someone. He was fully trained in hand-to-hand combat. He had a pistol but drew his knife, hoping he wouldn't need it.

Kline crept to the top of the stairs and peeked through the gap under the door. He could see feet—two pairs of shoes, one pair was a male's, the other belonged to a female. Casual shoes, not uniform shoes, so at least they were not police. He thought about waiting for them downstairs. They would certainly come down looking for any trouble with the furnace. Or would they? If they thought the family had been incapacitated by carbon monoxide, they would leave the house and call the gas company and an ambulance. He'd have to confront them quickly, before they left the house.

He looked around the door again and saw the man step into the great room. He hadn't heard that. Had he missed it? Had the man gone into quiet mode? He looked again and saw a large-caliber pistol in the man's hand. "Shit. What else can go wrong?" he wondered.

The Great Room

Maria and I had gone tactical. In the great room I checked the pulse of the first person I came to, Ruth. She had a pulse, although it was slow. I stepped over to Carol and checked her as well. Her pulse was stronger and she was breathing OK.

I looked around for any sign of what happened. Why was everyone unconscious? And why was every window in the house open?

I signaled Maria that they were alive. She had checked the men then moved into the kitchen and had her phone out. Two things cops never leave home without—a gun and a phone. As she called 9-1-1 she softly called out to me, "Address?" I gave it to her and she quietly told them to send at least two ambulances and backup. She also said there were two cops in the house and that we were searching.

We were in full cop mode. It's instinctive. We were in a house where something had taken out five people. We didn't know if it was environmental or if there were one or more bad guys around. Given recent history, I was thinking bad guys. If bad guys, had they left? If they hadn't left, how many and where were they? We needed to search the house.

There are two schools of thought on searching a house. One is "Are you trying to catch the bad guy?" The other is "Are you trying to clear the house to make sure he's gone?" Right now I figured the best way to get effective help for my friends was to find out what had put them down. And the best way to find that out was to find whoever did it.

The Basement

Kline was trapped. The man upstairs moved like a professional. He was no neighbor and no civilian with a carry permit. He was a cop. And there were two people. Was the other person a cop too? No way to know and no time to find out. It was an abort. Failure. No big paycheck this November. His best outcome at this point was to evade and cut his losses. Just go home. Nothing he'd be leaving behind would point to him. He'd just be back on Bald Eagle Lake with a Bushmill's before the Cowboys played, beginning to feel constipated.

He knew the house did not have a walkout basement. Likewise, there were no egress windows, windows whose bottoms are about waist high. There were, however "garden windows," short, wide windows mounted high in the wall to allow in a little daylight. He saw some chairs and boxes that could be stacked so he could escape through a garden window. He knew the cop upstairs would search the house. The man was a pro; he wouldn't wait for backup. Kline knew he couldn't wait. If more cops showed up, the first thing they'd do is establish a perimeter. How much time he had depended upon which way they went first—up or down.

Main Floor

Maria came into the area of the great room near me. We stayed separated as is prescribed by proper tactical search procedure. There was an office on the main floor where anything of value to a burglar would be. If this was the same guy who had hit Pete's house, he'd have been there rifling through drawers. We moved silently down the hall that runs to both the office and the mud room/laundry off the garage. I signaled Maria that I'd go in high and she would go in low. She nodded understanding. I signaled with my fingers one, two, three and we took the door.

Basement

Kline just about jumped out of his skin when he heard the door upstairs slam open. He nearly dropped the chair he was carrying. "Jesus Christ" he mumbled to himself. He caught his breath and continued his work.

Main Floor

As the door opened, Maria threw herself into the room low and to the right. I threw myself in high and left. We swept the room and came up dry. No bad guys. Good. I really didn't want to have to shoot anyone in Ruth's house.

Now the decision—upstairs first or down? Again, thinking this must be related to Pete's break-in I decided up. If the perp was still here, he'd be there.

We went back through the great room and I saw Pete moving on the floor. He was still out of it, but at least he was moving. That was a good thing.

At the bottom of the stairs I moved close to Maria.

"The house is a standard design. There are four bedrooms upstairs and two baths. One bath is off the master bedroom. We'll go up and work the rooms leapfrog style as fast as we can. If you see anything go ahead and lay down suppressing fire and I'll follow your fire into the room."

Again she nodded her understanding.

We headed up the stairs. At the top I hit the first room on the right. She peeked in, then stepped in and swept the room. Nothing. I went in while she kept watch, and checked the closet and under the bed. Nothing. We moved to the next room.

Same story for the next three bedrooms and the baths. I said, "I guess that leaves the basement." That was when we heard the crash.

Basement

The makeshift ladder was almost assembled. Kline had a chair and two boxes set up so he could climb up to the window, which was about eighteen inches high by three feet wide. The window's mechanism looked like it hadn't been touched for years.

Kline carefully climbed the wobbling stack until he was high enough to push open the window. It took a solid hit with the palm of his hand but it did move. Three more smacks and it was open far enough to get through.

Kline pulled himself up toward the window but was just a bit too low. He'd need to push himself up to get through the opening. He gave a careful hop and was almost there. One more good shove and he caught himself in the opening. But the shove caused the precarious ladder to fall to the floor with an ear-splitting crash. The pistol in his pocket caught on the window frame. He was stuck.

Upstairs

We ran down the hall and vaulted down the stairs. Maria rounded the corner to the basement one step ahead of me and I grabbed her by the tail of her jacket.

"Hold on," I said in a loud whisper. "We don't know what's going on down there. We need a plan."

"OK. Here's the plan," she answered. "I jump the stairs and you come down as fast as you can. This guy hasn't shot anyone yet and you said that Grams' murder was probably spontaneous. I can vault down four steps at a time and that will distract him. You come down as fast as you can and I'll tell you where he is."

"OK."

Maria took a deep breath and said, "Here I go."

I watched as the most important person in my life disappeared into the lower level. I heard her hit the floor but before I could follow, she yelled, "He's going out the window!"

Backyard

Kline freed himself from the window frame and scrambled through, leaving all his tools behind. He wasn't worried about fingerprints, because he'd worn gloves and the tools were untraceable. But he was worried about the stuff in the gully by the creek. He had worn gloves all night but might have left some other trace. You can't sit for ten hours in one place and not leave some of yourself behind. Another small failure, but they were starting to mount up.

Kline rolled down the hill, hoping to be out of the sight of anyone who might pursue. At the bottom of the hill, he quickly gathered everything together. His training had driven him to pack everything up in case a quick retreat was necessitated, so all he really had to do was grab his duffel and backpack and run for the car.

On the deck

I came out the sliding door onto the deck, gun in hand, just in time to see a figure roll over the hill. The deck was only about six feet off the ground, but combined with vaulting the rail, it would be at least a ten-foot drop. I knew my fifty-something-year-old knees couldn't take that sort of impact any more. I used the steps on the west side of the deck. As I reached the point where the hill broke downward, I could see a man picking up something. I yelled out, "Stop! Police!" as loud as I could, then started down the hill. Not my best idea.

In the gully

Kline heard the man yell, "Police!" "Big fucking deal" he muttered as he reached into his pocket and retrieved his nine-millimeter pocket gun—a small gun but it was loaded with the same lethal ammunition police departments use. Its compact frame held only six rounds. He fired one round up the hill in the direction of the cop in an attempt to stall him, not really planning on hitting anything with the un-aimed shot. He didn't want to hit him. He knew if there is any way to guarantee pursuit over the long run, it was to shoot a cop.

Coming down the hill

I saw the man look up my way when I yelled and then saw him draw. "Come on," I thought. "This guy can't be armed." If there's one thing a cop can count on it's that burglars don't go armed. There's no reason for it. Of course, if there's one other thing a cop can count on it's that the guy they're sure isn't armed will be armed.

He snapped off a shot my way with the nonchalance of someone familiar with firearms. I looked for cover. As I dropped behind a tree, I heard two quick loud reports from behind me.

At the top of the hill

Maria reached the top of the hill in time to see the man pull a compact pistol from his pocket and loose a round in Dan's direction. She went into automatic pilot and did what any cop would in the same situation. Her partner was taking fire. She returned fire.

Maria returned fire with a standard two-round group known as a double tap. Shooters do this because the first round, even a .45-caliber round, may hit something on the target that negates its effectiveness, like heavy clothing or even body armor. In some cases, the target may be on narcotics that render the individual impervious to pain. In either case, two hits from a .45 ACP at a range of less than seventy-five feet will put down pretty much anything from drugged-up crazy people to most large game. It did in this case.

In the Gully

After shooting the one round to make the man duck, Kline intended to return to the business at hand—recovering his gear and making his escape. Out the corner of his eye, he saw movement on the deck at the top of the hill. Another person. "Must be the woman," he thought. "She won't be any trouble." But when he saw her move in a familiar manner, just as he had been taught, bringing up her hands and crouching as if preparing to fire, he blurted, "Not another cop!"

It was a statement of frustration, not fear. For if there was one thing that George Kline knew it was that most cops "couldn't hit a bull in the butt with a bass fiddle," to quote Nimitz. As he brought his gun around to send another covering shot her direction he saw two quick flashes and felt the result.

George Kline caught both rounds center mass, right in the ten ring. His heart was shredded as the expanding hollow-point bullets ripped through his body and out his back. He was physically stunned by the blows and flew over backward. As he fell he had one final thought.

"Failure."

By the time Dan Neumann reached him, he was dead.

Chapter Thirty-five

I saw the man at the bottom of the gully take both of Maria's shots in the chest. He went down hard so I jumped from behind the tree and sort-of hopped my way down to him before he could recover and return fire. I knew he'd been hit hard, but you never know about these things.

Some guys can take a lot of hits and keep going. I remember one bad guy on meth who shot it out with three cops. They hit him fourteen times before he went down. Of course the cops were using standard department-issued Glock 17s, which are 9mm, not .45s, like Maria's. Oh well, you know what they say about the 9mm—it's a .45 set on stun.

I kicked the gun away from what I soon learned was the dead bad guy. Maria's two rounds had gone straight through him. He was lying face down. His back was a mess. From the look of his jacket I knew he couldn't have survived, but you do what you can anyway. I rolled him over and checked for a pulse. There was none.

About this time Maria made it down the hill. I could hear sirens wailing in the distance. She took one look at the dead guy and did what most cops do after they've ended a human life. She threw up.

It's not like in the movies. Nearly all of us find taking a human life repugnant. It is part of the job on rare occasions and it would be unrealistic to think that cops can just drop a bad guy and walk away untouched. There's a reason departments force a cop to take leave after a shooting. It's so they can get really drunk, really far away, and really over it. Some never do. Every cop's life is changed if they are involved in a shooting, whether they actually shoot someone or not. They are never the same; I know I wasn't. I looked at Maria and knew what she was going through. In all her years she had never had to shoot a person, even though she had prepared for it her entire career.

That's what it comes down to. FBI statistics say that the vast majority of gunfights happen at a distance of fifteen feet or less, with three to five rounds fired, and they're over in less than 3.5 seconds. A cop prepares every day for those 3.5 seconds. It's something he hopes he'll never have to do. But he has to be ready. He straps on that gun every morning and prays, "Not today, Lord. Just get me home tonight."

Most are never put in that shooting situation. But for the few who find themselves there, the training can be the difference between life and death—theirs and the bad guys.

I looked up the hill and saw an Apple Valley cop peeking over it. I pulled my badge case from my pocket, flipped it open and held it up in one hand. In my other I held my gun by the barrel so he could see I wasn't pointing it at him and yelled, "Police. We're clear down here but we're going to need an ambulance." I'd already determined the guy was dead, but that's procedure and procedure would be the byword for the rest of the day.

I holstered my pistol and hung my badge on my belt so it was visible. Maria was finishing her bout of nausea so I went to her and knelt down.

"You OK, honey?" I said, knowing she wouldn't be OK for quite some time.

"*Jesús Cristus*, no, I'm not all right!" she cried, wiping her mouth on her sleeve.

I held her other arm. "Do you want to sit down?" I asked in as soft a voice as I could manage in my agitated state.

"No, just let me go." She shrugged out of my grip and started back up the hill, her jacket flapping open as she walked, revealing the .45 auto hanging on her hip. I followed her and looked at the startled Apple Valley cop and tried to mentally send him the message that it would be wise to just step aside. He was too young and too single to catch my body language. All he saw was an armed woman storming the hill with a little spittle still clinging to her chin. He challenged her.

"Hold it right there," he said, his hand on his holstered pistol.

I shook my head and yelled up the hill, "She's on the job; let her go."

Maria just ignored both of us and proceeded past the youngest member of a metropolitan police force I had ever seen. He had to be even younger than the kid out at Pete's. At this point the kid looked at Maria, his eyes as big as billiard balls. He let her pass.

I crested the hill. "Wise move right there, officer. I'm Dan Neumann, MPD," I said, again showing him my shield. "You did the right thing letting her pass. Saved me having to explain to your boss how you got shot by an Arizona sheriff's deputy."

Two other squads had arrived. Two more cops with quizzical looks on their faces appeared. I said, "Let's all go in the house and see how the victims are doing."

Chapter Thirty-six

As more local help rolled in I went back into the house to see about the families. The air seemed OK. I took a few breaths to convince myself, but something had happened to these people. We'd need toxicology to determine just what.

Maria had finished opening the windows and was in the kitchen downing a large glass of clear liquid. I walked in hoping it was water and not vodka. The way she was taking it down she'd either have to pee or she'd be dead in the next twenty minutes.

"It's water," she said with a gasp as she finished it off.

"Good thing or I would be feeling bad about not increasing my position in Skye Vodka stock," I replied.

We both went back to the family room and started assessing the family's health. All were conscious or semi-conscious by now and the medicos had oxygen masks on them. An ambulance had arrived to augment the fire department's EMTs who had shown up just after the backyard excitement. One had gone down the hill and confirmed the results of Maria's marksmanship, saying, "Nothing to do down there—two right in the chest, look like big ones. Nothing but net." The other EMTs were checking pulses, blood pressures, pupils and other vital signs. The oxygen was working and they were coming around. Jim, the biggest guy, and certainly the fittest person in the room, was recovering the fastest. I walked over to him.

"Hey, guy. You coming back to us?"

Jim looked at me through bleary eyes. "Dan, Uncle Dan?" he mumbled through the mask. He's always called me Uncle and I kind of liked it, not having any kids of my own.

"Yeah, it's me, Jim. Any idea what happened here?"

"I don't know, Uncle Dan. We'd just finished dinner and were sitting around watching the ball game."

"Come on, son. They're teaching you to be a U.S. Naval officer. You are trained to notice things, notice changes in a tactical situation. You must have noticed something else."

"My dad. I saw my dad get a funny look on his face. Then he tried to get up and just fell over the table."

"How long had you been sitting here?"

"Only a few minutes, I think. We came in the room, sat down and it happened. I had just sat down when it happened," he said, repeating himself.

I asked, "Did you notice anyone breathing funny, or that your fingernails were turning blue? Anything like that?

"No. Just that funny look on my Dad's face."

The EMT taking care of Jim's oxygen mask read my mind and said, "If you're thinking furnace problem, it's the right time of year. But if it's carbon monoxide poisoning, the victim's fingernails will turn bright pink, not blue. Blue is what happens with carbon dioxide poisoning."

I gave him a "really" sort of look. He nodded. You never stop learning in this job. I went back to Jim.

"Anything else you noticed? Come on, Jim, think."

"Yeah, there was sort of a sweet smell. I thought maybe Aunt Ruth was baking cookies but I looked over and she was sitting right there in that chair. I could see into the kitchen and the oven wasn't on."

"Then everyone just passed out?"

"Yeah, really fast, too."

"Too fast for carbon monoxide," I said to Maria.

"You're right," Maria said. "That takes longer and people usually become nauseous. Couldn't have been CO."

I looked at her and said, "Then what was it and why was the bad guy in the basement?"

She looked at me and said, "I've got a better question for you. Why didn't it get us?"

Chapter Thirty-seven

A little while later we had some answers but even more questions.

By piecing together what little evidence the recently deceased had with him and had left in the house, it appeared to be a very elaborate attempt to kill an entire extended family and have it look like an accident.

I had a chat with Apple Valley's chief of police, Stephanie Kirmeier. She had shown up in mufti with a little flour or something on one of her sleeves, looking like she had been pulled straight out of her kitchen. I told her about the connections to the other cases. With this many people involved and my information that Pete's grandmother had been murdered in her home a month ago, Stephanie immediately agreed to bring in an outside crime lab, in this case, the Dakota County CSI since Apple Valley is in Dakota County. I made a play to call the Hennepin County people, since they were the ones who had the first two crime scenes but the chief wouldn't go for that.

It would take a little while for the CSI team to arrive; after all, it was Thanksgiving Day. During the wait I slipped on some rubber gloves and had a look around.

In the basement I found another tool bag. It bore no resemblance to the one found at Pete's house. This one was well worn, like one would have just to hold odds and ends. It was old but careworn. A rubber mallet was lying on the floor by the bag.

The dead guy had been doing something to the furnace. I found the cover off and the wall switch had been turned off. One thing about wall switches beside furnaces in Minnesota. The way furnaces are installed here they put a switch nearby, usually on the closest wall, or a bare stud if the area is unfinished. It looks like an ordinary light switch but it's a master switch for the furnace. Its purpose is to provide a repairman with a quick and easy way to shut off the furnace as opposed to finding the circuit panel and throwing a breaker. The reason I know about it is that people sometimes accidentally shut it off mistaking it for a light switch, or just bump it off, then take off for a late fall vacation, thinking the furnace will kick on if the temperatures drop. Of course the temps do drop and the house gets cold and that's when the pipes freeze and explode. Pretty soon water is running everywhere and the cops get called. You learn an awful lot of useless crap when you've been a cop for thirty years.

So the switch was off, meaning the dead guy turned it off. What was he doing to the furnace? I found a gas mask on the floor around the corner from the furnace, just out of sight from where we'd been looking before.

It was very apparent that he'd used some kind of gas to knock everyone out.

Outside, I'd seen a hose connected to the back of the house. It went from the house over the precipice down into the gully where the guy had his little campground set up. The other end of the hose was connected to an unmarked tank, which looked like a small version of a typical propane tank you'd have for your backyard grill, but it had no identifying label. It did have some strange cryptic markings that made no sense to me.

The gas mask next to the furnace and the fact that the bad guy wasn't wearing it while he was still in the house made me believe that whatever was in the tank was fast-dispersing. Otherwise, he wouldn't have been working in the basement without wearing the gas mask. But I'm no expert on gases and I had no idea what the stuff was. My choices were to take a good huff on the hose and see what happened or wait for the lab work. I decided to wait.

Already outside I saw a few cops down by the guy's body. Across the creek bed I could see trampled grass and weeds. I went down the hill and crossed over to that area. The cops gave me a quick wave as I passed but seemed more interested in the dead guy than me.

This could be an overwatch point. I put myself in the killer's position and looked around. From this spot he would have had a reasonable view of the street and could observe traffic going past the house. He could also see right into the Hammer's great room and kitchen.

Hidden near the point where the body had fallen I found a makeshift campsite containing a duffel bag, which I quickly inventoried. There was the usual stuff I'd take on a stakeout—energy bars, water, a very nice camo blanket made of some kind of synthetic material, very expensive binoculars and another tank. This one was labeled—carbon monoxide. I whipped out my phone and took photos of the markings on both canisters.

I reassembled the duffel, left it for the CSIs, and hiked back up the hill. In the house I noticed that Ruth, Pete's sister, was missing. I asked about her and the EMTs said she had not been responding well so they put her in the first available ambulance and sent her off to Regions Hospital, the closest Level 1 Trauma Center. The EMTs had everyone else looking well enough to be transported to the hospital by the two ambulances that had just arrived. I caught the eye of the Apple Valley chief and signaled her over.

"Stephanie, I've got an idea what happened here."

She gave me a look that said, "Go ahead, Mr. Big Shot homicide investigator." We had never met but she'd said she knew who I was when I introduced myself earlier. She wasn't very excited that I just happened to be there.

"OK," she said, "give me your 'big city' view."

I knew that, like Edina, Apple Valley had about one murder per decade, so I made her the same offer I'd made Chief Houkkinen.

"First off, I'm working the Edina murder case for Dave Houkkinen and the Edina PD for one dollar. I'll give you the same rate on this: one dollar and full access to everything from the associated cases."

"Deal," she said immediately.

I led her out onto the deck overlooking the backyard. Maria, whose coloring was looking a bit better, came with us. She hadn't been with me on my treasure hunt down the hill, so this would all be new to her too.

"Here's what I see so far. The dead guy must have snuck in last night and set up his camp down in the gully. He also, probably last night, rigged the hose to the house. Then he sat down there, on the opposite bank. There's some matted grass that looks like it could have been a deer bed but I think it was our guy. From that spot he could see when Pete Anderson's family got here. And he could see right into the house so he'd know all his targets had arrived. "From here on it's hypothetical."

She said, "That's all right, I speak hypothetical."

My kind of chief.

I went on. "I think he did just that. Waited for Pete and his wife and son to arrive, then turned on the mystery gas in tank one. I don't know what it is; we'll have to wait for lab work. Then he entered the house and opened it up to air out the first gas. From here on it's really speculation, because he didn't get that far."

"Thanks to you two," Chief Kirmeier said, nodding to Maria and me.

I think he was doing something to the furnace to make it leak CO. Then, he would close the house back up and exit, switch the hose to the CO tank and open the valve. As you know, that would kill everyone within minutes."

"Why not just use the carbon monoxide to start with?" the chief asked.

"Because it's not fast enough," Maria said. "We have CO problems in Arizona too. People use space heaters on those rare cold days. Sometimes they use gas or kerosene burners or just crank up the gas stove. But the effects take time and, if people are awake they'll usually notice that they're starting to feel dizzy or sick to their stomachs, so they get out of the house."

I said, "He had to knock them out with something that either wouldn't leave a trace in their systems or would be covered up and ignored as soon as the coroner found the high CO levels in their blood."

"Yeah, he did his homework. He just didn't count on more people coming for dessert," Maria said.

Stephanie looked at Maria.

"You're the shooter, right?" she asked.

Maria replied, "Yes. I suppose you'll be wanting my firearm." It was a statement, not a question.

"I'm sure the lab people will want it eventually. Since you're the only one who returned fire," she said, looking at me somewhat derisively, "I think you can hold onto your weapon for now."

"Thanks."

Well, now that the ladies had made it clear who had saved whose butt, I figured we could go to the hospital and see after the family.

Chapter Thirty-eight

One of the docs at Regions is a friend of mine. I hoped she was on duty.

We trotted out to the driveway and I opened the trunk of the Mustang. Wrapped in an old shop rag and tucked tight into a corner of the trunk was a magnet-based rotating red flashing light, just like in the police shows back in the 1970s. I grabbed it, slammed the trunk shut and hopped in the car.

"Here," I said, handing the light to Maria. "Unwrap this, plug it into the cigarette lighter and stick it on the roof."

She pulled it out of the shop rag, looked at the antique, then at me, and rolled her eyes in disbelief. "This thing come with the car as original equipment?"

"No, I found it in the storage room down at the motor department's service garage. It works just like you think. Try to get it as far toward the center of the car as you can before you set it down." I threw the car in reverse and hit the gas.

She plugged it in and, just as advertised, the light came on and it started rotating.

Maria yelled "Stop!"

I'm a typical male who wants to know why we are doing things but I'm also an experienced cop who knows that when your partner yells "Stop!" there's a reason. I stopped.

Maria pushed the door open, hopped out and stood on the open door sill. I saw her lean over the roof and heard a subtle "clunk." She climbed back in.

"What did we stop for? You could have just reached out the window to do that."

"I didn't want to risk sliding it and scratching the paint."

I shook my head as I dropped the transmission into drive and gassed it toward St. Paul. Worried about the paint. What a woman.

The trip north required us to travel a section of Interstate 35E that is posted 45 m.p.h. While I did blow the low speed limit into dust, I took it easy on the turns in deference to Maria's recent gastronomical episode. No sense pushing my luck and having her vomit in my car. That would be a bad thing, both for the car and for our relationship. Our relationship had had all the stress it could handle for one day.

When we pulled into Regions we could see three ambulances parked away from the normal ambulance entrance. They were over to the east near the small parking lot reserved for doctors. I could see a guard standing by an oversized door. This wasn't the normal place to bring in emergency patients. I wondered what was up.

I pulled into the doc lot and put my police business card back on the dash. Hopefully the guard would give me a break, Mustang or not. I walked over to him and asked, "Is this where those three ambulances dropped off the patients?"

"Who are you?" He answered with a question of his own. Good guard.

Anyone could have a flasher on his car. I pulled out my creds and showed him. "Minneapolis Police, I'm on this case."

"Sorry, you'll have to go in over there," he said, pointing to the patient walk-in door. Accepting this inconvenience, we walked around the corner of the building to a set of automatic doors that led into Emergency Receiving.

I walked over to a booth next to the receiving desks where a St. Paul city cop was seated.

"Dan Neumann, MPD," I said as I held out my shield for his inspection.

"Afternoon, Inspector" the cop replied. "What can I do you for?"

"Those three ambulances out there," I said, pointing through the wall in the general direction of the ambulance entrance, "contained five victims of an attempted murder. I'm on the case and need to see them as quickly as you can get me back there."

That got his attention. "No problem," he said, jumping to his feet. "Need anything else like recorders or cameras?" he asked.

"Yeah, if Dr. Day is on, I'd like to see her."

The cop looked over at the tunic-aproned volunteer manning the nearest check-in desk. She had been eavesdropping and said, "Dr. Day is here. I'll page her."

While the volunteer called Dr. Day, I used the moment to take Maria's hand and give it squeeze. "I'll bet you don't have Thanksgivings like this in Phoenix!" I commented.

Chapter Thirty-nine

I've known Sarah Day for about twelve years. I had the pleasure of meeting her professionally when I was brought to Regions after a car chase that started in Minneapolis and ended in a crash in St. Paul. While the bad guy wound up with a nice smile in his forehead the exact arc of a General Motors steering wheel, I only had some sore ribs, thanks to my habitual seatbelt use. Since then, I've consulted with Sarah on two of my books on forensic ballistics. She has a wealth of knowledge on the effects of gunfire on the human body; she did her trauma residency in DC.

Sarah is an intelligent, thoughtful, attractive woman in her forties, tall, with a figure like a runway model. In fact, it is rumored she worked her way through med school modeling. If you saw her anywhere but the hospital you'd think she was an actress or some rich exec's trophy—just about anything but a trauma specialist.

"Hi Dan. You working in Apple Valley now?" Sarah asked as she walked over to us. The hospital volunteer must have told her why I was there.

"No, the vics are very good friends of mine and I happened to be the one who walked into this. I thought I would be watching football all afternoon."

Sarah looked at Maria. "Hi, I'm Sarah Day," she said, holding out her hand.

I jumped in, "I'm sorry, ladies. Sarah, this is Maria Fernandez of the Maricopa County Sheriff's Office. Maria, this is Sarah Day. She is one of the top trauma docs in the country."

Sarah shook Maria's hand. "You only say that to add gravitas to your books. Makes it sound like you have real experts advising you."

I looked at the two women. I'd never dated Sarah. Even though we were both available and seemingly interested, it had just never happened. We had struck up kind of a sibling relationship that worked well. Good friends, I'd say. Now looking at the two of them, I wondered if it was because she was so Minnesotan and somewhere deep in my genetic code I had a pre-programmed need to stir the gene pool.

Sarah and Maria were as opposite as they could be. Tall, lithe, blonde, blue-eyed, and fine-featured, Sarah would be lost in the crowd on the streets of, say, Stockholm. Maria was not short at five foot five, but had a different build, more solid, certainly not fat, very fit, dark hair, eyes and skin. But both had an intelligence in their eyes, in their manner, that could not be denied. They looked each other over and reached an immediate opinion that they liked one another.

"What brings the deputy to Minnesota?" Sarah asked.

"I'm here visiting Dan. We met last summer on a case and it was my turn to visit," she said, establishing the ground rules. Sarah took it in stride.

"Well, you lucked out on the weather. You never know what it will be this time of year. I always figure it's fifty–fifty whether or not we'll be skiing by Thanksgiving."

Sarah looked at me with raised eyebrows as if asking, "Is she the one?" I gave her a wink and got back to the case.

"My friends were brought here, should have gotten in a few minutes ago. They were knocked out with something in their home."

"Well, that explains the decon," Sarah said.

"Decon?" I asked.

"Yes, your friends were brought in through our decon facility. It's right next door." She turned and started walking, motioning us to come with her. Her long legs were walking so fast that I was very nearly running to keep up.

We passed through an area of treatment rooms that didn't look all that different from a regular doctor's office.

Maria asked, "Is this your emergency receiving area?"

"For less serious cases. The bad ones go into our trauma center. This is pod A. We have four, A through D, although currently D is just empty space. We'll grow into it soon, though. This is one of the busiest ERs in the Midwest."

"But they look like regular examining rooms?"

"That's because most cases don't require a full-blown treatment room with all the bells and whistles. Most cases, whether walk-in or ambulance, wind up in one of these pod rooms. Only the most urgent stay in the trauma rooms. We're getting there now."

We passed through a short hallway and the level of intensity increased by an exponential factor. Here, surrounding a central triangular admin desk was much larger, and from the look of all the electronics hanging from the walls, much better equipped, treatment areas. There were perhaps six of them. Three had their curtains pulled and activity could be heard within.

We walked through another hallway and reached an alternate receiving area. A sign announced that this was the "Decontamination" facility. We walked through the door.

There were two stainless-steel archways that looked not unlike the metal detectors you have to walk through at the airport. They formed narrow four-foot-long hallways equipped with showerheads. Along the side of the last one was a metal and plastic gurney where you could apparently get your shower lying down. The floor was wet, as was the metal gurney, indicating recent use. Both of the shower stalls had their curtains pulled. We could hear the water running. Two emergency room technicians were standing by.

"You said that they appeared to have been knocked out. When we receive a patient who has been exposed to an unknown material, in this case some kind of gas, we run them through here to decontaminate them," Sarah said by way of explanation.

The shower stopped and the medicos swept open the curtain revealing a thoroughly wet and naked Jim Anderson.

"Uncle Dan!" he said with a start, grabbing the shower curtain as he noticed Maria at my side. She was suddenly fascinated by one of the instructional placards on the far wall.

"How you feeling, Jim?" I asked, as the ERTs helped him dry off and handed him the standard open-backed gown.

"I'll take it from here," Sarah said to me. She told the attendants, "Take him over to Pod A where the rest of the family is. I'll be right behind you."

As they left the area, the second shower shut off, the curtain slid open and revealed a naked wet ambulance EMT. The remaining assistant handed him a towel.

Sarah looked at him and said, "What are you doing in there?"

The EMT sheepishly replied, "I got a little groggy on the ride in. Your people made me go through the decontamination routine. I suppose my uniform is in a bag somewhere."

The decon attendant said, "You got that right." He turned to Sarah and said, "The two men in the ambulance with him were also pretty groggy, including the guy that just left. This fellow," he said, indicating the EMT, "just about fell out of the back when I pulled the door open."

"Cross contamination?" Sarah asked.

"Looks like it to me. So I had him go on through the shower and we bagged his clothes."

"Who came in with the kid?" she asked, referring to Jim.

"His father, Mr. Peter Anderson," he said, consulting a chart.

"What about the two in the other ambulance—Mrs. Anderson and Mr. Hammer?" Sarah asked.

"No problems. We ran them both through the shower, robed them and sent them over to the pods. They were both coming around nicely and their EMT was normal."

Sarah looked at the formerly groggy, but now just embarrassed, EMT. "How were the patients before you brought them in?"

"They seemed fine. Both were pretty big strong guys and didn't even want to come in to the hospital. The others were more affected by whatever it was, so we sent them in first. Mrs. Hammer was still out of it so she came in on her own, lights and sirens."

Sarah went on, "So Mrs. Hammer was the most serious, and she went first, presumably on a stretcher. Mrs. Anderson and Mr. Hammer, who were affected, but not as severely, went next, presumably on stretchers. Last came the biggest and, apparently, least affected patients—Mr. Anderson and his son, Jim. They were doing pretty well, didn't see the need for the ambulance ride and came along reluctantly. That about cover it?"

The EMT said, "Yes, that would seem to sum it up nicely."

"And since they were already ambulatory, and reluctant passengers, you probably thought, 'What the heck, let them ride in seats instead of strapping them onto stretchers, right?'"

The EMT started to speak but suddenly stopped, rolled his eyes and said, "Oh . . . shit."

"It's OK, I can understand the mistake. Go get cleaned up and learn from this," Sarah told him.

He left and I asked Sarah, "Learn from what?"

She shook her head and said, "It was a simple error. The most serious patients had been transported first. The last two were looking fine. BP, pulse, respiration—all were normal, no outward signs of distress, so this guy let them ride sitting up, like any normal healthy person. Why humiliate them by strapping them onto a stretcher for a ten-minute car ride that they certainly thought they could make for themselves. They were probably a little ticked off that they were going to be looking at a transport charge and have no way of getting home."

"So what happened?" I asked, still confused.

"Very simple and something that we train for. Whatever knocked everyone out at the scene was introduced into the house as an aerosol. It's still there on all the surfaces and in the fabrics. It probably has dispersed to the point that it is ineffectual, but it was on the victims' clothing. The first two ambulances transported the patients properly; they were wrapped in sheets and strapped onto stretchers. But this last guy, who was just trying to be nice to Mr. Anderson and his son, let them sit in the back of the ambulance. Now they were in a confined space. The material outgassed from their clothing in a strong enough concentration to re-affect the patients and also affected the attendant. We're lucky he didn't let one of them sit up front with the driver. I hate to think what might have happened then," she said, looking down the hall at the retreating EMT.

She returned her gaze to me. "Now, tell me what you found at the scene when you arrived."

"When Maria and I got there, they were all out cold. We discovered someone in the basement. It looked like he was tinkering with the furnace."

"Was he conscious?"

"Very much so."

"Was he wearing a gas mask?"

"No, but there was a mask at the scene. He had pumped some kind of gas into the house."

"Any idea what it was?"

"No. But there were two different canisters. One was marked 'CO.' The other had markings I didn't recognize."

"Hmmm, could have been something that has a very short half-life. A little chat with him would be nice."

I looked at Maria, who started turning pale again. "I think maybe you'd better sit down, honey," I said, as I guided her over to a chair. Sarah took an arm, too, and looked at me, her eyes asking, "What's this?"

As Maria sat I looked at Sarah and answered the question in her eyes. "You won't be able to talk to him unless you're the Ghost Whisperer."

Sarah looked at Maria and in a soft voice said, "You got him, huh?"

Maria had just enough energy left to nod her head. Then she deposited the last of her Thanksgiving buffet dinner on Sarah's shoes.

Chapter Forty

Some of the ER staff saw our little episode and two came running over with some towels; another brought a glass of water. Maria went into an apologetic fit.

"Oh God, I'm sorry," she said as she wiped off her mouth.

"No problem. I buy special puke-resistant shoes. In fact they're resistant to just about anything we get in here."

This produced a giggling fit from Maria, who was now crying and laughing at the same time.

"That's good, honey," Sarah said. "Just let it out. Dan's got plenty of money from the books I write for him. He can buy you another meal."

This resulted in what I knew had to be the last of Maria's breakfast appearing. I didn't know someone could toss their cookies while laughing. I guess "laughed so hard I puked" is for real.

One of the staff brought over a small empty bucket. Maria swished some of the water around her mouth and spit it into the proffered pail. She did this three times, then drank a swallow. Her color was returning and she looked less frazzled.

"Let's go find a conference room where you two will be out of the way while I check on everyone."

We made our way back to Pod A.

Maria and I had about five minutes to recover from her laughing-puking fit before Sarah entered the room with another doctor.

"Dan, Maria, this is Mike Taylor. He drew the first cases that came in."

Dr. Taylor shook hands all around. He was a good looking young black man, maybe mid-thirties, with dark hair, dark eyes, and broad shoulders that indicated some time on a weight bench. He was wearing maroon scrubs and had a stethoscope around his neck in the usual manner.

"I understand you are friends of the family?" he asked.

"They're practically family," I replied. "I'm also an investigator with the Minneapolis Police Department and I'm consulting with the Apple Valley Police Department on this case. Investigator Fernandez is too."

The new guy was obviously weighing things in his head, things like could he talk to us about the case even though we aren't really relatives versus this is the police department and how much am I going to have to watch what I say in case things go badly for that woman in Treatment Room 3? Unfortunately, doctors have to practice defensive medicine 24/7.

"Do you know if Mrs. Hammer was on any kind of medication?" he asked.

"I'm not sure, but I know that she was in excellent health. They all are in excellent health."

"Did you happen to notice what she ate today? Any muffins or cookies?"

"I didn't get a good look at the menu." This guy was starting to bug me—cookies?

Maria answered, "I was in the kitchen and all I saw were regular bread dinner rolls. No lemon poppy seed or anything like that." Maria had apparently figured out where this was going, even though I was still looking for a roadmap.

"Thank you," Taylor said to Maria. He looked at Sarah and said, "The EMTs report that all victims had constricted pupils upon their arrival on scene. Mrs. Hammer was unconscious and she was having difficulty breathing. The EMTs intubated her, started an IV and transported her stat. On the way in, they put a pulse oxymeter on her and got a high normal reading. Of course, that's what they'd get if it was carbon monoxide poisoning. But there were no other CO poisoning indicators—no pink fingernails or very pink gums, stuff like that," he said to us. "The report also states that the responding Apple Valley Fire Department personnel did a CO check and found none present."

"The EMTs also ran a quick blood sugar and it was normal. When she arrived here she was run through decon and brought into Room 3. When I first saw her she was normal for blood sugar, blood oxygen, pressure and pulse. She was coming around, but had constricted pupils and was in an altered mental state. So I gave her one milligram of Narcan."

"OK. I was fine up to the altered mental state and the Narcan." I looked at Sarah. "In English, please."

Sarah explained, "An altered mental state is a term we use for someone whose vital signs all appear normal but they are still woozy, look a little drunk or, perhaps, stoned. Mrs. Hammer was like that when she got here. The normal thing to do is to try a drug called Narcan. It's used to counteract opioids. These include the obvious things like heroin but also include prescription pain relievers like OxyContin." She looked at Taylor and asked, "How did she react?"

"It did the trick. She popped right out of it. Whatever was affecting her is an opioid. So we did a quick U-tox." He stopped, looked at me, then said, "That's a urine toxicology screening, and it came up blank— no opioids."

I shook my head. "I've known Ruth for twenty-five years. She has an abnormal aversion to medication in general and especially to any illicit drugs. She had a roommate in college who died from an OD. She doesn't take aspirin, let alone anything narcotic."

"That's good information to have," said Taylor, "but it leaves us with a mystery. A prescription narcotic like OxyContin would have hit on the U-Tox. It means that whatever is affecting these people no-shows on the U-Tox."

Maria asked, "You mean that the gas that was pumped into the house was an opium derivative?"

"Gas was pumped into the house?" Taylor asked, confused. He hadn't heard the entire morning's events.

"Yes," Sarah replied. "Detective Neumann and his partner found a gas canister connected to a hose that was running into the house. The gas canister was unlabeled."

"I took a picture of some markings on the canister if that would help."

Taylor and Sarah both nodded, so I pulled out my phone and, after a few seconds figuring out how to retrieve the photos, showed them the markings.

"Beats me," Taylor said after viewing the markings.

"Me too, but I think I know who to call," Sarah said.

"Who?" asked Taylor.

"James Likevich."

Chapter Forty-one

James Likevich turned out to be a tall stocky man with an olive Eastern European look. He looked to be in his mid to late forties, wore his hair cropped close to his skull and, even in the baggy labcoat, appeared extraordinarily fit. This guy could have been Arnold in his good days.

Sarah made the introductions. "James, this is Maria Fernandez of the Maricopa County Sheriff's Office and Dan Neumann of the MPD. Maria and Dan, Dr. James Likevich, our head of toxicology"

Dr. Likevich shook Maria's hand delicately and said "Enchanté." He took my hand in a vise-like squeeze and said, "Neumann, I understand you're a friend of Wolf Hutchens."

I did my best to maintain my composure as my hand was converted into oatmeal. This guy could crush golf balls if he wanted to. The rapid numbing of my hand wasn't enough to distract me from the reference to a man I'd met once and was mightily impressed with.

"If Dr. Hutchens referred to me as his friend, I am highly honored. I've only met him one time, but it was an eye-opening experience."

"Wolf told me all about it. He was very impressed with you."

"Then it is my great privilege and honor to call Wolf my friend. I'd really like to get together with him again, sometime, to go over the outcome of the case we discussed."

Maria knew about my meeting with Dr. Fred "Wolf" Hutchens. He was a friend of Pete's whom Pete had called in to give me some insight into the personalities of warriors. Wolf, now a psychiatrist specializing in post-traumatic stress disorder, was a former Special Forces team member. He had quite a history of combat experiences in Viet Nam and elsewhere. To be called his friend filled me with pride. This guy was one great American hero.

Sarah, however, did not know of my brief association with Wolf.

"You know Dr. Hutchens?" she asked.

"Just met him that one time last summer, working on the same case that took me to Phoenix where I met Maria. It was an interesting case that has had some lasting effects on me," I said, looking at Maria.

"He's something of a legend around here," Sarah said. "The work he does with returning troops is miraculous."

Dr. Likevich chimed in, "Well, enough of the Wolf Hutchens mutual admiration society meeting. He'll be intolerable if he hears we spent all this time beatifying him. What can I help you with?"

While Dr. Likevich was being tracked down, Maria had figured out how to email the photos on my phone to Sarah's hospital email address. Sarah had printed them off. She handed the photos of the unidentified gas canisters to Dr. Likevich as she presented the case.

"A family of five, all adults, had just finished Thanksgiving dinner and sat down to watch football when they were, apparently, gassed with material from this container. The would-be assassin then entered the house, opened doors and windows in an apparent attempt to ventilate the house, then went down into the basement to do something to the furnace. He was down there when Dan and Maria showed up. They found the family unconscious, called 9-1-1 and searched the house. The bad guy made it out a basement window but, unfortunately, died in the ensuing gunfight. Dan found another canister in his effects. Here's that one," she said handing over the picture.

"One of the victims, who presented unconscious, was then in an altered mental state when she began to come around. She reacted posi-tively to one milligram of Narcan. We did a U-Tox and came up blank for opioids. The others are being tested now. All other parameters show normal—BP, pulse, blood sugar, etc. The other victims all came around without assistance."

Dr. Likevich looked carefully at the photo of the unknown material. As he did, a scowl darkened his face. "I know what this is; it's very, very bad news. It's HaloRemi 35."

Chapter Forty-two

"This material was developed for the U.S. military as a crowd control and situation inhibitor," Dr. Likevich said as he looked around the room at each of us. He was clearly upset and very serious. "As I'm sure you can understand, the need for less than lethal weaponry is something that we have been working on for many years. Many events occur that would benefit from the availability of a less than lethal option. Things like CS gas—tear gas—were developed for these situations. But those materials cause strong reactions in people exposed to them. They inhibit behavior but do not render those exposed unable to react. The availability of a viable knockout gas is something both the military and the police forces have long sought.

"You probably remember some years ago in Russia when some Chechnya nationalists took about 800 people hostage in a Moscow theater. After a few days of negotiating the Russian military used a gas on those people to end the standoff. We believe we know what they used; something they had worked on for years.

"There are two types of gas used in this field. One is an inhalational general anesthetic, the other a narcotic. The inhalational general anesthetics are only effective when they are present. That is, as long as the material is still being breathed, it keeps the person knocked out. Its advantages are that it is instantaneous, meaning one good lung full and you're sleeping. And you don't really have to worry about dosage. But, if you shut off the gas, its effect wears off in seconds. So, to keep the intended sleepers down, you have to use something else with it.

"We believe the Russians used a blend of two gases. The first was a knockout gas. We believe it was Halothane, which is widely available and is used in anesthesia. We believe that they backed this up with an opioid called Carfentanil. Carfentanil is intended for use only on large animals because its extreme potency makes it inappropriate for use in humans. This didn't stop the Russians, though. The problem was dosage. Those who happened to be sitting closest to the air vents when the material was introduced wound up dead, about 180 of the total. It would be just like OD-ing on heroin. You would just go to sleep and never wake up. Obviously, this would be a problem for us here in the U.S. I guess the Russians felt it was worth the risk," he added with less than subtle cynicism.

"So, we chose another route, using Remifentanil, a commercially available product called Ultiva. This material is blended with Halothane and two or three other materials to aid in the aerosolization process to make HaloRemi 35. It is a fast-acting knockout gas that produces about a twenty to twenty-five minute period of unconsciousness after it is removed from the atmosphere. The idea is to give unprotected personnel the opportunity to enter the area and subdue the individuals who've been incapacitated. One of the characteristics of fentanils in general, and Remifentanil in particular, is that it shows blank on the standard U-Tox screen. A specific screen is required for this material."

I was amazed. This stuff could revolutionize law enforcement. Just think, something you could pump into a house or building that would simply knock out everyone without having to worry about them dying or choking on their own puke. It would save a lot of lives—good guys and bad guys.

"How can we get some of this stuff for police departments?" I asked.

"That's kind of a problem right now. It's experimental. The U.S. military is supposed to be the only place with access. I heard that some of the stuff got "lost" in Bosnia about two years ago, but that was just a rumor."

Sarah interrupted. "Harris is an active reserve officer in the Army. That's how he knows this stuff and why I wanted him to look at your canister. He's also the best toxicologist in the state. It's a nice combination."

"That would explain how he knows Wolf," I thought.

"Thanks, Sarah," Dr. Likevich said as his bona fides were established. "You're always too kind."

"So we have a bad guy using a classified and unavailable gas that he could only have gotten from the Army? Is that what I'm hearing?" I asked.

"That would seem to be the case, unless he has friends in Bosnia and got the bottle from them. I will make a few phone calls. The markings on the canister are lot-specific. If this one came from the missing lot, we'll know," he answered.

"Great," I thought. "Now we've got a killer who has access to international terrorist connections trying to knock off Pete's family." I knew one thing for sure. I'd never forget how I spent this Thanksgiving.

Dr. Likevich went off to do his research and call some friends whose wardrobe is primarily in shades of green and tan. I wanted to take a walk around and try to think. Maria got up with me and we excused ourselves, ostensibly for a bathroom break.

"Tell me what you're thinking," Maria said.

"I've got to talk to Pete about this. I'm thinking that none of this makes any sense. First Grams gets killed by a would-be burglar who takes nothing from the house, then Pete's dog runs off another—probably the same guy—burglar. I'd call that guy a semi-pro. He was good, had a good plan and equipment, but I don't think he was experienced."

"Why not?" Maria asked.

"Because a real pro would most likely not have made the mistake of going in while Grams was home. And he would have taken some things of value to cover his real intentions. Plus, he would have known about Pete's dog and taken precautions.

"Now this. This had to be a pro. Gotta be a different guy. What the hell is going on here?"

We walked out of Emergency to a wide staircase winding upward. At the top was a small café called The Overlook. We headed for it.

"Buy you a cup of something?" I asked.

"Sure, but what I need right now I doubt they have. I'll settle for a nice double espresso and a cruller."

"Sounds good, I'll get two."

Maria sat at one of the tables. The choices were wide-open, not much traffic on Thanksgiving Day. I ordered, waited, and paid for our high-octane coffee and sugar-laced rolls.

"Any thoughts?" I asked, setting the tray on the table.

"Start at the beginning. Someone breaks into Grams' house, takes nothing, but kills her in the process. Next, the same person, we think semi-pro, breaks into Pete's house and Pete's dog runs him off. Two break-ins, nothing taken, and you can't find anything anyone would want in what's left, other than the obvious stuff—jewelry, artwork and other things that the first guy had plenty of time to take, but left behind.

"Today, the target is the whole family. Not something in the house, but the people. The bad guy here had to be someone different than the first two incidents. This guy was a super-pro, you said. This guy had too much equipment and too good a plan to be some bumbling burglar. The game has changed and we have to figure out why."

I nodded my agreement. The game had been ratcheted up several notches. It was no longer a property issue, it was people—taking out people. I tried hard to think. What had changed?

Maria and I sipped the espresso and I could feel the caffeine kicking in. My head started to race. "It" was right in front of me. But what was "it"? What was the difference between this attack and the others?

I started to think out loud. "The break-ins had nothing in common. One had been at night, one during the day. This was during the day. One was at Grams house, one at Pete's. This was at Ruth's. In the first break-in it looked like the intruder was rifling the office; the second one didn't get that far. I almost wish the dog hadn't been home that day and the guy could have gotten whatever it was he was looking for. Maybe that would have been the end of it."

Maria was lost in thought too. She said, "There is a difference. The first two crimes were committed by a semi-pro, as you called him—but not this guy. Today's was a professional assassin. He wasn't interested in anything in the house, just the people. And he had it set up to look like an accident. That's why the carbon monoxide was there. He was trying to kill an entire family in one place at one time and make it look like an accident. They were the targets, not some piece of property. That could mean that whoever is behind this has given up on getting whatever it is he was looking for. Now, he's just trying to kill everyone. What's the connection there? Why would someone switch from trying to steal something to trying to commit mass murder?"

The buzzing in my head said that I'd already seen the answer. "It" was right in front of me. What had I seen? What had I seen that was worth murdering five people?

Chapter Forty-three

The family was coming around nicely when Maria and I returned from our coffee break. Pete and Jim were standing by Ruth's bed in the treatment room; Carol and Steve were seated. I looked at this family, my family, and asked myself again, "What is the common straw? What was there about all these strange events that wound its way to this trauma center?" Things were going to get weird now, as I expected three or four very expensive suits to walk in at any moment.

Though Maria and Ruth had never been formally introduced, they knew each other by reputation. I watched as Maria went to Ruth, leaned over the bed, took her hand and said something to her. I saw Ruth smile and laugh and decided I'd ask Maria what the joke was later. Steve must have overheard it as he added a smile to the conversation.

Sarah came in. "Everyone is doing much better, I'm glad to say." She looked at the victims and said, "However, you will all be staying the night for observation." A few hands went up and grumbles were heard but she simply held up a "stop" sign and said, "No discussion. You've been unconscious and that's never normal. You'll stay overnight and, most likely, you'll be out of here in time for all the sales tomorrow."

I knew Pete's biggest concern would be Sinbad, so I went to him with my hand out. "Give me your house keys. I'll take care of that walking security system you call a dog."

He chuckled, then grabbed a pad and pen and jotted something down. Handing me the note and keys he said, "Here's the alarm combo."

I stepped to the door and used a crooked finger to ask Sarah to join me. We stepped outside the room and out of earshot.

"I don't know what to say, but thanks."

"You're welcome, Dan. Next time, let yourself be knocked out and you can stay over too. Who knows, maybe I'll be on call." With a little wink, she turned and powerwalked away.

I returned to the group and everyone stopped talking. I guess they were waiting for my brilliant analysis of the situation. Unfortunately, I had none.

"I can tell you this. Whoever is doing this has raised the stakes. They are now going after you instead of some thing. Whatever the guy was looking for in Grams' office doesn't matter anymore. Now they are relying on your deaths to get them what they want. The problem I'm having is figuring out what kind of profit or gain they could find by killing all of you. This would be the same profit or gain they thought they could gain by getting whatever they were looking for from Grams' house or your house, Pete. Now, it's not property, it's killing you that will advance their position. I just don't know what that goal is. What kind of goal or gain can someone get by another person's demise?"

I turned to Pete. He could hold the key to this. I told him, "You have to find whatever it is that they're after. They thought it was at Grams' and then at your house. At that point, their goal could have been reached by stealing something. But they gave up on that and decided they could also reach their goal by killing your entire family. What is the goal?"

The group now had something to chew on. These were very intelligent people and I was confident that they would work that problem until they found an answer. In the meantime, I was determined to prepare for the arrival of the suits. With the attempted murder of an entire family by what appeared to me to be a professional killer, one that involved some kind of secret military gas that may have been stolen in Bosnia, of all places, the events were sure to attract the attention of my old nemesis. Call them what you will, they had a nose for anything that could turn into a big-time case and, therefore, big-time publicity. They were the original Men in Black, the FBI.

Chapter Forty-four

Maria and I left the hospital and headed back toward Apple Valley. Along the way I made a phone call. In police work, like in life and football, a good offense is often the best defense.

"Will Sanford," the voice answered. He was formal even on a holiday.

"Will, Dan Neumann."

"Dan! How is my favorite local lawman this fine Turkey Day?"

"Great, Will, just great. Listen, I've caught a case that I think will be landing in your office. I'd appreciate it if it was assigned to you."

"So you can keep your fingers in it?"

"You have always impressed me with your quick take on situations."

Will Sanford was one of the Men in Black. He'd been with the FBI for about fourteen years; at least I'd known him that long. We had collaborated on cases in the past and Will had been, for my money, the best feebie I'd ever worked with. Most feds worry too much about how the outcome of the case will reflect on the Bureau in general and on themselves in particular. This parochial focus tends to cloud how they think and how they act. Will is more pragmatic. Cut from the same cloth as his father, a career cop in Philadelphia, Will has a higher regard for getting the bad guys, even if someone else gets the credit. I wanted him on this case and an early notice would give him a head start when the Bureau's internecine rivalries started kicking in.

"So what is this hot ticket that you're sure I'll want to grab hold of and ruin what has been an otherwise lovely holiday afternoon?"

"Let me ask you this. Would your team be interested in a crime that consisted of an attempt to murder five members of a local family?"

"Not normally. Why do I suspect there's more to this than attempted murder?"

Like I said, he's quick. "How about if the attempt involved use of a gas that is supposedly an experimental military weapon and the killer was a pro?"

"You have my attention," was Will's simple reply. I gave him the address in Apple Valley and told him I'd be there in ten minutes.

"I've got to get away from the party. I'm at a neighbor's. They'll understand. See you in about a half hour."

Will would be coming from near his home in Woodbury, a nice suburb on the east side of the metro area. His friends were used to his sudden departures and I figured that it would take him less than the forecasted thirty minutes.

"And why are we bringing in the competition?" Maria asked. She had listened to the phone conversation with obvious interest. Local police don't normally like the appearance of the feds and certainly don't invite it.

"We know they'll be on this after today. The Apple Valley chief will have to inform them. Even if she doesn't, the Dakota County crime lab is going to have to call the state Bureau of Criminal Apprehension on those gas canisters. When that happens, the first thing the BCA is going to do is call the feds to help identify them. If it goes that way, we have no say in who the feds assign. This way, we give Will a head start. He's a good guy and won't do the usual fed thing by trying to pull the entire case away from us."

Maria was pensive. She knew what I meant about the feds pulling the case. They did it all the time, usually after the locals had a lot of sweat and effort invested. She also knew that she didn't want to be a bystander. She was more than involved; she was committed to this case. She knew that simply pulling the trigger would normally get her removed as an investigating officer if she'd been a local. But she was not local, she was an out-of-town peace officer here on vacation. Her involvement was no different than if she'd been a civilian with a carry permit. She was now completely shut out from this investigation unless she could find a way to keep her fingers in it. Obviously, I would keep her in it, and having

Will on the fed side would keep me in it. She was willing to go along with the counterintuitive idea of inviting the feds to the table.

We walked up the Hammer's driveway for the second time that day. It was late afternoon and the sun was disappearing. I had to park on the street down the block because the place had been circled with yellow crime scene tape and there were still several vehicles in the driveway. Along with three Apple Valley squads, one of which was Chief Kirmeier's, there were two trucks from the Dakota County crime lab, one light truck from the Apple Valley Fire Department and a minivan labeled "Dakota County Coroner." At least there were no TV vans yet. We walked around the collection of vehicles, flashed our creds at the Apple Valley uniform guarding the door and reentered the house. I saw Stephanie Kirmeier talking to one of the crime scene techs. When she saw me, she broke off and came over.

"Any news on the victims?" she asked.

"All have recovered and the outlook is that they'll be fine. The hospital did an amazing job of figuring out what was wrong with them and how to counteract it. They will be staying overnight but should be out tomorrow morning."

"We're very lucky to have a facility like Regions so close. A lot of lives have been saved by those people," Stephanie said, obviously relieved at the news.

I nodded. "Chief, the top toxicology guy at the hospital has tentatively identified the gas canister. I thought you and the lab would be interested."

"We sure are." She called over to a man in a white HAZMAT suit. "Freddie, you should come over and hear this."

The guy came over and introductions were made.

"Freddie, Dan went to the hospital with the victims. He has a report."

"What have you got?" he asked.

Before I could start there was a small commotion at the front door. Will had arrived and the cop on door watch was conflicted over letting in a guy whose credentials identified him as an FBI Special Agent and getting his butt chewed by his chief for allowing a fed into the building. I bailed him out by waving at Will, saying, "He's OK, I called him."

The chief waved to her officer and gave me a look that said that I had some explaining to do. Will came over and I made introductions.

"I was just going to give a rundown on what happened at the hospital."

"By all means," Will graciously replied.

"The hospital toxicologist is also a serving officer in the Reserve. He identified the markings on the gas canister that apparently knocked out everyone as something called HaloRemi 35, an experimental military crowd-control gas. He also said that it's unavailable to the public, but that there was a rumor that some of the stuff that was being tested in Bosnia had gone missing."

Will took this information stoically. I couldn't tell if he knew what the stuff was or was hearing all this for the first time like the rest of us. Remind me not to play poker with this guy.

"The material is a combination of a regular anesthetic called Halothane and an opium derivative called Remifentanil," I said, consulting my notes. No way I was just remembering all this stuff.

"He said that the Halothane knocks them out and the Remifentanil keeps them down for about twenty-five minutes. After that, it would be metabolized and the victims would wake up."

"Unless the bad guy had already started pumping carbon monoxide into the house," Maria said.

"Carbon monoxide?" Will asked.

I brought Will up to speed with the Readers Digest version of the day's events. He stood there, nodded at a few things, and absorbed it like the pro he is. Nothing registered on his face. He would make a great Bridge partner.

Freddie, the crime scene guy, was interested in the furnace and the gas. "If this guy pumped gas into the house, gas that has an opioid component, we should be able to get trace remains of the opioid off just about everything in here—the furniture, the walls, the carpeting, everything. We're going to need a furnace guy, though. If the bad guy was trying to make the furnace produce CO, I don't know how he'd do that."

Chief Kirmeier said, "My furnace guy lives pretty close to here. I'll see if he can come over."

Will, who had said little up to this point, said, "I'd like to see the dead guy, if he's still here."

The Chief said, "He's in the garage. The techs moved him there after the coroner got here and took a look at him in situ. He took a look, decided he was dead, and wanted to take him but I decided to keep him here on-site until we wrapped things up. It's not like he needed to be anyplace quick."

I nodded, knowing that in a suburban homicide investigation the chief would have the last say on that.

Will and I went through the house to the garage entry door. Maria stayed with Stephanie. I guess she'd seen enough of the dead guy already.

The body, covered by a white sheet, was on a gurney ready to be rolled into the back of the coroner's minivan. The coroner was watching the football game on Steve's garage TV. It looked like the Lions might win one game this year.

We ID'd ourselves to the coroner, a labcoated, balding, middle-aged man named Jesse Carlisle, by his tag. He walked with us over to the gurney and pulled the sheet back so we could get a look. The man was average in the extreme. No marks or scars, on his face anyway, and kind of a peacefully surprised expression. Will produced a digital camera and took a picture of the man's face.

After looking at the picture to approve its quality, Will pulled a gizmo from his jacket pocket, an electronic device about the size of a short paperback book. It was black with a white glass panel on one side and a rat-tail cable hanging off the end. He turned it on, read a message window, then reached for the killer's right hand. Spreading the assassin's fingers, he carefully applied all four fingertips to the window. After a beep signified the device's satisfaction, he repeated the process with the right thumb. Focusing on the device, he punched more buttons then plugged the cable into his camera. After a few more keystrokes, he unplugged the camera and plugged the device into his cell phone. A little more tinkering on the phone and he was happy, saying, "His picture and prints will go to our ID section in Washington. We'll find out if anyone is working today."

Once again, I was amazed at what billions of taxpayer dollars could accomplish. It wasn't that big a deal, though. Most patrol cops have a similar system in their squads. It was just that this one was pocket sized. What a country.

Carlisle had pulled the sheet down far enough that we could see the entry wounds where Maria's 230-grain hollow points had hit the man. Both were high center chest, one mid-sternum, the other slightly out-board—right where you could cover them both with your hand while singing the national anthem. I knew his heart was hamburger before he dropped. No heart surgeon on this planet could have helped this guy.

"I'm guessing cause of death will be gunshot wounds," the coroner said. "Just a guess, though. Won't be sure until the lab work is done." I suppose being a coroner on Thanksgiving would give you a bit of an edge. Will shook his head at the cynicism and we went back into the house.

Will went around the house taking pictures with a digital camera. He then went outside and got shots of the dead guy's campsite and his equipment, including the gas canisters. When he came back up he found me watching him from the deck overlooking the hill.

"I've got what I need for now. I'll have to stop by the hospital to talk to your friends. I'd appreciate it if you could give them a call to let them know I'm coming and that I'm a good guy."

"No problem. You'll keep this tight for now?"

"I'll do what I can. It will depend on several things. The gas thing, obviously, will get someone's attention. And I don't know if that will mean keeping it even quieter or blowing the thing open. A hit on the hit man may blow it open. Just depends."

"Thanks, Will. I knew you were the guy to call."

"I'll wait with my thanks to you. This could be great or this could be radioactive. I won't know until the SAC calls me into his office to tell me about the wonderful opportunity I've been given to advance my law enforcement career in, say, the Aleutians. They have a real problem with seal poaching up there."

I said goodbye to Will and found Maria in the kitchen eating some leftovers. At least her appetite had returned.

"How you doing, baby?"

"Pretty good," she said between bites. "Sorry about before. I really didn't expect to react like that."

"Everybody does," I said. That wasn't true, though. I had been involved in two shootings as a cop. The first one was a reaction thing where two guys came out of a store and one of them was shooting. I reacted like Maria did and wound up killing the shooter. The other one was different. I dropped a drug dealer/murderer one hot spring afternoon and didn't miss a meal or any sleep on that one. Different situation, different reaction.

I got Maria a glass of water to wash down the turkey and dinner roll sandwich she had eaten. She was looking better. The adrenaline had worn off and her color was back to its normal beautiful self. I sat and just looked at her. The idea that she had very possibly saved my life by risking her own was just settling in with me. I'd had many partners over the years and we'd covered each other the way partners are supposed to. Today, she was my partner. Of course, I'd never slept with my previous partners, even the women. That made this quite of bit more intimate. As close as I'd gotten to my partners in the past, no one had ever made me feel like this. What did this feel like? I'm going to have to figure that out.

I heard a conversation at the front door. The furnace guy had arrived.

Chapter Forty-five

Chief Kirmeier was talking with a man wearing what I call Minnesota casual, blue jeans, plaid cotton shirt and waist-length leather jacket. A helmet was dangling from his hand. He was about five nine, 165, and rugged with dark hair tousled from the helmet, and a stubbly three-day beard that may have looked that way on purpose, in a Hollywood sort of way. A backpack hung from one strap over his shoulder.

I walked over. The chief turned my way, saying, "Dan, this is Rick Bryant. He's a heating and AC contractor who has worked with us before."

"Good to meet you, Rick" I said.

Rick took my hand in a solid grip and said, "Good to meet you too, Inspector."

Maria came out from the kitchen where she had been finishing her replacement Thanksgiving Dinner. The chief introduced her as well.

I asked the chief. "Worked with you before?"

"Yes. We've had Rick involved on a couple of house fires that looked like they started in the furnace and one carbon monoxide case. He knows his stuff well enough that I trust him with my own furnace work."

Rick was blushing. Nice to see that could happen in a full-grown man these days. So few of us are in touch with our sensitive side.

"So what is it this time, Stephanie?" Rick asked, using the chief's first name.

Chief Kirmeier went over our assumed version of the day's events, stopping just before the point where Maria and I arrived. She told him about the tools in the basement and the first gas canister outside. When she finished, he asked what she wanted him to do.

"We want you to take a look at the furnace and tell us what he was trying to do to it before he was interrupted."

"Okay. Let's go downstairs."

Stephanie led the way as we all trundled down the steps. I was reminded that just a few hours ago I was standing at the top of these same stairs with my pistol in my hand, formulating a plan to flush a bad guy out of this basement. That plan had gone to shit when Maria threw herself down the stairs and flushed him out the window. Funny how days turn out sometimes.

The basement was typical of a Minnesota house. Unfinished, it showed its structure in the bare pine two by four studs that presented a preview of future rooms. The exterior walls were covered in plastic vapor barrier over pink blankets of fiberglass insulation interrupted by the edges of more studs. Here and there light switches and electric receptacles poked through the plastic, which was seamed with bright red tape. A workbench along one wall of the future amusement room was joined by racks of storage shelves aligned in two rows on the bare concrete floor. Stacks of boxes littered the rest of the area except near the mechanical features. The furnace, water heater and water softener were together in an area that was tucked out of the way near the stairs.

Bryant walked over to the furnace and took a quick look at the tools the assassin left on the floor. There was a small screwdriver set, two adjustable wrenches, a rubber mallet, a small battery-powered combination drilling-sawing tool called a Dremel, and the gas mask. He looked at the furnace and pulled off the access cover, revealing the guts of the machine. He flipped the switch on the wall and the furnace lit up.

Bryant dropped his backpack on the floor and fished out an electronic meter of some sort. While the furnace came up to speed, he turned on the device and unwound a cord with a foot-long metal probe on the end. There was a shiny silver tape patch on one of the white pipes coming out of the furnace, which he removed, revealing a hole from some previous work. He inserted the probe into the hole, looked at the meter and waited.

After about a minute he shook his head and said, "Looks like he'd already done something. This furnace is running terribly. The combustion is all wrong and it's producing very high levels of carbon monoxide. Strange, though. It's pretty new and everything in here looks just as it should."

He pulled the probe out of the hole and scratched his beard with it. You could see the analysis going on in his head as he worked the problem. "I've got an idea," he said.

Bryant set the meter on the floor, switched the furnace off and, after looking at the direction the pipes went, headed up the stairs. We followed.

We went out the back patio door onto the deck, down the stairs and around to the east side of the house where the pipes exited the siding. Bryant dropped down on his knees and peered up into the intake pipe.

"Yep. Figured it out," he said, standing up.

Chief Kirmeier said for all of us, "Tell us in language we can understand."

"Well, this furnace is a very good brand that is pretty much foolproof, reliable and economical. I don't do much work on them because they just don't need it. Downstairs, I was trying to figure our why it could be running so bad. It's early in the heating season; maybe the furnace hasn't even run much before today. What can happen over the summer that could screw up the combustion so badly?"

Well, I didn't know and I was certain Maria didn't know. Maybe the chief could answer this question, but I doubted it. Bryant helped us out.

"Sometimes, over the summer, we'll get wasp nests. It looks like a colony of wasps built their nest in this intake pipe. That would choke off the supply of combustion air enough to produce high levels of carbon monoxide in the exhaust, without completely stopping it up. If you do that, the furnace senses it and shuts down."

Chief Kirmeier got down on her knees and looked up into the pipe. "Yeah, there's a nest in there."

Maria and I took our turns and confirmed it.

"Pretty convenient that the wasps did something that would produce CO in a house where someone wanted a family to die," I said.

"Too convenient," said the chief. She called over one of the county CSI techs and told them to document and recover the nest, that it was considered evidence in the case.

"Chief, if you'd like, I could cut that pipe off so your people could take it to their lab and look at it. And, I could repair it right now so the house wouldn't be without heat."

Kirmeier thought it over and asked the CSI tech, "What do you think?"

The tech agreed. "It would be a lot easier to analyze in the office than it is here. And chain of custody would be maintained as long as I'm here during the removal."

Chief Kirmeier nodded her consent and Bryant said to the tech, "After I'm done looking at the furnace, I'll run home and get what I need from my truck and meet you back here."

Chief Kirmeier said to all of us, "All right, the guy screwed up the furnace. What was he doing downstairs?"

We all made our way back downstairs and Bryant looked carefully at the furnace, talking as he examined it.

"Just making the burner work inefficiently enough to produce CO isn't enough with this kind of furnace. You have to have a way to get it into the house. This is a sealed combustion unit that draws air from the outside to the burners, then exhausts the combustion air back outside. So, unless the heat exchanger is cracked, he would have to make a way for the exhaust to get into the house, and this furnace is much too new for that to happen."

Bryant looked again at the exhaust pipe, then pointed to the rubber mallet. He asked, "Can I pick this up?"

One of the CSIs was there and said, "Why?"

"I think the marks on this pipe were made by this mallet."

The CSI gingerly picked up the mallet with two gloved fingers, holding it close to the head, where the bad guy, presumably, would not have held it. He lifted it close to the pipe.

"Chief, look at this," Bryant said.

The mallet was close to, but not touching, the exhaust pipe. There were several black marks on the pipe that matched the end of the mallet in size and shape.

"How about he cracks the pipe with the mallet, then leans the ladder against it, maybe even smacks the pipe with the ladder to leave an imprint. It would look like the ladder fell against the pipe and cracked it."

We looked at each other, nodding. That could be exactly what he'd done.

"I think he was hitting the pipe with this to crack it," he said. He looked around the room and gestured toward a ladder that was four feet away. "That would allow the CO into the house, although not that much. It would take a long time to put enough CO in to kill people."

"Not if you had another tank of gas that you could release into the house. That would finish them off, then there would be plenty of time for the crack to work," I said.

"Another tank of gas?" Bryant asked.

"Yeah, he had two tanks. One of some kind of sleeping gas and another labeled CO. We think he knocked them out, came in here to do something to the furnace, then was going to use the CO to kill them."

"That should have worked. Why didn't it?"

"Because Mr. Neumann and his friend got here in time to put a stop to all this. Otherwise, I would have been calling you tomorrow to come over and figure out how this relatively new and very reliable furnace killed five people," Stephanie replied.

Chapter Forty-six

We finished up our quick course in furnace mismanagement and went back upstairs. Bryant left to run home to get what he needed to remove and replace the intake pipe for the CSI Tech. I guess he hadn't planned on an actual repair when he decided to ride over on his motorcycle.

We had a brief summary meeting to wrap up the events at the home. "Maria and I will be heading out. I'll stop over and make sure that the Hammers and Andersons get home OK tomorrow," I announced.

Will gave us a quick wave and said, "I'm going back to my neighbor's. Hopefully, I'll make it in time for dessert." He shook my hand and to me said, "Thanks for the call. This will be interesting." He walked out the door.

Stephanie nodded and said, "I'll be heading up to the hospital with one of my investigators to talk to the victims. You think they're up to an interview?"

"Yes, they were fine when we left. Keeping them overnight seems a little over-protective to me, but you know doctors."

"What about your federal friend?"

"He'll be on this the rest of the weekend. I figure he'll have to let his superiors know about it by Monday. We'll have at least until then to get what we can from him. After that it will depend on whether or not they leave him on the case."

"What do you think the chances are of that?" asked Maria.

"Pretty good. He's an experienced field agent with a good record. They'll know that someone local brought him into this even if he doesn't tell them, which I think he will. He's got to be able to explain why he came out here on Thanksgiving. Nothing's been on the news or wires yet. And he's worked with me before and we've been successful. That counts for something with the feebs, whether you want to accept it or not," I said, mostly to the chief. I didn't know what her experiences were in working with the FBI but most local longtime law enforcement officers had a horror story or three from past federal interference. Federal agents just don't have a rep for being all warm and fuzzy. .

I had certainly had enough fun for one day. I told the chief, "We'll stay in touch. I'd appreciate anything you pick up."

"I'll put you on the circulation list for everything, including the lab work when it comes in. We'll probably be having a task force meeting on this tomorrow morning. If you want to come and brief us on the history, that would be welcome."

I agreed to meet with them in the morning. Maria and I headed toward the car. After strapping in and firing up the 429, I asked her, "So, what now?"

Any officer involved in a shooting is given at least a week off on what's called "administrative leave." If she were at home, that would be starting right now. She would then go home, quite probably get drunk and try, unsuccessfully, to sleep.

I'd always heard that married officers had it harder than the single ones because their spouses didn't really understand what they did for a living. This would be one of those rare cases where the officer involved was going home to another officer, one who, presumably, understood what she was going through.

After both of my shootings I went home alone and got drunk. In fact, I got drunk for almost the entire week I had off after the first one. After the second, I just got blasted that first night, sort of out of respect for the custom more than anything else. I spent the rest of the week working in my wood shop and built a nice side table.

Of course, my two shootings were very different. In the second one I was first on the scene where a very bad guy had just beaten a college girl to death. Her offense had been getting robbed of the drugs she was smuggling for him. When I got to her she was still tied, naked, to the chair where he had literally whipped her to death. He had a gun in his belt and the official report showed that he had drawn it. I shot him with as much remorse as if I'd stepped on a bug on the sidewalk.

My first shooting was of an armed burglar who came out of an electronics store shooting. That one was all reaction; it was him or me. That one still bothered me and its parallel to today's events told me that today's shooting would bother Maria for a long time. Now was the time to let her decide what she wanted to do.

"Take me home and make love to me" she said, staring out the window.

Chapter Forty-seven

Friday, November 28
Robbinsdale, Minnesota

Friday dawned as bright and cheerful as the previous day. I knew today would be much different, however. We had yet another major case to work in cooperation with, now, three local police departments, two county crime labs and the FBI. We were at the point where I would most likely get tossed off the case.

The situation: The first crime occurred in Edina, the second in Shorewood, the third in Apple Valley. The hit man, having used a super-secret gas that only the military was supposed to have, ensured federal interest. My only hope of staying involved was the fact that I was the only person, law enforcement or otherwise, to have seen all three crime scenes and I was the only LEO who had been involved in the investigation from the first day. I was the point of continuity and I was going to use that to stay in the game.

Chief Kirmeier had called the South Lake chief and Edina's chief, Dave Houkkinen, and arranged a meeting at 11:00 in Dave's office. She let Dave have the site since he had the first crime and he was the most centrally located. And though she probably hesitated, she also invited Will Sanford.

The meeting took place as planned with each of the chiefs bringing along a deputy who would be handling the day-to-day follow-up on the cases. Each deputy went over his individual case and brought the entire team up to speed. I didn't hear much that I didn't already know.

I noted that the families needed additional security. We'd handled that with plans to send Ruth and Steve on a golf vacation. Pete's son, Jim, would be back at Annapolis where the Navy had been advised of his situation and the Marines charged with security at the Naval Academy would be sure to take this assignment very seriously. Pete and Carol would stay in their house, but would now lock the doors, arm the alarm, and Pete would carry his Kimber. Plus, they had Sinbad. I didn't think individuals would be threatened since the killer was clearly trying to get the whole family, but you never know.

Will heard a lot that was new to him but just sat and took notes. It's a kind of creepy fed way they have about them. They just sit and nod and don't say much. Then a few days later you hear that you're off the case because it's been taken over by the feds. I didn't think that would happen here, but I'd have to stay on Will.

We wrapped up with a plan to meet once a week at each department's office on a rotating cycle. Next week would be out by the lake. I hoped to have something new to present by then. I still didn't know where I was going with this, but the existence of Grams' love letters hadn't interested anyone. I was going after those.

My next stop was Regions where I picked up the family and took them back to Ruth and Steve's house in Apple Valley. They were all ready to go, so we loaded up my Denali and headed south for some home cooking. I knew Steve's sister had been at the house since early morning cooking, and Chief Kirmeier had a car in front, so I felt comfortable leaving them in their care. I promised Pete I'd keep him on top of things.

I'd reluctantly left Maria at home this morning. I knew how alone a cop could feel after a shooting and, although she didn't get blasted last night, she'd had a few. Our lovemaking was very gentle and sweet and mostly just holding each other. I needed it too. She'd literally saved my live. You get attached to people who do that for you.

I partially justified my departure with the knowledge that Maria wasn't really alone. We had stopped by Pete's house on the way home from Apple Valley yesterday and picked up Pete's dog, Sinbad. He and Maria had hit if off right from the start. She and Sinbad were stretched out on the couch watching "Ellen" when I left.

While I was driving home, Sharon Rademacher called.

"Hey sweetie, how was your holiday?" Apparently even she hadn't heard yet about the events in Apple Valley.

"The usual Thanksgiving dinner. You know, a big meal followed by attempted murder and a good shooting. How about you and the sheriff?" I asked, referring to her husband.

"I saw something on TV, but not that you were there. Somehow, I don't think you're kidding me."

"I'm not." I gave her a quick abridged version of the mass murder attempt at the Hammer household. She was amazed.

"Not only do you live a charmed life, you now have a partner who is not only beautiful, intelligent and available, but willing to save your life. How do you do it?"

"Clean living and a true soul," I replied.

"Clean living, my ass. You're just lucky."

"Sometimes you're the windshield and sometimes you're the bug. It's good to be the windshield. So what are you calling me about this morning? I thought you'd be out at the sales."

"I never go on Black Friday. Too much work fighting all those professional shoppers. I'm at the office. I wanted to let you know I got a hit on that name you got from the church ladies."

I had asked Sharon to track down June Ingberg, the name I'd gotten from Norma Eckmann, who had said that June might know the name of "Forever Yours," the letter writer.

"OK. What do you have?"

"I found seven female J. Ingbergs and Engbergs that should have been about the correct age. Three are deceased. Doesn't mean one of them wasn't the right one, just that you can't talk to them. Two of the remaining ones live more or less local, then there's one in Mora, Minnesota, and one in Fargo, North Dakota. I'll send you an email with the contact info I have."

"You're still the best, Sharon."

"I know, but you can still tell me. Is Maria still in town?"

"Yes."

"You think maybe I could call her, see if she'd like to get together and go out for lunch?"

"What for?"

"I thought she might like to get away for a little while. Besides, tough sheriff's deputy or not, she's still a woman and she might just like to have a woman to talk to right now."

"OK, but give me about ten minutes to get home. I don't think she'll answer the phone."

"All right. Talk to you then."

I pulled my Denali into the garage at the rear of the house and walked in to find Maria in the kitchen, wearing an apron. The countertops were covered with baking apparatus. I smelled cookies.

"Aren't we domestic this fine day?" I commented.

She was pulling a sheet of cookies out of the oven when she heard my voice. She carefully set them on the top of the range to cool and turned to me. "Since you wouldn't let me go with you this morning, I decided to mess up your kitchen. How'm I doing?"

I grabbed a cookie from a previous batch, took a bite, and said, "Just fine. Keep 'em coming."

"Nope. This is the last batch. I made six dozen. You'll be nice and chubby and ready for the cold weather when I leave."

This brought up a subject that had both of us wondering. Maria was scheduled to be back at work on Monday but, because of the shooting, she had to stay until released by the Apple Valley PD, in case they had any more questions for her. I'd asked Chief Kirmeier about it at the meeting earlier and she said she was ninety-five percent sure that Maria could make her Sunday night flight; she' let me know by tomorrow afternoon. I gave her the news.

"Damn. I was hoping for a few more days off."

She would get administrative leave for as long as we needed her here. Her boss, a famous southwestern lawman who knew good publicity when he saw it, was more than happy to have one of his officers involved in a case in another state, as it reflected well on his department.

"I think I'm going to be doing a bunch of running around on this thing anyway. And you know that the feds are going to want to keep you away from it to keep out any conflict of interest."

"I know, but I could help you. You're going to need a partner."

She was right. Since my status with the MPD was loose, to put it best, I'd need some help and they wouldn't give it to me. I worked as a contract investigator, primarily for the MPD, but in cases such as this, for other departments too. Technically, I was under contract to both Edina and Apple Valley so they would be expected to supply support. I could have gotten my usual MPD guy, Robert Smith, but I knew he was tied up with another case and not available. So, Maria's help would have been useful.

"I'll just have to get by without you."

"Just don't go rushing into any more fights. I won't be there to cover your nice little round butt and I'd hate to see anything happen to it."

She was recovering nicely. I said, "So, since it looks like you'll be leaving on schedule, I suggest we get back to our agenda of how to best burn your vacation time."

As I was saying this, the phone rang. It was Sharon.

After answering and acting surprised, I handed the phone to Maria. The two had really hit it off last summer when we were working on that other case and I wasn't surprised that Maria took Sharon up on her offer.

"You get to clean up. Sharon and I are going out for lunch," she said, taking off the apron.

"OK, but I'm not taking responsibility for these cookies. If they're gone when you get back, it's on you. And grab a coat. It's colder today."

Winter was descending on us as it usually does, in increments. We'd had a little snow overnight, but that was gone with the warm daytime temps. Last night it got down into the teens. I knew Maria was not acclimated to that.

Sharon arrived a half hour later and the two most important women in my life left for their excursion into the world of Black Friday restaurant exploration. Normally, given the circumstances of the past day and a half, and some unexpected free time, I would have gone to my favorite men's mental health center, Bill's Gun Shop and Range but, being a holiday, I knew it would be very busy there. The thought of spending an hour in a shooting range between two people who didn't know enough not to be there today was unappealing. Still, I needed something to take my mind off . . . what? The case? Yesterday? Maria shooting the suspect? I wasn't sure. I decided to go downstairs to my man cave as soon as I cleaned the kitchen.

My basement has the usual mechanical room with a furnace and water heater and a big storage room that is about ten percent smaller than I need. A friend of mine who sells real estate says it's one of Murphy's laws—whatever size house you buy it will be ten percent smaller than the space required to store your stuff. I'm single, I have 2,800 finished square feet including three bedrooms and three bathrooms, a den, kitchen, living room, dining room, family room and rec room, a two-car attached garage and a four-car garage and shop out back and I still need ten percent more space for boxes of junk, many of which I haven't opened in the ten years I've lived here. I'm not a hoarder; I don't go out and buy things and just pack them away. This is all stuff that I've used at least once. Why don't I get rid of it? I don't know. Maybe I could join the neighbor's annual garage sale. Something to think about, especially if I might, someday, maybe, possibly consider moving to Arizona.

The rest of the basement is definitely proof that a man lives here. The slightly L-shaped room includes a big screen theater area, a game table for poker nights, a wet bar, a workout area with a club-quality treadmill and weight machine and, the *coup de gras*, a bathroom with a sauna. There is also a small shop area in one corner where I can see the big screen while working on things I don't like to leave in the second garage, things like firearms. I have a small, perfunctory gunsmithing area set up, one simple enough to limit my ambitions to things I've been trained to do, preventing me from attempting to build things like, say, a rifle that can accurately shoot a little sabot'd dart a mile. I also have a loading bench.

A loading bench is a requirement for someone with my kind of shooting habit. I go through about 20,000 rounds a year in practice and competition and the cost at retail would put me in the position of having to choose between shooting and my Harley, not a choice I want to have to make. So, to save money, I load. The process is simple.

My setup includes a multi-station hand-cranked autoloader. Simply put, it's like a merry-go-round. You load your cartridge cases by hand in the first station and pull a lever. The turntable rotates and you load in another cartridge and the cases go around and come out the other side all ready to fire. I can crank out about twenty rounds a minute.

It's important to pay attention to the process so it's a good activity to take your mind off troubles. I had left the unit set up for .45 ACP, my most common round. So I just flipped on the TV, set my coffee on the bench, made sure all the feeders were loaded and sat down on a bar stool. After that, it's just load and pull, load and pull, just like sitting in front of a slot machine. While I loaded I watched the annual state high school football tournament on the tube. Minnesota has six or seven levels of competition. It's all-day nonstop high school football and I love it.

Two and a half games later I had about 1,500 rounds cranked out. The light was fading and I started wondering when Maria would get home. That's a nice thought—Maria would get home. Could this be her home? I don't know. She is such a product of the Southwest. Maybe I could move there? Or we could become one of those couples who spend the year in two places, winter in Phoenix and summer in Minnesota. Oh well, none of those things are happening anytime soon. She is still young and active in her work and I'm still working, sort of. Could I handle Phoenix in the summer?

My coffee was long gone and my cookie lunch was wearing off so I went upstairs in search of sustenance. As I opened the refrigerator, I heard the door open and the laughter of women's voices. They were back.

"Hey you two. How was lunch?"

Sharon answered, "Great, and so was the shopping."

That explained the long day. "I thought you didn't do Black Friday?" I asked rhetorically.

Sharon answered, "Not a chance. But we spotted a cute pair of shoes that turned out to be incredibly on sale. Then we went to the store next door—and then . . ."

Maria laughed. Her laugh filled me with a feeling that she had made progress today, could see that the normal world would go on. That's important after a shooting. The officer involved needs to do normal things. I was glad for Sharon's friendship and her call.

That night we made love, knowing that Maria would be leaving on Sunday afternoon. We spent the rest of the weekend together at home, cooking, eating, sleeping, and loving. We didn't talk about the case and I didn't answer my phone. Nothing would change until Monday when the feds would come in, and nothing would prevent that.

Chapter Forty-eight

Monday, December 1
Minneapolis, Minnesota

Monday came.

There is nothing subtle or finessed about the entry of federal authorities into a case. They are always the 800-pound gorillas in any room and they like it that way. In the post 9/11 world, they have personnel, technology, and financial resources unparalleled by any other law enforcement agency in the history of the planet, save, perhaps, the old KGB. And they flaunt it. My only hope was that by bringing Will in early we would still hold onto a shred of the case, enough to stay in the game and be able to keep the feds focused on it. They have a tendency to become distracted and move on to bigger and more visible cases when things don't progress fast enough.

The week went by rather quickly. The federal machine was processing little tidbits of information and, true to his word, Will kept me on top of things. I don't know if his boss knew that, but I knew Will well enough to know that he'd keep his butt out of the line of fire. By Friday's meeting we had a few things to talk about.

It was South Lake's turn and that chief decided to make it a lunch meeting. We met at Scotty B's, an independently owned place in neighboring Mound that features American cuisine—burgers and homemade soups at lunchtime. Good salads for the non-burger crowd, and reasonable lunch prices. A small meeting room in the back provided some privacy.

Since I was the common law enforcement thread, I re-introduced everyone, in case they'd forgotten someone from the first meeting. Dave Houkkinen brought Randy O'Falvey with him and, like the other assistants, he was eager to learn how a multijurisdictional case was balanced by several agencies, all of whom wanted their local case at the top of the support pile in terms of whatever the other agencies developed. They also wanted to hang onto the case and not wake up one morning to discover the entire thing had been federalized.

The food arrived while we were still in the small talk phase of the meeting. It turned out that there was not much new to report. The South Lake chief had nothing new. All the evidence from the break-in at Pete's had been turned over to the county crime lab and they were just waiting for the DNA work on the blood trace found on the stairwell wall, which had been sent to the FBI lab in DC. Dave Houkkinen from Edina had nothing new from his investigation. Again, all the physical evidence was at the county. And the new player, Stephanie Kirmeier, said everything she had was at the BCA. Her interviews with neighbors had turned up nothing. The car that was found parked in the play area parking lot was stolen from White Bear Lake and was absolutely clean, confirming our thoughts that the dead assassin was a pro, probably from out of state. The rest of his effects had been taken to the BCA crime lab and much of that had been taken away by the feds when they officially entered the case on Monday. The BCA's representative merely reiterated the chief's reports and wrapped up things.

I'd worked major cases before, and I'd seen task forces made up of people from a variety of jurisdictions and agencies work together to get things done. But this was different; these people were focused. The suburban police chiefs and their assistants all exhibited a sense of determination and commitment that I'd come to expect from departments that are unaccustomed to violent crime. They are used to burglaries, traffic accidents, and occasional domestic violence, but they are not used to this level of violence and having such a sophisticated criminal in their backyards. They were all, to a man and woman, dedicated to solving this case. I knew they would not rest until it was solved. When the suburban reports were complete they looked around the table at their counterparts as if soliciting an unspoken promise from each other. That brought us to Will Sanford.

As usual, Will had listened silently through the other presentations, as lacking in information as they were. He made no notes, just sat and sipped a glass of Michelob Ultra, the first time I'd ever seen a fed drink on the job. Granted, the case can be made that drinking Ultra isn't really drinking on the job, but still. It was very nearly a major faux pas as far as I was concerned. When Stephanie finished it was his turn.

Will carefully placed his glass on the table and opened his notebook. He hadn't brought copies of anything to distribute, an indication that what he was giving the team was more or less unofficial. Normally, when the feds give you information they hand you a polished and published booklet with all the i's dotted and t's crossed. Everything they do speaks to their financial resources.

"We have identified the fellow who attempted the mass murder on Thanksgiving Day," Will began.

He had our undivided attention. In fact, in all my years in law enforcement I had never seen a meeting of high-end LEOs go silent so suddenly.

"He is, rather, was, George Kline, of White Bear. He owned a house on the eastern shore of Bald Eagle Lake."

I noted that he did not say, "lived on Bald Eagle Lake." The feds are very precise in their use of language. What this meant was that they had found a property that the man owned. Owning a property does not prove residence. Whether or not he lived there was yet to be determined, or maybe it had been and Will would reveal that later.

Will continued. "He was born in Boston, Mass, in 1966 to a mother who was distinctly left leaning. His father is unknown. Her activities included anti-war protests. Apparently Kline's education included spending some time during the mid-1980s in Northern Ireland where, it is believed, he was trained by the IRA.

Upon his return to the United States, Kline began a long-term association with organized crime. He started out, as many future hoods do, working on a crew, but it was soon realized that his training and demeanor had prepared him for some very creative work. He became a specialist for a family in Boston but they didn't have enough work for him. A mob can only knock off so many people before attracting too much attention. So, being the exception that proves the rule, he left that family to become a freelancer. He has been sought by the Bureau for about seventeen years as a suspect in a total of sixteen very sophisticated hits, resulting in the deaths of a total of forty-three persons, none of them anywhere near Minnesota.

"He was a specialist in arranging the deaths of groups of people and, in most cases, making them look like accidents. Only a few pieces of evidence have ever been collected from his previous crimes, but those have been enough to eliminate the possibility of accidental death and prove homicide. There has not been enough to bring an indictment or an arrest. In fact, until now, we didn't know he lived in Minnesota."

"How did you figure that out?" I asked.

"We had a name but little else except a right ring-finger print on file. We made a preliminary ID from the body, but we still had no photo or address. Even the best trained eventually make a mistake. He left a receipt from a hardware store in Winona in the bag that was recovered at the site. We tracked it down and found that the store had a security camera that was strategically out of sight. They had video of him making the purchase of the hose and rubber mallet and we were able to add those images to his identity package.

"We made his address by the conversation he had with the hardware store clerk. They had talked about fishing and the clerk said he remembered that the customer said he lived on Bald Eagle. I guess he figured he was far enough from home that a little fishing talk wouldn't matter. But the clerk remembered him because of that. He thought it was a bit odd that a guy who lived on Bald Eagle would be visiting a small hardware store in Winona to buy a hose and a mallet."

Sometimes that's all it takes. One little slip-up like telling a guy you're not from around there and it sticks in his mind. I've gotten the start on cases with less than that.

"So we had a photo and a starting point and we canvassed the lake."

I knew that meant that the feds went door to door and talked with everyone who lived on the lake until they found the killer's neighbors—another testimony to the power of big budgets.

"We were able to identify him through those interviews. We obtained a search warrant for his house. He was apparently in residence as we found fresh food and clean clothes in the house. Two cars in the garage were registered to a Harvey Periwinkle, which is the name the property is registered to. The neighbors ID'd the photos from the hardware store and of the body. Same guy."

I sat shaking my head. Why would someone hire this guy to take out Pete's whole family? This connection pointed us toward a well-funded and well-connected organization, someone who could contact and pay a professional hit man. Who, with those connections, would want to hurt Pete's family? I had to answer those questions before I'd get any farther.

Will had one more bomb to drop. He dropped it after we all went through the decision process on whether or not to order dessert. I ordered a piece of French Apple Pie with a slice of cheddar melted over it.

"I also have the lab reports back from the break-in at Mr. Anderson's. The blood trace came from a male. The sample was cross-matched against samples taken from the residents of the house. It does not match the deceased Mr. Kline. It also does not match any of the usual occupants of the house, nor the responding officers from that day. However, comparison of all the samples does indicate one rather unusual fact: the man who broke into Mr. Anderson's house shares a grandparent with Mr. Anderson—they are cousins."

"Whooooah, wait a minute," I said. "Cousins? The burglar is Pete's cousin? Pete doesn't have any cousins. I know for a fact that both his parents were only children. His dad used to joke about it as being proof that no one should have only children because they grow up like him. And Pete's mom was an only child, too. This doesn't make sense."

The table was quiet, pondering what this meant. I didn't know, that much was for sure. I knew what I knew and that was that Pete was an only child. He had no cousins.

"You're confident in these lab results?" Dave Houkkinen asked.

"One hundred percent," Sanford answered. "This type of testing has gotten to the level where it's as accurate as fingerprinting. There is no question about the match. The question is, 'Who is Mr. Anderson's cousin?'"

Chapter Forty-Nine

I was picking at my pie, trying to wrap my brain around this last tid-bit of data. A cousin? I'd known Pete literally all my conscience life. I'd known his parents, his grandparents, vacationed with them, celebrated holidays with them, all the usual events where relatives would appear and I was certain he had no cousins. The rest were eating their desserts with gusto while I, normally a power eater when it comes to pie, was playing with mine. I noticed that the conversation had stopped and everyone was looking at me.

"You're sure about the no-cousins thing, aren't you, Dan?" Dave Houkkinen asked.

I nodded but before I could say anything, Will spoke up.

"That's correct. We've already checked it out. Mr. Anderson has no cousins. That is what makes this very interesting. We are looking for a second generation descendent of this common grandparent. We don't know if the grandparent is from his mother or father's side. But we do know that this grandparent did produce at least one other child by a different partner. Using the information from the two break-ins and the known lifespans of Mr. Anderson's four grandparents, we can esti-mate the individual's age at between eighteen and fifty. That makes the timeframe for the indiscretion between about 1935 and 1970. You don't happen to know if either of Pete's grandmothers was pregnant during that time, do you Dan?"

"Obviously, both were at least once" I replied. "But I don't know about more than once. I'm going to have to talk to Pete about this and see if he has any thoughts. I'll be real surprised if he does, I'll tell you that."

"I'd like to come along for that chat," Will said.

The rest of the group wanted to come along, too, but that wouldn't be necessary, according to our federal representative. He'd distribute any information we got to everyone as soon as it was available.

The meeting broke up and I called Pete. His voicemail said he would be in a meeting most of the day and would return calls later. I left a message to call me a.s.a.p.

As we left, Will maneuvered me away from the group and told me, "I didn't want to let this out to the rest of them, but the gas canister was confirmed to be part of a lot that was reported missing in Bosnia. Our friend Kline somehow got it delivered to his home in White Bear. We traced a UPS international shipment from Germany to his home about a year ago. Apparently he obtained the material in advance for an occasion like this."

"How would he know the stuff was available?"

"There is a market for things like this. People with the right connections buy and trade in this market all the time. It's one of the things we track to help us with homeland security."

"Did you know he had bought the stuff before now?" I was incredulous.

"No. We knew it was stolen and that some of it had been shipped to customers. But we didn't know he was a customer or where he was. If we had, we could have raided his house and recovered the material."

"How could he get hold of it?"

"He had very extensive contacts with overseas groups of all sorts of philosophies. In fact, searching his house has already produced leads on twelve cases, two of which are domestic in nature."

"Domestic in nature?"

"Tell your Arizona friend she may have prevented a nerve-gas attack. You'll read about it soon, maybe as soon as this afternoon."

With those cryptic words, we parted company.

Chapter Fifty

5:00 p.m.
Still Friday, December 5
The Sunshine Factory Restaurant
New Hope, Minnesota

Pete was on his way home when he called me about 4:30.

"What's up, buddy?"

"I just wanted to fill you in on the task force update meeting we had today. You doing anything for dinner?"

"Carol's in Chicago at a book signing, so I'm free."

"Let's meet at Sunshine," I said.

"Sounds good."

I'd taken Pete to Sunshine before. It's a nice combo sports/news bar and grill. They have an American menu and typical décor with a quiet dining room and a rowdy bar with lots of seating and TVs that are set to either sports or news channels. The screens are equally split between news shows and ESPN. The delightful aspect to the place is that they have a real chef, who does a daily specials menu sheet that can have anything from blackened swordfish to portobello ravioli, all handmade and good.

Five o'clock is early enough to beat the rush and we were able to get a table immediately. Menus were passed and drink orders taken. I was thinking this was going to be an important discussion and I wanted to stay clear so, for a moment, I considered ordering raspberry lemonade instead of my usual single malt. Fortunately, common sense won out and I ordered a Glenlivet, double, with a little ice. Pete ordered the same.

Our drinks arrived quickly, accompanied by a bowl of cashews. The crew here knows me well enough to bring them along with the scotch. We ordered dinner and each gave our glasses a good swirl then took a healthy sip, followed by the required lip smack and "Ahhhh." Nothing like a good single malt.

"So, tell me about the meeting. You guys making any progress?"

"Bringing Will Sanford in was the smartest thing I've done in awhile. Nobody else had anything new. He was able to track down the identity of the uninvited guest."

"No shit. So who was he?"

"He is, was, a professional hit man originally from Boston, who lately resided in White Bear over on Bald Eagle Lake. He was wanted by the FBI for at least a dozen murders, mostly on the East Coast."

"Hit man! And he was living on Bald Eagle? What kind of hit man lives in Minnesota?"

"The kind that is interested in maintaining a low profile. The FBI believes he did one of his jobs in northwest Iowa. They think that he probably did some traveling through the area and decided he liked it, so he settled here. The house was purchased seven years ago, which was just after the Iowa murder. The theory is that he flew in through MSP, rented a car and did his reconnaissance, then came back later for the hit. He may have spent some time living here while he was scoping things out and decided to come back and look for a place to live."

"And the feds had no idea he was here?"

"They knew he wasn't on the East Coast anymore. They didn't know where he'd gone. Will told me that the theories ran from Mexico to Alaska to the Bahamas. None of them included Minnesota. Will said the neighbors they interviewed thought the guy was a freelance writer for some fishing magazines, at least that's what he'd told them. That would explain the lack of an apparent work schedule and the occasional long absences."

"This is nuts. Why would someone hire a guy like that to go after my family? That's got to be a lot of money, doesn't it?"

"The old rule for pros like this one was a hundred thousand dollars. That's kind of a base price now. The mobs still do a lot of their own dirty work, things like popping some poor sap with two behind the ear, but that leaves a lot of evidence. In those cases, they just don't care or may even be sending a message by being less than subtle about it. A guy like this, a guy who could take out five people and make it look like an accident, would probably go for one to two million plus expenses."

Pete sipped his scotch, trying to wrap his head around the fact that someone thought it was worth a million bucks or more to take out his family. It was mind-boggling.

Pete said, "I just don't get it. What could someone hope to gain by killing us? I keep thinking of one of the episodes from the old *Star Trek* series where Kirk has to solve a murder that takes place on the Enterprise while they're transporting a bunch of diplomats to some conference. The suspect was an Andorian, I think they called him, a guy with light blue skin and antlers."

I nodded. Pete had been a big fan of the late 1960's TV series. At the time I thought he'd take a shot at becoming an astronaut because of it.

"Kirk and Spock were trying to figure out the logic behind the murder. The suspect's boss, another blue guy with antlers, told them, 'Don't look for logic in this crime; look for reasons of passion or gain. Those are motives for murder.' I'm trying to figure out a motive of passion or gain. I know for a fact that passion doesn't fit. Ruth and Steve have a solid relationship and so do Carol and I. Jim's too busy at the Academy to have anything else going on. So that leaves gain. But what is there to gain from all of us dying in an accident?"

"That's the million dollar question, isn't it?" I said. "I think if we can figure that out we'll break this thing open. You have a will someplace, right? Anything in there that could prompt someone to take a shot at you?"

"Sure I have a will, and so do Carol and Ruth and Steve. But everything I have goes to Jim if Carol and I both check out. Since Ruth and Steve don't have any kids, they have their stuff set to go to a couple of charities and their church. That's the line I was thinking but it just doesn't compute."

The waitress came back with our meals. Pete had gone with the crusted walleye and I was having a chicken Caesar salad with a light dressing in deference to the fall season. My body, which is preprogrammed by hundreds of generations living in country that gets cold this time of year, was doing its best to load up for the long winter ahead. It's a fight I have every year. The days get shorter, the weather gets colder, and my body gets thicker. The fight is getting harder every year, but this year I have real motivation. About five-and-a-half feet of motivation. Maybe I should lay off the scotch and cashews?

As we were finishing the main course, I decided it was time to lay the real bombshell on Pete.

"Will had one other piece of information that was valuable and we have to track down."

"Yeah, what was that?" Pete asked.

"He said they finished the DNA work on the blood sample taken from your stairwell. It was a male."

"I guess we figured that. Was it the same guy that tried to get us at Ruth and Steve's?"

"No. But there was one thing of interest. He said that whoever the blood in your house came from, he shares a common grandparent with you. He said the burglar is your cousin."

Chapter Fifty-one

Sunshine Factory Restaurant
New Hope, Minnesota

Pete was flabbergasted. "Cousin? I don't have any cousins. I don't have any aunts or uncles. Both of my parents were only children."

"I know and that's what I told Sanford. He said the test is ironclad, that they can figure out your ancestry with these tests now and that the burglar is your cousin, in the biological sense that you share a common grandparent. He said they can't figure out which side of the family he comes from, just that it is so. We are going to have to figure out who had an indiscretion."

"I don't know. I'm thinking Gramps did a lot of traveling when he was working for General Mills. I suppose he could have spread a little seed around. It's got to be on that side of the family; otherwise, why break into Grams' house?"

"I agree that it must be on your dad's side of the family. But I think we have to consider something less obvious here. I think we have to consider Grams."

"Are you nuts? Grams was as straight as the day is long. She was the very model of virtue. She was also always home and involved in all those church projects. Besides, one of the church ladies would have said something if she'd had a kid out of wedlock. Some of them knew her for nearly fifty years."

"Yeah, they knew her for fifty years after she moved to Edina. Before that, she lived in Fargo and before that in Alamo. You and they are looking at the adult Grams. This would have happened longer ago, maybe even in the 1940s. Hell, I don't know, maybe even before that.

Someplace along the way she had a friend, a friend named "Forever Yours." I think we've got to find out who that person was and what their relationship was. I think that's the connection we've been looking for, something that goes back to North Dakota."

"The letters! The letters are from someone who really loved her. Someone before Gramps. Maybe she had a baby before she and Gramps got together."

I agreed. "Either Grams had a baby before she knew Gramps or she had one while Gramps was away at war. She could have left the kid with his or her father, then moved away from North Dakota with Gramps. Now that guy's grandson is trying to kill your whole family. We've got to find out who 'Forever Yours' is and track down his grandson."

Still obviously reeling from this news, Pete looked at me and said, "You're the detective. How do we do that?"

I thought for a moment. "The church lady, Norma, said that some-one named June Ingberg was Grams' closest confidant. I found a June Ingberg in Fargo. We have to go and interview her."

"So when do we leave?"

"Let me do some more digging. I'll find out just where she is. And I want to check with Will Sanford again and see if he can stay in touch with us while we're out of town in case anything comes up on this end. How about we blow out of here Monday morning? It's only about three-and-a-half hours from here. Pack for a few days, in case we have to stay over in Fargo."

"Sounds good. I'll let Carol know what's up. She'll be coming back from Chicago tonight."

I knew this was the trail we had to follow.

Over the weekend, on Saturday evening, at the usual time, I called Maria. We talked about how things were going in our lives. She had a few small cases that she would close in the next week or so. She asked me about Pete's case.

"You know I can't talk to you about that. You're a material witness," I kidded her.

She knew I'd talk to her about it. Anything that happened after her involvement at the Hammers wouldn't have anything to do with what happened before and during. Besides, since we'd started seeing each other I'd found her to be a valuable asset. She brought a distant perspective to cases and was able to see the forest in spite of the trees. Sometimes I get too close to the trees.

"We found out that the person who broke into Pete's is his cousin."

"I thought Pete didn't have any relatives besides Carol?"

"So did he. It was a shock, to say the least, but the DNA says they have a common grandparent."

"Wow. That's going to shake things up a bit."

"And we are going to Fargo on Monday to interview a woman who was Grams' best friend back in the days when she was getting those love letters. We're hoping she might be able to tell us who 'Forever Yours' is."

"Why wouldn't she? Emma is dead and there's no one else who could be hurt by it."

"The problem is that June, that's the lady we're going to see, is in a retirement home with Alzheimer's. I don't know if she'll be able to talk to us or not. Her daughter says she has good days and bad."

Maria paused for a moment, then said, "Dan, my grandmother had Alzheimer's. She got it early, when she was only in her sixties. People didn't call it that back then; they called it senility or dementia. She also had good days and bad. On her bad days she couldn't do anything for herself. Couldn't eat, couldn't go to the bathroom, could barely talk. But on her good days she was just like you and me except for one thing."

"What was that?"

"She thought she was in her thirties. She thought it was the 1940s or early '50s. She would talk about the news of the day, like Truman running for president or the war in Korea where my dad was serving. If you pretended that you were someone she knew then, she'd talk to you as that person. I remember her talking with me as if I was my mother. We talked about my dad's letters from Germany and Korea. She'd talk about the Dodgers moving to Los Angeles, things like that. And she was coherent. She knew the facts like she'd just read them in that morning's paper. If you can get June to talk at all, pretend you're whoever it is she wants to talk to. Then you'll learn what she knows."

I gave that some thought and decided to talk to the guys about it on the way up to Fargo on Monday.

Will Sanford had talked his way into our little expedition over the weekend. He wanted in on any interviews we conducted that would shed light on the case and he pointed out that we were going to another state; his federal credentials might come in handy. I can usually get what I need from other LEOs after they make the connection between me and the author of the ballistics book most of them have in their offices, but not always.

Chapter Fifty-two

7:00 a.m.
December 8
Pete's House
Shorewood, Minnesota

I made my way out to Pete's in my Suburban. We had decided to make the road trip in this vehicle, rather than Pete's. Mine was marginally more comfortable and got a little better gas mileage. But the clincher for me was that it has XM radio, something I can't go without on the road. Plus, since it was my vehicle, I could claim most of the driving rights, only turning them over when I felt like it. Not that I don't trust Pete's driving; I'd just rather do it myself. It's a guy thing.

The temp was near twenty degrees but it was still technically fall. No snow cover yet, except the man-made stuff on the ski hills. The sky was dark at 7 a.m., but showed signs of lightening to the east. I anticipated a dazzling sunrise. Fortunately, we'd be driving in the opposite direction.

As we loaded up, Will's nondescript dark blue sedan pulled into Pete's driveway.

Some law enforcement people view my reputation as making me no longer part of the club. To them, I'm a big-shot out-of-town expert who comes in to tell them how to do their jobs or, in the case of paid testimony, how they didn't do their jobs. It can go either way.

Having a fed along wouldn't hurt. Plus, I knew him to be a pretty good guy and we could play the cop game of "top this." That's a storytelling game that cops all over the country play. If TV writers ever figured it out, they could just follow real cops around at some cop convention and get more material than they'd ever be able to use. The only problem would be that much of it is so far out that even TV audiences would think it's BS.

"Morning, Will. How's my favorite fed this fine day?" I asked.

"Still asleep. Do you know how early I had to get up to be here at this hour?"

"Hey Will," Pete said as he grabbed a bag from Will's hand. "Come on in and have a cup of coffee. I've got some on and got some packed to go."

Pete tossed Will's bag in the back on my rig and we all went inside for one last cup and bathroom visit. Will had never been in Pete's house so I took a moment to fill him in on the locale of the attempted break-in. During the tour, Sinbad came over to check out Will.

"So this is the home security service?" he said, patting Sinbad's head.

"He was that day," I said. "We believe he knocked the bad guy down the stairs, which resulted in the blood trace that your people say came from a cousin Pete never knew he had."

"You two ever come up with any theories on that?"

"Just that we have to follow-up on the letters."

I had left the letters out of my early multijurisdictional task force meeting's agenda. I hadn't made any connection at that point and they were too personal to just throw out there. After the cousin thing came out, I made the connection and called Will. That's when our traveling party became three.

Pete came over with a cup for Will, then went to say goodbye to Carol.

"Carol catching up on some beauty sleep?" I asked.

"No, this is normal. I usually get up around 5:00 and she usually sleeps 'til about 7:00. Gives me a little private time for reading, catching up on the business news, that sort of thing. Then we have breakfast together."

I knew better. He gets up at 5:00 for the same reason I do, to take a leak. But he's nice enough to not risk waking Carol by going back to bed. He could say it's private time but I knew Pete well enough to know that he was just being nice to Carol. Maybe that's how marriages stay fresh. He probably takes coffee to her at 7:00. Nothing like crawling into a woman-warm bed.

Will and I climbed into the Sub. Will took shotgun; Pete got the back seat and the snack duties. He had the coffee thermos and the bag from Bruegger's Bagels. Once Pete climbed in we headed out.

From the Twin Cities the best way to get to North Dakota is I-94. The problem was how to get to I-94 from Pete's. I zigzagged on county roads, which was better than dealing with the rush hour traffic on I-494. And it's a pretty drive. The fall colors were mostly done but a lot of trees still held their leaves. We passed several lakes with ducks, geese and even swans. They'd all be heading south soon, though. We could see the ice forming on the edges of the lakes.

Most of the ice we were seeing would go away during the day. Wave action from the wind and the sun's light would push it back into submission. That's the game this time of year—water versus sun.

Playing that game can make ice a genuine threat to human life. It looks solid, but there is no way to know how thick it really is just by looking at it. For a native Minnesotan, especially one who has ice-fished and been in law enforcement, like I have, it's no big deal to drive a four-thousand-pound car onto a lake. But it had better be thick enough.

Before it's thick enough, it looks the same. The only way to know you can't walk or sled or drive on it is to go out there and drill a hole in it or take your chances and walk, sled, or drive on it. Unfortunately, the second method is used by lots of people in the fall, often with fatal results.

As we cruised up I-94 toward North Dakota, a place that contained both Pete's future and past, he began reading the letters that had led us this direction.

My Beloved,

Today we are celebrating the birth of a grandson. It is exciting and deeply touching to look at this miracle and see that some part of you is going to continue on after you are gone. I know that you have already had this experience and now I understand why you were so moved by it.

As I grow older, I realize that the things we believed were important so many years ago are indeed insignificant when compared to the simple things like family and faith. The only parts of life that matter are those we receive at home. What we do for a living, where we live, how much money we have, none of these things is more important than the family we surround ourselves with.

So join me from your beautiful home in celebrating this moment in my life. I know that it would have been different if you had been here, but I wanted to share it with you as best I could.

I will always be,

Forever Yours
Williston, North Dakota
August 14, 1973

"I think he must have sent this after my cousin was born. This is strange, reading a letter to Grams from some guy she knew way back when," Pete said, as he perused the letters. "He's telling his life story. Here's an interesting one."

My Beloved,

I have received your latest missive and I am delighted to read that your grandson has achieved such a notable recognition as a National Honor Scholar and is seen as one of the future leaders of our country. Truly, I am confident that he will accomplish great things in his life, especially if he continues to pursue the science education he shows such aptitude for. Perhaps he will someday be an astronaut and walk on the moon. I couldn't be more proud if he were my own grandson.

Our fall season is upon us and, as I do every year, I went out to the park near Alamo on the anniversary on our meeting there. This year the weather was just as I recall from our last picnic in 1938. The sun was bright and the wind still, at least as still as it can be here on the northern prairie. Again I ate a sandwich and drank lemonade, as we did those many years ago. I could feel you there with me, enjoying the warm breeze and the singing of the birds.

Indeed, there are many times that I feel my move to Williston was a mistake. My soul will for all time be in Alamo, as will yours.

I am, as always,

Forever Yours,
Williston, North Dakota
August 28, 1974

"Pete, wasn't that when you got that award?" I asked.

"Yeah, summer of '74. I did that big project for school on the space program and the need for travel to other planets. This is just plain weird to read about it this way."

Each of us was lost in our thoughts as to what lay ahead as we covered the miles to Fargo.

Will was pursuing the case. For him this was business, a business that included murder, conspiracy, theft, smuggling and, ultimately, usage of a secret government gas weapon and attempted mass murder. It included the hiring of a professional killer for what had to be an extraordinary fee. Will knew that this was one of those cases that could make his career.

For Pete, it was the possibility of some twist of personal history, a twist that had come to life in a terrible and destructive way, with the murder of his grandmother and the attempted murder of the rest of his family. Had something happened all those years ago before Grams knew Gramps? Had Grams produced another child? Could she have had an affair while Gramps was away at war? And what about Gramps? Had Gramps been involved in some illicit liaison while on some business trip, a liaison that was now coming home to roost? What connection was there to the family today? This last question was certainly most important to him.

For me, it was a mystery. I'd spent my entire career chasing down mysteries and this one was no different on that level. But it was personal on the most intimate level. The killer or killers had targeted people I consider family. My people were in harm's way and I didn't know why. All I had to go on was the sophistication of the crimes already committed and the love letters from some past flame of my best friend's grandmother. How were these connected? I had to learn that before anything else would fall into place. And when I did, I had to follow that connection wherever it led. Even if it led straight to the gates of hell, I'd follow. Whoever was on the other side of this, they'd made this personal for me.

Part Two

North Dakota

Chapter Fifty-three

December 8
On Interstate 94 heading to Fargo

Once the caffeine kicked in, Will and I started exchanging case stories, kind of a game of "Whose is bigger?" It started when Will asked me what I'd been doing lately.

"Before the call from Pete telling me about Grams, I had just finished a small part of an investigation of a marijuana-growing operation in southern Minnesota that was just about unbelievable. This guy had been in the business for nearly twenty years. He owned a hobby farm on the outskirts of Jackson but also had a few businesses in town—a gas station, a barbershop and a liquor store. He was making an OK living but not really enough to explain how he supported his lifestyle. He owned a lot of stuff. He had two boats, a couple of very nice motorcycles, a lake place, an RV, eight or ten cars—we still aren't sure how many—plus the property. The state patrol was pretty sure that he had some other enterprise going on but they couldn't put their fingers on it.

"Anyway, the guy decided it was time to put new carpeting in the house. One of the guys putting in the carpeting had to get something from his truck. There had been a storm the previous night and a big tree had fallen across the driveway, so the carpet guys had parked out on the county road. The guy going to the truck cut across the yard and retrieved whatever it was he needed. On the way back he felt nature's call and decided it would be easier to just pop behind the barn to take a leak.

"When he rounded the corner behind the barn he was greeted by a row of nice healthy six-foot-tall marijuana plants growing under a row of trees that were doing double duty as both a wind break and camouflage for the weed.

"When he went back inside, he told the other carpet layer, who was also his brother-in-law, about his find. They decided to sneak back later that night and remove a few of the nice tall healthy plants for their own medicinal use.

"That night they executed their plan. It came off perfectly—right up to the point where they were pulled over by a state patrol officer for having a busted taillight.

"Now, I realize that crooks are dumb. But these guys may take the cake.

"When they were pulled over by the trooper, he ran the car's plate. The only thing that came back on the car was that its owner had two DUIs and had once been busted for a minor possession charge that was pled out with no jail time.

"He approached the car and asked for and received the usual driver's license and insurance information. After checking them with his computer he walked back to the car and asked the two to get out. He hadn't smelled any alcohol but since the guy had the DUIs and a drug history, he just wanted to be sure by talking to them a bit.

"Both guys got out of the car. He told them he'd pulled them over for the taillight. They were contrite and on their best behavior but the trooper continued his questioning.

"He asked them if they had been drinking. They said no. He asked them if there were any weapons in the car that he'd have to worry about. They said no. Then he asked them if it was OK if he searched the car just to make sure. They said yes."

"They consented to a search knowing what was in the car?" Pete asked.

"Yup. This is about the time that a smart bad guy would have stayed with the 'no' answers. Of course, with the previous drug bust, the trooper's next move would have been to call for a dog to check the car from the outside. Drug dogs are wonderful things. If the dog gets a hit on your car, it's search time whether you consent or not. But even that wasn't necessary—the guy said yes.

"When they popped the trunk the trooper found five six-foot-tall marijuana plants neatly arranged crosswise along with two shovels. He asked the carpet layers if the plants were theirs. They continued with their truthfulness and said 'No.'

"Now, if you ask anyone with more than two months on the job if bad guys will lie to you, you'll find out that most cops say they will and they do. The trooper expected them to say no so he just went along and asked, 'Then whose are they?' The carpet guys told him.

"What followed was a state BCA and state patrol case that resulted in busting the grass farmer. That's when I was brought in.

"This guy had some fully automatic rifles. As you two know, the AR-15 is a very popular rifle with many people. It's basically a civilian version of the Army's M-16 but it won't fire fully automatic. Unfortunately, it's not that hard to change that situation. It takes some good gunsmithing but it can be done. Oh, and there is one other way to get it to rock and roll—don't take care of it."

Pete, who owned an AR, was now paying attention.

"In the trigger group of the AR there is a thing called a "disconnector" and this thing has to be taken care of. Its job is to make sure that the trigger disconnects after only one round is fired. If you don't take care of it, it will wear and you risk the rifle going full auto by accident. In fact, this happened to a fellow in Wisconsin awhile back. Unfortunately for him, it happened at the range and there was an ATF guy shooting there. The ATF guys take their job very seriously. You can imagine the surprise on the agent's face when the shooter two lanes over ripped off half a magazine in about the time it takes to spit. It's an automatic ten years in a federal prison and ten grand for just possessing a rifle that fires full automatic. Last I heard the poor sap with the rifle was appealing a federal conviction. Heck of a price to pay for neglecting a little maintenance and less that fifteen dollars worth of parts."

Will nodded in agreement. "I heard about that Wisconsin case. Really seems like a case of neglect by the gun owner, but ATF is super-serious about full-up automatic weapons."

I continued, "So that 'Gee, I just forgot to lube it and it wore out' case was made by the defense for the fact that the grass farmer's AR would shoot full auto. Just bad maintenance. I was called in to examine the rifles and testify as to bad maintenance or altered on purpose.

"It's a close call. The work done to modify can look like bad maintenance but this guy had four rifles that would rock and roll. The odds that all four of a guy's rifles would fail simultaneously are beyond calculation. I think that was the clincher."

Pete and Will chuckled at the thought of trying to sell that defense to a jury of the guy's neighbors, people who lived in rural Minnesota and probably knew a thing or two about firearms. The case wasn't quite over but I figured the verdict would be against the pot farmer. Juries of neighbors can be hard that way.

About three hours after leaving Pete's we crossed into North Dakota and proceeded on I-94 to exit 346A, made a quick stop for gas and a bathroom break at a handy BP Station, then took Sheyenne north to 13th into West Fargo, a suburb of Fargo proper. My GPS led us to the retirement home containing one June Ingberg.

As we pulled into the driveway of the retirement home, I reviewed our plan. June was supposed to be Grams' confidant, as far as the letters went. We would let Pete do most of the talking since he would be the connection. I'd set up the appointment through Mrs. Ingberg's granddaughter, Julie Burrier, and she was meeting us at the home. Her job would be to introduce us and keep her mom interested in the conversation. Julie told me that this was going to be a challenge as her mom had advanced-stage Alzheimer's. She said that mom was in and out of the present but usually could relate events from the past pretty well. I silently hoped today was one of those days.

When Maria told me about her grandmother's affliction, I did a little quick research. I went over what I learned with Pete and we decided that, if June was living in the past, as her granddaughter had said she often did, Pete should play the part of his grandfather, Elmer. He would know June and would try to get her talking about their shared past. In that way she could relive her own history and, perhaps, fill us in on what had happened way back then.

Chapter Fifty-four

December 8
Williston, North Dakota

Simon Turner was happy. He had spent the last two days eliminating any possible connection between himself and that idiot "hit man" he had been referred to by the man he had met at a well-drilling conference in Texas. The braggart said he knew a mob hit man from New Jersey. Over gin and tonics in a Dallas bar it made for interesting talk. Simon never thought he'd have the need, but he kept the oilman's card for over six years. The need had come up a month ago.

He'd started thinking about a professional for the job after that klutz Paul Swanberg had messed up the first try to get the deed. That Paul had killed the old woman and walked away clean planted a seed in Simon's mind. Maybe just kill them all and go ahead with the mineral lease. That would be the easiest, as long as all the deaths looked natural or like an accident. That had been the problem, and the reason to hire a professional.

But it hadn't worked out. Simon had been monitoring the news websites and the story of the failed attempt was hot news. As soon as he heard that, he went into damage-control mode. Fortunately, he hadn't had to do much because from the beginning he had handled the money as if it could explode.

Working with wildcatters and roughnecks who preferred to have some of their fees sent to offshore accounts, he knew how to handle such transactions. He knew that even though the authorities could find the money transfers, it was all untraceable. The transfers wound through several different banks, ending up in the Bahamas. He destroyed all printouts of emails he had exchanged with his Texas connection and did the same with the emails to and from the killer.

The final step was to get rid of his computer. Simon was a typical twenty-first-century computer user, meaning he knew how to operate one, but not how it worked. His laptop had been selected for him by the company's tech specialist who, until recently, was a quiet little dweeb among the millions of quiet little dweebs plotting their takeover of the planet. He had worked in a windowless room in the center of the building under the constant hum of the magic boxes he tended. But Simon was not without imagination. He knew that computers could reach out and bite you in the ass because he'd seen it on TV. He knew it could be a problem from watching *CSI*. He'd learned on the TV shows that an expert could recover deleted files, so he knew he couldn't just erase the hard drive. He bought a computer identical to his old one, with the same applications and software, copied all his personal files except the Outlook email files from his old computer onto a thumb drive and loaded them into the new unit. He rechecked everything to be sure that all his emails were erased, then took the old computer apart, ripped out the drive and beat it to death with a hammer.

He put all the parts in an old pillowcase, threw in a couple of bricks for weight, and tossed the bag in the backseat of his Toyota 4-wheeler. He drove several miles and tossed it from the bridge into the center channel of the Little Missouri River.

Satisfied, he headed home.

While Turner was drowning his deconstructed computer pieces and Dan and company were driving into West Fargo, 2,000 miles to the northwest, a storm was forming over the north slope of Alaska. It would collect itself and glide southeasterly across western Canada, gathering speed and force, growing into a storm system that would make it into the North Dakota record books.

Chapter Fifty-five

Monday, December 8
10:45 a.m.
The Western Horizons Retirement Home
West Fargo, North Dakota

I parked in a visitor space near the front entrance. The building, set on the griddle-flat prairie of eastern North Dakota, was shaped like a large open "V." The center of the building was administration and cafeteria, an exercise room, meeting and common areas, with residential rooms in the two wings. The open entrance was inviting but I noticed a security station tucked away behind dark glass. Many retirement homes have these now after it became obvious to bad guys that people in these homes were usually unguarded, well-off and lonely, and easy targets for con men and outright thieves.

We were all dressed in what I call business casual travel wear, which in the Midwest is heavy slacks in khaki or another earth tone color, comfortably loose shirts of some cotton blend and a loose sweater and/ or jacket suitable for concealing a sidearm.

Minnesotans are congenital layer dressers so we know how to prepare for a trip into unknown territory in the winter. My Sub also has a winter survival kit in the back, a duffel with various food snacks that are impervious to age, a few candles, road flares, a survival blanket, a flashlight with a battery I check religiously, a set of those triangular reflectors, jumper cables and a tow strap. I've carried a kit like this for as long as I can remember, probably as long as I've had a driver's license, and never had to use anything besides the tow strap and the jumper cables, and never had to use those on my own vehicle. It's something I'm proud of— no winter driving mishaps. But I still carry it.

We went into the admin office and were greeted with a friendly Midwestern "Hi." The greeter was a tidy looking late-middle-aged woman with a touch of gray hair done up in a bun behind her head. She wore a comfortable looking flowered dress and a cardigan sweater that was probably hand knit. The sleeves of the sweater were twice rolled up her forearms and she had a Kleenex tucked under the left cuff. She held out her right hand for a greeting handshake. Her nametag read "Lois."

"Hi, Lois. I'm Dan Neumann from the Minneapolis Police Department. This is Will Sanford of the FBI and Pete Anderson. We talked last Friday about visiting with Mrs. Ingberg." I'd had a long phone conversation with Lois, explaining why we needed to talk with June Ingberg and asking for advice about the best approach. Lois confirmed my research that advanced Alzheimer's patients can have very lucid conversations with people from their pasts. If the information we received from Norma Eckmann was correct, and this was the right June, June had known Elmer when they were both in their teens, before Elmer married Grams and went off to war.

"Yes. We've been expecting you. June's granddaughter Julie has been here for a while. She's with June now. We're hoping that this is one of June's better days."

Better days? We'd driven 250 miles to talk with this woman and we really needed to get some information from the only part of her memory that was still accessible. I'd told the other guys to pack for a couple of days but that was a just-in-case measure. I'd hoped to be home for *Monday Night Football.*

"I'll take you to the meeting room where June and Julie are now," Lois said.

She led the way out of the office and down a short hallway past a pair of restrooms. At the next door we turned right into a meeting room that looked big enough to hold grand jury hearings. One wall, the back of the facility, I surmised, was full windows, the sides were paneled in light oak and the rear, hallway side, of the room was stacked with additional chairs and folded tables. We made our way across the carpeted floor to the corner where two women were seated at a cozy table for four. There was a coffee carafe and a tray of sweet rolls on the table. Lois pulled out a chair and sat down.

"June, isn't it a nice morning?" she asked.

Thirty years of cop training told me that the two women seated at the table were related. While their hair was different, their ages years apart and their clothing generations apart, they had the same eyes and turn of the mouth, sort of a cupid's bow with one side a bit more pronounced, alluring in a cute sort of way. Granddaughter Julie looked at me, then at Pete, while June formulated her opinion of the morning.

"Yes, it is. Every day is great." She was looking at Pete with the interest of a long-lost friend at a high school reunion, not quite sure if the person she was looking at was the person she remembered from school. Julie had agreed to introduce him.

"Mom, you remember Elmer Anderson, don't you?" Julie said.

She said, "Elmer?"

I pulled the remaining chair out and waved Pete into it. Time for the play to begin.

"June, how are you?" Pete said as he sat down.

Pete and I had dug up as much history on his Gramps as we could find, including one very long phone call with his sister, Ruth. We hoped he had enough background to carry his part of the conversation.

"Oh Elmer, how long has it been? You look different. I know. You've shaved off your mustache."

Pete and I looked at each other. Neither of us had ever seen Gramps with a mustache, not even in any of the old pictures Pete had dug up. Pete went with it.

"Yes, I did. It was too itchy."

June leaned forward and said in a conspiratorial voice, "Well, I'm sure that Emma is grateful. You know, she always hated that thing."

Again, exchanged glances. This was almost fun. I started to wonder where it would lead.

"Yes, she told me after I shaved it off. I would have shaved it sooner if I'd known."

"Where is she? I'm surprised she isn't with you."

"She's in the Cities. She asked me to stop in and see you while I'm up here on business."

June nodded her understanding. She leaned back in her chair and looked out the window.

"I always think of her in the fall. Winter's almost here you know."

"Why do you think about her in the fall?" Pete asked. Unconsciously, I leaned forward in my chair to listen more closely.

"Well, that's obvious, isn't it? The winter of '34–'35, when we had the big flu epidemic. Emma and I were about the only two in the whole town who didn't get it. It started around mid-December, almost right now, isn't it? What with everyone down sick, she would come to town every day and the two of us would take hot soup around to everyone who was housebound. My mother, bless her soul, would make the soup. Pa would close up at noon and come home from the bank and help get the soup ready, then he'd drive us around to deliver it. Those were awful days. The Depression was still in full force. The dust storms were awful all summer, even some in winter. Then that horrible flu. So many people sick, so many funerals. I wonder how we made it through."

June's granddaughter Julie had told us in our pre-visit phone call that one of June's favorite things to talk about was the flu epidemic. So we had checked that out. Pete's grandmother and her friend June had been up to their necks in sick and dying people—all at the tender age of fourteen. June's family was a town family, meaning that they worked and lived in town. By the standards of the times, they were rich. June's father ran one of the two banks in Alamo. He had a car and their house was one of the few with indoor plumbing. Grams and June were best friends even though Grams was a poor girl living outside of town on the family farm. Teenage friendship must have been much less dependent upon social status then than it is now.

"June," Pete said. "This is Dan, a good friend of mine and Emma's, and this is Will. He's also a friend. Can you tell them some of the stories about you and Emma? I know they'd like to hear them from you."

"Why don't you tell, Elmer? You know them as well as I do."

"Yes, I know all of Emma's stories, but you've known her longer than

I have. Emma and I didn't really get to be close until we decided to get married. And then there were all those years I was off to war while Emma stayed home with little Karl."

June's eyes started at the mention of little Karl. He'd struck a nerve. Pete saw it too and stayed on topic.

"What did the two of you do all that time I was gone?"

"Why, we did what everyone else did, we supported you boys off at war. We grew vegetables and walked to save gas and rubber and had a pot drive to collect aluminum for the airplanes. Some of the girls went off to the big cities to work in the factories or be Doughnut Dollies. Why, I remember Ethyl Fredericks went off and started flying airplanes. She was in the WACs. Every now and then she'd just drop in on us out of the blue. She would be delivering an airplane from the factory in New York, I think it was. Yes, that was it. It was the Grumman plant on Long Island and she would fly fighter planes out to San Diego or Seattle, where they'd load them onto a ship and send them off to the South Pacific. She couldn't land them in Alamo, of course, but she'd fly low, she and her friends, buzzing the town and waggling their wings. Sometimes there were a dozen of them. Then they'd fly down to Williston to stop overnight and her parents would go and get her and the other girls who were flying with her and bring them up to town for dinner and a place to sleep. She was a real hero to us. Not like you, of course, but a hero for us women. We were all devastated when we heard about her crash."

June shifted her gaze from Pete's face and looked out the window at the winter sky. It was a low-overcast gray day, heavy and threatening. She seemed lost in her thoughts about the woman flyer, as if she'd just heard the news for the first time. In a way, maybe she had. Her affliction caused time to become fluid and changing, not the constant the rest of us live in. She could skip from point to point in her life with the smoothness of an Olympic ice skater changing an edge. A moment ago she was with us here in her present, about 1955 by my estimation, then she was back in 1944, hearing about the death of the town's heroine. She stared aimlessly.

Two or three minutes passed and Julie said "Well, that's it for today."

Lois agreed and told us, "When she's done for the day, she does this, just kind of drifts off. She won't be able to help you any more until tomorrow. I suggest you try to get here earlier. She's really best first thing in the morning."

I looked at Pete and Will and we all rose simultaneously. Pete asked, "Should we say goodbye?"

"No real reason to. She doesn't even know you're here now. If she asks later, I'll tell her that you had to leave for a business meeting but you'll be back tomorrow. She'll be happy to see you again."

Lois led us out to the lobby and I shook her hand.

"Thank you for what we have so far. What time should we be here tomorrow?" I asked.

Lois said, "After 8:00 would be fine. That's right after breakfast. I'm sure tomorrow will be more productive."

With that we said our goodbyes and went out to the Sub. I pointed it east toward the city of Fargo. We took the 13th Street cutoff and rolled on down until I saw an Olive Garden. I cut across traffic and parked in the lot.

After being shown to a table in the back, we discussed the morning interview/trip down memory lane.

Will sensed the dismal state of mind both Pete and I were in and said, "I think this morning's talk was very interesting. It's clear that June recalls things from the past very well. It's highly likely she'll be able to remember both if Emma had a child after Elmer left for the Marine Corps, and with whom and when. That will give us a leg up on identification. In the meantime, I've got our people working on the material we found at Kline's home. We are tracking down his emails and phone calls from the last six months. That may give us direction as well."

When our soups and salad arrived, I asked Pete, "Did you know about Gramps' mustache?"

"Not at all. Every picture I've ever seen of him he's clean-shaven. That whole thing was just weird for me."

"You did great," Will said. "You were playing the part perfectly. When we resume this tomorrow, just keep her going on the past. She went a little further back than we need, but maybe you can work her up to the war period. That has to be when Emma had the baby, if it was Emma who produced your cousin's parent. From that we can work on birth records and adoption records. There were a lot of kids adopted because of war casualties. People often adopted the children of brothers lost in the war. Plus a lot of children were produced as the result of last-minute "I'm going to war tomorrow" trysts.

"I've got an idea that I want you to consider," I said. "We need to know who 'Forever Yours' is, right? How about we say that Emma is ill, that she has Alzheimer's, and that you were going through her things and found the letters? You aren't mad or upset about it, you just want to find out who it was so you can let him know that she's ill and that you thought maybe he'd want to visit, that a visit could help her condition?"

"That's a good approach, Dan," Will said. He thought for a moment, then looked at me. "You knew Emma pretty well, right? Another approach would be that you could say you're a doctor from the Cities and that you need to know who wrote those letters so you can contact him to talk about Emma's condition."

Pete was reluctant. "I don't know. It seems wrong to use Grams like that, like she's still alive. What if I slip up and say she's dead?"

"Don't," Will said. "Just be Elmer. You're here to talk to June about Emma's health and you need to know who 'Forever Yours' is to get some information to him about Emma's illness."

After lunch we loaded up and headed back out onto 13th. A little further east we came to a Holiday Inn Express. I pulled in and we walked into the lobby.

The desk clerk greeted us with, "Good Afternoon. Do you have a reservation?"

"No. Have you got any rooms?" I asked.

"Just happens that we do. I have just about anything you want. Mondays aren't real big around here. Wednesday through Saturday you can't get in, but today's not a problem. What would you like?"

Will stepped up. "These two are very close, but I'll need something in a single."

We all laughed, even the desk clerk.

I said, "Do you have any suites, something with two rooms?"

"Yes, we do. Our best room is a suite with two rooms. One is the bedroom, which has two queen-size beds; the main room has a living area, couch, game table and a small dinette. The dinette has a fridge and a microwave. I can let you have it for our off-season rate of $120 per night."

As I was thinking "Fargo has a season?" Will stepped in and said, "The rate should be the federal rate. We are all here on business of the federal government." He flashed his fed creds, complete with FBI badge. The clerk was suitably impressed.

"With those, you can just about name your rate. How about $45 per night for the suite and $30 for your room?"

"Sounds good."

We got our keycards and took a look at the room map. Both rooms were near the front of the hotel so I just moved the Sub out of the lobby lane to a nearby parking space and we unloaded from there. Pete and I pulled out bags and Will took his, which turned out to be a suitcase in disguise. It looked like a duffel, just like Pete's and mine, but it had wheels on one end and a pullout handle, just the thing for the yuppie lumberjack look. I don't know, I think if it looks like a duffel, you should have to carry it.

I told Will to stop down as soon as he got settled. Pete and I got the door open and found our way into the suite. I tossed my bag on one of the beds, unzipped it, and pulled out my stuff. One of the dresser drawers was quickly filled with a couple of extra sets of underwear. I hung up a shirt and a spare pair of slacks. I put my bathroom kit in the head, then pulled a rolled towel from the bottom of my bag. Pete walked in as I was unrolling the towel, which contained a bottle of Glenlivet and a Tupperware container of cashews.

"Now there's a man who's prepared," Pete said. "I'll get the ice."

Pete reappeared with Will in tow and a square plastic bucket of hotel machine ice. I'm not a big fan of hotel machine ice. I understand the reason the ice cubes are so small and useless because the machine has to produce them quickly to meet the demands of thirsty hotel guests.

But they melt too fast. I like a little ice in my scotch, but I don't like it watered down. I'd rather drink it warm than watery. I took the bucket from Pete and put a single layer of ice in the bottom of a hotel glass, which, thankfully, was real glass, then covered it with about two inches of single malt.

"I guess we're watching *Monday Night Football* in Fargo," Will said. "Who's playing anyway?"

Pete had picked up a "USA Today" in the lobby and had it open to the TV listings. He said, "Looks like Carolina and Tampa. That should be a lot of points."

We sent out for pizza, drank good scotch and wondered about the next day. Would the mystery be solved? Would we learn who "Forever Yours" was? Would the game be high scoring? Pete was right about that—Carolina 38, Tampa Bay 23.

Chapter Fifty-six

Tuesday, December 9
Fargo, North Dakota

The next morning came too early for me. I made my usual 5:00 a.m. piss call, then went straight back to bed. This is becoming the routine for mornings after parties as I mature. I used to be able to work all day, party hard all night, and I mean hard in the most suggestive way, and still rise and shine early the next morning. We used to make jokes about it. A bunch of guys would go off to a conference about some new body armor or some revolutionary new radio system, and we'd sit in classes and training sessions all day, maybe even spend time outdoors running through a shooting course with a new firearm, then party late into the wee hours. I mean wee hours. We'd get back to the hotel around 4:00 or 5:00 in the morning, catch an hour of sleep, take a shower and go back to class. We called it the $20 shower because, back then, the cop room rate was $20. I could do that for a week, sleep all weekend and be at work on Monday morning raring to go. Now, one moderately late night, a little scotch, bad pizza and football talk and I'm ready to sleep 'til noon. What happened to me?

Anyway, it happened to all of us, although I think Will went for a run. He's younger than Pete and I, so I'll allow it.

A complimentary continental breakfast used to be bad orange juice, overcooked coffee and your choice of stale plastic pastries. It's been upgraded recently, but I've always been a cereal guy, unless I'm entertaining. I hit the Cheerios and grabbed a banana. The other guys were already finishing up when I sat down.

"Finally woke up, I see," Pete said.

"I've been up for hours. Where've you been?"

"I've been out running with Special Agent Sanford. We got two miles in."

Will had the good manners to stay quiet. He chuckled at our banter but after a few minutes I could see he had other things on his mind. I asked him about it.

As we walked out to the parking lot, Will said, "I'm concerned about our line of questioning. We've got to rehearse this a bit. Going in there cold risks the possibility of a stumble that will make Mrs. Ingberg suspicious of us."

In the Sub on the way over to the retirement home we reviewed the game plan.

"So I just keep up the Elmer routine and see if I can talk her into telling us who 'Forever Yours' is?" Pete asked.

"Right," Will said. "Dan and I will try to help you out by directing questions when we can, but you need to carry the load on this."

"We aren't doing anything that's going to cause a problem later in court, are we?" Pete wanted to know.

"That is actually a very good question," Will replied. "I've been thinking about that. How a chain of information is put together will be brought up in court later on. The fact that Mrs. Ingberg has Alzheimer's is sure to be brought up by the defense, who will be questioning her capacity as a witness. The fact that we are leading her down this trail by pretending to be someone from her past will be a negative. But I believe that a good prosecutor will be able to show a jury that it was the only way to give her the chance to tell her story. As we've seen, she remembers the past very well. In her mind she's living in the '50s. And she remembers those days in the '30s and '40s as if they just happened.

"I recorded Monday's conversation with June," Will continued. That was the first I'd known of that. He pulled a very compact digital recording device from his inside jacket pocket. He passed it around. It was the smallest, lightest recorder I'd ever seen.

"This thing gets it right?" I asked, using the cop phrase for a clean recording.

"Clear as a bell. You just have to be sure it's not too close to your heart or you get heartbeats, too."

Pete gave it a professional look. His business background included some electronics design, though not like Ben Harris. I bet Ben would have something to say about this gizmo, like maybe he designed it. Pete gave it back to Will.

"Well, let's get this show on the road. No sense delaying it."

Unfortunately, it was not our day. June Ingberg was incoherent when we arrived at the retirement home. Her granddaughter told us that after really good days, like yesterday, she sometimes can be out of it for several days. She said that she would stay with her all day and call us if she came around, but not to get our hopes up.

So goes the life of an out-of-town murder investigator. We spent the balance of the day shopping, took in a movie, and went to the airport to see an old plane museum, which pretty much meant we'd hit all the highlights of Fargo culture. Actually, it was kind of nice to take a day off. We'd all been going pretty hard since this thing started and an unscheduled down day forced us to slow down. We went out to a Timberlodge Steakhouse, where the advertising slogan is, "Hope you're hungry." They mean it. I ate much too much and forced myself to try out my new swim trunks in the pool. I did twenty laps, then went to the room to crash.

Chapter Fifty-seven

7:00 a.m.
Wednesday, December 10
Fargo, North Dakota

Wednesday was another cold gray day. The weather guessers were saying something was coming in from Canada and would be here by the week-end. I didn't care much because I expected to be back in my woodshop by the weekend. I dressed in a pair of dark brown woven slacks and a wool shirt with a subtle blue and brown plaid pattern that I was able to cover with the sweater I'd worn on Monday's drive. I knew the retire-ment home would be warm so I'd switched to a shoulder holster under the ample shirt. I'd be able to remove the sweater and not spook the residents with a big black pistol hanging from my hip.

We met again for breakfast in the hotel's dining area. This time I went with the self-made waffle, mastering the waffle flipper on the first try. More fresh fruit and coffee and I was good to go. "Anything new in the federal world today?" I asked as I sat down.

Will had news.

"I received a message to call my office early this morning. They've tracked emails from Kline during the period he would probably have been setting this up. Emails people send and receive leave a trail. People get them and think that they have the "original" but they don't, they have a copy. The original is still out there in cyberland someplace. The Bureau is very good at following these leads; it's something that we've been developing since 9/11. So far, we think he was talking with some-one in Williston, North Dakota. The messages went to a server there but the end user is off the 'Net. The boys in the lab think they can nail down the exact address, and I mean the physical address, not virtual address, of the receiver. But it's going to take another day or two."

"So whoever hired Kline lives in Williston?" Pete asked.

"No way of knowing that. Only that someone there was in communication with Kline prior to the attempted murders."

"So that's our next stop?" I asked.

"Probably. But I want to see what other information we can get from Mrs. Ingberg. Hopefully, she'll be with us today and we can get to the bottom of who 'Forever Yours' is."

"Yeah, I sure hope she's back in her world today and we can talk to her," I added.

It was only a ten-minute drive to the retirement home. On the way over Pete, who had been somewhat reserved at breakfast, made an announcement.

"I got a call from my brother-in-law Steve last night. He's been checking around to see what the mineral deed might be worth."

"Yeah? Any luck?" I asked.

"He says he's got a friend who has a friend up here in Bismarck that does that sort of thing. He sent him a copy of the deed and the guy got back to him yesterday saying that he'd be more than happy to broker the rights. I asked him what the rate would be and Steve said the guy told him he'd do it for 5% of the lease. So Steve asked him what the lease was worth."

By now Will and I are hanging on every word. I gave Pete a "Get to it!" look and said, "Should I be pulling the car over for this?"

"The guy told Steve that there are two types of leases—exploratory and production. Production leases are based upon a percentage of production, but they don't use those until the land has proven that it will produce. An exploratory lease is a set amount for the right to drill. Those are based on potential. The guy told Steve he thought he could lease most of the area. Some of it's already been ruled out but some if it is prime. He thought the total for a five-year exploratory lease would run between $250 million and $350 million."

The car went silent. Even the engine seemed quieter. No wonder Pete had been quiet this morning. Over a quarter of a billion dollars just to explore! And Pete and Ruth get it whether the driller finds anything or not. Presumably, if the wells came in, production leases would be worth even more.

"Well, shit," I muttered.

I parked in the same visitor space and we went inside. Lois was in the office and said that Julie, June's granddaughter, was already there and it looked like it would be a good day to talk to June.

Chapter Fifty-eight

8:00 a.m.
Wednesday, December 10
Western Horizons Retirement Home
Fargo, North Dakota

June Ingberg was seated at the same table with her granddaughter. It was as if the first meeting had only been interrupted by a few minutes instead of days.

We walked over quietly. Pete took the lead, sitting down next to June. She looked at him and smiled.

"Elmer, how are you? You look wonderful, especially without that scratchy mustache."

We weren't picking up where we'd left off; we were starting over. Pete could use what he'd learned at the first meeting as if it was his own knowledge.

"Yes, I finally shaved it off. How are you?"

"I've been just fine. You know, I'm visiting my daughter Judith here. She's been living here for two years now. We're planning her wedding."

Apparently June was in the year 1958. We knew that Judith lived in Bismarck, North Dakota, in '58, just prior to marrying and moving to Fargo.

"I know. We are so happy for you, Judith," Pete said to Julie. Julie nodded with an understanding sigh. She knew that today she was her mother in her grandmother's eyes. That was all right with her.

Pete continued. "June, I'm here because Emma asked me to talk to you."

"Where is she? When I saw you, I thought I'd see her too. You two are never far from each other. I've always admired that about you, that you and Emma stayed so close to each other. Where is she?" June repeated.

"Emma is ill. She had to stay home in Minnesota this trip."

"Oh, dear. I hope it isn't anything serious. You know, she and I were about the only two people in Alamo who didn't get the flu the winter of '35. She and I helped my father deliver soup to the people who were afflicted. That whole winter she never got sick even though she was seeing sick people every day. I hope it isn't anything serious."

"June, unfortunately, Emma is quite ill. She has cancer and it doesn't look good. She has been making her manners to everyone she's known throughout her life to let them know how she is and that she is safe in Jesus' arms and looks forward to seeing them again someday in heaven."

Pete is a man of great faith and I know that he was confident that his grandmother would have said just this if she'd known her fate. He wasn't acting when he told June that Emma wanted her to know that she would see her again.

"Oh, dear. Does she have long?"

"The doctors say just a few months. That's why she is trying to say goodbye to everyone."

"That sounds like Emma—always confident, always positive."

"But she can't reach everyone and she asked me to stop and see you when she learned I was coming here on business, to ask you for help on contacting some people."

"Here we go," I thought. Pete and I had come up with a list of people from Emma's past from an old church directory he'd found in her effects. We picked some folks that he could ask June about. This would get her talking before he got to "Forever Yours."

"June, do you know whatever happened to Oscar and Ida Johnson?"

"Oh yes. Oscar died a few years ago, 1955 I think it was. Ida moved to Corinth."

"How about Roy and Eilene Dullum?"

"I remember them from the old days in Alamo. They were married during the war, you know. Quite an event at the time. Not many people got married during the war." She paused, thinking. "They may have moved to Williston. Their daughter Linda and her husband did awhile back. Move, that is. You know, their children wound up all over the place. Their son moved his family to Vancouver, Washington, and their daughters are living in Oklahoma and Connecticut. They have a terrible time deciding what to do for the holidays."

This was going very well. June was on a roll. She remembered these details like she was reading them from the church directory. It was almost time to spring the big one.

"June, Emma wanted to contact Mr. Storbakken, you know, old Ole. Do you know what happened to him?"

"Ole Storbakken? He's still alive as far as I know. Did you know he came from Norway in 1905? He was twenty-three years old. It took him two years to get from New York to Alamo with his wife, Anna. She passed in '32, but Emma knows that. I think he moved west, some small town. Appam, yes, that's it, Appam. It's just a few miles from Alamo. That's where one of his sons lives. He'd be seventy-six now."

We had a time reference to pinpoint June's memory. If Ole had come to the U.S. in '05 at the age of twenty-three, he must have been born in 1882. If he's seventy-six now, she's living in 1958. Perfect. I nodded at Pete, indicating he should go ahead and drop the bomb.

"June," Pete leaned in close, "Emma has one more person she wants to contact. And I don't know who it is. She has letters from someone from her past. She told me to find him and let him know that she's ill. But I don't know who wrote the letters. All I know is that the writer signed each one 'Forever Yours.'"

June leaned back in the chair. She looked into Pete's eyes and tilted her head. A deeply sorrowful expression came into her eyes and she visibly slumped in the chair. I thought for a moment we'd pushed too fast, that she was going to drift off and we'd lose her again, maybe for days or even weeks. She drew herself together and leaned forward toward Pete.

"You knew, didn't you?"

"Of course. A man knows. No one knows Emma as well as I do."

"And all these years, what has it been? A dozen years that they've stayed in touch. That was all right with you?"

"I love Emma more than anything else in this world. I can forgive her anything."

"I tried to tell her to let go, but she wouldn't. All those letters. She would write to him and he would write to her. They both wrote to me, really. They'd send the letters to me and I would forward them. We had to do that after he came back from the war and found out that his family had intercepted all the letters from him to her and vice versa. He'd tried to send letters to her through his family but they just tore them up. She was already married to you and she didn't know what was going on with his family here in Alamo. Then the two of you moved away right after the war so by the time he got home Emma was really gone. When he came back he found out what his family had done, keeping all his mail away from her. That was when he sent the first one to me and I sent it on to Emma. I know it was a bad idea, but I had to. Emma is my best friend."

"So you are the go-between?"

June nodded.

"And he sent letters all through the war?"

"Of course. He was still in love with her. He didn't know what happened to Emma until he came back and tried to find her. He finally got in touch with Emma's family and they told him about you and the baby."

"Me and the baby?"

"Yes, of course the baby. After all, he came only six months after you two were married."

"Karl?"

"Yes, Karl. Emma told me that you knew she was pregnant with Karl when you married her. Since you had been courting on and off for over three years everyone said it was all right if the engagement was short. And no one was really surprised when Karl came so quickly. It wasn't that uncommon for two people who'd been courting a long time to have a baby soon after the wedding. You know what your mother used to say—'The first one can come anytime, after that it takes nine months.'

"Emma told me that you weren't the father, couldn't have been because you two had never, well, you know, been 'together.' It was so good of you to marry her anyway, and take Karl as your own. I'm sure she must have told you who the father really was."

Pete hesitated, not knowing where to go with this line. He punted.

"Of course," he lied.

"Then you know who it is."

Chapter Fifty-nine

Pete looked at me, then Will. I gave him a slight shrug of my shoulders. Clearly, I had no idea where to go with this. I looked at Will and he was as lost as both of us. Julie recognized our dilemma and helped us out.

"Mom, I don't know who this person is. You've never told me about him. Tell me about him now."

June looked at Julie and smiled.

"He is the kindest man I know, present company excepted, of course," she nodded in Pete's direction. "He's older than Emma and me, so I suppose we both were taken with him back in those days. When you're a young girl on the prairie you spend a lot of time thinking about your prospects. He was always at the top of all the girls' lists, town girls and farm girls alike. After all, he was handsome and his family had property and money. That was something in the '30s, what with the Depression and all. The last time I saw him, he was still as handsome as when he was young, no scratchy mustache for him. He even looks a bit like you, Elmer," she said, looking at Pete, "only you've always had a stronger build. But that's to be expected, what with you a farmer and him a town boy.

"You know," she said to Julie, "I set my cap for him, too. Even though Emma is my best friend, I knew that whoever caught Frederick would be making the catch of a lifetime. But he never really showed interest in any girl except Emma."

Frederick.

"If he showed interest in Emma, why didn't she catch him?" Julie asked.

"Well, the families, of course. I think Emma's family would have been all right with it, but not his. After all, his family was a town family. His family owned a big part of Williams County; they own even more now. Even before the war, his father always had plans for him. That's why they sent him away to school when he was eighteen." She leaned forward and said in a conspiratorial hush, "They really sent him away to get him away from Emma."

With a knowing nod, June leaned back and went on. "They could see what was happening even if the two of them, Emma and Frederick, thought no one knew.

"He was going to be the first in his family to go to college, and he did. They weren't going to let him take up with some girl of a poor farm family often living on 160 acres.

"So he went off to college in the fall of '38, and graduated in '42. He was supposed to come home after college and prepare to take over the family business, but the war interrupted everyone's lives. He could have come home then, many young men did because this part of the country is agricultural and those men were exempt from military service, but he saw his duty and went straight into the service."

"What did he do in the service?" Pete asked.

"Why Elmer, I thought you knew. He was in the Navy, a fighter pilot. He served in the South Pacific, same as you did. After the war, he and I were friends, as you might suppose, since I was his Cupid, so to speak. I asked him about his war experiences. Then, when Emma and I talked, we compared notes. It turned out that you and he were in a lot of the same battles. Of course, he was on a ship and you were a Marine on the ground. But Emma and I think that you fought in some of the same battles."

"Do you know which battles?" Pete asked.

Pete had become obsessed with his grandfather's service record after we found his decorations in the safe at the house. After that discovery, he had done a lot of research. He found the original citations, read them and, after comparing them with his grandfather's journals from the war, knew which battles they were for. June was telling him that his grandmother had a relationship with a man who might have been in the same battles.

"I think there was one on an island called Peleliu. I'm not sure how to pronounce it. You were there with the Marines and he was there flying from a ship called the *Essex*. He flew an airplane called a Hellcat. I never liked that name, didn't sound right. They were flying Wildcats before that and I thought that was a good name. But that new plane's name, I don't mind telling you, a lot of people did not like that name.

"Anyway, we read about it in the Williston paper before we knew the two of you were there. It said a group of Marines were pinned down at the bottom of the only hill on the island and Frederick attacked the hill until he was out of ammunition and almost out of gas. He told the other planes coming in where the enemy was so they could protect the Marines. He had to leave or crash his airplane. But what he did was enough. The Marines escaped and he received the Distinguished Flying Cross for his flying that day."

Pete was deep in thought. He remembered the citation for his grandfather's Navy Cross. It was for holding a position on Peleliu under withering enemy fire long enough for Navy fighters to come in. Then, because his radios were out, he used smoke grenades to show the fighters where the machine-gun nests were. The citation read, "At great personal risk to himself, Captain Anderson pinpointed the enemy positions for the Navy fighters, resulting in their elimination."

"I remember that day. My platoon was pinned down. We couldn't move because the Japanese machine gunners had us covered. They were moving in snipers, climbing the few remaining trees to get a shot at us. Normally we could get air support from our own Marine flyers, but they had been in the fight all day and had to refuel and re-arm. The Navy flyers were responsible for fleet-defense, fighting the Japanese bombers and the Zeros. A few of them were let go to come and help us. If the Hellcats hadn't come in and rescued us, I'd still be there."

"Then that's it. Emma used to say that both her men were in peril that day and that God brought them both through safe and sound."

"So after the war, when Frederick came home and found that Emma had married me, he still sent letters to Emma and she sent letters back to him?" Pete asked.

"Yes. He came home and he was very upset with his mother. She was the one who had engineered their separation in the first place, then prevented their letters from reaching each other during the war. I heard there was quite a hubbub. It was the talk of the women's groups for a couple of weeks, then Margit, Frederick's mother, settled down and things got back to normal."

"Margit, Frederick's mother," I thought. I looked and Will was writing a note to himself on his iPhone.

We were close. We had a first name, we had his mother's name, we knew he was from Alamo and had returned there after the war. We knew he was a little older than Grams and that he'd flown fighters in the Navy in World War II. And now we knew he was the biological father of Karl, which would make him Pete's biological grandfather and that might explain the burglar-cousin connection. It was all coming together but we didn't have the rest. Without an identity we didn't know who, in today's world, could have perpetrated these crimes.

The biggest question was still, "Why?" Why had someone done these things? I went back to *Star Trek*—"Look to passion or gain, these are the motives for murder." Julie tried to help us again.

"Mom, this man sounds very interesting. Is he still in Alamo? How can Elmer get in touch with him?"

"I have his address right here." She tapped her temple, indicating the location of the address. "I've been mailing letters to him for over ten years."

Chapter Sixty

Our collective breaths stopped. An address! That would be fantastic. Will, Pete, and I all looked at Julie, mind-thrusting her to get that address.

Pete asked her, "Can you tell me his address?"

"It's a post office box in Williston, number 4205. That's where I send the letters so his wife won't get them at home. Pretty sneaky, huh?" June lowered her head and winked at Pete over this bit of subterfuge.

Of course, that wouldn't help us. We needed an address. Once again, Julie helped us out.

"Mom, Elmer needs to talk to him. He can't live at the post office. Where does he live?"

"In Alamo. The big house right on Tallman Street, right down the block from the Zion Lutheran Church. His family owns the biggest house in town. All us girls dreamed of living in it with him, raising his children and growing old with him. He was the best catch in town."

June looked out the window as she had on Monday, almost visibly drifting back in time to her childhood in Alamo. We were done for today.

We had collected several valuable clues. His name was Frederick, his mother's name was Margit, he'd served in the Navy as a fighter pilot and had been awarded the Distinguished Flying Cross—they don't just pass those out, so we should be able to narrow that down. We knew that his family lived in a big house on Tallman Street in the block with the Lutheran Church. We practically had a GPS location to "Forever Yours."

I looked at Julie and she nodded agreement that it was time to leave.

We all got up, thanked Julie and left her with June. In the hall I thanked Lois for all her help.

"Do you think this will help you find Emma's killer?" she asked.

Will answered, "I think it will tell us who wrote the letters. We still have to find a connection to Emma's murder."

Back in the Suburban Will said, "Pete, get out that letter from 'Forever Yours,' the one about your getting the National Science Honor. Read it again."

Pete flipped through the letters and found the one in question.

He read it aloud, again.

"My Beloved, I have received your latest missive and I am delighted to read that your grandson has achieved such a notable recognition as a National Honor Scholar and is seen as one of the future leaders of our country. Truly, I am confident that he will accomplish great things in his life, especially if he continues to pursue the science education he shows such aptitude for. Perhaps he will someday be an astronaut and walk on the moon. I couldn't be more proud if he were my own grandson."

Will interrupted, "You both caught that line about 'couldn't be more proud if he was my own grandson' didn't you?"

We both nodded agreement.

"I think that was a clear reference that Pete is his grandson. He knew, but apparently they didn't talk about it openly in the letters."

We all went silent. Pete was trying to wrap his head around the idea that his grandfather wasn't his grandfather, that his father was the result of a pre-marital fling. I was trying to construct a family tree in my head—I've always been very visual—so I could place the different names in the proper places. And Will was digesting what to do next and where this would lead.

What Will didn't say to us was that what we'd learned today should lead to the murderer and, with some luck, to whoever was behind the attempt to kill Pete and his family. If we can find that person or persons we might learn the why behind all this, and why was still the biggest question of all.

Chapter Sixty-one

We checked out of the hotel and packed up the car. I figured lunch was in order so I wheeled us over to a place called Culver's. As we ate I asked the boys the "Now what?" question.

"Why don't we go down to our local office? They may have some more on Mr. Kline by now," Will responded between bites.

"You have an office here?" Pete asked.

"The feds are everywhere, omniscient, omnipresent, ubiquitous, everywhere," I said with mock reverence.

"Yes, we have an office here. It's sort of a branch of our Minneapolis office, which is a regional office," Will said.

As we mounted up yet again, I said, "Give me the address and I'll put it in the machine."

I entered the address into the GPS and the gizmo worked its magic, pointing us east on 13th. After a zigzag course necessitated by Fargo's rail lines, we arrived in front of a typical product of governmental architecture—a five-story building, three brown brick floors above two plain concrete floors. There was angled parking across the street with open slots. I guess the feds didn't get that many visitors. The building had a large round seal of the federal government of the United States of America hanging at the second floor level and the words "Federal Office Building" embossed into the concrete wall protecting the entrance from errant vehicles.

We crossed the street, entered the lobby and found the elevators for the ride up to the fourth floor. There, we passed through the glass doors into what looked like the entrance to any law office or accounting firm. That impression was correct in this case, as nearly all FBI agents are either lawyers or accountants. The only big difference in this office was the presence of a large American flag, an equally large flag carrying the seal of the Federal Bureau of Investigation on a blue background, and the fact that the receptionist was quite obviously armed.

Will got the three of us through the reception area, a process that included checking all three of our weapons. Normally, private citizens, like Pete, are forbidden to carry a weapon onto federal property, no matter what they had for permits, but neither Will nor I liked the idea of leaving a gun in the car. So Will said he'd get Pete's gun OK'd and checked without any hassle.

Did I mention that Pete has a carry permit? His Minnesota permit, which is not recognized by North Dakota, is accompanied by a non-resident New Hampshire permit, which is. Between the two permits he is licensed to carry in twenty-seven or twenty-eight states; I'm not sure which ones. Anyway, he checked his .45-caliber Kimber Pro Crimson Carry II, I checked my .40-caliber Springfield XDM, and Will checked his popular-with-the-feds FN FiveseveN. Three completely different firearms, all made for the same purpose—close personal defense.

An agent came out to meet us and take us back to a conference room. The room looked like any other I'd been in during my career—rectangular, about twelve by twenty, with a long dark-oak table surrounded by comfortable swiveling office chairs. A computer terminal sat on each end of the table. One end of the room had a combination white board and projection screen and one of the long walls had windows that were covered with semi-translucent drapes, presumably to keep out prying eyes. They also had blinds in case there was a need to darken the room. The overhead lighting was harsh fluorescent and the beige carpeting was clean but worn.

A local FBI agent, Kyle Harms, had a file for Will. Clearly, he'd known we were coming. That's one of the wonders of working with the feds. They have sort of a Big Brother cuteness to them that will rear its ugly head every now and then. Just when you think they're keeping you in the game, you find out that they had a completely different game going on. We were about to be given a case in point.

Pete and I waited for Will and Agent Harms to start things off. Pete waited out of courtesy; I waited out of experience with these people. We were on fed turf now and we would be playing by their rules, at least until we got our pieces back and cleared the building.

Don't get me wrong. Will has always played straight with me. I just have plenty of other fed experiences that make me a little nervous. You want to put one hand on your wallet and the other on your dick just to make sure you don't lose anything important.

Will looked through the file Harms brought and started us off with a zinger.

"Mr. Kline was paid one million dollars through six different wire transfers into an offshore bank account. We can reach that conclusion by looking at his bank activity for the past four months. The last eight transactions on that account included six deposits and two withdrawals. We are working on the withdrawals now. We want to determine where and for what that money, roughly $28,000, went."

"Somebody was willing to pay a million bucks to knock off my family?" Pete asked.

"Looks that way. Actually, it was probably more. This was probably the down payment with the balance paid upon successful completion of the contract. The question is still why?" Will said.

Will went on. "I want to talk about the stuff we heard today, about figuring out Pete's family tree. Did I hear her say that Pete's grandmother was pregnant when she married his grandfather?"

"Yes, she said that Grams was pregnant and Gramps knew about it and went along with it. She said that Grams and Gramps had been courting—I love that word—for a couple of years, so no one was suspicious. She said that 'Forever Yours' had knocked-up Grams and then left town. I don't think I like this guy," I added.

Pete said, "I'm not sure that's how it went. I think she said that Frederick's family sent him away to college and he left without knowing that Grams was expecting, that he wrote her all through the war but his family didn't want the relationship to succeed. He didn't know about the baby until he returned after the war. Then he got in touch with Grams through June.

"I've read all the letters and they don't say anything about the baby—my dad, Karl. The letters were very general, talking about their personal lives and not about any family at all. Why is that, do you think?"

Will answered. "Oddly, in cases like this where there is a long-term relationship, and I've worked them before, the two participants usually follow one of two scripts. Either they discuss nothing but their families or they never discuss their families. I read most of the letters you copied for me. In this case, it looks like they did discuss their families, but not exclusively. They also discussed their relationship. They wanted to stay in touch but didn't want to bring their own families into it. They wanted to know what each other was doing personally, things like church, work, travel, education, but not who they traveled with. That was too personal, perhaps too painful, too strong a reminder of what they didn't have together. So they developed a relationship sort of like very good business partners—concerned with the other's well-being but not going into a lot of details."

I thought this was pretty insightful for a guy who was yet to turn forty. Maybe there was a new kinder, gentler Bureau I'd never seen before. He went on.

Looking at Pete, he said, "I think that 'Forever Yours' is your biological grandparent, the one you share with the burglar. I think when we figure out who 'Forever Yours' is, it will lead us to the burglar and we will be able to figure out who hired Kline. Then maybe we'll be closer to why this is all going on."

Will turned to a computer at his end of the table. He said, "I'm entering the information we have on 'Forever Yours.' From here on, I'm going to call him Frederick. We know that he would be about eighty-nine if he is still alive, but we don't think he's alive based upon the last letter he sent."

"You don't think that's proof he died?" Pete asked.

"It's a probability. But it's not proof. Could be that he just decided to break it off and that was the easiest way to do it. You know—'I'm dead, so don't write anymore.' He was probably born around 1920 in the area of northwestern North Dakota. His family lived on Tallman Street in Alamo. That would have been in the '30s. He went to college. He flew in the Navy, was probably awarded the DFC for service in the South Pacific, probably on Peleliu. He returned to the Alamo area after the war, probably picked up the family business, very high probability that he married and produced at least one child, and that child produced at least one child."

Will finished his data input with a flourish and hit the "enter" key. With that motion, the entire data processing force of the Federal Bureau of Investigation was looking for "Forever Yours," aka Frederick. He looked at us and said, "Let's head west. I think we'll find our answers there."

Chapter Sixty-two

2:00 p.m.
Wednesday, December 10
Williston, North Dakota

Winter was definitely nearby. You never know in this part of North America. Some years you're shoveling snow by the end of September, other years you're still playing golf in December. Granted, you have to wear a jacket and gloves on both hands and the ball gets a nice bounce off a very firm fairway, but it's still golf and you are outdoors. This year was somewhere in between. No real snow yet, temps had vacillated between freezing and thawing so the lakes and ponds were still not really frozen; some even opened up during the day. That wouldn't last. Simon had lived here all his life and he knew that winter was unstoppable, that it came at its own pleasure and stayed however long it pleased, kind of like bad relatives. And like bad relatives, it was frustrating, annoying and expensive.

As Simon sat at the desk formerly occupied by his brother, he pondered a family photo that included him. It was the one memento of his brother's that remained from the days prior to his unexpected death. Why Simon left it there, he didn't know. It was a reminder to Simon of happier times, times where it was easy to be number two in the business. Those times were over.

Simon had adjusted well to all the changes. As he gazed at the picture, he realized how surprised he was that his brother's widow, April, had adjusted as well. She was a strong-willed, intelligent woman who was looking out for her children's future. She didn't want Simon to cut them out of the family's growing business. She wanted a spot for herself in the company.

In the seven short months since his brother's untimely demise, she had not only adjusted to her loss but had found herself that place in the organization. Actually, Simon had decided to create one for her. First he had to determine her skills. She had some business savvy but certainly not enough, in his opinion, to deal with clients. She had rudimentary secretarial skills, but he knew she'd be insulted if he offered her a desk and a computer terminal. "Computer terminal" had triggered an idea. The company had recently changed its computers and had gone to an upscale central server system tied into the Internet. Each user had an assigned terminal in their office or cubicle, but there were shared terminals in the meeting rooms and off site computers in employee's homes. In their home offices, employees could log into the central system and use their own desktop computers to work on files. Luckily, the techno-dweeb who had been running the system was leaving, so the system needed a caretaker, someone who could keep it running and up-to-date with the latest technology. Perfect, he'd thought. He'd sent her to the suppliers training center in Bismarck and she took over the computer system, drawing a nice salary, keeping her husband's health insurance for her kids and feeling like she was making a contribution.

April had returned a month ago and he was surprised by her attitude. She was excited and had dug right into the job. In the last two weeks she'd already instituted upgrades that made their contract processing faster, their debt collection more timely and streamlined, and she'd straightened out the employee payroll/tax deposit system. She was happy.

Simon was happy, too, but not just because the system had been improved and certainly not because April had found fulfillment. His opinion of April was the same as his opinion of all women. Give them something to do, something that was boring or undemanding, and keep them happy. The job would keep April occupied and involved without letting her have any real decision-making power in the company. He'd take care of her, but that was all. He'd run the company the way he saw fit.

When he saw her in the break room two days earlier, though, she was visibly upset. She said that she wasn't sure, but she thought that someone outside the company had tried to break into their system. She had just updated the firewall protection program and on Monday afternoon had intercepted a message. She didn't know what the target was, maybe their oil lease contracts, maybe something else, and she was getting help from the support service to figure out the nature of the attack. They had said it was probably just some college kids hacking for the experience. Whoever it was, she was determined to find them.

He wasn't going to tell her, but Simon thought he knew what the break-in was about. Monday was the day he'd replaced his computer. The guy at the computer store had told him that no one could tell the difference between his new one and his old one, that he'd be able to plug it into the company's system and go right to work. If it was his computer that had somehow caused the glitch, he would tell April about the replacement and just say that he'd dropped the old one and the screen went out or some such. That would work for her. She wasn't a hardware expert; she had only enough training to make her an operator with some rudimentary programming skills. She'd never figure it out.

She hadn't mentioned anything since. Simon was glad because he had another problem to deal with. Paul Swanberg had just walked into his office.

Paul arrived at the office exactly on time, which was his nature. He was never early or late. He wore an expensive wristwatch that synched to satellites, not because it was stylish, but because it was the most accurate timepiece he could carry. It was part of Paul being Paul.

"Hello Paul. How are you today?" Simon asked with a fake sincerity that belied his real feelings. He didn't really care about Paul's condition today or any other day other than how it affected his ability to do business with him.

Paul took the chair in front of Simon's desk, but before he sat he checked to make sure the seat was clean. Simon had expected this and checked it himself about ten minutes earlier. He needed Paul comfortable and conversational. Simon spun around in his chair and poured a cup of coffee from a carafe on his credenza. He had preplaced a coaster for the cup. He knew that if there wasn't one there, Paul would hold the cup for the entire conversation rather than put it on the unprotected desk. Paul wasn't worried about hurting the beautiful wood desk; he was worried about the cup picking something up from the desk. Such was life with an obsessive-compulsive person.

Simon could see that Paul was upset. His usual control of his head bobbing was lacking today, and he could see that Paul's usual subtle rocking was more pronounced than normal. Paul was agitated.

"Paul, I think we've come to the point where we have to just go ahead with the leases. It's clear that you are never going to recover the original deed. We don't know if the original recipient of the deed even knew what she had." Simon decided not to say that she never would know now.

"The deed was never recorded and for all we know, it was destroyed. She could have received it and burned it out of spite. She may not have known what it represented and lost it out of disinterest. In any case, by alerting her family, all we've done is start the possibility of litigation.

"They may or may not have it now. We just don't know. But if they do, it's important that we act now. I think you should go ahead and just sign the leases before they do anything. Timeliness is of the utmost importance in cases like this, you know—who got there first. You have a clear, recorded title on all that land, including the mineral rights. If they find the old deed and bring it here to file it, they will be coming late to the table. We'll be able to question the provenance of the deed. We must go ahead with the filings in order to establish a timeline that puts you in front. I'll get the leases taken care of and you'll get the money."

"It's always the money with Simon," Paul thought, as he sat and listened, staring silently at the wall behind Simon's head.

It had always been that way with Simon. All through school Simon had been distant, cold, only interested in what was in it for him. He didn't understand the need for order, the need to do things according to a set of rules. The rules said that a deed was a deed and Paul knew, even if Simon wouldn't acknowledge it, that violating the rules would ultimately lead to failure. Paul wondered if he hadn't already started some kind of karmic failure sequence by what he'd done.

Though Paul didn't realize it, Simon had rationalized the entire sequence of events by telling Paul that this was the only way for him to protect his inheritance and, therefore, his legacy to whatever progeny he might produce in the future. Simon thought privately that Paul would never produce any progeny and he had planned on adding small print to the contracts that would leave himself in a position to control the land after Paul's death, whenever that might occur. He had even taken the chance of asking Paul to sign the leases before they had recovered the deed. Paul had refused that on the basis that doing so would be out of the proper order of events. So Simon had gone back to plan "A."

The key had been to convince Paul that pursuit of the original deed was imperative to going forward. He'd told him that only by assuring that the original recipient of the deed was out of the chain of title could Paul be sure that there would be no possibility of losing control in the future. In retrospect, Simon knew that had been a mistake.

Paul had argued that since there was so much money involved, they should approach the woman in Minnesota and offer to share with her. Simon was not a big believer in sharing. For all he knew this woman was just some one-night stand that old Frederick had had when he was a kid. "Hope she was worth it," Simon thought.

But he pretended to contact her. He told Paul he talked to the Minnesota woman and made the offer. After an acceptable amount of time went by, although he had done nothing, he told Paul that not only had his entreaties been rejected, that she was determined to totally close Paul out of the transaction.

Paul wasn't completely put off by this, as he was still very wealthy, so Simon concocted a tale that the Minnesotans were going to use the deed as evidence that they were, in fact, the rightful owners of the entire Swanberg holdings in North Dakota and that they were determined to leave Paul penniless.

This was Paul's motivation to break into the Edina home and find the deed. By invoking the importance of his legacy he made it a hierarchical question for Paul. In Paul's world it was all right to break a rule in order to uphold a more important rule. By saying that no one would know and that he was upholding a higher priority rule, it wasn't really a violation of the rules. Killing the woman, even though it was "accidental," was the result of that chain of bad karma telling him that it knew he had broken the rules. The dog running him off at the grandson's home was further proof that karma was still not on his side. Paul knew that the only possible course to success was to go to the remaining family members and make things right with them. If that meant that he had to go to prison, so be it. He was ready to do that. The only roadblock was Simon.

"I've thought about it and I think I should go to the authorities," Paul said. "That's the only way to make this work out right. I'll just have to tell them what I was doing and that Mrs. Anderson's death was an accident. Maybe I'll only get some prison time, but I checked the Minnesota criminal code and, as a first-time offender, it's likely that I could get by with a plea of unintentional homicide and a sentence of only a few years at a minimum-security facility. I could get out in time to still enjoy some life after."

This was not what Simon wanted to hear. Paul didn't know about the attack on the Andersons and Hammers. If he did, he'd be concerned about a little more than a few years in the slammer, to say nothing about his own complicity. Simon quickly debated the pros and cons of telling him now. He decided not to.

"Paul, I know that you worked hard to try to get that deed. I know that it was personally very tough for you to do what you did. But it seems that there is no trail back to you. There have been no inquiries, no calls from the authorities. If there was any official interest, I'd know. My contacts at the police department would have called me if anyone was asking questions about you. I've asked them to do that."

This much was true. Simon had friends on the Williston PD and he'd asked them to keep an eye out for anything concerning his old friend Paul. After all, Paul was a "special person," with a special problem but was also a leading member of the community and he needed people to keep an eye on him. His police contacts had agreed.

Paul wasn't convinced that the authorities weren't already on to him.

"They could be watching us right now. I've been keeping a close eye out for anyone strange in the area and I haven't seen anyone yet, but you can never tell. I think it's time for me to go to the authorities."

Simon tried to keep the exasperation he was feeling out of his voice. "Paul, you don't want to do that. You can always go to them later. Let's give it another week or two and see what happens, OK?"

Paul thought for a full minute before saying, "All right. We can sit tight for another two weeks. But if anything looks like the authorities have figured it out, I think it is in my best interest to go to them first. That looks proactive and will help me in court."

Simon got up, saying, "Then it's settled. You go home. I'll get the leases prepared so we can still make that year-end deadline for tax purposes. Have a good Christmas. Say hi to your parents for me."

Paul got up to leave. "Do you think we'll still get the prices we've talked about?"

"Sure. Why not? The oil is still there and they still want it. Maybe we should hold out for more."

Paul walked out and Simon sat back down. "Now what am I supposed to do with him? If I can't calm him down he's going to go to the cops and that will lead them straight to me, unless," he muttered, "I can lay that stupid Kline on him. Then I'd still be out of it.

He started thinking about that.

Chapter Sixty-three

4:00 p.m.
Wednesday, December 10
On Interstate 94, between Fargo and Bismarck, North Dakota.

On the way out of Fargo I decided our little road trip needed some healthy competition. I came up with an idea and got the ball rolling. I hit two numbers on my phone.

"Detectives. Sharon Rademacher speaking."

"Hey babe, how they shaking?"

"Like you'll ever find out. How about you? You keeping your nose clean?"

"Barely. I'm on the road with Pete Anderson and some suit from feddieland."

"That's got to be fun. How are you staying awake?"

"Good question. Listen, I've got a bet with our friends in black here that I, meaning you, can find someone faster than they can. I'm going to give you what we have and turn you loose. The other guys have about an hour head start on you."

"That won't be enough. What do you have?"

We're looking for a white male, born circa 1920 in northwestern North Dakota, probably in the vicinity of a town called Alamo. He would have at least one child and at least one grandchild. He was in the Navy in World War II, flew fighters in the Pacific, was at the battle of Peleliu and was awarded a Distinguished Flying Cross for action in that battle. His first name is probably Frederick, mother's name Margit, spelled M-a r-g-i-t. He lived on Tallman Street in Alamo and his family was probably well known and well-funded."

"Sounds like a piece of cake. That fire in Missouri might slow them down. I'll let you know. How much is on the line?"

I looked at Will who had been eavesdropping with great interest. Without consulting him I said, "$100."

"I'll take another $50 if he's got the stones," she answered.

Will nodded. I guess it was in the Bureau's budget to cover wagers when protecting their reputation as the finest research organization on the planet.

"He'll take it. Call me."

"You seem pretty confident about that bet," Will said after I hung up.

"You betcha. What you don't know is that there exists another intel network, one that isn't all computers and files. It exists between people like Rademacher and her counterparts in police departments all over the country. While your guys are looking in the record books, she will be calling people in Williston and Bismarck, asking them for favors. Maybe she'll just look it up on Ancestry.com. I don't know. But she'll have it before we get to Bismarck."

"We'll see," he said with a touch of disdain in his voice.

Pete asked, "What was the talk about a fire in Missouri?"

Will answered. "Back in the '50s sometime, I'm not sure when it was, there was a fire at the main Defense Department storage center in Missouri. A lot of the personnel files from World War II were destroyed. It's plagued the Bureau and other law enforcement agencies looking for records on veterans ever since."

I chimed in, "And, that's why she'll win. She'll be talking to locals who will surely remember a Navy DFC flyer whose family is rich. She'll have it first."

We drove on in silence, each of us cogitating on the last three day's events. I squinted into the late afternoon sunset. The land here was as flat as the clichés, the sleeping fields chilling in the declining daylight. The sky was clearing and the setting sun was the first we'd seen of it since we'd left the Cities. The low sun created a full-horizon pallet of reds, oranges and yellows. As we rolled along at over eighty miles per hour, the local custom, we were all wondering what the next day would bring. We were chasing something across the northern tier of the United States like some old-time U.S. Marshals. I was glad I had federal authority with me, and I was starting to wonder if I should have brought Pete on this part of the ride. What would his reaction be if, in the next day or two, he came face to face with the man who had killed his grandmother?

Over northern Alaska the storm was getting its act together. It was a bit larger and stronger than most winter storms, but not completely out of the ordinary. It slowed and built its strength as it crossed the border into Canada, before it started sliding southeast along the Yukon–Northwest Territories line. Its destination was a point on the map where the borders of North Dakota, Montana, and Alberta meet, just thirty miles northwest of Alamo, North Dakota.

Chapter Sixty-four

On I-94 between Fargo and Bismarck

As we rolled west on I-94 I flipped on some music. I've got an "on the road" collection in my iPod that's plugged into my car's radio. No, I don't actually know how to do this; my nephew, who is, like most kids under ten years old, an electronics genius. I told him what music I like for what collections and he did the loading or programming or whatever it's called. All I have to do is turn the thing on. I leave the device in the car all the time so I don't have to worry about charging it or losing it. The gizmo itself is so small, about the size of a business card, that if I took it out, I'd lose it. The way my nephew has things set up all I have to do is turn it on and wheel the thumb switch around to what I want to hear. I needed Bob Seger.

We reached Bismarck in time for dinner. Along the way, Pete called ahead to the Best Western Ramkota for two rooms. I've stayed at the Ramkota in Sioux Falls. It's a nice Best Western-type hotel, meaning that it will have a restaurant, a workout room and a pool along with decent rooms. Once again, we got a single for Will; Pete and I would share a suite.

Pulling into the drive in front of the lobby I was struck by the architecture, which was sort of a combination of Prairie and Spanish Southwest. The overhang above the drive had tapered stone pillars supporting a faux timber gable that matched the gables on the rest of the hotel. We walked into the lobby, took care of the paperwork and agreed to meet in the restaurant in twenty minutes.

Pete and I found our suite; it had two rooms, separated by a double door. The main room had a couch that I assumed was a hide-a-bed, a table with four chairs and another loveseat. The colors were muted browns and tans, good colors considering these rooms were occupied by hunters every fall. The earth tones would help hide stains from mud and pheasant or goose blood. I tossed my bag on the couch and told Pete to take the king-sized bed in the other room. He's a lot taller than I am and I doubted he could fit on the hide-a-bed. We did a quick unpack and headed to the bar.

The restaurant had a definite upper-end men's club feel with heavy wood crown molding and coffered ceiling. The chairs were upholstered in tapestry fabrics and the carpeting had an old-fashioned dark-flower pattern. At 6:30 in the very western edge of the central time zone there was still just a hint of sunlight coming into the room. It would be dark before the salads arrived.

We had just started on the evening's first round of drinks when my phone rang. It was Rademacher.

"Hi sweetie, did we win?" she said brightly.

I hit the speaker button on the cell phone. "Depends. You find our guy?"

"Of course I did. It was easy as pie. I just called an old friend in the Williams County Sheriff's Office and told him what I was looking for. He checked around and they found the name, Frederick Yates Swanberg."

"She has an old friend in the Williams County Sheriff's Office?" Will asked. She heard it.

"Honey, I have friends everywhere. You ever hear of the International Police Games? Well, about six years ago my husband Sam was competing in weightlifting at the games when they were held in Vancouver, Canada. While we were there we met law enforcement people from all over the world. Most were from North America, but there were people from Europe and Australia and everywhere. Anyway, you know me, I kept a journal and it's right here at the office, just in case I ever need to call one of them. Joe Eid from Williams County was also in weightlifting."

Will shook his head. "Nothing will ever replace good old-fashioned personal contacts, will it?"

"You can have your computers, honey. I'll keep my notebook," Sharon said.

I asked, "Anything else on this Swanberg guy?"

"Yes, he's deceased. Joe said he knows the family and thought that Frederick passed around the mid-1970s. He had a son who is still alive, but retired early and moved to Arizona. His name is Oscar. And Oscar has a son who now runs the family business in Williston. His name is Paul Swanberg, age mid-thirties. Joe said that Paul has a reputation of being a bit odd, that the word was that Paul has a little OCD. He said one time he found him sitting at a stop sign, not moving. When he asked Swanberg what he was doing Swanberg said he couldn't go until thirty-three cars went by. He was counting them."

"Counting cars?" Will asked.

Sharon said, "That's what he said. I know a little about OCD. One of Sam's nephews has it. People with OCD will sometimes have a number that is special to them. They use it when they need to count things. In this case, I'd say Paul's number is three. When they are under stress, they will get "locked up," so to speak, and sit and count things over and over until something breaks them out of it. I asked Joe if he knew of anything that had happened in Paul's life the day he was counting cars and he said that it was the day Paul's mom, Betty Swanberg, had been diagnosed with cancer. She's still alive and the thought in the sheriff's department was that her illness was the main reason Paul's parents retired early and moved to Arizona."

"Did you happen to find out the family business?" I asked.

"Of course. It turns out that the Swanbergs own a huge chunk of land north and west of Alamo.

"How much land is a huge chunk?" asked Will.

"He said he thought it was around three quarters of a million acres. That's a big chunk in Minnesota."

"That's a big chunk in Texas. You have any contact info in Williston?" I asked.

"Not yet. I'll have something for you tomorrow."

"Great work, Sharon. I'll collect your bet for you" I said and disconnected the call.

"OK guys, I, for one, would like to meet Pete's long-lost cousin."

"So would I," Will added.

Pete sat lost in thought. I wondered how I'd handle a massive data overload like this. Hope I never have to find out.

"I think I'd like to see Alamo first," Pete said. "Do you think we could drive up there on our way to Williston?" he asked.

"Why not? I'll take a look at the map and plan it out," I said.

Will added, "I'm not in all that big a hurry to get to Williston anyway. I can wait to confront this guy until we have more solid evidence from my lab and the intel guys," Will said. "I'll check with my people here in the morning and see how the search is coming for the money source on the hit."

"Sounds good," I said. "We can stop at your office, then head out to Alamo."

Pete picked at his salad. I could see the revelation was still bugging him. I wanted to vent this now instead of waiting until we were driving tomorrow.

"Pete, are you still thinking about this burglar cousin of yours?"

"First off, we don't *know* anything. We *think* he's my cousin and we *think* he's the same guy that was at Grams'. We think he hired someone who tried to kill my family. We don't *know* anything," he repeated.

"It's looking pretty good to me," Will said. "We know a relative of yours was in your house. We know that Kline tried, very nearly successfully, to kill you. We know that someone paid Kline one million dollars as a down payment to kill you and your family. If we can connect the dots between Swanberg and Kline, that will tie things up rather nicely. The only thing we don't know is why? If we can figure that out, we'll be closer to an answer."

Pete said, "You know the OCD thing? I've had to fight that all my life. My son Jim has it, too. OCD is not restlessness or a short attention span. It's an attention to details that most people don't have. But that attention made me a better engineer and it will make Jim a better Naval officer. It doesn't have to be what people saw in that Howard Hughes movie. It's not always debilitating.

"Dan, have you ever noticed that the pictures hanging on the walls of my house are always perfectly plumb and true? You ever wonder why? Because they're screwed to the walls so they won't move. That's how I have to install them so they don't drive me nuts. You ever notice me straightening the pictures at your house?"

In fact I had. I nodded.

"You know how Carol is in the kitchen—all the latest equipment. She must own a dozen pairs of potholders. Have you ever noticed that I never use two that don't match? I can't. If two unmatched ones are on the top of the pile in the drawer, I have to dig until I find a matching pair.

"When Jim was a little kid, he had to line up all his Hot Wheels cars in a perfectly straight row. If you moved them, he'd go back and fix them. That's how it is with him. A certain order is necessary to keep us happy."

Dinner came and the discussion switched to football and the Vikings' chances. Will likes them; Pete loves them. I don't know. I've been disappointed too many times. Sort of like the times I put a little faith into someone I knew was a bad guy. You try to give them a chance to redeem themselves and they still go bad. While the other two were talking about quarterbacks, I was wondering about tomorrow.

Chapter Sixty-five

Thursday, December 11
9:00 a.m.

After three days on the road and too much time interviewing, thinking, and scotch, we all crashed early Wednesday night. A little extra sack time was appreciated by all. About 9:00 the three of us staggered into the hotel restaurant for a late breakfast. The buffet was over, which was OK with me. I'm all right with hotel buffets but only if I'm there when they open up. By the time the buffet is set to close, the food has taken on a unique texture that's hard to describe, sort of a cross between leather and rubber, and the taste has left the building. We ordered from the menu, all of us having nearly the same thing—eggs, toast, ham or bacon, hash browns, juice and lots of coffee.

"You guys check out yet?" Will asked.

"No, but we're packed. We can be out of here ten minutes after we're done with breakfast."

"Sounds good. We can stop over at our office here. I'd like to check in and see if they've had as good of luck as Sharon. We may have pictures, maps, and other info."

We finished off the coffee, paid up and headed to our rooms to get our bags and check out. Out in the parking lot I felt the cold chill of the northwest wind. A gray scud layer was starting to obscure the blue sky and I wondered if the forecasted weekend storm would hit a bit early. You get that way when you've lived in the Midwest all your life. You develop a sixth sense that tunes you into the weather. You start to watch the sky and pay attention to things like the birds and the squirrels loading up on food. Empty bird feeders mean a storm is on the way. I loaded our bags into the Sub and we pulled out onto 3rd Street heading north toward downtown Bismarck. At East Broadway I hung a right in compliance with the GPS's voiced instructions and went one block. The FBI offices were in a building shared with a Wells Fargo Bank. The architecture was similar to the Fargo office—solid, safe, and boring.

We took an elevator to the second level. Will again led the way through the check-in process. He left us in a conference room while he made his manners with the local boss, the Special Agent in Charge, or SAC. He's the local Capo, or boss in English. To others in law enforcement, the word SAC is appropriate enough to describe this position, but I've also heard non-fed fans describe them as the MFC for Mother Fucker in charge and MFCC for Mother Fucking Chief in Charge. These nomenclatures were not arrived at randomly; they were developed after long personal contact with the MFCCs by people who can recognize when an individual has an intuitive ability to cover one's ass, congenital skill at claiming credit for everything that goes right and ducking everything that does not, and an over-developed sense of self importance. In most, but not all, cases, the labels were highly accurate.

Will came back and sat down in front of the computer terminal. He was actually on a videophone call with one of his Minneapolis people where he could see and talk. Neat stuff, but I prefer a regular phone. That way I can still scratch where it itches without grossing out the person on the other end of the conversation. I stayed out of the computers camera's line of sight.

"You get anything on that info I sent you last night?"

The guy in the computer said, "Yeah, it looks like your source is correct. All the data plays out to be a Frederick Swanberg of Williston, North Dakota."

I looked at Will with a "What's this?" raised eyebrow smirk on my face.

He looked back at me and said, "I sent a possible ID to the Minneapolis office last night based upon that source we found. Looks like it panned out."

I shook my head. Even in the face of success and cooperation, it's tough for the feds to admit defeat. I wondered who'd be paying off the bets.

"Anything else on the Kline follow-up?" he asked.

"The tech guys have tracked down the source of both the emails and the cash transfers to a company in Williston. It's called Turner Mineral Leases, LLC, a company that specializes in brokering leases between drillers, oil companies and landowners. Basically, it's about a dozen or so people who sit in an office and generate paper. We haven't contacted them. I wanted to talk to you about it first."

More coordination. The feebies like to CYA with the best of them.

"Send me the contact info and I'll go see them when we get to Williston. We're heading there as soon as we're done here, but we're going by way of Minot, so if you need me before noon, you can send stuff to Minot for me."

Will looked at me and said, "We have an office in Minot, in case they send me something."

Again I replied with a shrug. I was ready to get going right now. This was all interesting info but I wasn't seeing the advantage of talking to Minneapolis on the Batphone. We could be on the road right now.

Will signed off and said, "Just give me a minute and I'll be ready."

He walked over to a printer that had started humming, waited about four seconds, then took a sheaf of documents out of it.

"Let's go."

We checked out and left. Walking out to the Sub, I knew some kind of storm was coming our way. I wasn't sure what it was—Mother Nature or something else.

About one thousand miles to the northwest, the storm hit the city of Edmonton, Alberta. Schools and businesses were closed early in a place that celebrates snowfall with as much relish as Acapulco celebrates sunshine. The snowplows were pulled off the roads when it was determined that lack of visibility caused a plow to drive off an overpass and fall forty feet onto a city bus. The storm was losing no strength as it continued to roll south.

Chapter Sixty-six

On US 83 heading north between Bismarck and Minot

We made our way north through Bismarck to pick up US 83, which would take us to Minot, closer to Canada and, ultimately, to today's destination, Alamo. As we drove I asked Will about the data he'd picked up. He leafed through it.

"Looks like a little of everything. I have the contact info for the company in Williston where the emails to Kline originated. They also apparently wired some money to an offshore bank in the Bahamas that Kline was using. We also have the family history of the Swanbergs, including whatever was available regarding Frederick's war record and the family company, which is named Swanberg Holdings, Inc. And some on Swanberg's son and his grandson, who is still listed as living in Williston and is currently the CEO of Swanberg Holdings. Swanberg Holdings is listed as a hay and beef producer, owning or controlling nearly one million acres of northwestern North Dakota. Grandson is one Paul Frederick Swanberg, age thirty-five, named for granddad, no doubt. He is single, never married, no military experience, graduated at the top of his class at South Dakota State with a B.S. in geological engineering. Also has an MBA from the University of Minnesota."

"Interesting combination of degrees," I commented. "Why would a guy want that kind of education if his family is in the hay and beef business?"

Pete had the answer. "Only one reason you go to school for geological engineering—oil and gas drilling."

I thought back to the meeting we had at my house with Steve and

Ben. They had both been interested in the oil and gas angle and the deed from F.Y.S. Land and Cattle. The buzzing that had started back then was getting louder.

"Didn't Sharon say that Frederick's name was Frederick Yates Swanberg?"

"Yes," Pete said.

"And that deed we found in Grams' safe-deposit box, that was from something called F.Y.S. Land and Cattle, wasn't it?"

Again, "Yes."

"Frederick Yates Swanberg—F.Y.S. You think maybe it was Frederick Yates Swanberg Land and Cattle?"

We all looked at each other. Bingo. Will called his office and gave them the information, asking them to check the name of the current company against any previous names.

We rolled north past a series of small towns that typify the north central part of the U.S., towns that had once served as centers of commerce and society but were becoming fewer and farther between as transportation got faster and production became more centralized. In the 1930s, when this chain of events started, most people never traveled more than twenty-five miles from the place they were born. That was how far it was from the most remote part of the county to the county seat. It was also about how far you could comfortably drive in the conveyances of the day on the roads of the day. Most families still traveled by horse, though Henry Ford's reinvention of motorized travel had lowered the common denominator to a point that many could afford at least a used car.

As we crested a hill south of Underwood, I saw a house in the distance on the west side of the highway. As we drove, the house appeared to move. I shook my head and blinked to clear my eyes. As I watched, the house moved again.

"Hey, guys. Is it me or is that house up there moving?"

They both looked. We were maybe a half mile south if it by now. It moved again. As we approached I could see a long structure like an arm moving with the house.

"It's an excavator," Pete said.

"A what?" I asked.

"A dragline excavator," Pete said again. "For mining. I saw one of these on a Discovery Channel show. It's as big as a house. There are only a few of them in the entire world."

As we approached, we could see the machine working. The arm was a boom that held a bucket suspended on a cable. The house swiveled as we drove past. The machine was enormous; the house itself was bigger than most people's homes. It was a large-sized two-story that would have totaled over 4000 square feet, and here it was turning and moving with ease. The bucket scooped up a load of whatever it was mining with the grace and effortlessness of a body builder sweeping his towel off a weight machine. We couldn't see where it was dropping the load, but the house spun and the bucket spilled out its contents in one smooth move.

"Lignite, I bet," Pete said. "That's what it is. It's a form of coal. I read about it when I was looking up mining in North Dakota. The website said that there is an 835-year supply of the stuff up here."

"835 years? Why are we having an energy crisis with that much coal around?" I asked.

Will offered, "Because cars don't run on coal?"

I guess that made sense. "This entire landscape looks alien to me."

"It's a little different. You have to remember that, geologically speaking, this is some of the youngest land on the planet. The last Ice Age was only about 10,000 years ago, a blink in geological terms. It left the land scoured flat with enough depressions to form lakes and with great topsoil for farming. It also left a lot of coal, lignite, near the surface. And where there is coal, there's often oil and gas."

That quieted things down for a while.

We made Minot about lunchtime. There'd been no messages from the Minot branch of the feds, so we skipped that optional stop and swung into a McDonald's drive through.

Pete asked, "You know why this outfit is so successful?"

Pete's always good for a conversation starter when things quiet down.

"I doubt it's the sophistication or health aspects of the cuisine," I answered.

"No, it's the consistency of the quality. You can go into a McDonald's anywhere in the country and it's the same."

Will added, "I went to the Far East on a case once, about twelve years ago, pretty early in my career. We were investigating a drug smuggling operation. We stopped into a McDonald's in Hong Kong and I ordered a Big Mac. It was the same as if I'd gotten it near my home in Woodbury."

We headed out of Minot on Highway 52 north as the lesson of the day concluded. We went up the road to the Highway 50 cutoff to go west to Alamo.

The sky darkened as we rode west on Highway 50. The lifelong Midwesterner in me was whispering in my ear to keep an eye on the sky. Something was coming and this time of year it wasn't going to play nice. I hit the scan button on the radio to try to find a forecast. No luck.

Minot was about halfway to Alamo. As we cruised west Will received a call from his office that filled in a few more blanks.

"OK. We've got home and business addresses on Swanberg. I've been thinking that maybe he has a business relationship with this Turner Mineral Leases company and he was using one of their computers for the money transfers and to set up the hit with Kline."

"Yeah, that would explain why the emails and transfers were coming from there," I added. "I think we should go there first thing tomorrow to see if there is a business relationship between Swanberg and Turner."

Pete was quiet. I'd never seen him in this mood. He was obviously working through some very heavy thoughts, trying to balance the idea that some relative he didn't even know he had would actually attack him and his family. Was it just for money? Was Paul Swanberg somehow not responsible for his actions because of his OCD? These were thoughts that he'd have to reconcile before facing his "new" cousin.

The drive was on a two-lane highway that weaved its way between low hillocks and frequent ponds and small lakes. Many of the fields were strewn with large rolls of baled hay while others looked like tall grass gone to seed.

Pete commented, "I looked at aerial photos of this area. In summer the fields are beautiful. The clover and alfalfa blooms in bright lavender and saffron."

I tried to add those colors to the landscape but the thickening overcast hindered the effort, pushing everything into gray scale.

The first sighting of an oil well changed the atmosphere in the Sub from one of "Are we there yet?" to anticipation and quiet excitement.

We began seeing more and more bobbing oil well heads, silently rocking up and down in the distance. Next to each well was a row of short stocky tanks that served as collection and storage centers. These tanks were located near an access road to facilitate the trucks that would haul away the millennia-old black gold that had been produced by the decomposition of late Paleozoic forests. One such set was right next to the highway. I pulled over and we got out for a look.

The well pump made a moaning squeal as it rose and fell. It was a uniquely mechanical sound, accompanied by a rhythmic clank and thump from some other parts of the apparatus. A faint smell of oil floated in the breeze.

"So this is what it's all about?" I asked.

Pete answered, "Yeah, this and a million dollars per year in royalties for each well."

We loaded back up and continued down the road.

About an hour and a half later we crested a hill and could see down into the valley beyond. Pete said, "There it is."

Chapter Sixty-seven

"It" was a collection of buildings at the west end of a small lake. I could see the tall buildings of a feed grain elevator operation and the markings of some old stock pens paralleling what must have been a rail line along the north side of the town. The tracks were no longer there, just the dusty trail of the old roadbed.

The town was laid out in typical western-American style, with a main street running perpendicular to the former rail line and the entire town cocked a little counterclockwise, due to the slight southward angle of the rail line as it passed through town from east to west. After they tore up the tracks the town stayed cockeyed for no apparent reason.

The ever-prepared Pete had Google-mapped the town. There were a total of twelve city blocks making up the former metropolis, three blocks north to south and four east to west. Main Street ran north to south through the center of town, with Tallman and Parker streets to the east and Willard and Kenney streets to the west. Railroad Avenue ran next to the now-abandoned rail line, with 1st, 2nd, and 3rd Avenues running east to west, each a block south of the other. Pete had shown me a rough plat of the town, circa 1920, which showed buildings and homes no longer here. In fact, today there was little sign of human life at all.

The town was about a half mile north of Highway 50, so we turned off on County 11 and entered the town on the west end. I drove around the perimeter, going up Kenney Street to Railroad, then east to Parker and back south to 3rd. We didn't see a living soul. There were signs of life—homes with cars in front, kids' toys in the yards and trash cans with bulging lids. As I came down 3rd we saw an elderly woman raking leaves in the front yard of one of the last homes. I pulled over.

"Pete, go tell her that your family used to live here. We'll back you up. Try to find out whatever you can about Swanberg and any history she knows."

"Good idea," Will said.

Pete just nodded and we bailed out. Pete took the lead. An oddly warm wind was blowing from the south, a precursor to the incoming low. We kept our hands on our pockets to hold our jackets shut so she wouldn't see our firearms as we approached her.

"Hi! I'm Pete Anderson. My family used to live around here and I was passing through on business and thought I'd stop by and see where I was from."

Pete held out his hand in greeting and she stopped raking. She had an apprehensive expression and clutched her rake like it was a combination cane and Japanese shinai. I guess they didn't get a lot of visitors here.

"I was hoping there was a chance you might have known them?" He kept his hand out. She took it.

"Maggie Nygaard," she announced. "What did you say your family's name was?"

"Anderson. Elmer Anderson was my grandfather, Emma—my grandmother. Her maiden name was Bjornstrom. I know that Elmer's family had a farm and that Emma's did too, but I don't know where they were or anything else. I guess I'm trying to find my roots."

Maggie thought for a moment as if considering both the answer and whether or not to answer. Finally she said, "Emma was a good friend of my older sister Dorothy. Very nice people. But they've been gone so long. Elmer went into the service and Emma moved to Fargo to work in a bank. They never came back. I never heard from either of them after the war. Emma's family sold the farm and moved to the Southwest somewhere and Elmer's family just slowly died out. His parents sold their farm in the '50s and they moved into town."

"Maggie, is it OK if I call you Maggie?" She nodded. "Maggie, do you know anything about the time around the war, before Emma went to Fargo?

Maggie looked at the ground. She was thinking about long ago, thoughts that had not stirred in nearly seventy years.

"Let's go in for a cup of coffee." She led the way into her home.

The house had that smell of an older person's abode; not a bad smell, just the combination of years of living, cooking, fires in the fireplace and the must of old things. The walls were lined with so many photos and knickknacks that determining the paint color was nearly impossible. There were hand-crocheted doilies on the side tables and hand-knit afghans over the backs of chairs. There was an old console model television, but the home had a state-of-the-art Bose Wave radio-cd player, indicating that Maggie had a taste for music. We looked around and made a silent group decision that the easy chair in front of the TV was Maggie's. We sat, two on the couch and one in a wing chair.

I could smell coffee. If she was like Grams, she kept a pot on all day. It was a crapshoot as to whether it would be great coffee or motor oil, depending on its age. You could usually figure it out before you drank it by its viscosity. If the spoon stood up by itself, look out. If the spoon dissolved, well . . .

Maggie came back with a tray filled with cups and cookies. She set it on the coffee table in front of the couch. The cookies were homemade, half chocolate chip, half sugar. The coffee was already poured, removing the opportunity to determine its age by watching it flow into the cups. It was black. I picked up a cup and took a sip. It was great. Strong but great.

Pete introduced the rest of us.

"Maggie, this is Will Sanford and Dan Neumann. They are traveling with me." He left out the law enforcement thing. "The real reason I'm here is to find out anything I can about my family. We've had some things happen that are causing me to try to track down some information from Alamo regarding the time my family lived here. Can you remember anything from those days, anything that happened here that, maybe, Grams or Gramps wouldn't have passed on to my parents?"

Maggie looked pensive, lost in thoughts of the past. It was time to break the news.

"Maggie, I'm a detective with the Minneapolis Police Department. Will is a Special Agent with the FBI. Pete is my best friend, I've known him my whole life and Emma was like a grandmother to me when I was growing up. The reason we are here is that back in October someone, we think a burglar, broke into Emma's house in Minneapolis and killed her."

I stopped to give Maggie a chance to process this bit of info. She took it well. I guess at her age nothing really surprises you anymore. I continued.

"Then, about two weeks later, someone broke into Pete's house. No one was home and Pete's dog ran the burglar off. Nothing was taken in either of these burglaries. Then, on Thanksgiving Day, a man tried to kill Pete and his family at his sister's house. Fortunately, he failed. We've been following the evidence in the case and it has led us here. Rather, it's led us to people who lived here during and after World War II. That's why we need to know what happened so long ago. If you can help us it could be the thing that breaks this open."

Maggie looked at Pete and then at Will and me. "I'm not sure how I can help. What is it you're looking for?"

"That's part of the problem," I said. "We're not sure what we're looking for. We'll know it when we see it, but until then, we're just asking questions in the dark. Here's what we know."

I looked at Will, who gave me a nod. We were on the same page.

I went on. "Maggie, we know that the person who broke into Pete's home is related to Pete. We have DNA that shows that the burglar is a white male and is Pete's cousin. We don't know how he's Pete's cousin but we think it must have something to do with Alamo. We think that, maybe, after Elmer went to war, Emma might have had an affair with someone here."

I adjusted the story a bit from what June Ingberg told us. Cops do this to see if they can get the same story from a different source. She'll have to correct me to make it consistent. If she could deliver the same story she'd be a good backup to June's story. A defense counsel could easily convince a judge or jury that June's statements were inadmissible because she was living in a different century.

"We think that affair produced a child who would be Pete's uncle or aunt. And that person, in turn, had a child. Do you know anything about that?"

"Well, it didn't quite go like that."

Maggie sat back in her chair and looked us over like she was trying to decide if we could handle the truth.

"I was, let's see, about fifteen years old in the fall of 1938. That's when this all happened. People who lived through those days, the war days, remember the years very clearly, even the years leading up to the actual war. Most of us knew that war was coming, what with the problems in Europe and the things the Japanese were doing in China. So we paid attention to things. In the fall of '38, Emma was in love. I know this because she used to come over and sit and talk to my sister Dotty and June Ingberg about it, though June wasn't an Ingberg yet then, she was a Brockstad. They'd sit in our room when I wasn't around and talk about things they didn't want me to hear. But I was sneaky," she said with a wry smile. "We lived in a two-story house and I used to shinny up the cottonwood tree outside the house and climb onto the roof. I could sit right outside the bedroom window and hear everything they said. It was quite an experience, let me tell you. They talked about Emma's love life and who she was seeing and who she wasn't. She was seeing two boys—one who wanted to marry her when the time came and one who she knew she'd never marry. She knew way back then that it just wasn't to be."

"Why wasn't it to be?" Pete asked.

"Because of the families. She was a poor girl from a small farm and he, well, his family owned half the county. She wanted to marry the rich boy. Who wouldn't? My sister sure did. So did June. Every girl wanted to land Frederick Swanberg."

"Why?" I asked.

"The same reason his grandson Paul would be such a good catch today—he was handsome, witty, and his family had money. That was a big thing during the Depression. These days Paul's family owns even more land than they did then—a big chunk of Williams and Divide counties. Whoever gets Paul will have all her worries taken care of. And he's a pretty good looking young man, too."

"Why hasn't anyone caught him yet?" Pete wanted to know.

"Well, he is a little odd. He has dated girls and everything so I don't mean he's odd that way. He's just odd."

I thought she must be referring to the OCD, so I asked her "You mean with the counting and all that?"

"Yes, that's what I'm talking about, the counting and the straightening and the cleaning and such. But he'd be worth it if ever some girl catches his eye. Everyone says he's just like his grandfather. He even looks a bit like you, Peter. You two could be brothers."

That last comment is what's known as a stopper in the cop business. Not much to say after that.

We wrapped things up with Maggie, asking her to keep our visit to herself. She nodded her understanding and we thanked her and headed out to the Sub for the drive to Williston. I figured we had about forty-five minutes of processing time before we had to talk about it.

I took the county road back down the mile or so to Highway 50 and headed west to US 85. That took us the last leg to Williston. Along the way, Will got on his crackberry and made reservations at a place called the El Rancho Inn on the main drag in Williston. I'm not big on chain sleeping rooms, the places bereft of amenities that cater to those who are just looking for a place to crash, shower and leave. I guess Will isn't either. This place, Will relayed, had a coffee shop, a restaurant and a lounge. I liked the idea of a lounge.

We found it easily enough, checked in and dropped our bags in our rooms. Then it was down to the lounge for a strategy session. It was about 6:30 on Thursday evening and the place was pretty empty. It was an almost square room with a pull-tab setup on one wall and the main bar at the end. The end opposite the bar was open to the lobby, divided from it by a knee wall and a header that dropped from the ceiling and supported a row of large flat screens. The flat screens circled the entire perimeter of the place and contrasted with the retro vinyl and chrome seating, giving it a combination of anachronistic charm and bad taste. A lot of naugas died to upholster this joint.

When the barmaid came by, I ordered a very light beer, Mich Ultra, while Pete and Will went with diet soda. We'd had enough power drinking back in Fargo. There was going to be a lot of work tomorrow and we all had enough travel experience to know when to pull in the reins. I was even thinking Cobb salad for dinner. Will had been checking his email on the way in so I inquired.

"Anything new from mother fed?" I asked.

"Still nothing more than what we had this morning. I think it's on us to take the next step."

"And what's that going to be?" Pete asked

I said, "I think we drop in on this Turner Lease outfit first thing tomorrow and ask to see the boss. We tell him or her that strange emails have been coming from their server and that we want to figure out who sent them. Most top management people don't have a clue how their IT stuff works, so he'll turn us over to his IT staff. I've found that IT staff can be very helpful when you let them in on what's going on. They love puzzles and will do the work for us."

Will wasn't sure. "I don't know. Our normal procedure would be to seize everything and have our own people look it over. That way you don't have to worry about the IT staff destroying anything we need. There's always the chance that one of them is in on it. Maybe Swanberg ran his communications through there because he was sleeping with the IT manager. Maybe the IT manager is his cousin. We don't know. But I like the idea of going there first."

"So what do we do?" Pete asked again.

Will said, "Let me call Bismarck and see if they have anyone they can send over. I can also start the warrant process in case the Turner people are less than helpful. We should use a federal court judge in Bismarck for that. That will help keep it quiet here in Williston. The agent from Bismarck can bring a search warrant with him. That way, we can begin by saying please and thank you but we'll have paper coming just in case."

I laughed. Will was right and I knew it but I couldn't resist the opportunity to give him the needle. "You guys just don't understand the value of goodwill and personal relationships. You get all papered up and go in there with specialists and it's no wonder that people don't like it. My way, you make friends with your suspects, you develop a relationship and they just give you what you want."

"Yeah, but my way, we know we will get what we want," Will said, refusing to allow his chain to be yanked. During this friendly law enforcement banter, Pete looked on in silence. He was thinking that he might be meeting his never-known cousin tomorrow as he was arrested. His cousin, who might even look like him and who had, maybe, killed Grams. I could see that Pete didn't know how he'd react and decided right there that I'd better confiscate his .45-caliber Kimber before that moment came.

Pete and I hung out in the lounge after dinner watching our choice of NBA or NHL games on the impressive collection of flat screens. Will joined us around 8:00 with the news that he'd been talking with the SAC of the Bismarck office and had arranged for a computer specialist to come over. That person would also bring a search warrant for all the computer equipment on the premises of Turner Mineral Leases, based upon the research on the emails to and from Kline that the FBI had completed. Everyone had a nightcap and we crashed, exhausted, before the 10:00 news, so no one caught the weather forecast.

Chapter Sixty-eight

Coffee Shop of the El Rancho
Friday, December 12, 9:30 a.m.

The hotel had a surprisingly decent breakfast buffet and we all loaded up on eggs, bacon, hash browns, biscuits, juice, fruit and coffee. I made the supreme sacrifice and passed on the sticky rolls that were obviously fresh and just as obviously contained an entire day's worth of calories. We were all on the coffee when a young woman entered the coffee shop and looked around. Will said, "Here she is," and rose to wave her over.

I was immediately struck by the woman's appearance. She was about five foot seven with a lean curvy figure that her winter coat couldn't hide. She had perfectly styled blond hair and the face of a beauty queen. I knew that the feds didn't hire idiots, that most federal agents were either accountants or attorneys, and some were both, so I began to think that maybe she was one of those supermodel lawyers like you see on Fox News. I had long ago come to the conclusion that any newswoman on that channel had to have knockout looks and a 140+ IQ as a job prerequisite.

We rose as one as she walked over, moving fluidly through the chairs scattered akimbo by departing diners. She smiled broadly as she approached and held out her hand to Will. She must have gotten a look at his photo; she didn't give either Pete or me a second glance.

"Agent Sanford, I'm Molly Foss, Bismarck office."

"Call me Will. This is Pete Anderson and Dan Neumann. Dan's with the Minneapolis PD." He left it there without explaining Pete's involvement. She didn't let it pass.

Molly shook my hand and took Pete's, asking, "And what organization are you with, Mr. Anderson?"

Pete clamped. He didn't know how to answer without making it seem as if he shouldn't be here. Will bailed him out.

"Pete is the reason we are here," Will said. Molly cocked her head with a this- sounds-interesting look and waited. "Didn't you get a copy of the file?"

"My instructions, which I received at 7:00 this morning, were to pick up this file," she held up an envelope for us to see, "and to be here now. This is probably a copy of the case file, but reading and driving don't mix well."

Will frowned. I'm sure he thought Agent Foss would have been up to speed. Now he had to fill in the blanks.

"Here's the short version," Will said. "Mr. Anderson's grandmother was murdered during the commission of a burglary at her home in Minneapolis. There was a subsequent attempt to burglarize Pete's home and a very sophisticated attempt to assassinate Pete's entire extended family on Thanksgiving. Email communications and money transfers have been traced to the computers at Turner Mineral Leases, here in Williston. We also believe the burglar is a resident of Williston or Alamo."

Molly accepted this and said to Pete, "I'm sorry for your loss." Pete recovered and thanked her.

"Thank you. Good to have you on the team, Agent Foss."

"Please, call me Molly."

We sat back down and Will offered Molly coffee, which she accepted.

"I hope it's strong. It was a little longer drive than I thought it would be."

She wrapped her hands around the cup, warming them, and blew on the hot surface. She still had her coat on and I thought she looked like a little kid with a cup of hot cocoa just in from the ice rink. After a tentative sip, she stood and removed her coat, revealing the previously poorly hidden figure and a bare ring finger on her left hand. I had to remind myself that A: I was committed to my relationship with Maria, and B: I was old enough to be this woman's father, almost. B was the clincher. I wondered if young bachelor Will might be interested.

The look in his eyes told me he was thinking about it, but being the fed he is he went right to business, going back to the inadequate briefing.

"They really didn't brief you on any of this?"

"I was told to meet you here this morning, that you were working a case that has led to some electronic devices that may need investigation. I am a specialist in electronic forensics and I'm here to assist you any way I can."

"Well, that's a start." Will filled in the blanks for Molly on the break-in at Grams and the fact that nothing was taken, the attempted break-in at Pete's, where again nothing was taken. Finally, the attempted murder at Ruth and Steve's and the subsequent investigation that identified George Kline. He covered Kline's background with the IRA and his history as a hired gun with the East Coast mob. Then he went over the use of HaloRemi 35 gas at the Hammers. He told her that the email communications had been tracked to the Turner company and our theory that Paul Swanberg had used a computer there for his communications.

"We are planning to go over to Turner this morning, serve the warrant and check their computers. If we can find what I think must be there we'll have enough to arrest Swanberg and turn the whole thing over to a federal prosecutor."

"So my role will be to go through Turner's computers and see if one of them sent the emails in question, correct?"

"Correct. Hopefully, you've been given the background on the emails and their sources so you can track them."

Molly opened the packet of information and flipped through the pages. "Looks like I have everything I need here."

"Great. Do you need some breakfast or are you set to go?"

"Actually, I just grabbed a breakfast bar on the way out the door this morning. OK if I hit the buffet?"

"Go ahead. We've got time."

Molly got up and headed over to the buffet line. I commented, "She's a pro. Where do you find these people?"

"Since 9/11 we've had a much easier time with recruiting. Most of the new people have a connection, either a parent or relative who was in the military or law enforcement, or just a strong desire to serve that recognizes the danger that is still out there. Most of the kids are from the center part of the country, away from the biggest cities. Personally, I think this gives them a better perspective and a less jaded view of our country's position in the world. They're bright, motivated and good team players."

"And great to look at, too," Pete said.

"I noticed that. I think I might need to call an FBI-only meeting tonight for dinner. You guys cool with that?"

"Knock yourself out," I said. "Just don't distract her from what she's doing here."

"I'm not worried about him distracting her, I'm worried about her distracting him," Pete said.

"Don't worry, gentlemen, I'm a professional."

We passed the next half hour making small talk with Agent Foss, filling her in on our own backgrounds and other tidbits about the case. She was especially interested in the use of a radio jammer on Pete's neighbor's security system. Will said he'd send her the write-ups from the Twin Cities FBI office that covered the investigation of that particular event. Molly finished her eggs and fruit and we prepared to leave. Pete paid the bill and we headed out the door.

It was only a five-minute drive to the offices of Turner Mineral Leases LLC in Williston. We parked in the lot next to the brown brick one-story building and went inside. Our group of four looked normal enough to the receptionist. We were all smiles as we walked up to the desk. Will looked at the nameplate that identified the receptionist as Amy Opsal. She was all smiles, too, until Will produced his fed creds and announced our intentions.

"Good Morning, Amy," Will said pleasantly. "I'm Special Agent Will Sanford with the FBI. I'd like to speak to the owner, Mr. Turner."

The receptionist froze. After two long blinks she recovered and answered, "I'm sorry, Mr. Turner isn't in right now. I can have him call you when he returns or you can wait."

"When do you expect him?"

"I don't know. Mr. Turner spends a lot of time out of the office. I don't really know if he's coming in today or not. He didn't tell me he had any appointments today."

"All right, we'd like to see the next highest ranking person on site and the head of your computer department," Will stated.

"That would be Mrs. Turner. She's both. I'll call her."

Will stepped back from the desk with a neutral expression on his face. He'd served enough warrants to know that these things could go many ways, anywhere from polite compliance to a shoot-out. Start with polite, but firm, and you usually get your way.

The receptionist put down her phone and said, "Mrs. Turner will be here in a moment."

I asked, "Is Mrs. Turner Simon Turner's wife?"

"No, April's husband was the president until last spring. He died." She paused, then went on. "It was so bizarre. He slipped on an ice patch on the sidewalk and hit his head. They said he died instantly. Anyway, April needed something to do and wanted to stay in touch with the company, she is half-owner after all, so she went to computer school and now she runs IT. It's a lot better since she took it over, too."

My one real gift as an investigator is that, for some reason unknown to me, people open up to me. I get them to tell me more than they should. I don't know why, or how to teach it to other people, but it's always been that way. Maybe it's my smile, or maybe because I always try to start very non-confrontationally. Whatever it is, it has served me and law enforcement well. I sensed that there was more to be mined here and pursued it.

"So Simon recently became president?"

"Yes. Before Matt, that's Simon's brother who died, Simon was in charge of "wining and dining" we used to say. You know, customer entertainment. But I think that was just because Matt had to find something for him to do. He was good with the clients but not very nice to work for, always ordering people around and calling for coffee and having us place phone calls for him like he was the president of the United States or something." She hesitated as if she suddenly realized she was talking out of school. "I shouldn't be saying all this," she said, and actually put her hand over her mouth.

We had gotten some useful information. Mrs. Turner, April, whom we were about to meet, was only recently involved with the company and she was the one in the best position to help us. We'd have to discern her feelings for her brother-in-law, the absent Mr. Turner. There might be some latent animosity between her and her brother-in-law or she might be eyeing him as the next father for her children. And, she could be involved in the case. Cops all believe there are only three types of people—victims, suspects, and witnesses—and some people fall into more than one category. Either way, she might or might not be useful, depending upon how she balanced her commitment to the company and her loyalty to her family. Were they one in the same? Time would tell.

April Turner appeared from a hallway to the left of the lobby. She was a tall handsome woman who looked to be about fortyish. She was wearing business casual, wool khakis with a light sweater over a light blue button-down blouse. Her dark hair was just short of shoulder length and she wore just a touch of daytime makeup. Her expression was all business. She went to the receptionist first and exchanged a brief conversation with her. Then she came over to us.

"I'm April Turner," she said as she offered her hand. Will led the way.

"I'm Special Agent Will Sanford with the FBI. This is Agent Molly Foss and this is Pete Anderson and Dan Neumann of the Minneapolis Police Department."

I noted how he ordered the introductions to make it sound like Pete was a cop, too.

"How can I help you?" Mrs. Turner said with concern in her voice.

"Do you have a conference room where we could have a little privacy?"

"Sure. Amy, we'll be down the hall," she said to the receptionist.

April Turner led us to a nicely appointed room with the standard conference table and chairs. All in all it looked like about ninety percent of the offices in the country. We let her take the chair at the head of the table and we surrounded her on both sides.

Will began. "We're here on an investigation that began in Minneapolis and has led us to your computer systems." He pulled the warrant from his pocket and served Turner Mineral Leases, LLC, in the form of April Turner. "We are here to determine if some electronic communications both originated and were received by a computer here, communications that were involved in an attempted murder and the use of stolen U.S. Army weapons."

That's the sort of message that will get your attention. We had April's.

"Are you sure you're in the right place? Our computers used in a murder and stolen weapons? That's absurd."

That's the reaction we'd expect, especially if the person we're talking to knows exactly what's going on. Or, it could be real. After all my years in law enforcement I'd been lied to so many times that I admit I'm a little cynical. That said, I began to have doubts about April Turner.

Molly took over. "Could you describe your systems to me, server type or types, terminal types and number, that sort of thing?"

April was in shock, but that often makes for a good interview. Without really thinking about it, she began describing their system. As she did, Molly took notes and jotted items she'd want to ask about when April was finished. She also interrupted now and then to ask April to elaborate on some technical point. As I watched I could see that April was comfortable with the course of the discussion. She was in her area of expertise and obviously knew the company's system inside and out. A very bright woman, she was also hedging some of her answers, limiting them to simple yeses and no's. So far, even my limited understanding of the subject matter was enough to tell me that nothing of value was being discussed. The two women were framing the details of how the system worked, not what it contained. We'd see if Molly would pursue topics that would knock April out of her comfort zone.

Chapter Sixty-nine

Simon Turner's home
Williston, North Dakota

As soon as April Turner took the group of investigators back to the conference room, Amy, the receptionist, did what April had instructed her to do. Amy called Simon Turner on his cell phone. He recognized the number and answered accordingly.

"Yes, Amy, what do you want?" he gruffly responded.

"Mr. Turner, Mrs. Turner asked me to call. There are people from the FBI here and they are asking her questions about the company's computer system."

"What!" he exclaimed. "Who the hell are they to come barging into my business asking questions?"

His statement was rhetorical, but Amy answered it anyway.

"They have a search warrant, Mr. Turner."

"A search warrant!"

"Yes, Mr. Turner."

"How do you know that?" Turner asked.

"I was in the hall outside the conference room and I could hear them talking."

Being the receptionist for any company brings you into contact with everyone who has any contact with that company. The gatekeeper must present the company in the best light to visitors and properly filter those visitors, controlling their access to the people at the company. Matt had taught Amy early on that she was very important and that he expected her to be the face the public saw as Turner Mineral Leases, LLC. She took this responsibility seriously and the company benefited from it.

When Matt died and Simon took over, the entire culture of the company changed. While Matt had always taken the approach that his employees were his greatest asset, Simon treated everyone equally as serfs. Amy developed a loathing toward Simon. He was impolite, had boorish sexist friends and business contacts, and treated her as chattel.

He believed that employees needed to be reminded of their place in the organization. And that would be beneath Simon. Within three months of Simon's taking over, key people started looking around for a change of venue. Fortunately, April's entrance into the business started reversing this trend. Her upbeat, appreciative nature, very much like her husband's, gave those mistreated employees reason to believe that maybe things could be like they were before. Even though her official position was IT director, arguably not a prominent one at Turner Mineral Leases, her mere presence as a half-owner brought back much of the culture that had dominated the company in the time the employees called B.S.—Before Simon.

Amy Opsal took some perverse pleasure in Simon's apparent discomfort. She didn't get many opportunities to piss him off and get away with it and she was going to milk this one as far as she could.

"Yes sir, Mr. Turner. The leader of the group had a search warrant and identification that said he's a special agent with the FBI. There's another FBI agent and two people from the Minneapolis Police Department. They are talking with Mrs. Turner in the conference room right now. She wanted me to call you and ask if you could come into the office and deal with them yourself, since they asked for you."

"They asked for me, personally"

Amy thought for a moment. They hadn't actually asked for Simon Turner by name, they had asked for "Mr. Turner." "Yes sir, they asked for you by name."

Amy felt Simon's discomfort through the phone line. She was really enjoying this.

After a pause, she heard Simon say, "Well, April will have to handle it. It's her department they're interested in. Not much I could add to that. I won't be in this morning. I have to see some people, so hold down the fort and tell April to call me when those people have left."

He hung up.

Amy hung up the phone with a feeling of satisfaction. She had given the boss the needle, a huge needle, and there was no possibility of repercussions—all in all, a nice start to the day.

Simon Turner's mind went into overdrive. What was the FBI doing at the office? What would they find? How could he deflect interest to Paul? That was the main question. That had been his damage control plan after that idiot Kline has screwed-up the hit, a million-dollar screwup.

Now there were FBI agents and Minneapolis Police at his office looking at his computer system. That shouldn't be a problem. His new computer didn't have any of the problem emails on it. So, how could he get the feds interested in Paul while they're here? Maybe he should go into the office. He could handle damage control better, get a feel for what they were looking for, and spin interest toward Paul. That was a good plan. He jumped out of his chair and went to his bedroom to change into power-business clothes. Fifteen minutes later he walked into the lobby.

Simon Turner marched through the lobby, past Amy Opsal's reception desk without as much as a "Good Morning," surprising her since, just minutes before, he had told her he wouldn't be in. He strode down the hall to the conference room and entered without ceremony.

Chapter Seventy

Conference room, Turner Mineral Leases, LLC

We were about to find out who had access to the system when the door burst open.

I saw a good-looking man of average height in an expensive black cashmere jacket with a pink open-collared button-down single-needle cotton shirt and dark gray wool slacks that held a neat crease. He wore burgundy tasseled loafers that had to be tough to keep shiny in the middle of a North Dakota winter. He had a world-class smile that spread over his face but did not include his eyes, which were penetrating and unfriendly.

"Hi, I'm Simon Turner," he said as he approached the table.

April said, "I'm glad you could join us."

"Well, Amy called and said that you had guests and that you wanted me here, so here I am," he said, his big smile intact. I noticed that April did not look at Simon with affection but with more of a "Where've you been?" look that wives save for tardy husbands—that look. I had an immediate impression of a strained relationship.

"So, what's up?" Simon asked.

Will took the lead. "I'm Will Sanford of the Minneapolis office of the FBI." He held out his identification as he spoke. Will then introduced the rest of us. We did the customary card exchange.

I noticed that Simon gave Pete a hard, lingering look as he shook his hand. Will then briefly went over where we were so far in our discussion with April.

"We need to determine if someone at your firm or someone who may have had access to your computers was the one who sent emails related to the case we are investigating."

"Can you tell me what the case is or is that top secret?" he said with a smile. Look or not, his manner was so amiable that I started to like the guy. That's a big no-no in this business.

Will answered, "It's an attempted murder case using stolen military weapons. That's what brought the federal interest."

"Wow, stolen military weapons! But just attempted murder so no one was killed?"

"Yes. Actually it was Detective Neumann who interrupted the attempt. If he hadn't come along it's entirely likely that the attempt would have been successful."

Simon Turner cast a gaze in my direction that changed from friendly to animal in an instant, and for only an instant. In that second I decided he was trouble. You don't get a look like that from someone who is simply interested in a case from an outsider's perspective. It erased any thoughts of my liking him. The look told me I'd have to watch my back around him.

Recovering, Simon said, "So, how can I help you?"

"April is doing fine on that," Molly said. "We just have some technical things to cover so we don't need to keep you. If you'll let the receptionist know where you are, we can find you if we have any questions."

"Sounds good. I'll stay in touch. April, give me a call when you're done here, OK?"

April nodded. She had also seen the various changes in Simon's demeanor and she was cautious as well.

Simon left.

"That went well, didn't it?" I asked the group.

We shared a look of befuddlement, which, I suppose, indicated that none of us had a real hold on what had just transpired.

I spent the next hour or so listening to a conversation between Molly and April that might as well have been spoken in Martian. Molly asked April to describe the system they used at Turner and April said it was a main server with eighteen computers hooked into in. That much I got. Then they started talking about whether the company was covered by something called the Sarbanes Oxley law, which would require it to maintain archives, or if the company operated in an area where the government would require WORM Technology. I connected that with "Write Once–Read Many" after that phrase was tossed out. April said that they weren't under that type of legal situation, but that they did have a WORM system on the server because their work in brokering leases was so close to securities. She said that the WORM system was something that she installed after she took on her current position. Molly asked about email archives and April said that they could find those and could also find the exact computer the messages were sent from. I admit that I was drifting in and out of this entire discussion. I figured that when they got to something that involved an arrest they'd wake me.

Chapter Seventy-one

Williston, North Dakota

Simon Turner jumped into his Lexus and ripped out of the parking lot. He wasn't sure where he was going, just that he was getting away from the people in his office.

"What was that?" he asked himself. "The FBI is in my office asking about computers and emails? Good thing I got rid of that computer when I did. That twit April will never figure that out."

There was an opportunity here, though, he thought. The FBI guy had said that they were looking for someone who might have gotten access to the office's computers. That was perfect. He could point them at Swanberg and let them do the rest. All he had to do was give them a little nudge. "How can I do that?" he asked himself.

First, he had to let them know about Paul's interest in the deed. He had to explain that the deed was worth a lot of money to Paul. Then, he had to manufacture an opportunity for Paul to have been at the office using a computer. They kept a visitor's log. Surely he could add Paul to the days in question and make it look like Paul had come in for a meeting with him that Simon was late getting to. The staff would always let a client like Paul wait in his office, so that would be the same as access. He did a quick U-turn and headed back to the office.

"What were the days?" he asked himself. He had a daily diary in his briefcase that he diligently kept regarding his whereabouts and activities. His secretary knew about it so he'd have to turn it over if they asked for it. Better check that quick and make sure there were no problems there. He slowed and eased his way into the lot behind the building. He didn't normally park there, but did often enough that it wouldn't seem completely out of character. His key got him through the back door.

Simon proceeded to his office through the back hall. He didn't pass the conference room or the lobby. As far as anyone knew, he was still gone. He'd told his secretary, Angie Nash, that he wouldn't be in today and she'd stayed home, working from her home office as she sometimes did. He unlocked his office and went in.

The office was dark with the lights off and the overcast sky. He left the lights off as he went to his desk, retrieved his briefcase with the diary, and slipped back out, locking the door. Then he walked down the hall toward the lobby, stopping short of both the lobby and the conference room at a storage closet. He opened the door and removed the November logbook from a storage box on the top shelf. Quietly he slipped back down the hall and out the back door. He got back in his car and, this time, carefully pulled out of the lot.

He was on his way to the golf club where he knew he could work in peace. Since it was off season there wouldn't be anyone there besides some kitchen help getting ready for dinner, and perhaps the guy who ran the pro shop.

The golf club was north of town near the airport. He parked in the back of the main building near the entrance to the locker rooms, out of sight from the approach road. Using his key card to gain admittance, he entered the locker room, quickly walked through the area and exited into the hall that led to the dining room. He walked through the dining room to the bar, which had a nice view of the eighteenth hole. Taking a table near the windows, he opened his briefcase, took out the diary and began working his way through it to the dates he had sent the emails. They weren't written in the diary, but he had code for those contacts. It took him less than fifteen minutes to find the dates. All the contacts had been sent at the end of the day. Perfect. That's when Paul could have been in the office.

He then opened the logbook to each of the days he had emailed Kline or the contact who had connected him to Kline. Using what he thought was a good imitation of Paul's handwriting, he added a visit by Paul to each day. It turned out that Paul had visited one of the days, so he used that as a model and copied it each time he had to add Paul's name. There were four additions.

Now, how could he nudge the FBI toward Paul without implicating himself? He drove back to his office and replaced the logbook in the hall closet, then walked past Angie's vacant desk into his office to replace his diary. He walked back into the conference room just before lunchtime.

"So, how's it going?" he said, smiling.

Chapter Seventy-two

Conference Room
Turner Mineral Leases

I looked up as the door swung open and Simon Turner walked in. He asked how it was going.

"Fine, Simon," April said.

We had just completed about an hour and a half discussion about Turner's computer system. Most of it was mind numbing to me and I got the impression that Pete and Will were struggling too, but Molly and April were speaking the same language.

Simon said, "How about a lunch break?"

I woke from my previous stupor, looked at Will and said, "Sounds good. Just give me a second to run to the men's room."

Will caught the cue and joined me.

"What do you think, go to lunch?" Will asked in the men's room.

"Sure. Why not? I don't like the guy much from what little we've seen. He reacted when you said I interrupted the murder attempt at Pete's, but other than that, I don't have any reason to like him for the crime," I said. "Let's see how charismatic he can be."

Will said, "Can you call that sheriff's deputy Sharon talked to and see if he could come over and sit on the room? I don't want to leave possible evidence unattended."

"Good idea," I said, and made the call.

We went back to the conference room and announced our readiness. Molly had closed her rapidly filling notebook and Pete was up and had his jacket on. April was the only one who seemed confused. I gave her an out by saying, "You ladies want to make a stop before we go?" Molly took the lead and they left.

In the ladies room, Molly broke the ice.

"Mr. Turner seems like a nice fellow."

It was an open-ended statement that would allow April to answer any way she chose. She chose contradiction.

"He's nowhere near the man his brother was. Frankly, if I didn't feel the need to keep involved with the company I wouldn't have anything to do with that man."

"Really? Most brothers I know are very similar. How is he different?"

"He's an overbearing prick, to put it bluntly. He treats our employees with contempt, always puts blame on whomever is handy, never takes responsibility for mistakes, and he's made plenty, and takes credit for other people's work. The only reason he puts up with me is the same reason I work here—because I own half the company.

"His one talent is that he's great with clients. He lands a lot of business. But if he'd let me handle the reins we'd make a lot more money. Of course, some of that would come from cutting his expense account."

They finished washing their hands and April added, "I was really surprised when he came in and suggested lunch. That's very out of character for him."

"What's he usually do for lunch?"

"Beats me, but he's never asked me to lunch before and I'm ostensibly his partner. The only time we talk about anything is at meetings. He doesn't even talk to my children and he's my son's godfather."

Molly processed that as they left the restroom. The two women joined the men in the lobby.

I had just finished explaining the evidence situation to the group when Deputy Eid walked. After introductions, April took him back to the computer room. She came back out to the lobby.

"Why don't you ride with me, April?" Simon asked.

April just nodded and headed out the door. We followed.

As soon as the rest of us were in the Sub, Molly told us about her conversation with April in the ladies' room.

"She was very surprised to see him," she finished.

"I was too. I took him for the kind of guy who would stick his nose in and then take off to the golf course, if it was summer," I said.

Pete had an insight. "I've seen guys like him all my business life. He's a controller, but he doesn't really know what he's doing. He's typical of a second- or third-generation business owner. I've done business with lots of companies that were industry leaders when they were run by their founders, but went downhill after the funerals. You see it all the time. In a company where the founder is still running the place, he remembers what it was like to be poor, to be struggling. But he worked his butt off and made something for his family to enjoy. Then, the heirs turn things to crap."

"How do they do that?" Will asked.

"It depends on how long it took him to hit it big. If he hit it big later in life, when his kids were older—teenagers or in college—they might remember struggle, too. In those cases, the second-generation kid that goes into the family business usually still does well. But if Dad made it big before the kids were very old, say, before they were ten, and certainly for third-generation kids, they wouldn't remember anything but affluence. When they come into the business, they don't have that hunger, that burning need to do well. All they remember is private schools, big houses and vacations, the best in cars and clothes, and whatever they wanted, because their parents wanted them to have everything that they didn't when they were growing up. Those kids only have a taste for the good things in life without a real feel for how they got there.

"When they get hold of the family business they usually ruin it by alienating all the employees and customers. They take the attitude that they're different from regular people and that they deserve more respect and deference, not to mention money, than the vast unwashed who work for them."

That was interesting. "So, this guy is the founder's second son. He's also second generation. How does he wind up a prick?" I asked.

"What's the age difference between him and the older brother?" Pete asked.

Will consulted his notes. "Looks like about five of six years."

"So," Pete went on, "they both come from a typical Williston family, not poor but not wealthy. Brother Matt finishes school and starts working for dad at Turner Mineral Leases, thinking that it's a nice way to make a living up here in the north country, or maybe he had the insight to realize that Dad was right and that sooner or later someone would figure out how to the get the oil out of the ground and he could be in on the ground floor, so to speak. Another five years later, baby brother graduates and needs a job. In fact, I'll bet Simon didn't graduate in the normal four years. I'll bet anything that it took him longer and that he came to the company when it was already starting to roll.

"It was running well when baby broham needed a job. So Matt, being the nice guy I'll bet he was, brings him into the company after it's already going strong and making good money. He starts out with a salary and bennies that would make you cry, and the cost of living isn't that outrageous up here, so a hundred grand probably goes a long way. He's got a nice house, cars, women, booze, a country club membership—you name it. Talk about a big fish in a small pond! He's entitled, right away, but he hasn't done anything to earn it except swim out of the right end of the gene pool.

"He didn't work the long hours for little or nothing at the start like Matt did. He's a second-generation, maybe more like third-generation, owner if there ever was one. And I'll bet he's a narcissistic misogynist as well, from what I saw."

This was quite an analysis from about ten minutes total exposure. Will and Molly thought so, too, and chimed in, though with caution.

"I don't know. We really don't know that much about him," Will said.

"April did call him an "overbearing prick" in the ladies room," Molly added.

I said, "Take the sugarcoating off narcissistic misogynist and you get overbearing prick."

Pete just looked at them. I'd known Pete long enough to see that he was getting to something. I thought it was time to shore up his credentials.

"Pete has been in business as long as I've been in law enforcement. I know he has a reputation for his ability to read people in an instant. If he says the guy's a narcissistic misogynist, I'll go with it. Molly, no matter what happens at lunch, we need to go back to the office and you need to get April alone and check out this guy. If she called him an "overbearing prick" in five minutes in the ladies room, she'll say more.

"We need to get a handle on him. If he knows about the deed, he'll see the value in it. Let's make that our target at lunch. I'll try to get him to talk about any business he had with Paul Swanberg. I'll tell him that I have an interest in the area and might be able to do some investing. That might get him to go into salesman mode and say some things he shouldn't."

Pete disagreed. "Let me talk to him. I'll tell him my family is from the area and that I have land available."

"No. No way," Will said. "He doesn't know who you are. Right now he thinks you're a Minneapolis cop. If he is involved in any way and he knows you were one of the targets, you could be putting yourself in grave danger."

Pete thought for a second then said, "He's not involved. He's a drone. If he knew about the deed he would have just come to me and told me about it. What difference does it make to him if he's brokering the deal for Paul or for me? Let's tell him."

In spite of what I'd just told the group, I wasn't sure about that assessment of Simon. "Tell him what?" I said.

Pete answered, "Tell him who I am. Tell him everything. Tell him that Paul Swanberg is the target of the investigation. Tell him that I have the deed. He might try to broker the thing from me right there at the table. He might try to help us hang it on Paul. Maybe he'll have something that could help close this out."

Will was thinking and finally said, "All right, since this is formally a federal investigation, this is what we'll do."

We'd given birth to a plan.

Chapter Seventy-three

Our drive took us west to the edge of town and a rough industrial area close to the river. In the center of truck garages, warehouses and equipment dealers, Simon Turner turned into the parking lot of an old-style roadhouse. There was no telling how long this place had been in existence, or the date of the last visit by a state health inspector. Oddly, this was the type of place I preferred. Sure, there was the possibility of disease, bad service, or even a nasty-tasting meal but, more often than not, in my experience, these places had better than good food, acceptable service, and reasonable prices. I was smiling.

My car mates were not. With the exception of Pete, who knew about my hole-in-the-wall joint affliction, it seemed that the federales were expecting something a little more conventional. I'd noticed an Applebee's on the way over and I'd bet a pair of Vikings season tickets that they were wishing we'd gone there.

The parking area was gravel and the door creaked a low tone as it was pulled open. There was no light in the small atrium that acted as an air lock in the winter, keeping out the blustery north winds. The wind had been steadily growing throughout the morning and was now at the level that required that unique Midwestern hands-in-pockets slump-shouldered shuffle. Obviously, something was coming in.

Simon Turner held the inside door and we entered a dimly lit square room with windows on the south side and an old-fashioned bar on the east. There was no reception stand or staff person to ask the usual "How many?" question. The group stopped until Simon came through and led us to a table on the window side of the room. A young attractive dark-haired waitress materialized in black jeans and a cowboy-cut and-decorated shirt, complete with mother-of-pearl studs. Her nametag told us she was Megan.

"And how is everyone this fine fall day?" She greeted us with genuine enthusiasm as she passed out menus.

The group gave her a unanimous "fine," "good," and "great." Then she asked for drink orders. Pete, Molly, and Will asked for diet cola, and April and I went with raspberry iced tea. Megan left.

Will noticed that Megan had not asked Simon for his order and mentioned it.

"She knows what I'll have," Simon replied with the assurance of a regular customer.

We opened the menus and started the usual pre-ordering conversation, asking the locals what was good. Simon said everything was good; April said she'd only eaten here twice in her life, an interesting contrast in experience.

Megan returned with the drinks. She sat a short glass with a couple of ice cubes and two inches of dark liquid I recognized as bourbon in front of Simon. I used to be able to down a double of the hard stuff at lunch. I remembered being thirty-five. If I drank that now, I'd be taking a nap at 2:00. I hit my raspberry tea, hard.

Time to order. Everyone went with the typical lunch fare—burgers for Will and Pete and salads for April and Molly. Simon ordered the house special, meat loaf dinner, and I went with pan-fried walleye. It was advertised as local catch and I knew there were good fish in the local lakes. Megan scooped up the menus and waltzed off to the kitchen.

"So, tell me about this investigation that's brought you to Williston," Simon said.

Will started in. "About a month and a half ago, there was a break-in in the Minneapolis suburb of Edina at the home of a wealthy elderly woman, Pete's grandmother. In the process, the woman was killed. Oddly, nothing was taken from the house."

The mention of Pete's grandmother garnered him another long look from Simon.

"Two weeks later, Mr. Anderson's house was broken into. That break-in didn't last long. Pete's dog ran the burglar off. Finally, someone tried, obviously and unsuccessfully, to murder all of Pete's family on Thanksgiving."

"That was the attempt that Detective Neumann broke up, right?" Simon asked.

"Correct," Will replied. "The subsequent FBI investigation has led us to your computer system. Someone with access to your server sent emails to the hit man who made the attempt on Thanksgiving Day."

Molly took it from there. "What we know is that the messages were routed through your server. There are many possible ways that could happen and we're tracking them down with the help of Mrs. Turner."

"How can you track down emails? I thought you had to find the computer they were sent from?" Simon asked.

"Anything sent on the Web is there, virtually forever. If we can find a communication at any point in the transmission, we can track it both ways, to its destination and to its source. But we do run into dead-ends. This one ends at your server. We can only track it that far. With April's help, we'll take a look after lunch and see if we can figure out where, within your company, the messages came from."

"So you've got it as far as our server, but still don't know who sent it?"

"Actually, we'll never really know *who* sent it, just which computer it was sent from. Anyone with access to that computer could have sent it."

"April, we have pretty good control on who can use our computers, right?" Simon asked.

April answered, "Our policy is that they are for employees' use only, but you know that some people bring their kids or spouses in, and some clients occasionally ask to use a terminal to check email or a stock quote. We'll have to rule out any of those situations as well."

"Is there any chance that someone could have gotten into our system from the outside?" Simon asked.

"You mean hacked into it?" April asked in return.

"Yeah. What if someone got into our system and sent the messages? Would they be traceable?"

Molly answered. "It would be harder, but we should be able to find out if that happened. The most likely scenario would be if we can't find a computer on your system that sent the messages. That would be an indicator that it came from outside."

"Hmmm," Simon said. He knew that they wouldn't find the messages. So they would have to assume that it came from outside. Now, to start them looking at Paul. How to handle that?

Lunch arrived and everyone agreed that it was good and plentiful. The salads overflowed, and the burgers were half-pounders. Simon's dinner looked like it could feed a family of four and my walleye must have weighed around five pounds. Outstanding all around. The conversation turned to the meal and the local history. This gave Simon the chance to get into his game.

"Pete, Will mentioned that your family seems to be the target of this series of crimes, the break-ins and Thanksgiving thing and all. Any ideas why?"

"No, not really. At first we thought it was just a burglar who got spooked at Grams' house. She belongs, sorry, belonged, to a church group that took tours of B and Bs and went antiquing. It was on the church's website that the group would be on one of their trips when the break-in happened. She wasn't supposed to be home that night. We all figured that it was just bad luck that she was at home and interrupted whomever.

"But then, when my house got hit, we began to think there must be something specific that this guy was after. We went through all of Grams' stuff and couldn't find anything other than the usual things that a burglar should have taken right away—jewelry, art, coins—that sort of thing. Even when we went through her safe-deposit box there wasn't anything worth killing her over.

"The final straw was the Thanksgiving attack. It's clear that someone wants me and my entire family dead and went way out of their way to try to kill us all and make it look like an accident. Good thing Dan came along or it would have worked."

At the mention of my name, Simon looked at me again.

"Why did you just happen along, Detective Neumann?"

"Pete and I are old friends. I had been invited for a little after-dinner dessert and football and just stumbled in while the would-be killer was still there."

"And you arrested this person?"

"No. My girlfriend, who is also a cop, and I chased him. He opened fire. Maria dropped him."

"So you didn't get a chance to talk to him or find out who hired him?"

"No, we didn't. Maria's very good with a weapon. She used to head up her department's SWAT Team. She put two in the ten ring and he was gone before he hit the ground."

This news seemed to please Simon. He said, "Thank God you weren't hurt. There is so much crazy news on TV these days."

Simon turned back to Pete.

"So, no idea who's doing this or why?"

Pete saw the opening and made his play.

"There is one thing, although we don't really know if it's valid. My family used to live up here in Alamo. My grandfather and grandmother were both born there. After World War II they moved to Fargo and then to the Cities, but their roots were back here. In my grandmother's things we found a packet of letters, letters that had been sent to her from an anonymous admirer. All we had to go on was that he signed them 'Forever Yours.' We've been tracking down old family friends to try to see who might have sent them and we've come up with a possibility. Someone named Frederick Swanberg. Apparently he lived in Alamo, too, and might have been dating my grandmother before Gramps did, or maybe at the same time. We don't know. Anyway, she kept his letters and they helped us figure out that there used to be something called F.Y.S. Land and Cattle Company. We think that F.Y.S. was Frederick Swanberg. The question mark is a mineral deed we found made out from F.Y.S. Land and Cattle Company to my grandmother for mineral rights over a large bit of land. Now, we don't really know if it's worth anything, but it's all we have to go on."

Simon's head was spinning. They had found the deed but didn't know what the deed was worth! In fact, it sounded like they hadn't known the deed even existed until after Mrs. Anderson was murdered. He'd told Paul to just go ahead and lease the rights and they'd take care of the Andersons later, if they ever appeared. And now it looked like they never would have! They were well off by their own standards and the old gal didn't even know what she had in her hands. This entire disaster could have been avoided if only Paul had listened to him.

But he hadn't and now there was a huge mess to clean up. Simon knew he had to help them find out about Paul, but in a way that deflected interest in him. At the same time, he wanted to get the rights to broker those mineral claims. He'd have to play his cards carefully.

"You say you have a mineral rights deed?" Simon asked.

"Yes. I have a copy of it here." Pete fished through his briefcase, dug out a copy of the document and handed it to Simon.

Simon looked it over. It was identical to the copy Paul had found in his grandfather's effects, right down to the lack of a "recorded" stamp. The only difference was that Paul's deed was marked "copy."

Simon announced, "It looks legitimate. All the wording is correct and the legal description is correct for the time period in which it was created. There's no recording stamp, so, presumably it was never recorded. That will be the first thing to do—record the original. Do you have that with you?"

"Yes," Pete lied. The original was back in Grams' safe-deposit box. Pete was playing a hunch.

"Well, I could take care of that for you. That's what we do. Right April?"

April nodded, not sure where this whole thing was going.

"We could have this recorded and, if you'd like, I could see about turning your little piece of paper into some money for you. That's also what we do. We broker mineral leases."

I asked, "How, exactly, does that work?"

"It's very simple. Most people don't know this but we are sitting on a vast oil reserve, bigger even that ANWAR in Alaska. The problem has been that the nature of the geology here is such that it makes removal of the oil difficult. Over the years, techniques have been developed that are starting to crack those problems, so this area, the Bakken Field it's called, is now attracting development. My father and brother realized this years ago—that someday the engineers would figure out how to get the oil. That's why my dad started our company. He knew that when that happened there would be a lot of North Dakotans with mineral rights to a lot of land but no idea how to exercise them. I have contacts with oil drilling and roughneck companies who are looking for places to work. They look for areas that are promising, geologically, and drill test wells. Then, if the geological structure in that area is willing, the oil can be removed from the ground."

"So, what do you think this is worth?" Pete asked, pointing at the copy of the deed.

"That's the big question, of course. It will depend on where the land is and how much preliminary work has been done. The price will be set based upon potential. And there are several types of leases. At the beginning we go with what's called an exploratory lease. This usually covers about three to five years. During that time, the leaseholder has the right to drill test wells to see if there's any point in going forward with production wells. They may drill or they may not. We've handled leases for people who've received the entire amount of the lease and never had a hole sunk.

"If oil is found, a production lease would follow the exploratory lease. This is usually long-term, say up to fifty years, and is based upon actual production. Basically, the landowner gets a piece of the pie."

So far, what Simon was saying pretty much matched what Steve had told Pete about the deed. Now we'll have to see what kind of number he'd come up with. That would say something about whether or not we should trust him.

"A typical five-year mineral exploration lease around here would be worth about $250 per acre. There's a lot of land here," he said, referring to the deed, "and if we could lease most of it, you'd be in for a lot of money, say in the neighborhood of ten million dollars. Of course that would be after commissions and expenses."

The number was about a fifth of what Steve thought they could get. I was starting to mistrust Mr. Turner.

Pete picked up the conversation. "You think this piece of paper is worth that much?"

"Yes, I'm sure it is. I could get you a more accurate number with some time, but I think what I said is pretty close."

Will asked, "And that would be an exploration lease, correct?"

"Yes, a production lease could bring much more. Perhaps as much as twenty million per year, if the land produced."

Pete and I had talked to Steve about that, too. He said that producing land was paying royalties around a million per year per section. Granted, not all the land would produce, but there were 947 sections covered by the deed. That would max out at 947 million per year! I definitely would keep my eye on Simon from this point forward.

Pete looked at me and Will and, playing the part better than I could have ever coached him, said, "Maybe this is what Paul was looking for."

Simon asked, "Paul. Who's Paul?"

He said it so smoothly I thought he still might be in the dark. Will explained.

"We have reason to believe that a man named Paul Swanberg is involved. Do you know him?"

April and Simon exchanged glances.

Simon said, "Of course we know him. I've known him all my life, and he's one of our clients. His family owns quite a bit of land in the Bakken. We already lease much of it and it's producing. Now that I think of it, this deed could be some of the Swanberg land—the description looks correct. I can't believe Paul would be involved in anything illegal."

April agreed. "You have to know Paul. He's a little different, very black and white, never any equivocation. I don't think he's ever gotten a traffic ticket and I've known him all my life, too."

"Does Mr. Swanberg have access to your offices?" Will asked.

"Yes, he does. He comes in frequently when he's in town," Simon said.

"In town?"

"He lives up in Alamo. The family has a house here in Williston, that's where Paul grew up, but these days Paul spends most of his time at the old family homestead."

"Do you have any records of visits by clients?"

"We do but they're not always accurate. Amy doesn't always have them sign in," Simon complained.

"She does her best," April defended. "And Paul does sign in. It's a rule and he follows rules."

Pete asked, "What can you tell me about Paul?"

Simon took this break in the conversation to look at this watch and say, "Listen, I'd love to stay and chat about Paul, but I do have another meeting. I'll try to catch up to you at the office later."

Simon rose and made his way out. On the way he stopped and said something to the waitress who looked our way and nodded.

"So, you were saying about Paul?" I asked April.

"I don't know that he has a real affliction," she said, "but he has some odd habits, things he does. He's Simon's age, was in Simon's class in high school so they know each other from that. I've known who he is most of my life because he comes from one of the wealthiest families in the area. Like Simon said, they own land that can be tallied in the hundreds of thousands, maybe millions, of acres. A lot of it is in the area that is ripe for drilling but we've leased very little of it so far."

"Why do you suppose that is?" Will inquired.

"I don't know. Could be that Paul and Simon weren't exactly best friends in school. They went to different colleges but when you come back to a city the size of Williston, relationships go back to high school days and high school problems. People remember things that happened to them back then."

"So, Paul and Simon had problems back in high school."

"Yes, they did. Paul had trouble making friends in high school. He was quirky. Some of the other boys made fun of him because of his behavior."

I asked, "Was Simon one of the boys who would pick on him?"

"No, Simon ignored him. Simon ignored anyone who couldn't do him some good," April replied.

"Tell me about his behavior. What was quirky?" Pete asked.

"Oh, just little things. He always had his desk arranged just so; he always parked in the same spot away from the other cars; he dressed very nicely and would become upset if his clothes got dirty. In fact, he had a thing about cleanliness and would wash his hands repeatedly during the day. I always thought he was just a neatnik. I guess, looking back on it now, he might have a touch of OCD. But back then we didn't even know what that was."

In many investigations, there are times when you need the assistance of someone outside law enforcement. I'd done it when I called Ben Harris about the security system. It's a moment where you go with your feelings and decide to trust someone who could have ulterior motives or even be part of the case. In this case, I knew we were going to need someone who had more insight into the local elements than any of us did.

I'd planned to talk to the sheriff's deputy, Joe Eid. But Sharon had said that he was about her husband's age, which made him at least ten years older than Paul Swanberg. I doubted that he'd have the history April seemed to have with Paul. Without consulting Will who, I was certain, would have disagreed, I disclosed a piece of information to April.

"April, we have DNA evidence that Paul Swanberg is Pete's cousin."

April sat back in her chair and looked at Pete. Will and Molly looked at each other and quickly convened a private conference, the topic of which, I was certain, was, "How do we dump the local cop and get this investigation back on track?" Pete looked back at April.

"You know, you kind of look like him—a little taller, but you could be cousins."

I continued before the feds could intervene.

"We know this because he left DNA in Pete's house when he broke into it. We also have evidence that Paul was the one who broke into Mrs. Anderson's and killed her. What we don't have is a motive."

April was clearly shocked. Paul Swanberg a murderer? She shook her head and stared at the table.

"I, I, . . . Paul?" she stuttered. "I don't know how I can help you."

This is the answer you fear when you play this card. The surprise piece of info didn't stir some long dormant thought in the person you let in on the secret. In fact, it may have but they may have other loyalties. Maybe April had a thing for Paul. After all, she was single now and he was, by all accounts, a prime candidate in a target-poor environment for a single woman in her early forties.

Perhaps she'd had a revelation of some other kind, one that somehow threatened her, or her family. She wouldn't roll over on Paul if it would hurt her. Or, maybe, she just didn't make a connection and couldn't help us. I had to dig deeper, throw some trash her way to see if I could jog something loose.

"April, you may not think you know anything that can help us, but I'll bet it's in there somewhere. All I'm asking at this point is that you and Molly go back to the office and dig out the source of that communication from your computer system. While you're doing that, keep in the back of your mind that we are trying to find out why Paul would break into Emma Anderson's and then into Pete's."

"What about the attempted murder on Pete's family?" she asked.

"We can only directly connect Paul to the break-in at Pete's. We think he's the same person who broke into Emma Anderson's. On the attempted murder—we don't know, in the legal sense, that Paul had anything to do with that—only that there were communications from your computer system to the hit man. We're still trying to track down the money and motive there as well. Paul may have been the one who hired the hit man or he might not be, if someone else is involved. That's why we need to find the motive. Think power, money, passion; these are the reasons for murder," I closed with the *Star Trek* quote. Funny how things like that maintain their relevance.

She nodded and lunch was over.

I waved the waitress over and asked for the checks. Megan said, "You're all set. Mr. Turner took care of it."

"Great. That's all I need," Will said to the group. "Professional Standards will have a good time with that," referring to the FBI's version of Internal Affairs. I guess feebs aren't supposed to let possible suspects in murder cases buy lunch.

We all loaded into my Sub and I drove back to Turner's offices. On the way we decided that Molly and April would go in and hit the computer system again in search of the emails and Will, Pete, and I would talk to the sheriff's deputy.

Chapter Seventy-four

Simon Turner had to think fast. He had this going just the way he wanted. The cops were looking at Paul and he had created the "evidence" of Paul's visits to the office on the days when the emails had gone in and out. He could attribute motive to Paul. The deeds were already drawn up listing him as successor in title if anything happened to Paul. He knew that he could get the forged documents recorded with any date he wanted on them, courtesy of a contact in the recorder's office who had a bit of a gambling problem Simon had been funding.

All he had to do now was set Paul up in a no-win situation where he'd likely be killed. That would tie things up nicely. He thought about it and decided what he would do. First, he'd call Paul and get him to show up at the right place at the right time. Then he'd count on the cops to do what they did best.

The male contingent of the law enforcement group currently involved with tracking down a killer in Williston, North Dakota, decided that a stop at a local watering hole was in order. I walked into Turner Leases, relieved Deputy Eid from computer sitting and asked him to meet us in the El Rancho lounge.

He agreed and a few minutes later we were ordering a pitcher of Diet Coke.

As we were getting comfortable, Fred laughed and said, "You look just like Sharon said you would—average everything with a nasty disposition."

I laughed, as did Will and Pete, just a bit more heartily than I thought was necessary. That's what Sharon would say about me, all right. "Fred, this is Will Sanford from the FBI and Pete Anderson."

Hands were shaken. "Sharon said you're the guy whose family is under attack," he said to Pete as his face darkened.

Pete nodded, saying nothing. Will said, "We think we've got some pretty solid leads here in Williston. I think we'll be making arrests over the weekend."

"Arrests? You have more than one person in mind?"

"That's what we want to talk with you about," I said. "We have one target for sure and at least one, maybe two more. We need your feel for the local personalities and politics."

"What do you want to know?"

"Can you fill us in on local people concerning the oil drilling business? Who would be likely to have a hand in getting in on the ground floor of developing the Bakken field?"

Fred thought for a moment.

"Williston's like any other mid-sized city in the Midwest, meaning it's all business and politics. People have relationships going back for generations. My family's been in farming, mostly, since the early part of the last century, with some dabbling in law enforcement. My grandfather was a county sheriff and I've got a son who ran off to join the Secret Service after a stint in the Marines. All the rest of my people are still within a hundred miles of where they were born. It's like that for most people here. They have a good thing going and don't see any reason to leave. That leads to difficulties when there's trouble."

Fred was a talker and I encouraged him. "How so?"

"Say, you pull over a kid for speeding. He's the son of some local politician, which means he's also the son of some local big shot businessman, oilman or farmer. Politics isn't a full-time paying job, just a full-time job, if you know what I mean."

Will interrupted, "I'm not sure what that means. Can you elaborate?"

"People who get involved in politics out here in the hinterland don't usually do it as a steppingstone to moving on to some bigger office, say congressman or governor. The idea is to control the local laws and business climate. Some do it out of a sense of service to the area that has been good to them, but just as many get involved because they want to have a hand in directing the local ordinances that will affect them. Since local politics takes a lot of time but doesn't pay much, they all are either pretty well off or have jobs that will keep paying them even if they aren't working all that much. They're the only ones who can afford it.

"So, back to our speeder. If he's the son or daughter of one of these public people, as a law enforcement officer you subconsciously take that into account. By that, I mean that you weigh the hassle that's going to come down on you if you ticket him. A speeding ticket's not that big a deal, a lot of people consider it a rite of passage, and that probably won't be a problem. But if you bust the kid for drug possession or dealing, or maybe a little B and E, you're going to have questions to answer. Those sort of offenses can come back to bite mommy or daddy in the next election."

We nodded our joint understanding. Fred went on.

"Then there's another group of people. These people also want to control things but they don't have the need for public recognition. They stay in the background and do things like fund the campaigns or act as fixers when the kid gets picked up for dealing meth at the junior high school. They get little Johnny out of trouble so they can collect a favor sometime later.

"It's almost like the movie *The Godfather* where the Don takes care of a problem and says, "You don't owe me anything." But sometime in the future there's going to be payback. These people can be really danger-ous—not in a physical way, but in a way that subverts justice. I can tell you about plenty of cases where first-degree misdemeanors have been swept under the rug, even some low-end felonies. These people are used to getting their way and will do whatever they have to to get it."

For this to work, we had to find out if Fred might be someone who would keep Simon in the loop on what we were doing. Turns out Fred, like a lot of good cops, is a mind reader.

"Just in case you're wondering, I'm sure there are people in the sheriff's office who would keep certain people in the know on what you folks are doing. Not me. I take my job as seriously as my granddad did. You need any information, I'll do my best to get it to you and keep it private."

Will took the lead. "Fred, let me fill you in on what we have and you tell us if there is anyone around here you think could be involved."

Chapter Seventy-five

Computer systems room
Offices of Turner Mineral Leases, LLC

April and Molly were deep into the search for the emails. They had gotten as far as digging into the archives when things began to get weird.

"I don't get this," April said. She was looking at a listing of communications into and out of their server. It showed that the emails had been encrypted. Gobbledygook. Molly took a look.

"Yep, we've had that before. It's a pretty standard commercially available encryption system that our people in DC were able to break, so we got the content of the messages. Unfortunately, the messages also use a kind of code, no names, addresses or dates, but that sort of thing is easy to encrypt using something we call a one-time code."

"One-time code?"

"Yeah, you pick a book or something, for a reference. Popular books are frequently used because both parties can get one without much trouble. Then you just talk, using normal English. When you get to something sensitive, say, the name of a target, you go to the book. You code the name one time using the page, paragraph and letter number you want. For example, say you want to send Will's name. For the first letter you pick a page at random, say page 100, then go down to a paragraph that has a word that starts with "W," let's say that's paragraph four. Then you count over to the word that starts with "W," say that's word seventeen. Your code for "W" is 100 4 17. After you've sent the whole name once, you assign it another code word like "truck." The next time you need to say the person's name you just say "truck." Then, when the message is complete, you encrypt it and send it. The code is easy to read if you know what book to look in. If you don't have that, it's just about unbreakable."

"Wow. That kind of stuff was coming in and going out from here?"

"Apparently. We need to figure out whose computer sent the messages."

"OK. We're about at the end of my abilities here. You're going to have to help me with this to get any farther."

"No problem."

Molly slid into the system administrator's chair and began looking at the server. Like other servers, it didn't say whose computer was whose; it gave IP addresses, numeric strings that lead to a specific port in the building. After it identified the port it would also identify the device on the other end.

After about fifteen minutes of digging Molly said, "I think this is our device, the computer that sent all the messages."

She showed April the address she had found.

April let out a gasp. "Oh my God, Simon sent it!"

Molly had other thoughts.

"We don't know that Simon sent the messages. We also don't know for sure that they came from Simon's computer. They probably came from Simon's computer, but there are other possibilities."

"Such as?"

"A clone. Someone could have come in here and used Simon's outlet to link into your system with a computer that mimicked Simon's. That would make it look like Simon sent the messages. The only way to know is for me to examine Simon's computer. If the messages came from it, we'll know. That still won't prove that Simon sent them. Anyone with access to that computer could have sent them."

The two women went down the hall to Simon's office.

"I'm not sure about this," April said. "His office is off limits to every-one in the company, including me."

She had a slightly crooked smile on her face as she inserted a key into the lock. The restriction obviously didn't dissuade April from the task at hand. Molly thought she was getting a thrill out of violating the sanctity of Simon's space.

They went inside. On the desk was an open HP laptop. April went around the desk and fired it up. After about ten minutes of keying, April said, "I don't think he did it. I looked in his email files and I can't find them. Not only can't I find them, I can't find anything older than last week."

"Does he dump his memory that often?" Molly asked as they traded positions so she could look.

"I think he might. I remember he told me that he didn't want anything archived older than a month. He said that he'd read a magazine article that said that, in litigation, people were subpoenaing email records. He said that they could ask for and would receive everything on a person's computer over a specified period of time and he didn't want the company looking stupid if someone got sued and they found a bunch of kiddie porn or something on one of the company's computers. We sent a message to everyone advising them to start purging their files, but I don't think many people do."

"Well, he's sort of right. You can clear the computers but you can't clear a WORM system. Everything that's been done since that's been installed is still there. Those are usually cleared after seven years. But there's something screwy about this computer."

Molly started looking at other programs. The computer seemed to have everything it should have, software-wise. All the registers were in place with files going back about two-and-a-half years.

"Do you know when he bought this computer?"

"I wasn't here then, but I know all the computers were purchased in May of '05, right after Windows XP was upgraded again. I just checked the records because we are thinking about replacing them with something newer but there's a rumor that Microsoft is going to come out with another new operating system next year and we're waiting to see how that goes."

Molly flipped the computer over to look at the serial number.

"Do you have records of the serial numbers of each of the computers here?"

"I don't know. Like I said, they were all in place before I took over the department. Record keeping was a little lax back then. I don't mean that we were slack in backups or accuracy, just the records on what was purchased when are a little sloppy."

"That's OK. I know how to find what I'm looking for."

Molly removed her own laptop from her bag and set in on the desk next to Simon's and hit the start key. While it was booting up, she flipped Simon's computer right side up and turned it off. After it had shut down, she flipped it back over and, with a small screwdriver she had pulled from a tool kit in her bag, she removed the panel covering the hard drive. On a pad of paper she recorded the serial number of the hard drive. By the time she was done with this, her computer was ready.

She logged onto the computer and then onto the Internet. Through the FBI's system, she contacted someone in the FBI headquarters building in DC. They started to chat.

Molly: Hey Chuck, I'm at a business in Williston, North Dakota, on that case we talked about yesterday and I need some equipment tracked down.

Chuck: Anything for you, Mol.

Molly: I've got an HP laptop that I need tracked for manufacture date and hard drive date. I'd like to get the VAR ID as well.

Chuck: No problem. Send 'em when you've got 'em.

Molly entered the serial numbers from the PC and the hard drive and hit send.

Chuck: Got 'em. Should have your answers shortly. You want to chat or should I call you?

Molly: Call me. I might be off line.

Chuck: Got it. TTYL

April looked at Molly and said, "I know what the serial numbers are but what's a VAR and what good is knowing the manufacture date?"

"You said that this computer was purchased in early summer of '05, right?"

April nodded.

"Then it should have been manufactured a little previous to that, say early '05 or late '04."

"Makes sense."

"People sometimes replace computers or hard drives when they are trying to hide something."

"Oh, my. What about the VAR ID?"

"The VAR is the value-added reseller, or the store the company bought it from. Do you know where the company bought this computer?"

"Yes, they got the entire package from an outfit in Bismarck that does small LAN systems. It's a one-woman shop that specializes in HP equipment called Joyful Systems, Inc. I can call her if you need to talk to her."

"Hold off until we know a little more history."

Molly reassembled the laptop and returned it to its place on the desk. The two women went back to the conference room.

"It'll take Chuck an hour or so to get the info. Let's take a break."

"Sounds good."

April was having a difficult time comprehending everything. The thought that Paul Swanberg could be a killer was unfathomable. She thought she knew him. "But who knows?" she said to herself. "You hear about things like this on the news every day. But here in Williston? Someone I know personally?" That was the part she couldn't get together.

Chapter Seventy-six

3:00 pm
El Rancho lounge
Williston, North Dakota

Will finished his recap of the case. Fred took it in like the professional lawman he was. He'd seen plenty of the great and mighty fall in his years behind a badge; we all had. He listened, asked a few pointed questions and listened some more. Will sat back in his chair and waited for a response.

"There are a number of people who could be involved. You said you have at least one suspect. Who is that?"

I could see that Will was reluctant to share the information. Though he had told us he would play it straight, we had no way of knowing where Fred's loyalties really lay. I go with my feelings and I wanted him in the game. Letting the local guy in on this is also a way to get him on board, to include him, so to speak.

"We have DNA from blood found in Pete's house from an unknown subject who would be Pete's cousin by a shared grandparent. We have evidence that the cousin is Paul Swanberg, but we haven't tested his DNA yet."

"Paul, huh? So that's what Rademacher was calling about. She asked me if I had any background on Paul or his family. I've got to tell you, he's not high on a list of suspects for any crime higher than distracted driving and weird behavior. In fact, I'd have to rank him as one of the last people in town that I would have come up with for this."

"Fred, is there anybody who might have suggested this line of action to Paul?" Pete asked.

"Suggested?" Fred replied.

"Yes. I have the same sort of personality quirk, for lack of a better term, that Paul does, so I've done a lot of research on it. People with OCD tend to be very serious about rules. Rules are absolutes that must be followed, regardless of the apparent social or personal consequences. Normally, that would eliminate someone like Paul from considering breaking into someone's home, much less murder.

"But those rules can be overridden by other rules or perceived rules. A person with OCD can break one rule to enforce another rule. Paul might have been presented with a situation where he thought the right thing to do was to commit burglary if he thought it would enforce a more important rule."

"This sounds a little strange to me," Fred said.

It sounded weird to me too, I thought. Where was Pete going with this?

"It's a question of the hierarchical order of rules. I'll give you an example. A man is standing at a street corner. The light is red for him, preventing him from crossing. He sees a person jaywalking across the street while having an agitated conversation on his cell phone and there is a bus coming. It's clear that the jaywalker will be struck by the bus but the man on the corner doesn't want to break the rule against jaywalking himself and crossing against the light. In this case the man with OCD can override the rules against jaywalking and crossing against the light in order to follow a higher rule to save the man's life.

It's an odd situation. A normal person would have no problem running across the street against the light and out of the crosswalk, but that person would also probably not have the compulsion to save the jaywalker. He would just stand there and either do nothing or maybe yell at the guy to look out. The person with OCD has to battle the urges to stand fast or to save the jaywalker. If Paul was given the choice of breaking into Grams' house in order to follow some higher, more compelling, rule, he might do it."

Fred digested that bit of info and replied, "Yeah, Paul could do something like that. He has a very strong sense of right and wrong. I saw it in him when he was running for city council. He didn't get elected and I think it was because he refused to take money from some of the businesses in town. There were going to be some zoning things coming up before the council and the Chamber of Commerce people wanted their boy on the council. Paul wasn't that person and they knew they couldn't bring him around, so they backed someone else."

"Who'd they back?" I asked.

"Simon Turner. He didn't get elected either, a gal from the north side of town did, but they wanted Simon."

That was interesting. Simon and Paul had once been political opponents, after a fashion. I wondered if there was any animosity left over from that.

We had another round, switching to various non-alcoholic beverages, and I found some peanuts. Not cashews, but they'll do when there's nothing else. We talked about the locals and kicked around the idea that Paul was being coerced into doing what he had probably done. I say probably because I've never liked the word "allegedly." When a cop likes you for a crime, he's got a pretty good idea that you did it. Proving it is another question altogether. Anyway, the DNA made me like Paul for at least the first two break-ins and Grams' death. We still had the attempted mass murder to solve but even that was coming around. We'd have to see what Molly came up with.

Molly and April walked in around 3:30. Both had concerned looks on their faces. They sat down with us and ordered—diet cola for Molly, a Michelob Ultra for April, who looked like she could use something stronger.

Will started. "Any luck with the computer system?"

"I think so. It's clear that the emails were sent to and from the data jack in Simon's office, but we don't know if he sent them or if someone else did. Couldn't prove it in court."

Which is how the world looks to FBI agents. Nothing is real except in terms of how it will stand up in court. Fortunately, I don't suffer from that disease.

"How, exactly, do you know that it came from Simon's office?" I asked.

"The messages are still in the server's WORM memory. We've tracked them to the data jack in Simon's office. That's the connection in the wall where you plug in your computer. But it doesn't look like his computer sent them. There is no record on the computer."

"And what does that mean?"

"Someone could have sent them from another computer plugged into the same port, or he could have installed a new hard drive since he sent them, or even gotten a completely different computer. We're working on that right now."

"And, if you find out the computer's drive, or the whole computer is new, you'll be able to state, in court, that he sent them?"

"I'll probably never be able to do that. But If I can prove that he is now using a different computer or hard drive, that's pretty good circumstantial evidence that he did it. He had to have some reason to make the change."

Circumstantial evidence is what most criminal trials are based on. TV shows would have you believe that all bad guys confess and that there is a smoking-gun witness to every crime. That's pretty rare in real life.

The shows also say that there is DNA on everything and that the labs can pull a slug from a body and match it to a gun, then match that gun to a shooter's hand. That's pretty much true. But the slug, the gun, and the DNA are all considered circumstantial evidence. Most convictions come from circumstantial evidence. Our system ain't perfect but it's the best on the planet.

The ladies' drinks arrived and we returned to talking about Paul and Williston and what was going on. Pete asked April about Paul and if there was any chance he might have something going on that he might be trying to protect. She thought the only person he might be protecting was his mother, who had cancer and all the medical expenses that can go with that. But she didn't think he was short on money. Turner Mineral Leases did quite a large amount of business on his behalf and she was confident that he was making plenty of money from that. Plus she knew that both the cattle and haying businesses were going strong.

About 3:45 Molly's phone rang. It was Chuck from the FBI computer lab. She put her phone on speaker.

"Hey guy! What did you find out?"

"I tracked down the hard drive and the computer's manufacture date. Both were early this year. The computer was VAR'd through a place there in Williston called Bob's Tech Services. I've got contact info that I'll text you."

Molly looked at April as April shook her head. This was not where the company had purchased the computers.

"Thanks, Chuck. I'll look for the text." She hung up.

"April, that's not your supplier, is it?"

"No. We buy all our equipment from Joyful Systems in Bismarck, like I told you. That's where I went for my training."

Pete asked, "What does it mean?"

Molly responded. "It means that the computer on Simon's desk was bought recently. It's not the computer he was using previously and April doesn't know why. It was bought here in town at this Bob's Tech Services. We need to ask him who he sold it to. And we need to ask him if he knows why the previous computer was replaced."

I looked at April. "Do you think this place is open this late? It's almost 4:00 on a Friday." I figured a place called Bob's couldn't be very big.

"I'm sure it is. Bob Davis is the biggest HP dealer in the region. He has about twenty people working for him out of their office here in town. He'll be there."

The group stood as one and headed for the door. As we crossed the parking lot to our cars, I could feel a freshening wind cutting through my jacket.

Chapter Seventy-seven

4:15 pm
Simon Turner's home
Williston, North Dakota

Simon called Paul Swanberg's number. He'd have to play Paul very carefully if he were to lay the entire thing on Paul and grab the lease work from Pete Anderson. It was the only plan left with a real chance of success.

"Paul, it's Simon. Say, I really need to get together with you."

Paul was already in a high state of agitation. He had been since the failed murder attempts.

"What is it, Simon?"

"There have been FBI agents snooping around my office asking questions about mineral leases. I think they are looking for you."

"Oh my! What did you tell them?"

"Nothing, of course. They asked some questions about how mineral leases work and what kind of money could be had from them. In fact, they brought Pete Anderson, Emma Anderson's grandson, with them. He's talking to me about brokering the rights on your land."

"Oh no, they must have figured out the whole thing. I told you this was a bad idea. We have to surrender and tell them what happened."

"I agree. We both need some time to take care of our affairs, so tonight's out. I can set up a meeting for tomorrow morning. Where do you think we should meet?"

Simon had given this it quite a bit of thought. He knew that this part of the plan could not take place in town. He had to nudge Paul into wanting to meet away from the city. Fortunately, he knew Paul well enough to know that he'd want to be out of town as well.

"I don't know, Simon. Do we have to walk into the courthouse or police station like common criminals?"

"No. I think it's in our best interest to meet them away from town. Any ideas?"

"How about Alamo?"

This was the answer Simon wanted. He knew that Paul would feel most comfortable in Alamo, his hometown. Now to pick the place.

"Sounds good. How about the parking lot at the grain elevator? That's a nice open space where we'd have some room." Simon knew that Paul would not want to be without an exit, that he didn't like feeling trapped.

Paul jumped at it. "Yes, that's a good place. What time?"

"First thing would be best. I'll call them and let them know that we'd like to meet them at the elevator about 9:30 tomorrow morning."

Paul sounded a little calmer. "So, we are agreed. We will both turn ourselves in tomorrow morning at 9:30 at the elevator in Alamo. And we'll both tell them exactly what we did and why we did it. Mrs. Anderson's death was an accident. All we were looking for was the deed. I still wish we would have just worked something out with them for the deed like I suggested in the first place."

Simon thought, "Sure, and I'd have to pay them the regular fees instead of the fraction I was going to pay you." But he said, "Yes, you're right, Paul. We should have done that. But I tried that and you know where that got us. We can't go back, can we?"

"No. We can only go forward. We must go forward." More of Paul's double speak.

"This will all be over tomorrow and I'll be on my way to real wealth," Simon thought. He hung up and thought about the call he needed to place to Agent Sanford.

Chapter Seventy-eight

4:30 pm
Bob's Tech Services
Williston, North Dakota

On the way over to Bob's Tech we decided that April would go in first and ask for Bob, since she was local. If the staff gave her any grief we would pull our shields and make them uncomfortable.

April went in. We gave her about two minutes. When we entered she was waiting at the reception counter. As we approached, a man walked up to April.

"Hello, April. Am I finally going to get some of your business over at Turner?"

"I think you may already have gotten some of our business, Bob," April answered.

Will stepped up and flashed his fed creds. Molly, Fred and I all joined him. This can be a life-changing event for people, so I always closely observe their reaction to being confronted by a group of law enforcement officers. Bob went pale.

"How can I help you?" he managed to say.

"Let's talk in your office, all right?" Will said.

Bob nodded and led us to his office. It looked like any other office except for the computer setup that looked like something out of a futuristic movie. He had four flat screens arranged two on top, two below. Why you'd need four screens is beyond me. Maybe he could watch different football games on them.

Introductions were made and I could see that Bob was impressed by the jurisdictional diversity of the group before him.

"Since you know April, do you want to take a guess at why we're here?" I asked.

Bob was smart enough to get with the program. He also knew that he hadn't done anything illegal.

"I would guess that this has something to do with replacing Mr. Turner's laptop."

"Bingo." I said.

Will asked, "When did you do that?"

"Early last week, Tuesday or Wednesday."

"And why did he want it replaced?" Will asked.

"You know, I don't really know. There was nothing wrong with the one he had. He said he just wanted a spare, a duplicate, so to speak, in case anything ever happened to the first one."

"He didn't want an upgrade, a newer model?" Molly asked.

"No. He was adamant about that. He said he wanted the exact same one. He said that he'd dropped his laptop a few times and was worried that it might conk out one day. He didn't want April to know he'd been such a klutz. He said he wanted it to have the same programs and files on it as the old one with the exception of the email files. He said he didn't need those copied."

"Mr. Davis, didn't that raise a few questions for you, that he didn't want the email files copied?" Will asked.

"Sure it did. But what he wanted was understandable. Some people write or receive emails that are embarrassing and they want to get rid of them. He didn't tell me that, but it was logical. I asked him if he wanted them copied off on a thumb drive, just in case, but he said no."

"And you'll do that, copy everything but the emails, for a client?"

"Why not? It's not illegal. And it's not like someone good couldn't still find them someplace."

"Where would 'someplace' be?" Will asked.

Bob looked at April and said, "I think your server probably has a WORM system on it. They'd still be there if you're interested. I'd be happy to help you with the recovery if you'd like."

Will answered. "That's OK. Agent Foss is an FBI specialist in computer systems. I'm sure she'll be able to get whatever we need. Bob, this is part of an ongoing FBI investigation. I'm putting you on notice that if you talk to anyone, and by anyone I mean especially Mr. Turner, you will become an accessory after the fact. Do you understand?"

"Got it—don't talk to anyone."

On the way to the car Will's phone rang.

"Will Sanford."

"Will, this is John Mokowski in the DC office. I've been tracking some wire transfers for you on this attempted murder in Apple Valley, Minnesota. I've got a possible make on the sender."

"Go ahead, John."

"We were able to track five separate transfers through a total of seven banks, winding up in Nassau. The total was an even million in U.S. funds. They came from two banks in North Dakota, one in Bismarck and one in Williston. The owner of the sending accounts is one Simon Turner of Williston, North Dakota."

"Got it, John. Can you send what you have to the Bismarck field office? I'm going to need a warrant first thing in the morning."

"Consider it on the way."

"Thanks," Will said, and he signed off.

We were at the Sub. Will didn't tell the rest of us what his phone call was about, so we just loaded up and went back to the El Rancho. Deputy Fred had to get back on patrol, so we agreed to meet at the hotel at 7:00 in the morning and said goodbye. Will and I pulled April aside before she could get in her car.

"April, we're going to need to get back into the office tomorrow morning. Can you meet us here at 7:00?" Will asked.

"Sure. I can get the neighbor to watch the boys."

"And, just a precaution, if Simon or Paul calls tonight, don't answer the phone."

She nodded, with a bit of a fear in her eyes. We bid her farewell and headed inside.

Will let us in on the phone call he received. "That call was from DC. I didn't want to talk about it in front of Mrs. Turner or the deputy. We have tracked the million dollars sent to Mr. Kline's accounts in the Bahamas. The money was sent from two different accounts in the United States. Both of them belong to Simon Turner."

We went back into the lounge, which at 5:30 on a Friday was starting to show some life. A corner table was open, so we grabbed it, sat and waited for someone to speak. I've never been good at waiting, so I took the lead.

"So, let's go get him."

"Not so fast. I want warrants for everything in his home and office. It will take until morning to get those."

"How about Paul Swanberg?" I asked.

"We can put a warrant on him, too."

Pete was still uneasy about Paul.

"I think we need to find out if Paul planned all this or if he was just involved somehow through Simon."

"We can ask them tomorrow after the arrests."

Will's phone rang again.

"Will Sanford."

"Will, this is Simon Turner. Listen, I've been talking to Paul Swanberg. He told me that he did go to the Twin Cities and break into some woman's house. He said he was looking for that deed Mr. Anderson showed me. He said that it's a mineral rights deed for his land and he was trying to recover it so he could lease the rights out and make some money."

"This is all very interesting, Mr. Turner. Why are you telling me this?"

"Look, Paul is a good man and a friend. I convinced him that his best course of action is to surrender. I've talked Paul into turning himself in. He'd like to meet you tomorrow morning at 10:00 in the parking lot of the grain elevator in Alamo. He'll be alone."

"Why in Alamo?"

"That's where he lives. He didn't want to be brought into the courthouse in cuffs so I asked him where he'd be comfortable. He said Alamo."

"Sounds good to me, Mr. Turner. Tell him that we'll be there."

Will hung up and told us what Simon had said.

"So, what's really going on here?" I asked.

"That is a very good question, Dan. We know that Turner is involved and now he has set up a meet for Swanberg to turn himself in. He said that Swanberg would be there alone. Sounds too easy to me."

"If they're in this together, he won't be alone," I said.

"That's my guess. The meet's on their turf so they know the lay of the land. Turner says Swanberg will be alone so that frees him up to take us out. I don't much like this."

"Neither do I. So here's what we'll do."

Chapter Seventy-nine

6:30 am
Saturday, December 13
Williston, North Dakota

The four out-of-towners met in the hotel restaurant for breakfast at 6:30. As we ate, we went over the plan we'd hammered out late last night. Will had been on the phone with the FBI office in Bismarck and they were sending the warrants along with a half dozen more agents. They were an ad hoc assault team, as there was no FBI Hostage Rescue Team assigned to Bismarck. An HRT is the FBI's version of SWAT. While it was unlikely, there was a chance we'd need them to help us secure the properties and with the final arrests. I wanted to take at least four of them with us to Alamo, but Will was worried about getting them into the small town unseen. Our previous visit had revealed that there were few ways to approach the town without being seen.

Winter had finally shown up. Overnight, the storm I'd been feeling in my bones had swept in from the northwest—one of those fast movers that rolls down out of Canada and seizes the Midwest in a death grip for a couple of days. Its strong north winds piled frozen crystals into desert-like white dunes that swirled around buildings, parked cars, and trees—anything that stuck up and dared challenge the northern force. With it came an air mass straight from the North Pole and a concurrent ridiculous drop in temperature. It met all the textbook requirements of a blizzard.

Storms like this have to be respected or lives will be lost. In our case, it affected, eliminated really, any chance of sneaking some of the extra troops into Alamo overland on foot. On the other hand, if it got a little heavier the visibility would decline and it could cover a vehicle approach. Hoping for the weather to get worse is not my idea of a good felony arrest plan; after all, it could get so bad you couldn't even drive.

April came in a little before 7:00, followed immediately by Deputy Eid. They joined us for coffee. April and Molly started laying out their part of the operation, which included securing any evidence in the Turner offices.

The Bismarck contingent showed up, including the local SAC, Jules Whitman, who turned out to be an exception to the more typical SACs I've known. He was polite, recognized the importance of a Minneapolis cop to the case, and was deferential enough to leave Will in charge. But it was clear that his people were his people. In order to give him something important to do while simultaneously keeping him out of our hair, Will put him in charge of the two detachments that would simultaneously secure Turner's house and offices. Will is a pretty good politician.

The hotel had a conference room we could use for a quick briefing. One thing about the feds, they don't take a shit without a plan and a briefing. While I generally agree that going into a possible shooting situation requires planning and coordination, the level of detail in the briefing was enough to put me back in bed. On the other hand, the feds rarely make mistakes like losing hostages, good guys or bystanders. The final score counts and they have an undeniably outstanding record on that. So the briefing wasn't brief. It was forty-five minutes of non-stop information.

The first order of business was to pass out pictures of the people to be arrested. This included Swanberg and Turner, but the feds had pictures of April, Pete and me as well. Nice to know we made the scorecard. Everyone involved would be able to distinguish good guys from bad guys. Whitman would take a team of four of the new guys to Turner's. They would serve the warrant and secure Turner's house and anyone in it. If there were no complications, Whitman would leave the two agents to process the house.

home, Molly would meet April at a coffee shop a block from the Turner offices at 8:30. They would go together to the offices, where

Deputy Eid had arranged for one of his office's newer, thus least-likely-to-ask-questions, officers to spend the night sleeping with the computers.

There shouldn't be anyone at the offices on a Saturday, but you never knew. If no one was there, Molly would proceed to secure the offices. If one of the employees had decided to catch up on a little work, they'd be shown the warrant and asked to sit tight in the break room.

Deputy Eid would be on standby down the street in case local authority was needed. Whitman would then get there with two of the guys who had gone to Turner's house. That group of five—April, Molly, Whitman and the two agents from Bismarck—would process the offices, collecting whatever evidence they found. That left the last two agents to go with Will, Pete and me out to Alamo.

The town of Alamo, which we had unknowingly reconnoitered on Thursday, was laid out pretty much to the other side's advantage for this meeting. From the grain elevator on the north edge of town, anyone could see us approach from miles away and watch us make our way through town to the grain elevator. That kind of advantage is something that makes a guy nervous.

I thought we should split the group and have the two Bismarck guys circle around the town and enter from the north. We had overhead imagery printed off Google Earth so everyone could see what we were talking about. The still-operating grain elevator was on the north side of Railroad Ave. The open parking lot was on the south side. Swanberg would expect us to arrive from the south on County 11. If the back-up team headed north on Highway 50 at the last county road west of Alamo, then east on another county road, they could swing around in a flanking movement from the north. They would be behind Swanberg, and be in position to support us if there was any trouble.

On the Google Earth site we could see a rise in the road about a half-mile north of the grain elevator. They would see the elevator before they crested the hill, so they could slow down and creep up to the military crest of the hill. The military crest is the highest point you can climb a hill without being seen by the bad guys on the other side of the hill. Will told them to call when they got there and to wait until he called them for support or to block an escape or whatever was necessary. They had the back door.

It was approaching 7:45, and I wanted to get going. I knew that it was only about a forty-mile drive to Alamo, but the weather was getting worse and it could take more than an hour to get there. My desire was to arrive at 9:45, ahead of Swanberg and, maybe, Turner. With the time needed to get the back-up team in place, we didn't have any time to waste. Everyone, with the exception of the women, was going "Tommy Tactical" as we say—putting on their tactical vests and firearms. Pete, who was technically not coming, had his own vest, one I'd borrowed years ago from the MPD, and his own sidearm, which I'd decided to let him keep. I'd made it clear to him that I didn't want to see his gun unless Will and I were both down and out of the fight.

The decision to let Pete come along at all hadn't set well with Will. Law enforcement types rely upon each other with a faith based on training. They know that the other guy, whether he is police, sheriff's department, state troopers, federal agent or military, has had training in many areas, including firearms training, small-unit tactics, tactical hand signals to communicate with each other, fields-of-fire discipline, use of covering fire and many other needed skills for use in an urban combat situation. Pete had good firearms skills and had good fire discipline, but he was lacking in the other areas, especially the vital communication skills. I told Will that I'd keep him close. Will finally agreed, going with the theory that more firepower is always a good thing.

We mounted up—two cars going to Turner's house, one car to the coffee shop, and two cars headed north to Alamo. Will, Pete and I reviewed the plan as we drove, trying to think of anything we might have left out. A dude named Field Marshall Count Helmuth Von Moltke once said that "No battle plan survives first contact with the enemy" and I wanted to have the contingencies laid out in our minds for when they'd be necessary.

There was still the possibility that Paul would be there by himself, ready to turn himself in for the naughty boy he was. In that case, we'd just pull up, say "Hi!" to Paul, snap on the cuffs and take him away. Then we'd have to track down Simon. Maybe he'd be home when the feds called, maybe not, but I was willing to separate the two events.

That was the best possibility. Going down from there was that Paul would be there but not quite so willing to be taken into federal custody, or Paul would be there, armed and ready to take care of the nuisance we had become or ready to commit suicide by cop. Additional negative scenarios were basically the same, augmented by the presence of Simon Turner. A long shot was that Turner, who had already shown the resourcefulness to hire Kline, would have added more guns to the scene. I discounted additional pros because I didn't think he had had the time needed to bring anyone in, so any more shooters would be local. Two or more guys firing from cover would be a game stopper for us, necessitating the back-up team. Sun Tzu, the author of *The Art of War* said, "All war is deception." I'm willing to listen to these guys—they were always right.

About a half hour into the drive we got a call from Whitman. His team had the Turner house secured and were starting the search. There was no sign of Turner. They were on their way to the offices. Will relayed this info to Pete and me, and then passed the message to the other part of our team.

"Where he is?" Will asked.

"We know he's not at the golf course," Pete said, looking out the window.

"That's true enough," I agreed. The snow had picked up and was blow-ing sideways as we drove north. Visibility was down to under a mile. My nearly three-ton Suburban was being tossed laterally enough that I had to concentrate on the road. The snow was beginning to stick to the road. If it got much more slippery, I'd have to slow down from my already sedate forty miles per hour just to stay on the road.

Another phone call, this one from Molly to Will. They were at Turn-er's offices and, as hoped, no one else was there. They would sit on the place until Whitman got there for the evidence search.

Pete asked, "So, Turner's not there either?"

The question went unanswered. Since he wasn't at home or the office, where was he? There is always a chance in a situation like this that the person you are looking for has done something domestic, like gone to the grocery store, or for a haircut. But no one would be out in this weather unless they had to be. More likely was that he'd be waiting for us with Paul Swanberg. More worry.

We made the turn onto Highway 50 and proceeded east to the county road about two miles west of Alamo. The back-up team headed north and we slowed down. They were driving the classic black FBI Suburban and went speeding off into the storm with no apparent concern for the conditions.

"I hope those guys didn't just get assigned to Bismarck," Will said.

"You got that right. If this is their first encounter with this kind of weather, we might be on our own," I said.

We cruised east at about twenty miles per hour and pulled over just a little before we had to turn north on County 11 to get to Alamo. Our wait was short, as the Will's phone rang and we got the "in-position" call from the back-up team. I looked at Pete and Will and we all nodded. It was 9:50.

"Here we go," I said.

I turned north into Alamo. We cruised up County 11 to the point where it forks. I stayed to the left at the fork, preferring the perimeter of the town. This would keep any possible ambush sites to only one side of the car—the right. To the left there was only farmland. I turned right onto Railroad and covered the final two blocks to Railroad's intersection with Main. There, I had to turn onto Main, cross the old railway bed and turn right into the grain elevator's parking lot.

We were gunned-up and caffeined-up, making us amped up. I slowly slid the big car across the front of the grain elevator, staying as far from the buildings as possible.

The installation had two sets of buildings. One was a classic four-story corrugated elevator building that narrows to the lift house that climbs to about six stories. It looked to be about forty feet across the front and sixty feet front to back. It was separated from the other building by about eighty feet of open parking lot.

The second part of the elevator complex was a combination of three buildings; the center one was a virtual twin to the standalone building. The closest building to us was similar to the other two, only turned ninety degrees clockwise. The last building was a big brother to the others, half again taller and wider than its lesser cousins. I could imagine dozens of good firing positions within all those walls and there was no cover, save the Suburban, for us.

I cruised on, not stopping, but looking for any sign of Paul Swanberg. A gold Buick Lucerne was parked at the very eastern end of the complex, the kind of car I'd expect Paul to drive. If we got a little closer, I could get the tag number and Will could run it.

Will didn't want to wait. He said, "Pull it over here and let's get out."

"OK," I said, "you're the boss."

Chapter Eighty

Behind the main elevator
Alamo, North Dakota

Paul and Simon waited in the lee of the wind at the southeast corner of the larger building. Paul's need for privacy precluded standing out in plain sight. Simon was fine with that. He couldn't let anyone see him for his plan to work.

The pair wanted both cover from the wind and the ability to see any approaching car without being seen. It was a dicey compromise—trying to stay hidden from both the eyes of the law officers and the eyes of the storm. The best position would have been to be north of the buildings, but the howling blizzard erased that possibility. The storm made it necessary to watch the approaching car from the southeast corner, then retreat to the northeast corner to maintain cover when the car reached the parking lot. They saw the car pull over and three men get out.

"OK, Paul. I told them you'd come out first, then me. You go ahead and when you reach them, I'll come out."

Paul wasn't so sure. "I think we should go together."

"No, they'll feel more at ease if they only have to handle us one at a time. If we both go together, they'll think we're up to something. I told them one at a time and that is what they're expecting."

Simon knew the key to dealing with Paul was to remind him of the rules. A change in the rules was always trouble.

"All right. I'll go take a peek and talk to them to make sure they're ready."

Paul walked forward toward the corner of the massive grain elevator. He slowed as he approached the corner to take a look around it and announce his intentions. As he did, Simon unfastened his coat and produced his prairie dog rifle, an AR-15 with a thirty-round magazine. He was proficient enough to hit a prairie dog at two hundred yards with it, but this would be the first time he'd ever shot at a man.

I exited the Sub from the side closest to the building. Pete and Will got out from the passenger side. I knew the elevator building was less than 150 feet away, but the snow was so heavy and blowing so hard I could barely make it out. Will had passed Pete and was moving later-ally, creating a combat spread ahead about six steps past me. He had just opened his mouth to yell out for Paul Swanberg to show himself when a figure appeared at the corner of the building and a shot rang out. The round hit Will in his lower right abdomen, and he staggered away from us toward a pile of construction debris. I could see that he was going to make it so I dove toward Pete who was just rounding the front of the Sub. As I hit him with what I hoped was the best cross-body block I'd ever thrown in my life, I heard another shot. We tumbled to the ground and I yelled, "Are you hit?"

"I don't think so."

We scrambled on hands and knees to the cover of the Sub. I yelled out to Will.

"Will? Can you hear me?"

Will answered, "Yes. I'm hit but not bad. I'm calling the cavalry."

Will had made it to the pile of construction materials, a position of relative safety, all things considered. He pulled his radio from his pocket.

"Team Two. Team Two. Shots fired. Shots fired. Shooter or shooters located at the northeast corner of the east building complex. We are pinned down off the southeast corner of that building."

The back-up team responded, "We're coming in."

At the sound of the first shot, Paul Swanberg reeled in place and looked at Simon. Simon was holding his rifle and looking at the result of his first shot. Like many target shooters, Simon had made three mistakes. First, he was unprepared for the utter lack of visibility he encountered, which resulted in a complete lack of proper sight picture. Second, while he was accustomed to the rifle, he had been out in the cold for over twenty-five minutes. He was juiced up on coffee and over-anticipated the recoil of the rifle by pulling down and left with his forward left hand. This caused the round to go low left. Finally, Simon was then preoccupied with whether or not he had hit what he was shooting at. He couldn't believe he hadn't hit the man high center chest, where he had aimed and it caused him to pause for a moment instead of doing what a trained combat shooter would have done, pour fire down range. This pause saved Will's life.

His trance was broken when he saw all three of the targets moving. He got off one more shot without really aiming, then noticed Paul.

"Simon! What are you doing?" Paul shouted.

"I'm getting set to get rich, you little shit. All my life I've scraped while you had all the chances. And what did you do with them? Nothing. Well, not this time."

Simon lunged at Paul. As they tangled, Simon managed to hang the rifle's shoulder strap over Paul's head. Paul stepped back, aghast that the weapon was now hanging from his body. Simon pulled a pistol from under his heavy coat and lunged again, pushing Paul out into the line of fire. Simon leveled the pistol at Paul and yelled, "Get out there and die, you little prick!"

Paul fumbled with the strap as he staggered backward, flipped the rifle off, stumbled again, then caught his footing and ran for his car. It was only twenty feet away, so he made it in four or five quick steps. Simon watched the rifle fall to the ground and decided that was acceptable. There wouldn't be any fingerprints on it but it was the rifle that had shot that FBI guy. They had seen Paul run from the building with it and would put two and two together. He had already decided to tell them that he had sold the rifle to Paul months ago. He had even dummied up a sales receipt. That would establish ownership. As Paul ran, Simon waited for the sound of gunfire that would cut Paul down, ending his problems.

From behind the Sub, I saw a man with a rifle run out into the open. The rifle's shoulder strap was clumsily draped over his neck, not a proper position for firing. He was looking back toward the building, not at us. As he moved he fumbled with the strap, finally clearing it over his head and throwing the rifle to the ground. As the strap cleared his head, his hood came down and I could see the man's face. "He could be Pete's brother," I thought. He matched the pictures of Paul Swanberg.

He turned and ran to the car, threw himself into it and was struggling to get in position to drive off when I realized what was happening. I pulled my XD and readied to take the shot.

As the car started moving, I stepped around the front of the Sub and raised my gun. It would be a moving target shot, but I'd made them before. I also knew that it would take several rounds just to break out the glass in the windows, so I was ready to send all seventeen rounds my pistol carried into the car. This had all the ingredients of a righteous shoot, but before I could fire, I sensed Pete next to me. Just as I was pulling the trigger, he grabbed my arm and raised it so the shot would miss.

"What are you doing?"

"If that's Paul Swanberg, I'm saving my cousin."

"Are you nuts? I saw him. It's gotta be Swanberg."

The car sped by. I looked at the driver. He looked straight at us. He looked a lot like Pete except for the terror in his eyes. He turned south into town.

At the same time, I heard the sound of gunshots from the north side of the grain elevator. I said to Pete, "Go check on Will," then I ran toward the grain elevator.

Simon listened for gunshots but there were none. "What the hell," he said to himself. "Are these people stupid? I just gave them the prime suspect and all they had to do was shoot him. Why didn't they?"

With the frustration that drives men to impulse, he squeezed the .45 automatic in his hand, preparing to take a shot at Paul himself, if he got the chance. Paul didn't give him one, speeding off in his car.

"Shit!" he said through clenched teeth. He shook his head and started walking back to the north-side door of the elevator. As he rounded the back corner of the building, he saw a black Suburban careen into the parking lot. It slid to a stop in front of him and the doors burst open. Two black clad men with "FBI" lettered on their chests jumped out, guns drawn and ready.

"Drop the gun," the first man screamed.

"Hands on your head," the second one yelled.

Both federal agents had their guns on him. He complied with the second command before his gloved hand felt the weight and he remembered he was carrying his pistol. As he raised his hands, the pistol came up into firing position. The two federal agents were well trained and didn't hesitate. As one, they fired on the man who had fulfilled the definition of a lethal threat, striking him with three rounds each, center mass. All Simon Turner felt was the cold.

Chapter Eighty-one

The two agents came around the building and ran toward me. I pointed toward the cover pile where Will Sanford was and yelled, "Over there." We all ran over and found Will lying on his side, his pistol in one hand, his radio in the other. Over the history of human conflict it has often been debated which of these two devices is the greatest weapon ever invented. Today, the radio won.

"How you doing, man?" I asked.

"Just freakin' wonderful," Will answered. Not bad for a guy whose gut was bleeding. "What happened back there?" Will asked, indicating the elevator building.

The taller agent answered. "When we rolled into the lot a guy came around the back corner carrying a .45. We came out of the truck and ordered him to drop it. He raised it toward us and we stopped him."

"Who was it?" Will asked.

Good question.

The agents looked at each other and one of them said, "I think it was the other guy, Turner." He pulled a picture of Simon from his pocket. "Yeah, it was this guy. He was carrying a pistol and raised it toward us . . ."

Will cut him off before he could repeat the stock answer. "And his condition?"

"Down and dead," the agents answered, almost in unison.

Will nodded and the second agent added, "There's an AR on the ground back there."

Will gave commands. "Secure it and secure the area," he told the agents. He looked at Pete and me and said, "That's probably what he hit me with."

"Sounded like it to me," I agreed.

Pete and I rolled Will onto his back. I handed his firearm to the closest Bismarck guy, who cleared it and stuck it in his pocket with the practiced ease of an expert. Will's wound was through and through, as the trauma people say. There was a bloody hole in the side of his jacket. The round had somehow snuck in between the front and rear panels of his flak jacket. He had a messy exit wound. The rear panel of the vest had caught the round, making it a lot easier to find than waiting for the snow to melt in the field behind us. He was bleeding, but blood is like oil on the garage floor—a little can look like an awful lot. I gauged him as serious, but not critical and formulated a plan.

"Here's what's going to happen. You two are going to take Agent Sanford to Williston as fast as conditions allow."

Will tried to interrupt, but I cut him off.

"You are wounded and no longer in charge." I looked at the agents. "The weather is too bad for a chopper, so he has to be driven to the nearest hospital, and I'm guessing that's Williston. You two both need to go because someone has to drive and someone has to tend to Agent Sanford. Take it easy. The roads are getting bad and I don't want to have to wait until spring to find you."

"And what are you two going to be doing?" Will asked.

"We're going after Swanberg."

At that moment, I looked up in time to see a gold Buick racing out of town north on 11. Paul Swanberg had had time to decide what he wanted to do. Now he was doing it.

I said, "Let's go," and Pete and I jumped into my Sub. Swanberg had a head start but not much and I had a definitive advantage in terms of car. I fired up the big V-8 and we took off in pursuit.

Paul Swanberg knew the lay of the land but I had the horses and the traction. He was already out of sight, but I knew we could make that up quickly.

Paul Swanberg was in a completely reactionary state. His mind knew what he had just seen, that Simon had shot one of the policemen, but everything was surreal. Simon had literally thrown him out from behind the building into the line of fire. All he could think about now was running. He had jumped into his car and fled the scene without a thought of where he was going. He drove toward his old homestead, but then realized that he couldn't go there. That would be the first place they would look. So he did a quick U-turn and headed back north, into the storm.

He would go to Canada. He knew the people at the border station because he went into Canada frequently. He fished there and had business acquaintances there. The crossing was only forty miles away. Once there, he would figure out what to do next.

Clearly, he would have to hire a criminal lawyer and arrange to get back into the United States, but he would have to make sure that Simon was not going to try to get him killed again.

As he sped out of town, he saw four men near the wounded man and a black Suburban that hadn't been there before. He hoped the injured man was all right and wondered aloud, "Where's Simon?"

The storm was intensifying and visibility was down to a couple hundred yards. I thought we might run over Swanberg without a chance to slow down. That didn't happen.

What happened is something that, as a lifetime Minnesotan, I'll forever be ashamed of. Roads in this part of the country run straight north–south and east–west. We were running straight north and did so for about ten miles. I let the speed get up to about sixty, fast for the conditions when, out of nowhere, a ninety-degree left bend in the road appeared. I'm sure there was a sign but I didn't see it. Fortunately, there was a dirt road that continued straight north and I used it like a truck overrun in the mountains. But before I could bring down the speed, the Sub skipped left and hung two wheels over the left shoulder. We ran up against a dirt berm on the left side and the big rig slowed to nothing. We were stuck.

I looked at Pete and we both said the only thing appropriate for this situation. "Shit."

"I have a shovel and tractions mats in the back."

We bailed out and went to the back of the truck where I pulled out the shovel and the mats and we went to work.

The Buick

Paul was still moving at a good, but not reckless, speed. He'd negotiated the double ninety-degree bends safely, but was approaching another more subtle hazard, a simple bend in the road necessitated by a small lake. He was going over fifty when he lifted his foot off the gas pedal. Doing so turned the engine into a brake, but in his front-wheel-drive car that slowed only the front wheels. The sudden drag on the front end gave the rear end a chance to overtake the front. The car began to slide, first left, then right. It finally snapped left and, only about a mile and a half from the double bends where Dan and Pete were just starting to dig, Paul's car slid off the road out onto the lake. The ice held for a second then released under the weight of the car.

Paul's car went through the ice about twenty feet from the shoreline where the water was only a couple feet deep. He was able to open the door and get out but now he had a life-and-death dilemma. Paul knew from a lifetime of living in North Dakota that to leave the vehicle was sure death. He had planned for this his entire life, had read about it, and had packed for it. The "go bag," which was in his car from October through March every year, included his emergency supplies—a high-grade blanket, candles, energy bars, flares, a tow line, emergency reflectors, gloves, even a hand-crank generator so he could power his cell phone. He was ready for being stuck in the snow. He wasn't ready for being stuck in the water.

Being stuck in the water required him to leave the car. If he stayed in the car, he would stay wet and would die. But he knew that he couldn't leave his emergency kit.

He would have to do the one thing he was sorely equipped to do. He would have to improvise and change his plans. He would have to grab his kit, leave the car, and set up some kind of shelter on land.

After wrestling the back door open he got to his survival bag and tried to carry the heavy bag over his shoulder, but his footing was so poor he slipped and fell fully under the surface of the freezing water. Struggling back to his feet, he slogged to the shoreline.

He was close to the road, so it was only a matter of time. The next car that drove by would find him but in this weather, how long might that be? Shaking uncontrollably, he wrapped the blanket around him and held himself tight against the cold.

How long?

The Suburban

All told, it took only fifteen minutes to get us back on the road, but that's a long time when you're chasing someone. It's also a long time out in the cold. We had gloves and hats and were working physically, but I was numb. The Sub's thermometer said it was five degrees and I knew that the wind was running at thirty-plus gusts. Wind chill would be down near fifteen or twenty below. This is the cold that can cause frostbite in less than five minutes.

We drove straight ahead for about thirty yards to a stop sign. There was another county road that would take us west about two hundred yards to where it intersected the northbound County 11 again. I knew this because one of the things I did when we loaded back up was to turn on the GPS. Guess I should have done that before; maybe I'd have been ready for the turn.

I took it easier, figuring that we'd lost him, but I wanted to at least give it a try before heading back to Williston to admit defeat to the feds. I was guessing that Paul might be trying for Canada, but I thought that was a long shot, and even if that was where Swanberg was headed, there were a thousand ways for an experienced person to get across. You didn't have to go to a border station. In fact, that would be the worst way to do it. I mentioned this to Pete.

"But if he is headed north, a border station is how he'll do it. He has to. It's the proper way to go."

"You think so?" I asked.

"Only way he can. Let's call the feds and have them notify the Canadians."

"Good idea. Call Will's phone and see who answers."

As he did, I negotiated the bend around the lake on north County 11.

The Lake

Paul had wrapped himself tightly but was not getting any warmer. He looked for his cell phone, not sure it would even work this far out of town. No luck. Must have dropped it in the lake or left it in the car, he thought.

At least a half hour had gone by but there had been no cars. He started thinking about warm places like Florida and Arizona and began to feel warmer. Then, the strangest thing happened. He began to feel too warm. He needed to take off his clothes. He removed his gloves and his soaked jacket and felt better. He kept removing clothes. The more he took off, the better he felt. Soon, he was down to his underwear and he felt just fine. And sleepy. He wanted to sleep. He needed to sleep.

Paul Swanberg lay down under his blanket and closed his eyes.

The Suburban

Just north of the second bend, we came to a little curve that GPS said went around a lake. I slowed further, not wanting to repeat our dig out, and went right up the center of the road. About halfway through the mile-long curve I noticed the faint image of skid marks in the snow, then deeper tracks going off to the left. They had to be fresh. Skid marks had about a twenty-minute lifespan in this wind. I nudged Pete, who was just now getting a few bars on his cell.

"You see that?"

"Yeah," he said, flipping the phone off.

We kept our eyes open and I saw, just offshore, the top half of a gold Buick in the water. I stopped.

We got out and started searching. Pete wasted no time and ran straight into the water to the car.

"There's no one in the car," he reported.

"He must be here somewhere."

We searched. I saw some tracks and waved Pete over. We followed them and found a reflective survival blanket. Under it was Paul Swanberg. He was unconscious.

Pete reached down and checked for a pulse.

"He's alive," he said and started scooping him up in his big arms. I grabbed Pete's arm.

"If we leave him, or even just take a minute, he'll be gone. Hell, he's probably gone already."

"No, he's family. And if he's my family he's yours too."

"Pete, he's the guy who killed Grams. He's the guy who was at least in on trying to kill your whole family. Yeah, that's my whole family too. I say leave him for the coyotes."

Pete would have nothing to do with that. "We'll get him help and then find out what really happened."

He carried his cousin Paul to my Sub and loaded him in the back. There he pulled a blanket out of my winter driving bag, climbed in the back and wrapped Paul in it. I climbed in front.

"Turn the heat up full."

"Got it."

While Pete worked on Paul, I got the Sub turned around and we headed back to Alamo and Williston. It would be the longest hour-drive of my life.

Chapter Eighty-two

Mercy Medical Center
Williston, North Dakota

I called ahead to get the location of the Williston hospital. We rolled into the emergency entrance of Mercy Medical Center seventy-two minutes after leaving the lake.

All along the way, Pete had been wrapping Paul in my emergency blankets. He also found my supply of chemical warming packs, popped all of them and stuffed them around Paul's body under the blanket. I had the temp in the car up to about ninety with everything running flat out—front and rear. Finally, Pete had taken off his shirt and lay down next to Paul to warm him with his own body heat. When the doctors and ER folks opened the door that's what they found.

"Let us take over, sir," the lead ER nurse said.

"We found him nearly naked, wet from crashing his car into a lake," Pete said.

The staff of Mercy took over and we went looking for Will Sanford. We didn't have far to look.

There was a crowd outside one of the rooms. Molly Foss and April Turner were there along with the two agents who had been with us in Alamo.

I looked at Pete, knowing that someone was going to have to tell April that her brother-in-law was dead in the snow in Alamo. Deputy Joe Eid was there too. He'd been with April and Molly all day. I pulled him over first.

"You get the rundown?"

"Pretty much. I sent a car to Alamo to secure the scene for your people. I suppose you'll be wanting the feds to do the crime scene stuff."

"I'm sure that's what they'll want. It's a fed-involved shooting, so they'll want control. That's a little different than for you and me, huh?"

Fred nodded. When a local police officer or sheriff is involved in a shooting, the other department takes the lead on the investigation. I'd headed up several sheriff-involved shootings. But when the feds are involved, they investigate it themselves. Whenever you play poker there's someone with the most chips, and in our cases no one has more chips than the feds. The power of the big stack.

"I'll need to talk to Mrs. Turner," I said.

Fred nodded and asked, "OK if I come along?"

"Sure thing." I wasn't going to turn down any help for this.

We walked over to the treatment room and I looked in. Will Sanford was lying on his left side, naked from the waist up. He had a blanket covering his lower extremities and was probably pantless. His stocking covered feet stuck out from under the blanket. He had been hit about two inches from his right side, about four inches above the belt. I could see where they'd bandaged the wounds all the way around to the exit wound in his back. Nasty. He seemed in pretty good spirits for a guy who'd just cheated death.

He saw me and asked, "You get him?"

"Yeah, we brought him in. He'd run his car off the road into a shallow lake and was wet and unconscious when we found him. Pete gave him first aid all the way back to town. He was still breathing when we got here."

A tall doctor in a blue scrub cap and white jacket had entered the room while I was giving Will the rundown. The doctor looked at us and introduced himself. "I'm Jeff Neset, the on-call today. You brought the other guy in?"

We confirmed we did.

He shook hands with Pete and me as we gave him our names. He looked at Pete and me with sadness in his eyes.

Pete said, "All he had on when we found him was his underwear."

"Sounds like late-stage hypothermia. People sometimes think they are getting too warm and start taking off their clothes. Crazy, I know, but that's what they do. Usually it's the last thing they do."

"What's the story on his condition, doc," Fred asked.

"Touch and go. If he makes it, it will because of what you guys did."

"He's not out of the woods?" Pete asked.

"Not yet. We are doing a procedure called "gastric lavage," trying to warm him from the inside by pumping warm fluids into his body cavities. That's the best thing we can do to warm him."

He said to Pete, "Your makeshift warming procedure—taking off your clothes and holding him—is surely the only thing that got him here alive. His core body temp was still way down when he got here, but, in this weather, he would have been a goner if you hadn't done what you did."

"How much longer until he'll be out of the woods?"

"No telling. Even if he makes it, there's a chance of brain damage from oxygen starvation, but that is offset by the fact that he was hypothermic." He weighed the possibilities in his hands.

"It can still go either way. I'll go check on him," he said and he left. We told Will we'd be back after we talked to April.

April looked at us as we emerged from Will's room and I motioned for her to come with me. Fred followed us into a small waiting area. I began.

"April, here's what happened, at least what we know so far. As you know, Simon called Will last night and told him that he had arranged a meeting with Paul and us where Paul was going to turn himself in. We also found out last night that the money used to pay the hit man came from Simon's accounts. So we knew he was involved. What we didn't know was where Simon was going to be this morning. That's why we sent a team to his house and then to back you and Molly up at the office. But Simon wasn't in either of those locations.

"Our team—Pete, Will, the two Bismarck agents and I went out to Alamo to meet with Paul. When we got to Alamo, Pete, Will and I got out of the car and someone opened fire on us. That's how Will got hit. We all took cover. Paul ran out from behind the grain elevator and jumped in his car and left. What we didn't see was that Simon was behind the grain elevator with him. We had a back-up team in place and they came in from the north and ran smack into Simon coming around the corner of the building. He had a gun in his hand, which he raised. In the exchange that followed, Simon was shot and killed."

April shook her head. "I knew he was in on this, I just knew it. There was too much money involved for him not to be."

She was in a bit of shock, but asked, "Is he the one who shot Agent Sanford?"

"We don't know. There was a rifle on the scene. Ballistics will tell us more."

"Then Simon did the shooting," April said firmly. "Paul doesn't own a gun. He's not a hunter even though nearly everyone here is."

Interesting observation. We'd see when the crime scene team was finished.

"Are you OK, April?" Fred asked.

"I'm fine, Fred. I guess I'm the one who gets to call his parents then, don't I?"

"I'll take care of notifying them, if you'd like," Fred offered.

"Thanks, but I should be the one," April said.

We left April and Fred to talk about the family stuff as went back to Will's room. We intruded on a pleasant scene between him and Agent Foss. Molly was holding his hand.

"I'll check back with you later," I said.

"Sounds good," Will said, and we left.

I found the two agents and asked them if anyone had ordered up a crime scene team.

"Yeah, Agent Sanford wouldn't leave Alamo until a sheriff's deputy was there to secure the scene and we had a team on the way."

"Well, I guess we're done here for now," I said to Pete. "Let's go see if the hotel still has our rooms so you can change clothes."

Chapter Eighty-three

Monday, December 16
Williston, North Dakota

The storm cleared North Dakota by Monday morning after spending all Saturday and half of Sunday pummeling the area with high winds and snow. The resulting sunshine and crystal clear blue skies revealed a little over two feet of the white stuff that had drifted into magnificent house-covering mounds in Alamo. Investigating the shooting scene at the elevator was as difficult as any crime scene I'd ever been involved in. The feds brought in three big RVs for the investigators to use; one was a mobile lab, one was a communications center and the other was a warming shack, complete with a cook. They got the job done in spite of the conditions.

The crime scene team had found one thing we had not expected. Just a few steps inside the back door of the elevator they found a small hidden room stocked with supplies which would enable someone to hide out for some time. They found survival blankets, power bars, water, hand-heaters, even a book. Only a five-minute walk into town, behind the old high school, they found Simon Turner's car. Apparently he had planned to shoot at us, push Paul and the rifle into our line of fire, knowing that we'd return fire. He then planned to run to his hidey-hole. That would have wrapped things up rather tidily for Simon.

I had spent most of Sunday at the hospital talking with Will and waiting for word on Paul Swanberg, who was still unconscious and on life support. After the doctors had done everything they could to raise his temperature, they could only wait and see if he would come around.

Just after 5:00 pm, he crashed and, in spite of their very best efforts and expertise in dealing with hypothermia, Paul died.

By Monday we had a pretty good idea about the course of events that had led us here. In his Alamo home, Paul had left detailed notes that stated he had committed the two break-ins. Grams' death had definitely been unplanned. As we thought, he had expected her to be gone. When she interrupted him, he just reacted.

At that point, he thought it should end and had told Simon so. He also left a record of the conversations he'd had with Simon where he had first suggested that they simply contact Emma Anderson and discuss the deed with her. He relayed how Simon had convinced him to try to recover the deed, telling Paul that he had contacted Pete and Pete had insisted that Paul be cut out of the deed. Simon had told Paul that he could lose all his holdings.

The FBI team found little of interest in Simon's house other than several books on OCD and ADHD. There were notations in the books that indicated that Simon had been researching ways to understand and control the behavior of a person with those conditions. Oddly, the high-lighted passages in the books explained that OCD is not a debilitating condition, simply a way some people react to stress, and there is no way to control a person's behavior by exploiting their OCD.

They also found a sales receipt for the sale of an AR-15 rifle by Simon to Paul dated August 23rd. It had been signed by both people but the FBI experts quickly determined that Paul's signature was a forgery.

Likewise, the signatures in the daily log book at Turner Mineral Leases showed forgeries for the days when Paul supposedly sent emails to George Kline. The investigators also found mineral rights leases in Simon's office that would put Simon in control of Paul's land under terms that were a fraction of what Paul should have received.

Pete took a strange, at least to me, point of view of the entire affair. He had had a brother, after a fashion, for a moment. He had found him, come to hate him, then forgive him, and then lost him forever in just a few days' time. I hoped he'd be able to get over the combined feeling of loss and confusion the appearance of Paul Swanberg had brought to his life. Only time will tell.

Will stayed in Williston a few more days until the docs let him out. He had Molly there to sit with him.

Paul's parents flew back to Alamo to bury their son. Pete, joined by his wife Carol, stayed through Paul's funeral. Considering that Paul's father and mother, Oscar and Betty Swanberg, were his aunt and uncle, they had a lot to talk about.

Pete told Paul's parents that we were convinced Paul was basically a good guy who was led astray by the false information that Simon Turner had pumped into him. He had made his decisions based upon lies.

As I prepared to pack up and head back home alone, I thought about the years to come. I thought about "Forever Yours" and who he was. I thought about how his love had transcended the years and how his letters and his gift of the deed had brought us to this point, how love can stay alive even though both persons involved are gone.

While I have a sister and enjoy her children as an uncle would, I started thinking that maybe some additional family wouldn't be such a bad thing. As I headed out of Williston I called Maria and asked her if she had any time off coming. It was my turn to go south, and after the last two days of winter madness, I was ready for some warm weather and the touch of a warm human.

Maybe I should stop by my favorite jeweler before I get on the plane.

Epilogue

Saturday, April 18
Robbinsdale, Minnesota

Four months had passed since the unexpected turn of events in Alamo, North Dakota. On this spring Saturday afternoon, I was on my way to hang out at Pete's while he decided whether or not to move. He loved the house on the lake but it was quite a bit bigger than he needed and Carol was making noises about the kitchen not being right for the work she was doing. That was to be expected, as the home had been built in the 1950s and, in those days, even big homes didn't have kitchens that compare with today's designs. Pete was faced with the move or remodel decision.

Personally, I wanted him to remodel. The house was magnificent and its location on the lake was central, near good fishing, skiing water and boat-up restaurants. Most important, it was convenient for me to visit.

It wasn't like he couldn't afford it. He and Carol had been comfortable before last fall's events, but now they were approaching the "money is no object" level of wealth.

After things settled down Pete and his "new" family became good friends. Oscar and Betty Swanberg were very nice people who had no idea that Oscar's father had been sowing his wild oats, so to speak, before he married Oscar's mother, Margit.

April Turner took over Turner Mineral Leases, LLC, as sole owner, and soon approached Pete and Ruth about their mineral rights deed. Pete went to Oscar and Betty and offered to share the proceeds fifty–fifty. They recognized Pete and Ruth's legal and moral claim to all the riches and accepted his offer with grace. Within two months April had leased about half the area and had collected over fifty million dollars in fees. Needless to say, everyone was happy about that. As part of their agreement on the leases, the Swanbergs and Andersons decided to establish a fund to provide scholarships for people studying OCD at the University of Minnesota.

The final nail in Simon's coffin, so to speak, was his secretary, Angie Nash. She had kept, as she had for Matt Turner, a log of all phone calls made or received by the president of Turner Mineral Leases, LLC.

Matt had told her years ago that complete records were the key to any disputes over lease negotiations. She had a record of every phone call—the date, time and the phone number called or received by the man in that office. Over the next few months, her phone log helped lead to the arrests of thirteen people in four states on charges of conspiracy to commit murder, theft of government property, and various other counts involving secret weapons. This ultimately solved the riddle of the HaloRemi 35.

The combined evidence of the emails and wire transfers definitively showed Simon Turner to be the man behind the entire scheme. If it had worked he would have been a billionaire.

In life's biggest gambles you play for the biggest stakes. In this case, the gamble was wealth beyond the dreams of avarice versus death in the cold of a North Dakota blizzard. Simon Turner lost.

My own life had taken a bit of a turn. Shortly after returning to the Cities, I flew to Phoenix and spent a week with Maria. One night, after a long romantic dinner, we were back at her place and I popped the question. Down on one knee and the whole bit. She didn't say no.

She didn't say yes either. She said, "Not yet."

After some conversation to clarify her position, which was, "I love you and want to spend my life with you; I'm just not ready to marry you yet," I recovered and tried to look at the whole thing from her angle.

She is happy where she is, is in line for a promotion, loves her job, is close to her family and really likes having her emotional and physical needs tended to by a somewhat cynical German–American semi-retired cop from Minnesota. She's perfectly happy where we're at. So am I, I think.

Author's Note:

As a residential Realtor®, I get to sit in a lot of continuing education classes to keep my license current. It was in one of these classes that the seed of an idea was planted that grew into *Alamo, North Dakota*. It was "What would happen if mineral rights had been granted someone long ago when they were virtually worthless and now, eighty or so years later, something valuable was found on that land?" I had read something about an oil field in North Dakota that piqued my interest in that area.

I knew my family had once lived in Fargo, but that is almost Minnesota, certainly not a *real* North Dakota experience. Later, when talking about the idea with my dad, he said, "Put it in Alamo." I thought "Alamo? Alamo, North Dakota—what a great title."

"Is there an Alamo?" I asked Dad.

He said, "There was in 1918, when your grandparents lived there."

I went looking for Alamo and found it still exists. It's a little town with a population of fifty-one according to the 2000 census. I have a feeling that number may be a bit larger now. But just finding Alamo wasn't enough. In order to have Alamo as the central focus of this story, it had to be at least close to oil-producing land.

I began researching North Dakota oil production and found that the biggest and best-kept secret in American energy today is arguably the Bakken Oil Field. It stretches in a roughly east-west oval shape that covers much of northwestern North Dakota, northeastern Montana and southern Alberta. For the Alamo location to work, it had to be located somewhere in that oval.

Looking at a map I found the little town of my ancestry was smack in the middle of the Bakken Oil Field. It was good karma.

And the story began.

On Alamo and the Bakken Oil Field:

Alamo is in the heart of the oil-producing geological formations of the Bakken. But those formations are primarily shale, making extraction very difficult, read: they are expensive, and are so varied that no one method of extraction will work for the entire field. Some areas are easily exploited, others are nearly impossible to extract a drop of oil from, even though testing shows it's there. If the technology can be developed, there will be a lot of very rich North Dakotans.

On the 1934–1935 flu epidemic:

A worldwide flu epidemic did touch Alamo, but it was during the winter of '17-'18, not in the thirties where I've put it. The math on the characters' ages just wouldn't have worked out otherwise. But during the 1918 pandemic, which killed an estimated fifty million worldwide (more than died that year in World War I), my grandfather was the manager of one of the banks in Alamo and he did close up the bank at noon each day so he could go home and help my aunt and grandmother deliver soup.

On knockout gases and "HaloRemi 35":

Halothane is widely used in operating rooms throughout the U.S. Remifentanil is an opioid-based anesthetic that is used as well. It doesn't show up on toxicological screens for opioids. Both materials behave pretty much as described. It is believed that the Russians used carfentanil when they dealt with the terrorist incident in the Moscow movie theater and the results were as reported here. The material HaloRemi 35 is made up, but wouldn't it be useful?

On OCD and ADHD:

I am not an expert on this subject outside of what I've read, experienced in my own life, and seen in one of my grandsons. I guess I have it, too, if it includes habits like checking two or three times that the garage door is all the way down, straightening pictures and using matching potholders. I was the kid in the class who had to speak up with a question even when the class had been told to be still, and the one who'd be looking out the window when he should have been listening. The truth is I found most classes boring. This didn't keep me from graduating near the top of my class in high school or from becoming an accomplished musician, artist, writer or successful salesman. My inclusion of OCD as it affects an otherwise normal person is not meant to portray it as a life-hindering affliction, but rather that it is something that just is, like having brown hair or being tall or short. It simply is. That it affects people's lives in ways large and small is just another of life's mysteries.

On a gizmo to jump your phone line:

Beats me, but it seems to me that it wouldn't be that hard to do. My good friend Deb H., who works in that industry, tells me it would work.

On Wi-Fi security:

My research has led me to believe that use of Wi-Fi is OK as long as you use a sophisticated alphanumeric password such as the one I describe, along with a good encryption system. I've also come to believe that using "open" Wi-Fi systems, such as those available in public places like airports, coffee shops, and hotels is like posting your private information on the Net. It's insanity. And the police really are on the lookout for people sitting in cars apparently working on their laptops but who very well may be hacking into your Wi-Fi system. If you see someone sitting in a car in your neighborhood typing away on a laptop, ask them who they are and what they're doing. And don't be bashful about calling your local police department. They'd rather make a roof estimator feel a little uncomfortable than have you become a statistic in the fastest rising crime in our country.

As with *Dart*, I have many people to thank for their insight and expertise in writing *Alamo, North Dakota*.

Forensic technologist Zubin Medora for his help on the aforementioned Wi-Fi systems and their weaknesses and his expertise on how everything—EVERYTHING—you send on the Internet is still out there somewhere. (Just ask those irreproachable scientists who declared that the world is heating up. It turns out they were covering up, suppressing, and ignoring data that didn't agree with their conclusions. And now it's all coming off the servers and home to roost on their heads). All Internet postings are accessible by potential insurers and employers. It would be a good idea if we could teach today's children that fact *before* they post things on social networking sites that might embarrass them later, things they might not want showing up when they are, say, forty and running for office or are in competition for a promotion.

Denise Wedel, MD, of the Mayo Clinic's Department of Anesthesiology for her help on the gases Halothane and Remifentanil and inspiration to "invent" HaloRemi 35.

Koren Kaye, MD, of St. Paul's Regions Hospital, for her help with the how's and whys of emergency patient care at that world-class facility.

Brian Rickert, my own furnace guy, who showed me how a furnace could be made to kill people. As a lifelong Minnesota resident, I can't understand why people don't have their furnaces checked annually. A guy like Brian can save your life.

Mike Siitari, former Chief of Police, Edina, Minnesota. Mike is a longtime family friend who was kind enough to walk me through the process of investigating a murder in a relatively crime-free suburb. The crime statistics are as reported—they don't have many murders there and never did as long as Mike was Chief. Mike's wife is in law enforcement as well and she really did tell me to put my firearms in the dishwasher to clean them.

My editor Pat Morris and my book designer, Dorie McClelland.

My Brother Pete, who declared himself my unofficial publicist when I needed one.

My Dad, who thinks I should write a political thriller about how a third-party candidate wins the presidency in 2012. I'd like to do just that, but reality is overtaking me. Don't be surprised if a third-party rises and tosses out all the current lifetime career politicians.

And finally, my wife, Cindy, who has been single-handedly running our real estate practice while I indulge my dream of becoming a writer. Thanks Babe. I still do.

Phil Rustad's
insatiable curiosity and
"What if?" imagina-
tion have led him into
multifaceted experiences
ranging from making stained glass windows
to being an international AKC dog-obedience
judge to working with companies "that make
things go boom!" His natural storytelling ability led him to write the Dan Neumann mystery
series.

Phil and his family (including the four-legged
ones) live in Minneapolis.

Watch for the next Dan Neumann mystery,
Judge's Choice, in 2012.

Coming soon . . .

Judge's Choice

An early morning call from an old friend has Dan Neumann racing north to Minnesota's lake country to help in a murder investigation. The young woman's mutilated body is the latest message from the most difficult kind of serial killer to find—a traveler—one who kills over many years and many miles. Knowing he needs back-up, Dan enlists the help of his girlfriend, Maria, an Arizona investigator, and Will Sanford of the FBI. Together they follow the years-old trail of the killer and discover two things: wherever the killer strikes, a major league dog show is nearby, and the time between murders is getting shorter and shorter. Dan enters the cacophonous controlled chaos of the dog-show world to cut off a killer before he strikes again.

ALAMO
NORTH DAKOTA